The Echoes in the Cabin

ANNE WYN CLARK

avon.

Published by AVON
A division of HarperCollins*Publishers* Ltd
1 London Bridge Street
London SE1 9GF

www.harpercollins.co.uk

HarperCollins*Publishers*
Macken House, 39/40 Mayor Street Upper
Dublin 1, D01 C9W8, Ireland

A Paperback Original 2026
1

First published in Great Britain by HarperCollins*Publishers* 2026

A catalogue record for this book is available from the British Library.

ISBN: 978-0-00-876346-6

Set in Sabon LT Pro by HarperCollins*Publishers* India

Printed and bound in the UK using 100% Renewable Electricity at CPI Group (UK) Ltd

Anne Wyn Clark was born and raised in the Midlands, where she continues to live with her husband and a sweet-natured cat. She has three now grown-up children and six grandchildren. Much of her formative existence was spent with her head in a book, and from an early age, she grew to relish the sheer escapism afforded by both reading and writing fiction.

She has a love of antiquity and a penchant for visiting old graveyards, often speculating on the demise of those entombed beneath.

The Echoes in the Cabin is her sixth novel.

You can follow her on X @EAClarkAuthor

Also by Anne Wyn Clark

Whisper Cottage
The Last House on the Cliff
The Secrets of Mill House
The Shadows of Hill Manor
The Cottage in the Ruins

For Gemma, Natalie and Christopher, with love.
xxx

'La plus belle des ruses du Diable est de vous persuader qu'il n'existe pas'

'The finest trick of the devil is to persuade you that he does not exist'

Charles Baudelaire

Prologue

TEN YEARS EARLIER – October 2013

Anglesey

Three weeks after the storm

The views over the Menai Strait and Snowdonia were stunning. Alun, the helicopter pilot and tour guide, smiled to himself at the '*ooh's* and '*aah*'*s* emitted by the four passengers he was carrying above the crystal waters as he indicated the various landmarks to them, a middle-aged couple with their adult daughter and twelve-year-old grandson. Though he had seen it a thousand times, the scenery never failed to take his own breath away: the snow-capped mountains to one side, the huge expanse of sea to the other, wrapping around the place he felt privileged to call home and separating the island from the mainland. And the two huge bridges spanning the body of fast-flowing water: most of all, Alun had always loved the Menai Suspension Bridge, the *Pont y Borth* as the locals knew it, with its hefty, distinctive blue-grey chains. The engineer in him still marvelled at Thomas Telford's impressive design, constructed almost 200 years earlier. The sign at its approach: *Môn, Mam Cymru* – Anglesey, mother of Wales – welcomed him every time he returned home.

Môn – from the island's Roman name, Mona, with its patchwork of fertile green fields, dense pine forests and pale sandy beaches that stretched for miles – boasted a wealth of folklore and sites of historical interest. For Alun, it had everything.

The best way to appreciate the scale of the island and its beauty, especially on a day like today, was from above, with sunlight glittering on the sea and the sky a perfect azure blue. The chopper traced the coast as the young lad bombarded him with constant questions about the helicopter controls; the adult passengers strained to look below, the man busily snapping away with his camera, chipping in from time to time as the older of the two women gave a running commentary, often interrupting Alun as he pointed out places of particular interest, which was beginning to grate a little. Soon they had travelled virtually the whole of the shoreline clock-wise and it was almost time to fly back to Caernarfon Airport, leaving him half an hour or so for a tea-break before more tourists would be embarking. Alun hoped the next lot would be a tad less vocal.

They passed over a long shingle beach, silver in the afternoon light, beyond which a column-like edifice seemed to float above the water.

'Look, isn't that a lighthouse down there? I'm sure that's the one we saw on telly, isn't it?' The older woman bobbed excitedly in her seat.

'I think it is.' The man turned to Alun. 'Wasn't it on that *Countryfile* programme or something?'

Everyone peered down at the black-and-white construction standing proud of the teal-green waters, perfectly visible today owing to the ideal weather conditions.

'It's called Trwyn Du,' Alun asserted through his mouthpiece. 'You can't see it because it's under the water at the moment, but it's sitting on a rocky outcrop, part of the headland at Penmon Point.' He indicated the rocks beneath them. 'There's an ancient priory close by, well worth a visit. And that strip of land on the other side of the water is largely limestone – they used the stone from here to build the Menai Bridge, among other things.'

He waved a hand. 'You can see Puffin Island up ahead. There are often seals and porpoises around here, as well as the puffins and other sea birds.'

'Ooh – can we go a bit lower? I've never seen a seal before. Not in the flesh.' The older woman craned her neck expectantly. 'Will we get a good view of them from up here?'

Alun gritted his teeth. 'Not really. There's a boat trip that goes right up to the island, if you want to get up close and personal. I'll take us as low as we can safely go though, so you can all get a better look.'

The helicopter began to drop a little, bringing gasps and squeals of delight from the older woman as she peered below. The daughter, who had remained relatively quiet throughout, looked a bit embarrassed.

'Calm down, Mum.' She rolled her eyes at Alun, making him suppress a smile.

The mother appeared not to hear her. 'Look, look! I think I just saw a dolphin – coming up out of the water.'

But the man was almost out of his seat. He seemed suddenly agitated, his focus on something else entirely. 'Here – what's that – down there on those rocks?'

Everyone craned to look at where he was squinting, flapping a hand at the ground below. The woman's excitable chatter turned to sudden shrieks of hysteria as her horrified daughter quickly covered the boy's eyes.

'Oh, dear God. Oh my God. Is that – is that what I think it is?'

Alun glanced downwards briefly, then did a double take, suddenly filling with horror. Of course, there had been cases, plenty of them over the years. Usually holidaymakers, people enjoying themselves and forgetting that the sea was something to be cautious around. A sad suicide or two. But in the fifteen years he'd been in the job, he'd been fortunate enough to avoid seeing anything like this so far.

Towards the end of the promontory, partially covered in something red, lay the crumpled form of a human body, face down, limbs akimbo. The helicopter circled for a moment while Alun gathered his thoughts, all the while staring below. He pressed the radio to contact the coastguard.

'*Sut mae*. Alun Jenkins *syma*. Listen, I'm flying over Penmon Point at the moment – looks like a body's washed up on the rocks near Trwyn Du.'

He listened, his lips setting into a grim line as the gravity of the situation pressed down on him, nodding from time to time, while the operator responded.

'I remembered about that young lad going missing in Traeth Coch a few weeks back. He had a red jacket on, didn't he? Just wondered . . .'

Alun paused, then nodded again. '*Dim problem*.' He ended the call and promptly turned the craft around, doing his best to shut out the constant wittering from the older woman about how it had ruined the whole experience for them as they headed back towards Caernarfon.

Alun was a parent himself: it was painful to think that someone would be receiving the worst possible news later that day. He wondered what could have happened to the poor kid. Maybe they would never know.

Chapter 1

NOW – Monday 3rd April 2023

Elin

Elin felt the pressure of Cai's lips against her cheek as she lay, half-asleep in the early morning light, registering the waft of coffee coming from her bedside. Slowly opening her eyes, she rolled towards him where he sat, already fully dressed, at the edge of the bed. Elin winced, her foot twinging sharply to remind her that even after a fortnight, she still needed to be careful when moving. It was easy to forget when she was just lying there. Such a *stupid* thing to happen; who'd have thought something as innocuous as tripping over your own doorstep could result in a bloody fracture? And now she was incapacitated. At least she worked from home; but even though she'd be going to the archaeological dig Cai was planning near the beach where she'd grown up next month, she'd been hoping to take time off to travel back home to Wales this time with Cai too, stay with her sister Nerys for a few days while he was on his course. She felt guilty that she hadn't been back for so long. But her wretched foot had put paid to all plans for now. A long journey with a couple of changes by train felt like an ordeal she could do without.

'Morning, you,' he'd said softly. 'Don't get up. You need the rest.' He tipped his head towards the mug of coffee. 'I've left you a couple of Digestives, in case you need to take more painkillers – not a good idea taking stuff on an empty stomach. There's an almond croissant in the kitchen, but I thought it might be too early for you.'

She reached a hand towards his cheek, smiling. 'You're a diamond.' And he was – ever since the fall, he'd fussed round her constantly, asking if she was okay, whether she needed anything. Though it wasn't exactly his forte, he'd tried his best to do the housework, brought her meals on a tray. She'd adapted to the clunky boot the hospital had given her and was managing to do most things now, even if at a snail's pace. Apart, of course, from driving or walking any distance. Being confined to the house was starting to wear thin. She had to focus on the fact that it wouldn't be forever and she'd be able to lose the boot in a couple of weeks or so. It just felt like an eternity at the moment.

'If you've time, can you call on Nerys? Wednesdays are still her days off. I know she'd be pleased to see you. It must be so lonely for her now, since Nain passed away, and . . .' Elin broke off, realising that the far side of Caernarfon wasn't right on her sister's doorstep and that without the car, Cai would have to catch a bus, possibly two, and then make his way back again. It probably wasn't feasible. Maybe it wasn't really fair to ask.

Cai puffed out his cheeks. 'I'll do my best. Depends how tight the schedule is and whether they give us a few hours off for good behaviour.' He grinned, smoothing a strand of hair away from her face. 'Right. The fridge is well stocked, so you should be fine.' He paused for a second, his expression suddenly serious, then cleared his throat. 'I'll be back early Thursday evening – we can get a takeaway. Thai, maybe. Something to look forward to. That, and a hot bath.'

The thought of three long days stuck in the house without Cai, without the comfort of his solid presence, made Elin's heart sink. She sat up properly then and clung to him, pressing her face into his collar, breathing in the scent of fresh laundry blended with his peppery aftershave. 'I wish I was coming too.'

He'd laughed, gently prising himself away before taking both her hands in his own. 'Ha – you don't know what you're missing. No expense spared. Vending machine coffee. Sandwiches curling up by the time they're handed round. Sharing a shoebox in some hostel in the middle of nowhere with three other snoring, farting beasts who probably haven't changed their socks for a month.' He screwed up his nose. 'Not to mention hours of listening to Dr Baden prattling on in that monotone of his – I actually dropped off during his last lecture.'

Elin managed a weak smile. 'Yes, but the other stuff'll be fascinating. I'd love to see all the artefacts on display.'

And she honestly would. Funny – she'd never really been interested in archaeology or anything remotely history-related until Cai came along. His enthusiasm for it all was infectious.

'You'll be able to see everything soon enough. Most of it'll be exhibited in Birmingham Museum before too long. Anyway, I'll find stuff of my own once we start the dig at Traeth Coch next month. It's a dead cert.'

He widened his eyes, nodding encouragingly. 'And you'll be there to witness it first-hand.'

Elin flopped back onto the bed. She stared up at the ceiling, noticing with indifference a cobweb fluttering from the light fitting. Her grandmother, her lovely nain, would have frowned at that. Elin was usually meticulous, but hadn't been able to clean properly for weeks now. Ah well. It'd have to wait.

'Huh. Knowing my luck, it'll be a broken piece of twentieth century pottery.' She cringed inwardly then, thinking she must sound like a petulant child. But Cai laughed.

'O ye of little faith! One of the guys I was at uni with unearthed an Iron Age spearhead on his first day in Melsonby. I'm a firm believer in beginner's luck.' He glanced at the alarm clock and pulled a face. 'Shit. Gotta go or I'll miss my train. Look, I'll drop you a text when I get off the train, but it's doubtful I'll get a strong signal while I'm at the hostel, so don't worry if you don't hear from me. I'll be home before you know it.' He planted a soft kiss on her mouth, squeezed her to him for a moment. 'Love you.'

'Love you too. Have a good journey. And be careful.'

And that was that. Her parting shot, the words she always said whenever he had to go away, as though it would guarantee him safe passage; like a talisman to protect him against all evil. The door slammed, leaving her alone and slightly bereft for the briefest moment. But she brushed off the feeling: she ought to use this time by herself to get on top of things, wrap up some outstanding tasks. Her job as a telesales operator for a marketing company meant that she'd be able to work from Nain's cottage when they started the dig in a few weeks' time; Cai had bought a spare modem – all she needed to do was set it up and then she'd be up and running. There would be no need to hurry back to Birmingham at all. They'd even discussed going back to live on Anglesey permanently. During the time he'd spent on the island, Cai had grown to love the place, its wide open spaces, the huge expanse of sky. The sea, the quieter roads. He was tired of living in a city, he'd said. And he felt a real connection to the area owing to his mum having been brought up on the island.

'Once I've tied up any loose ends here, there's no need for us to stay in Brum a minute longer if we don't want to,' he'd told her only the other day. 'Just think, this time next year, once I've saved up enough, we could have our own home up there.'

Elin had wrapped her arms around him, her eyes filling with happy tears. He'd mentioned it briefly before, but this was a solid plan. Despite her initial desire to get away, after five years in the Midlands, she seemed to have got it out of her system and the yearning for home was growing stronger. Being back there with Cai would be a dream come true.

The next day dragged even more than Elin had expected, though she cleared up some overdue admin and responded to several emails she'd been putting off. She even managed to flick a duster round the living room, but couldn't face mauling the vacuum cleaner across the floor just yet. She received a brief one-liner from Cai on Monday afternoon, just to say he'd arrived safely and that he'd see her soon, but nothing since.

Elin did send him a few messages on the off-chance he could pick them up; some funny cat memes, and video clips from memorable occasions they'd shared that she'd scrolled through in moments of boredom. She'd come across the one from her last birthday, when Cai had surprised her by filling the living room with balloons and a banner, and had attempted to bake a cake. She remembered arriving home to the smell of burning, after he'd sent her to the supermarket with a ridiculously convoluted list – clearly to keep her out of the way for a while, she'd realised subsequently. He'd been flustered, which was so unlike him; she'd found Cai himself, plus the kitchen surfaces and floor, sticky with buttercream and flour. The cake had been a disastrous cremated offering, and he'd apologised profusely, before going out to buy another one. Apologised, after going to so much trouble! His thoughtfulness had really touched her. It was so typical of Cai, wanting to do something nice for her. They'd shared a takeaway pizza and a bottle of Prosecco, and he'd presented her with the beautiful sapphire earrings that she'd admired in a jeweller's in town. It had been the most perfect day.

She didn't have much else to report, though, being stuck looking at the same four walls.

By Wednesday, not being able to get out of the house, Elin had begun to feel more restless than ever. Though she wanted to speak to Cai, she wasn't entirely surprised when he hadn't called: it was nothing new. He was only going to be away for three nights, and the places he travelled to with his job were often remote. She assumed that, as he'd suggested, the signal may have been poor. He probably hadn't managed to visit Nerys after all – he'd have messaged while he was there otherwise, or Nerys certainly would. She wanted to speak to someone and decided to ring Nerys, explain her predicament. It dawned on her that they hadn't spoken for more than a fortnight, and she felt a twinge of guilt. But Elin knew Nerys would be pleased to hear that she'd be travelling up to stay with her as soon as her foot had healed, and they'd be able to catch up properly then. Hopefully she'd be fit enough to take part in the dig Cai and a couple of his colleagues were planning. Initially he had intended to excavate the area beneath Castell Mawr, the rocky limestone mound looming over the west of the bay, which had once been the site of an Iron Age fort; but having explored the locality further, Cai had decided to focus first on the overgrown scrubland sitting high above the sands on the opposite shore, saying that not having been disturbed for so long, it might be more likely to yield something of note.

Elin was confident that Cai knew what he was talking about and happy to go along with whatever he decided. She hoped that maybe Nerys would like to come along, too. Hell, she might even hit it off with one of the lads who'd signed up to help. It would be nice to see her settle down with someone – and would make Elin feel a whole lot less guilty for deserting her.

Shortly after Elin and Cai had first met, he had been so excited to learn about the history of Traeth Coch, the beach Nain's cottage overlooked. Known in English as Red Wharf Bay, it was a geologically interesting piece of the coastline with a dark past: the name born as the result of a Viking battle which had taken place in the twelfth century, leaving the sands awash with blood.

What had piqued Cai's interest, however, was hearing about the hoard of Scandinavian treasure, dating from around a thousand years earlier, discovered buried on the east side of the bay in the nineteenth century. Elin had never seen him so animated.

'There *has* to be more out there. One day I'll organise a proper dig.' He'd looked at Elin with shining eyes. 'You don't know how lucky you are, living right on top of a potential treasure trove. The historical significance of this place is astounding.'

Elin had never really considered it. The quiet bay was just home; safe but dull. There was never much newsworthy going on. Apart from— well, she didn't want to dwell on what had or hadn't happened to her mam. To poor Jac Parry. It was all in the past now.

Chapter 2

TEN YEARS EARLIER – October 2013

The night of the storm

Elin

Elin awoke to the sound of shouting outside. The room was in darkness, a small chink of light bleeding through the cracks around the door. As she made to turn over, everything began to spin. She let out a small groan. The memory of the two-litre bottle of cider sneaked from her best friend Catrin's dad's cellar the previous evening made her gut churn. It had seemed like a good idea at the time. Disorientated, she sat up, rubbing her eyes and reaching for the ceramic rabbit table lamp placed between the two beds. Elin's mouth felt parched and stale. At least she'd remembered to bring a pint of water up with her before she collapsed into a stupor. Glugging greedily from it, she peered at the small alarm clock. It was 2.20 a.m.

A chill suffused the air, sending goosebumps along her bare arms. Turning to question Nerys about the din, she saw that her sister's bed was empty, the covers thrown back; a dent in the pillow as though she had just been whisked away. Rain thrummed against the roof as the wind whined in the chimney, rattling the louvred shutter over the small fireplace that was no longer used. Lightning flashed across Nain's thin rosebud-patterned curtains, preceding a low rumble of thunder, which felt as though it was emanating from the very bowels of the cottage. Still, the voices persisted from beyond the walls over the sounds of the storm: not drunken brawlers or quarrelling lovers, but urgent, fearful voices. Their tone sent a stab of dread through her.

Shakily, Elin crossed the room and lifted one curtain to peer out into the gloom, wiping the condensation from the windowpane with her hand. The night sky was inky-black, the moon a curved, pale sliver against it. The smudged beams of several torches darted across the bay; even through the glass, the roar of the waves was audible as they crashed against the sea wall.

Grabbing her dressing gown from the foot of the bed, Elin headed for the door. Yellow light flooded the stairwell from below. She stood for a moment at the top, listening for evidence of activity inside the cottage. Nain was speaking to someone over the phone in the living room immediately beneath, her voice quavering.

Still muzzy-headed, Elin made her way downstairs. Nerys, dressed in her tiger-print onesie, looked up from the settee, hands wrapped around a mug, a tangle of dark curls framing her deathly pale face. There was a tall, uniformed policeman standing just inside the front door, hands behind his back, his head barely clearing the ceiling. He turned slightly, giving her a weak smile as she came into the room. He seemed quite young for a police officer, not much older than Nerys. Elin noticed that his left eye was twitching; whether from tiredness or nerves, she wasn't sure.

'What's going on?' Elin sank beside her sister on the settee, looking anxiously from her to the policeman and back. Nerys's eyes were glazed over.

'Nain couldn't sleep. She got up to make a cup of tea, then realised Mam hadn't come home. She was seen in the pub earlier in the evening – her car's still parked outside The Quay, but there's no sign of her anywhere and her phone's dead. They think . . .' Her voice snagged as she leaned to put down her mug of tea, still full, the cloudy surface suggesting it was cold. 'They've launched the lifeboat. They . . . they think she could have been carried out to sea.'

Elin's stomach rolled. She stared at Nerys in disbelief. Mam stayed out late sometimes – it was nothing new. Elin had been sitting on the bed only hours earlier, chatting to her about her day, watching as Mam wriggled into her new skinny jeans and applied a slick of pink lip gloss as she got ready to meet her new man in the pub.

'Here, do this up for me, will you, El?'

She'd lifted her ponytail for Elin to fasten the gold clasp of her tanzanite pendant, the one with the huge heart Bethan had given her that almost matched her eyes, like the one worn by Rose in *Titanic*. She'd shaken her long, streaked blonde hair from the scrunchie she'd been wearing, run her fingers through her locks and appraised herself in the mirror with a frown before blowing out her cheeks.

'I'm getting crow's feet. And I should've done my bloody roots. Do I look okay?'

Elin had laughed. 'You look hot, Mam. He'd better be worth it.'

Mam had grinned, clasping her hands to her chest. 'Oh, he's

definitely worth it. *Wonderful Will.* I'd go to the ends of the earth for a fella with eyes like that.'

Elin had rolled her own eyes. She'd wondered about Will, this latest man, but with no more than passing curiosity. For as long as she could remember, there had been a string of them: some lasting weeks, none more than a few months. And the longer relationships would inevitably be followed by a period when Mam emphatically declared herself 'off men'. Until someone new brought a gleam to her aquamarine eyes. Eyes that seemed to change with the weather. Ruled by the tide, that's what Nain always said of them. Mam was a free spirit: Nerys's father had never been on the scene and Elin's own hadn't stayed around for long. The girls had been raised in an all-female household, a tight-knit matriarchy. Their mam had yet to meet The One, the soulmate who could accept her unconditionally, with the baggage of two now teenage daughters and an ageing, often critical mother. But Elin suspected she didn't want to settle down properly at all. That it was always about the thrill of the chase. The anticipation of the gift, before the disappointment when the pretty wrapping came off.

Mam had glanced at the time on her phone and grimaced. 'Bugger. I'm five minutes late already and I've got to drive to Moelfre. Not a good start.'

She had pulled on her high-heeled ankle boots, shrugged on her favourite turquoise velvet jacket, and in a haze of citrus perfume and blown kisses, had torn from the bedroom and down the stairs, calling out her goodbyes and don't-wait-ups, before the door slammed, leaving silence in her wake. Leaving Elin to study her own reflection in the mirror – and appreciate the similarity in hers and Mam's appearance – and to hope that her own life wouldn't turn out to be quite as chaotic.

Chapter 3

TEN YEARS EARLIER – October 2013

The night of the storm

Elin

Elin studied Nerys, so different in every way from their mother – darker in complexion and curvier; hazel-eyed and placid. She was nineteen: four years older than Elin, born when Mam was just eighteen. Though Nerys was even-tempered and more tolerant than anyone else Elin knew, she had always been fiercely protective of Elin. *Her lovely big sister.* They were all so close, but Elin knew deep down that, though she tried to disguise the fact, Mam favoured her above Nerys. She wondered if Nerys sensed it too, and it made her feel slightly guilty.

Elin couldn't believe that Mam might have fallen foul of the sea. She knew the area like the back of her hand – she was always so careful. Hadn't she impressed upon them the dangers of the tide, the way it could creep all around the curve of the bay and cut you off? Hadn't she warned them time and time again, about the unwitting holidaymakers over the years who'd dropped their guard and paid for it with their lives? The way the weather could turn within minutes and transform the glass-like surface of the water into a seething, hostile mass, capable of drawing even the strongest swimmer down into its depths.

But though Mam stayed out late now and then, Elin couldn't remember an occasion when she hadn't come home. Mam liked her own bed; didn't sleep well in other people's houses, she'd declared. Whatever time she'd stayed out until, she was always there for her girls in the morning, laying the table, making a pot of tea, before setting off for work at her friend Bethan's little arts and crafts shop in Beaumaris, where she had served for as long as Elin could remember.

The feeling of dread began to mount. Mam would've called if she wasn't coming home for some reason; she wouldn't have wanted Nain to worry. This felt very off.

The sound of the phone clicking back onto the receiver made both Elin and Nerys look round sharply. From the far corner under the stairs and next to the kitchen doorway, Nain approached, shaking her head, her short white hair still flattened from her pillow. She drew her dressing gown around her more tightly.

'I was . . . I thought . . . she might've been with Bethan.' She looked away, her expression empty. Her jaw was tense, her nostrils flaring a little, as though she was trying not to cry. Nain never cried. Automatically, she picked up her knitting from the side table suddenly and lowered herself onto the armchair next to the low fire which had been resurrected in the grate. Soon the hypnotic click of her needles cut through the uncomfortable silence while the wind continued to wail eerily through any available crevice, rain pelting the windows and the roof. Elin sat back in her seat, fighting the nausea rising in her gut, still not quite sober, but enough to be grabbed by the gravity of the situation.

All she could think was how Mam would have rolled her eyes at her, told her she should've made herself tea and toast when she got home to soak up the booze. She would have regaled her with some story about her own exploits as a wayward teenager, of that time she'd been so drunk she'd actually walked into the wrong house and scared the wits out of poor old Mrs Williams, who'd been halfway up the stairs on her way to bed. Well, no one ever locked their doors round here, did they?

'We all make mistakes, El – the thing is to learn from something and not do it again. And again,' she'd have said. There'd be a suppressed smile, though: a feeling of 'that's my girl'. Elin had always been much more like her mother than Nerys had. Nerys was the home-maker, the sensible one. The one anyone could turn to in a crisis. But not tonight. Tonight, she looked like a frightened little girl who needed a reassuring hug. And though normally Elin would have put an arm around her, she felt oddly paralysed. The suggestion that something could have happened to their mother, the indomitable Meinir Owen, was unthinkable.

A rap on the front door made them all stiffen. The policeman opened it a fraction, clearing his throat. From where they sat, Elin couldn't make out who was on the other side. With an awkward glance back at them, the young man stepped outside, closing the door behind him.

'Oh God. *No*.' Nerys's voice was barely more than a whisper. She began to rock gently in her chair, her anguished eyes fixed on the entrance. Nain had paused, the needles still clamped between her hands. She set the knitting down on the side table, rising to place a knobbly hand on Nerys's shoulder. The lack of any reassurance from their grandmother told Elin that she was already resigned to the worst. A ripple of fear moved through Elin. She realised suddenly that her teeth had begun to chatter.

It felt like they waited an eternity, the three of them watching the door as if trapped in some sort of torturous tableau. Rain and the smell of seaweed gusted in suddenly, as the young constable returned, ducking under the lintel as he entered, dripping water onto the flagstone floor. His expression was grave as he wiped his feet on the '*Croeso*' mat. He was followed closely by Ianto Pritchard, a local man who had been at school with their mother and, Elin suspected, still held a candle for her. His face was alight whenever he spoke to Mam, leaning in and hanging on her every word. But Ianto's wide brown eyes were devoid of their usual spark, his mouth unsmiling. His dark hair was wet and he pushed it back from his round face, then ran a hand awkwardly across his beard as if he didn't know quite what to do.

He nodded briefly at each of them in turn, his eyes darting.

Elin had always liked Ianto. He lived alone in the fisherman's cottage where he had grown up, at the top of one of the two winding lanes that led from Pentraeth down to the far side of the bay. He had been an omnipresent figure as she grew up; usually so cheerful, always ready with a wink and a joke. He would often walk down with his placid border collie, Gel, and pop in for a cup of tea, to chew the fat with both Nain and Mam. His van took him all over the island and beyond for his job as a carpenter and he was well known as a good, reliable worker. A solid, salt-of-the-earth sort of man. The kind Nain would have liked her daughter to settle down with.

Ianto closed the door behind him. Elin watched as he shifted from one foot to the other, shooting an anxious look at the constable. He seemed to be doing some internal wrangling, as though mustering courage. Elin's mouth felt dry; her heart raced.

'Spit it out, man.' Nain drew in a breath. 'Have they found her?'

'No, Mrs Owen.' Ianto's face contorted into something like a grimace. His hand travelled to the back of his head now. 'They found one of Mein's boots on the far side of the bay. There's a policeman outside with it in a bag.'

Nain clapped a hand to her mouth. A strangled sob escaped her throat. She tipped towards the back of the settee as her legs seemed to give way. Ianto rushed over to help her, gently guiding her back into her chair, where she gripped the arms as though trying to ground herself. Elin looked on in disbelief, overwhelmed by a sick feeling of panic. This couldn't be happening. Surely they'd got it all wrong.

'But—but that doesn't have to mean . . .' Nerys remained seated, turning to Nain in desperation, her lower lip trembling. 'She could've just . . . taken it off, couldn't she?'

'In *this* weather?' Nain looked round abruptly. Ever the realist. Her eyes were glassy with tears. 'She's gone, cariad.' She raised a gnarled fist to her mouth as her voice cracked. 'My girl's gone.'

Nerys doubled over, arms wrapped around herself. A howl, animalistic and painful, came from somewhere deep inside her. Elin's chest contracted. She was going to throw up. She had to get to the bathroom. She tried to stand, but the room began to swim. And then everything went black.

Chapter 4

TEN YEARS EARLIER – October 2013

The night of the storm

Meinir

Meinir hadn't expected the evening to end on such a high note, given she'd decided within minutes of sitting opposite Will that the chemistry just wasn't there. He had already arrived and was sitting by the window, raising a hand to wave her over. He'd bought her a bottle of Peroni without asking – just as well she liked lager. No glass. She tried not to show her disappointment.

Despite the initial attraction she'd felt when he'd come into the shop the other day, once they'd started talking, she realised that it wasn't going anywhere. Will was nice enough, but the moment he brought his ex-wife, Ruth, into the conversation, he went off at a tangent about how happy they'd been and how bitterly he regretted not being a better husband and father. That familiar, puppy dog look glazed his lovely eyes, which had failed to light up when they fell on her, implying he would really much rather have been sitting there gazing at Ruth than at her. Meinir wasn't about to be anybody's consolation prize. And anyway, apart from the eyes, he wasn't as devastatingly good looking as she'd remembered, nor did they seem to have much in common. Funny how your perception of someone can shift so quickly. *Pfft.*

She finished her beer, weaved her way through the sea of customers to the ladies', then returned to make an excuse about something coming up at home, before making her exit. The Kinmel Arms looked out onto the shingle beach at Moelfre; though the evening air was cool, people were still sitting outside to admire the view as the sun went down over the gently lapping sea. Meinir stood in the doorway for a moment, feeling deflated. All dressed up and nowhere to go. Maybe she could nip into The Quay in Traeth Coch on her way home, see if anyone she knew was in. Thursdays were usually fairly busy. At least then she could have a couple of drinks without worrying about driving home.

She turned to walk up the steep slope leading to the small car park behind the pub and almost collided with a tall man coming round the corner. Meinir wasn't sure what happened but she swerved to avoid him, teetered for a moment, then fell back and landed hard on her backside, letting out an involuntary expletive.

The man had been carrying a towering, wide package wrapped in brown paper, half of it obscuring his face. 'Oh my God, I'm so sorry. I was focusing on not dropping this bloody thing – I didn't see you.'

Meinir felt more embarrassed than anything else. She attempted to regain her composure and hauled herself back onto her feet, sliding a little as the worn soles of her ridiculously high boots lost traction.

The man propped his parcel against the wall hurriedly,

reaching out a hand to help her up. His brow furrowed as he studied her face. 'You okay?'

'I'll live.' She forced a smile and released his hand, feeling a sudden rush of heat to her cheeks, conscious of her dishevelled appearance. He looked just a little older than her, with greying cropped hair and tanned skin which emphasised his intense blue eyes. *Oh God.* Why was she such a sucker for blue eyes? He was solidly built and wearing faded jeans and a crew-neck navy sweater.

Meinir brushed off her hands and the backs of her thighs, her gaze shifting towards the wall. 'What's in the package?'

The man scratched his head a little awkwardly. 'A painting?' It came out more like a question, as if he wasn't entirely sure himself. 'Um, it's one I did myself, of the bay. The landlord in the Kinmel displays work by local artists, and he gave this one the thumbs up, so I'm hoping he might find me a buyer. Bit of a captive audience in there.' He grinned.

'Ah, I've seen the pictures – there're some really good ones. You must be talented then, if they're going to put your work on the wall.'

'I'll just have to hope someone who comes in thinks so. I could really do with a sale – my van needs four new tyres, or it'll fail the MOT again.'

'Well, good luck with it. I'm sure it'll get snapped up. There are plenty of holidaymakers looking for a souvenir of the island to take home.'

He nodded and smiled again. 'Look, can I buy you a drink? Just to say sorry for almost knocking you flying. I'm Gruffydd, by the way. Griff.'

'And I'm Meinir.' She paused, screwing up her face. 'That's very kind, but I'll pass.' She tipped her head towards the pub. 'I've just made an excuse to escape my disaster date for the evening and it might look a bit odd if I go back in.'

'Oh dear. Didn't go too well, then?' Griff raised a questioning eyebrow.

'You could say that.' Meinir rolled her eyes. 'I'm heading nearer home so I can ditch the car and drown my sorrows.'

He straightened a little. 'If you don't mind waiting, I could always follow once I've handed this over,' he indicated the painting. 'You know, so you can drop your car off – I'll take you somewhere else, if you prefer.' Griff regarded her hopefully from beneath dark, velvety eyebrows, waiting for a response.

Meinir hesitated. She wasn't sure she wanted to get into a car with him, but a drink or two in her local wouldn't hurt. He seemed nice, and he wasn't bad looking either. At least the evening wouldn't be a total write-off. But it wouldn't do to appear too keen.

'You carry on, but if you want to come to The Quay in Traeth Coch, I'll be in there for the next hour or so.'

Griff's face lit up. '*Iawn*. I'll see you in a bit, then.'

Meinir nodded, then carried on up the path to the car park. She felt a tingle of excitement. So, he was an artist. Maybe she could persuade Bethan to hang a couple of his paintings in the shop if they were any good. There had definitely been rather more of a spark between them than there'd been with Will, she was sure of it. She just had to hope he wasn't still pining for an ex, too.

*

Meinir wondered if she should pop home to let them know she was just up the road if she was needed for any reason, but thought better of it. It wasn't as if the girls were babies any more – and she'd got her phone with her. She parked her little blue Ford Ka on the forecourt of The Quay. Judging by the number of cars, it was going to be busy inside. A couple of lads sat smoking at one of the wooden tables positioned next to the low fence in front of the rugged whitewashed building, but a chill had descended and no one else was braving the elements.

It was between tides, leaving a handful of small sailing vessels stranded at a tilted angle, on the strip of wet sand which would later become submerged again, beyond the sea wall and the shingle end of the beach. Several rowing boats lay upturned on the grassy embankment on the opposite side. Two men were leaning over one of them, securing it with a length of rope. One, a tall man with his head covered by a hood, had his back to her. The other, thick-set and white haired, straightened, peering across at her, then raised a hand in greeting. Meinir waved back, realising it was Peter, the man renovating the house next to their own. The Fowlers – Peter and his wife, Libby – had taken early retirement to the island and bought the rundown property almost three years earlier. Prior to them moving in, the old cottage, which had something of a dark history, had been empty for almost ten years after its elderly occupant had died. Peter had been working hard to restore the prefabricated building, which had once been a holiday let. Owing to the tiny birds nesting above the front door's canopy, he had mounted a smart sign with its new name: *Swift Cabin*, on the wall. But for Meinir, a change of name would never eradicate the knowledge that someone had once died in there under fairly horrific circumstances. She wondered if Peter and Libby knew about it. She wasn't going to be the one to break the news.

The couple seemed to have integrated into the community well: they were regular attendees at the church in Pentraeth and had become volunteers, Peter helping with the garden and general maintenance, and Libby with cleaning and arranging flowers. Peter was often in the pub, playing darts, and though Libby was more reserved than her husband, she always stopped to chat if she saw Meinir and the girls, even if it was just polite small talk. Libby's older sister had been staying with them when they first moved in, though the sound of raised voices from inside the cottage on a few occasions implied three was definitely a crowd. Things seemed more harmonious after the woman returned to Spain, where she'd emigrated a couple of years earlier, apparently. Peter was kind enough to trim their hedge whenever he did his own and had even put a lick of paint on the rusty old gate for them.

'It's no bother. Might as well, while the brush is wet,' he'd said cheerfully.

'Worth their weight in gold, good neighbours,' her mother had remarked, watching approvingly through the window as he'd got to work. 'I'm baking today – I'll have to send round some *bara brith* to say thank you. He won't take a penny, you know.'

And it *was* nice – not everyone was quite so accepting of them; of Meinir in particular. Small communities invariably meant a few small minds, and some of the older generation liked to gossip – the fact that both of her daughters were without fathers, and that Meinir made no secret of her liking for men, had earned her the occasional look of disapprobation and snide comment from behind a cupped hand. Much like Mam, Meinir didn't really care what people thought of her, but it hurt her to think that their negativity might impact on Nerys and Elin, who were just kids when all was said and done. People could be so thoughtless.

Chapter 5

NOW – Wednesday 5th April 2023

Elin

As she'd grown older, the thought of moving away to somewhere livelier and more vibrant had become increasingly appealing to Elin. It seemed to her that the island had little to offer the younger generation, unless they were born into farming families or ran their own business; so many of her friends had moved away to find work, lured by the promise of higher salaries and more varied careers with better prospects. Elin didn't really know what she wanted to do with her life, only that to carry on serving in a café would eventually drive her insane. She wasn't brilliant academically, but was practical and knew she could turn her hand to plenty of other things if she put her mind to it. She just needed someone to give her a chance.

Nerys was very much like Nain, in that she had always been content with her lot and dismissive of ambition. As long as the house was warm and food on the table, life was fine. One evening, after Elin had just heard that one of her classmates was moving to a mansion in Cheshire because her dad had won a sizeable amount on the lottery, she'd slumped down onto the settee, bemoaning her own mundane existence and lack of funds to do the amazing things that she seemed to hear about so often. The most exciting thing she ever had to look forward to was the occasional disco in the village hall.

'Kelly's so lucky,' she'd sighed, glancing round the living room at their worn, old-fashioned furniture, the yellowing paintwork. 'They're even having a swimming pool.'

'The grass is never greener in the end, cariad, you mark my words.' Nain had looked at her pointedly as she sat back in her armchair, knitting needles clicking incessantly. 'Money can't buy you everything. There's a lot to be said for peace and quiet, especially when you get to my age.'

Elin felt guilty then, for complaining. Nain had done her best for her and Nerys, and it hadn't been easy after they'd lost Mam. Elin herself hadn't been easy; she realised that when she looked back.

But even so, the thought had niggled: how nice it would be to be able to afford a few luxuries. And peace and quiet was for someone Nain's age, not hers. Meeting Cai when he came into the café in Traeth Coch that day five years earlier had been the best thing that could have happened to her. Though Cai's mother was from the other side of the island and his father hailed from Conwy originally where the couple had settled, they'd moved away when he was small, and he'd been brought up near Manchester. Cai was studying archaeology at university in Birmingham. Like her, he had lost his mum in his mid-teens, although to cancer rather than a horrible accident. He and his father weren't particularly close, and after his mum's death, their relationship had grown increasingly strained. The man had remarried and emigrated to France when Cai was nineteen, leaving him a small allowance to live off and a flat in Birmingham that his dad had inherited from an uncle. A flat with ample room for two. When Cai had taken her hands in his and looked into her eyes, there was no way on earth she could have refused his invitation to move in with him. Christ, she'd have gone anywhere in the world with him. She was besotted.

'So you're leaving us, then.' Nain's words had felt like a rebuke, the hurt in her green eyes evident as she stood in the kitchen doorway, looking over at Elin's bulging suitcase and the numerous carrier bags piled at the front door. Thinking back now, Elin realised she could have handled things better. Maybe done it more gradually, gone for weekends and eked them into weeks. Allowed both Nain and Nerys time to adjust to her not being around, rather than make her announcement as a fait accompli the very day she planned to go.

At the time, however, all she could think of was getting away, and that, plus her feelings for Cai, overruled everything. She was twenty: old enough to make her own decisions. And it had been a good decision, for the most part. Birmingham was the complete antithesis of Traeth Coch; she loved being swept along with the breathless pace of life; the buzz of the bustling streets, the huge selection of high-street stores, the nightlife. She embraced the diversity of the culture and foods she'd never even heard of before. Even lockdown had felt exciting, having Cai all to herself and a legitimate excuse not to go home or even leave the flat, come to that. It had been oddly liberating, though she'd felt slightly guilty when explaining to Nerys over the phone that they wouldn't be able to visit until travel restrictions had lifted.

'Nain's not so good at the moment,' Nerys had replied in a muted voice. 'I'm struggling a bit here, to be honest – do come as soon as you're able, won't you, El.'

And Elin had promised that they'd come the minute they could – but it had been a full four months until the Welsh Government's *Stay Local* policy was relaxed. Even then, Elin hadn't been in a huge rush to go home. Part of her had hoped that Nerys would be getting used to her absence and coping better. After all, she'd reasoned, she needed to start making a life for herself, not using Elin as a crutch. And when a further lockdown was imposed during the winter months, Nerys had sounded fairly resigned to it.

'I've got sort of used to the routine now. We managed last time,' she'd said, almost brightly. It had reassured Elin that she was learning to cope without her.

Although now, five years older and a little wiser, she was beginning to feel the odd pang of homesickness. *Hiraeth* – that's what it was. A deep longing for her homeland, the place holding all her childhood memories. Memories of her beloved mam; of Nain. Of things she ached for and could never have back – but returning to where she belonged, at least she'd feel more connected to them once again. So when Cai had excitedly brought up the plans he'd been discussing with a couple of his like-minded mates for the dig, it felt serendipitous. Her one deep regret was that now Nain would no longer be there to greet her.

Elin dialled Nerys's mobile and, as was often the case, the standard voicemail message responded immediately. She blew out a long breath. Nerys was frustratingly bad at remembering to keep the thing charged and she owned an ancient handset that seemed to die after only a couple of hours. Elin called the house phone instead. It rang out for ages, and she was about to hang up when it was finally answered, an older woman's hesitant voice coming down the line. An English voice.

'Hello?'

Elin paused for a moment, puzzled, wondering if she had misdialled. 'Sorry – is that Nerys Owen's phone?'

'Yes. Yes, it is. I'm afraid Nerys isn't . . .' There was a pause, an expulsion of breath. 'They've taken her into hospital. She's been quite unwell. I'm keeping an eye on things for her. Just until she can come home.'

'Oh God. What's wrong with her?' Elin felt a sudden wave of panic. Her sister was ill and she'd been blissfully oblivious. Elin's mind turned over every possible scenario: Nerys must have contracted some horrible, incurable illness. Or maybe she'd had a terrible accident in the house and had been found after lying unconscious for days. 'Who—who's that?'

'Is that you, Elin? This is Libby from next door.'

Momentary relief washed over Elin as she recognised Libby's slow, slightly sleepy tone. But the relief was quickly followed by a stab of anxiety. What had happened to Nerys? Why had no one informed her?

'Yes, I was just ringing to see how Nerys was doing – nobody let me know she was poorly. What's happened?'

'I'm sorry – we'd have called you a while ago, but we didn't have your contact details.' There was an audible sigh from the other end of the line. 'Poor Nerys. She collapsed last week. She's not been too good for a while now. I think it's probably exhaustion – she did so much for your grandmother, and well . . .'

The suggestion was left hanging, but the implication was clear. Elin flooded with guilt, hot tears pricking her eyes. Nerys had been lumbered with everything and it had obviously all got too much for her. Things must have come to a head now that Nain was no longer there. How could she have left her to deal with it all on her own?

Elin felt a surge of despair, followed by anger. She hadn't really kept in touch with either Bethan or Ianto, but why hadn't Catrin let her know? She had her on WhatsApp. Maybe she wasn't aware, having moved to the other side of the island – Elin knew she'd got a lot on her plate herself, now that she was a farmer's wife; then she had to admit to herself ruefully that she hadn't exactly been the best at keeping in touch either. She would have to give Catrin a call. Most importantly, Elin needed to go home. Fast. The buck stopped with her: even if it was long overdue, Nerys needed her support.

Elin's mind was flying. She'd have to contact Cai somehow, tell him what had happened and that she was going to be travelling up first thing the next day – Thursday. The same day he was due home – the day she'd been looking forward to all week. She was praying to catch him before he boarded his train, that he'd be able to come straight to Traeth Coch instead. Whatever the situation, she'd just have to manage, broken foot or not.

'Libby, d'you know whether Cai called round at all? He's on a residential course near Caernarfon at the moment and he said he'd pop by if he had a chance, but I haven't heard from him.' Elin was suddenly desperate to speak to Cai. She felt impotent, useless. What a time to be incapacitated.

'Cai? Oh, you mean your boyfriend?' There was a pause. 'Um, not that I know of. Certainly hasn't been a car here or anything – I'm sure we'd've noticed.'

'No, no, he's not in the car – he travelled up by train.' Elin thought for a moment. Cai had met the neighbours a few times – she remembered him chatting to Peter more than once outside the house – the last time discussing the dig he was planning. 'I'm sure he'd've knocked at your door if he didn't get a reply from Nerys. He wouldn't have just cleared off without checking if you'd seen her around, not after coming all that way.'

'It's possible we were out – we did go to the supermarket yesterday.'

'Yeah, maybe.' Elin couldn't think straight. She felt remorseful and helpless, and briefly annoyed with Cai – he could have made the effort to find *somewhere* to call her from, let her know what he was doing. 'Where *is* Nerys? Have they taken her to Ysbyty Gwynedd?'

'Um, they did in the end. Someone came to assess her from mental health services.' There was a shuffling noise from the other end. 'She's in the psychiatric unit. Hergest, I think it's called. The poor girl was in a really bad way, I'm afraid.'

Elin felt her stomach plummet. 'The *psychiatric* ward? I thought . . . didn't you say it was exhaustion?'

'I think – um . . .' The line crackled, then became muffled, as though the receiver had been covered briefly. 'I think she's probably had a breakdown, to be completely honest with you. She was very confused, almost hysterical when they took her out of the house. They had to sedate her. Distressing to see her like that, I'm sure you can imagine.'

'Have you seen her . . . since she's been in?' Elin had seen these places on TV. She pictured Nerys, doped up to the eyeballs and slumped in a chair, dribble running down her chin. A lump rose in her throat. Her sister had been floundering and she'd been oblivious. How could she have been so thoughtless?

'I've had a stinking cold. I didn't think it'd be a good idea to go passing on my germs.' Libby sniffed loudly as if to demonstrate. 'But we'll certainly go once I'm over it,' she added quickly. 'In the meantime, we've been keeping an eye on the house, watering the plants and stuff. I've had a whip-round with the Hoover and Peter's just given the back lawn a cut.'

Elin held her breath for a moment. While she was grateful that someone was looking out for her, Nerys having to rely on their neighbours to do things for her, for their family home, just wasn't right.

'Thank you, that's very kind. I'll ring the hospital now, see if they can tell me any more.'

Chapter 6

TEN YEARS EARLIER – October 2013

The night of the storm

Meinir

Heavy grey clouds were beginning to scud across the darkening sky, and as she looked out towards the horizon, Meinir saw that the waves were becoming choppier. She shuddered a little. From the way the wind was picking up, the electricity in the air, a storm was clearly brewing. She'd have to keep an eye on the weather – even if home was only a couple of hundred yards away, it was far enough to get drenched.

Meinir pushed open the door to the pub and was greeted by a welcome wave of warmth and the buzz of chatter. The smell of ale and food cooking permeated the air. It was humid and slightly oppressive, partly from the number of bodies but also, she suspected, the impending deluge.

Meinir scanned the sea of faces. The regular crowd, only a handful she didn't recognise. As usual, she received the odd smile and nod; a couple of blank expressions from people she didn't much care about. She spied her friend, Ianto, leaning against the far end of the bar. Seeing her, his face broke into a grin and he waved her over.

'What brings you in here this evening? Thought you had a hot date.' He raised one eyebrow, smirking slightly.

Meinir grimaced. 'Turned out to be tepid, to say the least.'

Ianto had been a good mate for as long as she could remember. Never a boyfriend, but someone she confided in and felt comfortable around. Someone, unlike a lot of blokes, you could rely on. The last few years hadn't been easy for him, trying to juggle his work commitments while caring in turn for his elderly mam and then his dad, who had now both passed away. Meinir had always suspected Ianto of having a thing for her friend Bethan, and vice versa. When they were at school together, Bethan had admitted she had a massive crush on Ianto and snogged him once outside the school disco when they were fourteen, but nothing ever came of it. Meinir often thought it would be nice to see the pair of them actually make a go of things.

But for now, all she could think about was the possibility of a romantic connection for herself. She gave Ianto's arm a gentle nudge.

'Hey, I've got another one lined up potentially – he's meeting me in here shortly.' She glanced back over her shoulder, hoping to see Griff walking in as the door opened. But it was just the two lads who had been smoking outside. She had only just arrived, to be fair. Give him a few minutes.

Ianto's eyes followed the trajectory of her own. He huffed quietly. 'Well, let me get you one in while you're waiting. Half a lager?'

Meinir turned back to him, smiling. She was close enough

to home that she could have whatever she fancied now without having to think about driving. 'D'you know what, I'll have a rum and black – and make it a large one, if that's okay.'

Ianto pursed his lips. 'Hmm. Think I can just about stretch to that. Got a nice little bonus today,' he said, winking.

'*Diolch*. Feel like something a bit more warming.' Meinir rubbed her arms, glancing about. Still no sign of Griff, but from the way he'd looked at her, she was quietly confident that he would show up. 'Bloody chilly out there now.'

She pulled up a stool next to Ianto, accepting the drink from Rhiannon, the dark-eyed girl behind the bar, with a curt nod, and scrutinising it briefly before taking a sip. Meinir had felt the weight of Rhiannon's stare as soon as she joined Ianto. She wouldn't have put it past the girl to deliberately give her a dirty glass – or even spit in it or something. Rhiannon was Elin's friend Catrin's sister, some five years older than the pair of them. Meinir liked Catrin, but found Rhiannon could be quite surly. The girls' mother had died when they were small and they lived with their dad, Derfel, whom Meinir had dated a handful of times a few years ago. It quickly became clear that they weren't a match made in heaven, and Meinir suspected that Rhiannon still hadn't forgiven her for giving her dad the elbow. Derfel was generally nice enough when he was sober, but enjoyed a drink rather too much and could end up being a proper bloody nuisance after a night on the tiles.

She had often sensed Rhiannon's hostile gaze upon her whenever their paths crossed, and though she tried not to let it bother her, it irked Meinir to think that the girl still held a grudge. Ironic, really, as she knew Rhiannon wouldn't have welcomed her, or anyone else, as a stepmother. But it was more the fact that her father had felt slighted – if the dumping had been the other way round, Meinir felt sure she would have remained quite friendly towards her.

'So, Rhi, what's your Catrin up to this evening?' Ianto leaned across the bar to hand over a ten-pound note, casting a brief wink in Meinir's direction. 'Looking proper grown up she is these days.'

'God knows.' The girl rolled her eyes. 'She was on the phone to Elin when I came out.' Her unsmiling eyes landed on Meinir once more. 'Hatching something, I expect.'

'As long as it doesn't involve boys, eh, Mein?' Ianto laughed, turning to her, taking a mouthful of his pint. 'You're a bit young for grandchildren just yet.'

Meinir spluttered. The very thought made her stomach turn over. 'Don't even go there. Caught Elin messaging some lad on Snapchat the other day. Can you imagine?'

Rhiannon muttered to herself as she turned away, just loud enough to be audible. 'Like mother, like daughter.'

Meinir scowled, flipping a finger towards the back of Rhiannon's head, but said nothing. Not worth getting into a slanging match with the silly little . . .

Ianto gave a small cough. He looked uncomfortable, and began tapping his fingers against his glass.

'So, Mein, how's work going? Busy in the shop?'

'So-so. Sales always tail off a tad in the early autumn. Tend to pick up again in the run-up to Christmas. But Bethan's got a handle on everything – she's got a great business mind. We go to town on the place around Halloween – always brings plenty of customers in.'

'Um, how is Bethan? Haven't seen her for a while.' His tone was casual, but there was an almost eager look in his brown eyes as he awaited the response.

Meinir smiled to herself. 'She's fine. Keeps herself busy, you know.'

Bethan had been married once, briefly and unhappily, and her husband deserted her for some floozy several years younger. The only plus side was that she'd been able to set up her little business with the alimony. Meinir wondered if, having had her fingers burned once, Bethan was reluctant to commit to anyone again. She always used her mam as an excuse: the old woman's health wasn't great, and Bethan spent a lot of time running around for her, taking her to medical appointments and making sure she always had clean clothes and a hot meal every night. But Bethan had bags of energy: nothing seemed to faze her. Surely a relationship wouldn't have been a problem. Meinir hated to think what would become of her if anything happened to her mam. She needed someone to come home to; someone *nice*.

Ianto had dated people casually, but remained a bachelor. It was as though the pair of them danced around the issue but had never actually dared admit their feelings, either to each other or anyone else. Maybe it was time Meinir tried a little matchmaking before they got too old to be bothered.

Ianto's gaze shifted sharply towards the entrance, making Meinir turn to see what he was looking at. Her heart lifted as she saw Griff in the doorway, casting around to find her.

She raised a hand to wave him over. 'Hiya.'

His face broke into a grin as he spotted her. He strolled across. 'Hello. Sorry I've been a while.'

'*Sut mae*.' He nodded at Ianto, who seemed to stiffen.

Ianto nodded back, smiling tightly. '*Iawn, diolch*.' He turned back to his pint and took a long swig, his eyes drifting at once to the clock behind the bar, then blew out his cheeks.

'Match is on in ten. Better get back or I'll miss kick off.'

Draining the last of his beer, he slid from the stool. 'See you, Mein. Say hello to your mam and the girls for me, will you? And Bethan . . .'

'Will do. Ta-ra.'

Nodding again at Griff, he disappeared through the crowd.

Griff stared after him, scratching his head. 'Was it something I said?'

Meinir laughed. 'He's a man of few words, our Ianto, until you get to know him. Always a bit awkward around strangers.'

'Ah well.' He shrugged. 'Anyway, what can I get you?'

Meinir tipped her head towards her almost-empty glass. She felt pleasantly relaxed now. 'I'll have another rum and black, please.'

'A double?'

Meinir thought for a moment. Well, he had offered. 'Yeah, why not. The last one's gone down a treat.'

Griff ordered Meinir's drink and one for himself. 'So this is your local, then?' His gaze travelled round the room. 'Nice little pub. I haven't been in here before – I'm from Llandygai, so not on the island that often.'

'Yeah, 's'okay. Pretty handy for me, anyway.'

Meinir saw Rhiannon smirking to herself as she measured out her rum, then poured the Guinness that Griff had requested. She placed the glasses on the bar and turned to say something in a lowered voice to the young lad who'd just brought back a tray of empties, whose cheeks reddened as he turned to look at Meinir. Meinir caught the tail end of the sentence, her temper rising now.

'If you've got something to say to me, Rhi, just bloody well spit it out.'

The girl's eyes narrowed, her face stony. 'I've got nothing to say to you. You're old enough to be my mother and you're still behaving like a flamin' lovesick teenager.'

'Oh grow up, will you.' Meinir's voice was louder than she intended, attracting a few raised eyebrows. 'Who the hell are you to judge me? I'm just minding my own business, trying to enjoy my evening. I'd advise you to keep it buttoned and do the same.'

'Think about Nerys and Elin,' Rhiannon hissed. 'You're an embarrassment to them.'

'An *embarrassment*? Don't talk to *me* about embarrassing parents.' She jabbed a finger across the bar. 'I'm not the one—'

Meinir stopped short of saying something she might later regret. Even if Rhiannon had an acid little tongue at times, Catrin was Elin's closest friend, and it wasn't their fault their father could be a pain in the arse. But still the girl's criticism had angered her. Meinir leaned forwards, feeling the warmth drain from her cheeks. More people were stopping to stare, and a hush had descended on the crowd assembled around the bar area.

Griff stepped back slightly. He looked awkwardly from Rhiannon to Meinir, raising both palms in front of him. 'Hey, come on, ladies. Let's cool it down, shall we.'

'*Cool it down*?' Meinir turned to him in disbelief. 'I'm sorry, but this has absolutely nothing to do with you.' She looked at her glass and then back at Rhiannon, who was still glaring. Meinir didn't appreciate Griff butting in like that when he knew nothing of their history. Knew nothing about her at all, come to that. Seeing the curl of his lip and the look of distaste on his face, her desire for male company suddenly evaporated.

'D'you know what, I think I'll call it a night.' She downed her drink in one and climbed from the stool, fixing Rhiannon with a cold stare.

Griff's mouth gaped as if to protest, but Meinir raised a palm. 'Thanks for the drink. You can stick the mediation.'

Before he could respond, she pushed her way to the exit and stepped outside, taking a much-needed deep breath. *Bloody men.*

Chapter 7

NOW – Wednesday 5th April 2023

Elin

Elin ended the call with the nurse on the Hergest Unit, a sick feeling swimming in her gut. It was as she had feared: the man she'd spoken to couldn't tell her too much over the phone, though he explained gently that Nerys was sleeping a lot and not communicating much. She'd been very confused when she was admitted, he said. Elin's need to get to her sister was suddenly overwhelming. Yet again, she tried to contact Cai, but it rang out for a while before the voicemail kicked in.

'Where the hell are you? Ring me back the minute you get this. *Please*. It's urgent.'

Elin cut the call in frustration, praying he would pick up the message soon. In the meantime, she needed to do something constructive. She settled on the settee with her laptop and a cup of tea to book a train ticket for the following morning, then hauled herself up the stairs to pack a bag. She would have to travel light – carrying anything was going to be tricky, hobbling around as she was.

Elin's mind was whirring. She tried to remember the most recent conversation she'd had with Nerys and wondered how on earth she hadn't picked up on her sister's fragile state of mind.

Elin could only recall it in fragments now, but tried to burrow into her memory, searching for what she might have missed. It was the day before she'd broken her foot. She'd been in the kitchen, she remembered, stirring pasta sauce, keeping one eye on the clock with the TV playing in the background. She had nearly ignored her phone when it rang out, but seeing it was Nerys, thought she ought to answer as it had been a while since they'd spoken.

Nerys had *sounded* fine. A bit quiet, perhaps, but sometimes she could be. Elin had filled the gaps easily, talking about Cai and the course in Caernarfon he was going on, about irritations around her job; about the bloody dinner she was making and what a faff the sauce had been. She realised now how the majority of the conversation had been about *her*; about what was happening in *her* life.

Nerys had mentioned something about trying to get on top of the paperwork that seemed to have mounted since Nain passed away, but Elin had brushed it off without thinking, saying not to worry; that she'd get through it eventually. She remembered steering the topic back to the oven timer and how she'd need to go in a minute to drain the spaghetti. Now she wondered why Nerys had brought up the paperwork at all. There had been a pause after Elin's reassurance, a pause she should have picked up on.

She'd heard a noise in the background, then – a sudden clatter. Elin had asked about it, half-laughing. Nerys had said she'd knocked a mug over.

'Is it broken?' Elin had asked.

'No, but I've bloody chipped it,' came the reply. She'd sounded frustrated. Elin had made a joke about it. '*Bacha byns*.' That was what Mam always used to say if they dropped anything. *Butterfingers*.

Elin found herself fixating on that moment. She could almost hear it now – the way Nerys had answered too abruptly, the way her strained laugh had come just a little too late.

Then there was the thing about the new cat. Elin bit her lip. Nyten, that's what Nerys had called her. That was the clearest part, somehow. How Nerys said something about her being hurt; that the vet had seen her but that she was back home now.

'Oh, that's good,' Elin remembered saying. She hadn't asked what had happened, or how bad it was, or how Nerys had managed. She had only asked what it had cost. That, more than anything, made her flinch now. There had been another pause after that. A longer one. Elin could remember turning down the heat on the stove, thinking about the sauce, not noticing that Nerys hadn't filled the silence.

The subject of Nain had come up, too. Elin had said she couldn't believe it had been almost five months already – as if mentioning their grandmother was the same as acknowledging her loss. Nerys had said the house felt very quiet. Elin remembered saying it would take time, but she was sure she'd get used to it. How could she have been so tactless?

And then – and this was the part that really made her cringe – Nerys had said she might come and visit. Elin closed her eyes, wincing in shame as she recalled her reaction.

It hadn't sounded like a concrete plan, not really. It had sounded tentative, as if Nerys was testing the water, hoping for an enthusiastic response. But Elin had answered without thinking, saying she and Cai would be coming up to Anglesey soon anyway, and it would be better to wait until later in the year. Nerys had agreed immediately. At the time, it had seemed like nothing.

Now it felt like a door Elin had slammed in her sister's face.

Cai would have noticed something was wrong if he'd been the one speaking to her, of that she was sure. He was astute like that, sensitive to people's feelings. It was one of the things she'd always loved about him. She recalled one occasion when they hadn't been seeing one another long and she still worked at the café in Traeth Coch where they'd first met. It was then that she'd realised she'd found someone very special.

It was the end of the Easter break and the café had been quieter than usual that afternoon. The constant drizzle made for a bleak, miserable day. Elin was standing behind the counter, wiping down the tiled surface while the tea urn hissed gently in the background. No one had come across the threshold in nearly half an hour. Catrin had nipped out for what had turned into a very long break, but it hadn't been a problem. Apart from Elin and Cai, two middle-aged women in the corner, who'd been in for lunch and seemed to be eking out their coffees, were the only people inside now. Soon the ladies got up to leave, smiling as they dropped a handful of coppers into the tip jar on the counter. Elin called out her thanks as the door swung shut behind them, rolling her eyes as she realised the gratuity only amounted to about twenty pence. Thankfully most people were rather more generous.

Cai sat by the window, half-turned towards the sea, a notebook open on the table in front of him. He'd been in for about an hour, scribbling intermittently, then stopping, as if the rain-misted view kept interrupting his thoughts. Every now and then, he would look up to stare through the window, twirling his pen between his fingers.

Elin watched him when she thought he wouldn't notice. They had only been on three dates, had only shared a few tentative kisses, and she found him increasingly fascinating. He'd brought her a polished piece of rose quartz in a little gauze bag when he'd turned up; handed it over nonchalantly, saying it was supposed to bring positive energy. Elin had been surprised but touched. It was an unusual, thoughtful gesture. She wasn't used to receiving gifts from boys. But he wasn't pushy and seemed interested in her without being overtly keen. As if he didn't expect anything in return. A complete contrast to her last boyfriend, Tom. Cai had that way about him – quiet, but not withdrawn. Perceptive. He gave her his full attention; asking meaningful questions without being the least bit nosy.

The bell over the door finally rang again and an elderly man shuffled in, bringing with him a gust of earthy, rain-infused air and the faint smell of damp wool. Elin recognised him at once – Mr Hughes, a widower who lived up the same lane as Ianto. He didn't come in often, and when he did, he always paid with a handful of loose change, apologising under his breath as if his very presence was something to be sorry for. He took off his cap as he walked towards her. Elin noticed how frayed the edge of the peak was, how unkempt what remained of his sparse grey hair.

'*Sut mae*,' she said, smiling.

The old man nodded, looking slightly flustered. '*Iawn, diolch*. Just a pot of tea please, cariad.'

'Not very nice out there today, is it?' she remarked, turning to lift a small china teapot and a cup and saucer onto a tray. Hearing the scrape of a chair, she glanced back over her shoulder to see Cai approaching the counter.

'Can you make that two, please?' he said, wriggling his eyebrows.

Elin looked beyond him, nodding towards his table with a grin. 'You're still on your first one.'

He smiled, his eyes twinkling. 'I know.'

She didn't question him. Pouring hot water into a second teapot, she set another cup on the tray, and popped a couple of pieces of shortbread onto a plate without thinking too much about it. When she brought them over, Cai had already pulled out the chair opposite him as the old man was crossing the floor.

'D'you mind joining me?' he asked Mr Hughes. 'I'm getting tired of my own company.'

The old man hesitated, clearly unsure. 'Oh, I wouldn't want to intrude . . .'

'Please,' said Cai. He sounded genuine, his eyes widening hopefully. 'You'd be doing me a favour.'

After a moment, Mr Hughes lowered himself onto the proffered seat. He still looked a little uncertain.

Elin lingered behind the counter, pretending to rearrange the sugar packets and paper napkins while she listened. Cai didn't rush the conversation. He chatted about the weather first, then asked questions about the history of the bay; about how long Mr Hughes had lived in Traeth Coch and what he'd done for a living, about his family. He listened properly to the answers, nodding; asking follow-up questions, never interrupting.

At one point, Mr Hughes laughed – an abrupt, croaky sound, as if it had been a while since he'd done it.

Elin felt something shift inside her. She'd seen plenty of people come through the café. Some were polite, some were friendly; some not so. Some were decidedly rude. Many were loud and full of inane chatter. But this – this quiet empathy – was different. Cai wasn't acting. He wasn't trying to impress anyone. He was simply making time for the old man, as though his stories mattered.

As though *he* mattered.

After a while, Mr Hughes reached into his pocket, pulling out a handful of coins. He counted them slowly onto the table.

'Oh. I was going to get the teas, but I've only got enough for the one,' he said, looking embarrassed. 'I didn't realise . . .'

Cai waved a hand. 'It's fine,' he said lightly, pushing the coins back towards him. 'My shout.'

The old man frowned. 'No, I couldn't . . .'

'Yes, you could,' Cai said, gently but firmly. He scooped up the coins and pressed them back into the old man's hand. 'Next time, you can tell me more about the area. You've told me lots of things I didn't know and it's been really helpful.'

There was a pause and Mr Hughes nodded, dropping the coins back into his pocket. When he left, he seemed to carry himself a little taller than when he'd come in, the hint of a smile on his lips.

Cai didn't look over at Elin straight away. He picked up his notebook again, as if nothing particularly significant had just happened. Elin walked over, wiping her hands on her apron.

'That was good of you,' she said.

Cai looked up. 'What?'

She tipped her head towards the door. 'You know.'

Cai pushed out his lower lip. 'He looked like he needed someone to talk to.'

'Well, it was a nice thing to do, anyway.'

He shrugged, his cheeks flushing a little. 'Anyone would've done the same.'

But Elin knew that simply wasn't true. She studied him then, properly. There was no trace of self-satisfaction in his face, no expectation of praise. If anything, he seemed slightly puzzled by her reaction. Something in her chest fluttered, but not unpleasantly.

A lot of people, she thought, rationed kindness, expecting it to be acknowledged when given. Expecting something in return. But it was clearly just part of who Cai was. A natural reaction; as unremarkable to him as putting on shoes before leaving the house.

She smiled, a rush of warmth rising in her. 'D'you want another tea?'

He grinned. 'Go on, then.'

*

Elin remembered how, as she'd turned back to the counter that day, she had looked forward to telling Nain and Nerys about him. Not about his sense of humour, or his enthusiasm for the archaeology, or even the way he'd brought her a gift. But about this. About the way he treated people.

It was Nerys who had summed it up perfectly when she'd told her later.

It was about the goodness of his soul.

*

Elin was feeling increasingly anxious that Cai hadn't got back to her. It was almost 9.45 p.m. and she needed to get an early night. Having made arrangements for her journey, she would have to travel whether she heard from him or not. It was really bizarre that he didn't appear to have checked his phone at some point. Surely he must have been able to get a signal *somewhere*.

Having finally given up on hearing from him, Elin left one last curt message and switched off the TV. Though her mind was still buzzing, she really had to get to bed. She was halfway up the short flight of stairs leading to the bedroom when the security light outside the front porch lit up the hallway. The doorbell rang out. Elin turned to see two figures in silhouette through the frosted glass.

Her heart quickened. Who the hell would be calling round at this hour?

She retraced her steps to open the door cautiously, the chain still in place. Cai had impressed upon her to always be careful, especially when she was alone. Coming from a place where people rarely locked their doors, during the day at least, it had taken some getting used to.

Through the gap, she could see two uniformed police officers;

a twentyish, tall, clean-shaven man with ruddy cheeks and a petite, olive-skinned woman, who looked about forty.

'Elin Owen?' The woman smiled diffidently.

'Yes?'

The female officer indicated her colleague, who appeared suddenly preoccupied with his shoes. 'This is PC Walker and I'm Sergeant Chowdhury. I wonder, could we come in, please?'

Chapter 8

TEN YEARS EARLIER – October 2013

The day after the storm

Elin

No one had slept properly. The storm passed, leaving the sky a bleak white-grey, the sea as calm as a millpond. Ianto went home to see to Gel then returned with the dog around midday, looking hollow-eyed and anguished. Nain was attempting to maintain some sense of normality, and had made a big pot of vegetable *cawl*. How she could concentrate enough to do anything under the circumstances was beyond Elin, who had been helped back upstairs by Ianto after fainting the previous night. A bucket had been left beside the bed, but thankfully throwing up once violently when she came round seemed to have purged her. She was grateful for the soup and sat now on the settee with a blanket wrapped round her, the steaming bowl on her lap, dunking a huge wedge of buttered bread into it. Nerys looked as though she had been drugged. She sat staring into space, hands in her lap, her eyes heavy and unfocused, refusing anything that Nain desperately tried to get into her.

Ianto had declined Nain's offer of soup, but perched on the edge of the armchair nearest the window clutching the mug of tea which she'd pressed into his hands, his eyes travelling outside periodically as Gel sat panting at his feet.

'Just heard young Jac went missing last night, too.' He took a slurp of tea, glancing back to the window as if still hoping Meinir might reappear. 'His mam's beside herself.'

Nerys turned her head, her brow creasing. 'Jac Parry?'

Ianto nodded. 'Seems he went on his usual walkabout – he'd been saying he wanted to chase the lightning when Delyth told him there was a storm on the way. You know what he's like, gets all animated with anything different, poor lad. Brightens stuff up for him, I s'pose.' He shook his head sadly. 'Sounds as if he'd been pestering her about it and in the end, she gave in and said he could go out for a while. I mean, it can't be easy for her all on her own with him. She still needs to keep a close eye on him all the time, even if he's a grown man now. I mean, he must be what – mid-twenties, at least – but he's still like a child in his head.'

'Oh *Duw*.' Nain stood in the kitchen doorway, wiping her hands on her apron. 'And there's been no sign of him?'

Ianto looked solemn. 'He'd popped into The Quay for half an hour last night, saying hello to everyone like he does, watching the fruit machine and that. I must've left before he got there. Rhiannon was working behind the bar. She said he'd been watching the storm for a few minutes, then suddenly got up and went.' He rubbed at his eyes with the heel of his hands, letting out a long breath. 'The coppers have been knocking on everyone's doors in case he'd gone into someone's house to shelter, but sounds like no one's seen him since he left the pub.'

‘That’s awful. I’ll go and see Delyth, offer some moral support.’ Nain relieved Ianto briskly of his empty mug and bustled into the kitchen. The noise of the running tap and clattering around implied she was in a hurry.

Ianto took this as his cue to leave. He stood up, shooting a brief, uncertain smile at the girls, the dog at his heels, tail wagging. ‘I’d better get back myself. *Diolch am y panad*, Mrs Owen,’ he called through to the kitchen. ‘Give Delyth my best, won’t you? See you soon, ladies.’

*

Nain filled a lidded Tupperware container with a generous amount of soup for Delyth. She placed it at her feet, then lifted her coat from the hook next to the front door.

‘Poor, poor Delyth. That lad’s her whole life. She’s got no one else.’ She looked pointedly at the girls where they sat, waiting for someone to offer to accompany her. Elin chewed the last mouthful of her bread and put down her bowl, shrugging off the blanket.

‘Give me a minute and I’ll come with you.’ Elin took the stairs two at a time to find her coat, which she’d draped over the chair in the room she and Nerys shared. She glanced into Mam’s room as she came out, an ache filling her chest. It was just as she’d left it last night, Mam’s half-drunk glass of squash still on the dressing table with a lipstick mark around the rim. Elin couldn’t bring herself to remove it. Not yet. Tears sprang to her eyes once more and she stopped for a moment to compose herself, before pulling on her coat and thundering back down the stairs to where Nain was already standing in the open doorway, letting in a blast of cool air.

Elin turned to her sister.

‘Nerys? You coming?’

Nerys paled, as though the prospect of leaving the house was something terrifying she dare not risk. She shrank deeper into the settee. 'I—I'll stay here. Just in case . . .'

Nain's eyes flickered but she said nothing.

Bringing the pot of soup in a carrier bag, Elin followed through the door, closing it behind them. As they passed out of the gate, they saw the snow-white haired Peter around twenty yards away lumbering across the quay in their direction, his focus trained on a cluster of gulls jostling as they pecked at something on the ground, their wings outstretched. Looking up, his gaze shifted towards Elin and Nain. He seemed to stiffen a little, glancing back over his shoulder, but then carried on towards them.

As they met halfway across the gravel path, Peter greeted them with a nod, smiling uncertainly.

'Mrs Owen. Elin.'

Nain nodded back in greeting. '*Bore da*, Peter.'

Elin shot a look at her grandmother. She looked exhausted and yet was still managing to hold everything together. Her strength was incredible.

'I just wanted to say . . .' Peter paused awkwardly, his eyes not meeting theirs, hands behind his back as though unsure what to do with them. 'Libby and I are so sorry. For your loss.'

Elin drew in a breath. So it was official. Everyone must know by now: word travelled fast round here. They were going to start receiving pitying looks wherever they went, or people would avoid them. She'd seen it before, when Mrs Williams's husband passed away. Well, she remembered Mam talking about it, anyway. How awful she'd thought it must be for the poor woman. Nobody knew quite what to say when someone's loved one died, she'd said, and many of them obviously found it easier to say nothing at all. Elin felt sure that Peter would have pretended not to see them, had they not met him face to face.

'I can't imagine what you're all going through. If there's anything we can do, anything at all, please don't hesitate to ask.' Peter leaned forward to shake Nain by the hand. It felt a rather stilted reaction to Elin, but Nain appeared to receive the gesture warmly.

'Thank you, Peter. That's much appreciated.'

Peter seemed to relax a little. He smiled, more confidently. 'I'll let you get on your way. Don't forget, we're only next door if you need us.' He nodded again and, releasing Nain's hand, continued towards his front gate.

Nain hooked her own arm through Elin's free one and they began to make their way around the edge of the bay, towards the lane and Delyth Parry's *bwthyn*, her ramshackle cottage.

Delyth was a small woman, her build so slight that she looked as though she might snap if someone hugged her too tightly. Her bobbed, mousy hair was thinning, grey creeping in at the temples. The clothes that hung from her were worn and faded from years of use. She must have been ten years older than Mam, but looked more like twenty. Life had been hard on her and it showed. The atmosphere in the damp little house was fraught. The woman kept shifting between tears and extreme agitation, constantly going to the window to check for evidence of Jac's return – or of someone bearing news. Nain tried to encourage her to eat or drink something, but to no avail.

'How can I eat when my boy's out there all alone somewhere?' she had wailed, her face twisting in despair. 'How could I have let him go out with a storm brewing? He kept nagging at me and I was just so tired yesterday evening – I'd been on the go all day. I just wanted an hour to myself to wash up after tea and watch *Coronation Street*. I thought he'd be back by eight. We were going to watch one of those *Harry Potter* films and he was looking forward to it. He just gets, you know – fidgety sometimes. Needs to get stuff out of his system.'

'I know, cariad,' Nain had soothed, patting her on the back. 'It's not your fault. You're entitled to some time to yourself and Jac's a good boy, he always comes home when you tell him . . .'

'So where is he then?' Delyth began to sob, covering her face with her hands and crumpling to her knees. 'Where is my son? What's happened to him?'

Chapter 9

TEN YEARS EARLIER – October 2013

The day after the storm

Elin

It had been awful. Elin stayed with Nain at Delyth's for about an hour, then made her excuses, saying she ought to go and check on Nerys. Which was true; she *was* quite worried about her. But that aside, she felt exhausted and needed to warm up, and the frigid atmosphere in the cottage was leeching into her bones. Her feet were blocks of ice, and with the hangover, plus the lack of sleep, the lure of her own cosy bed was increasingly irresistible. There was an intermittent drip from Delyth's ceiling, an old metal bucket placed near the small window catching the water beneath a patch of plaster with a huge stain spreading across it. The draughty little house remained freezing, despite the fire that Nain had managed to coax back to life in the ancient range. Stuffing poked through the worn, flat cushions of the wooden-framed suite and the old rag rug in the middle of the stone floor did nothing to block out the cold rising from the ground. Maybe Delyth was used to it and had become hardened to the chill. Elin's heart went out to the woman. Her son might not ever be coming home and she had nothing, not even any basic home comforts. It seemed so cruel.

The tide was out. From the end of the lane, Elin spied a group of around seven men gathered by the small boats anchored to the ridge of sand near the shore, in front of The Quay. As she drew nearer, Elin could see that Ianto was among them, along with Catrin's dad, Derfel, and Peter. Their heads were bowed and they all appeared to be inspecting the sides of the boats. There were raised voices and much swearing, their body language taut as though ready for a fight.

'Hey, Ianto.' Elin nodded, a little self-consciously, as the others turned to glance at her. Everyone's demeanour shifted, their expressions suddenly uneasy. No one spoke. Mam's disappearance was clearly a big, fat elephant in the room.

Ianto looked round, his expression grim at first, but he managed a brief grin as his eyes landed on her.

'Hiya, Elin.'

'What's going on?'

His face dropped again. He gestured over a shoulder with his thumb.

'Looks like someone's been at a few of these fellas' boats with something. They've got holes in 'em.' He shook his head angrily. 'Potentially thousands of pounds' worth of damage if they can't be permanently repaired.'

He explained that initially they'd thought the destruction could be attributed to the storm, but closer inspection revealed that the cracks in the boats' hulls were too similar, too uniform, as if caused by a heavy implement. Someone had deliberately sabotaged them. But of course, owing to the weather, everyone had been indoors. Nobody had seen a thing.

Elin approached, her eyes scanning the damage. It was a horrible thought, that someone could have been so malicious. Particularly if it was someone who lived among them.

'Why would anyone do something like that?'

Derfel turned to her, his face puce. She knew that one of the boats belonged to him and was named after Catrin's mum, Sali-Mai.

'Because they're a twisted bastard, that's why.' His voice was an angry hiss, but there was an underlying tremor. His huge fists were clenched like rocks at his sides. 'And if I get my hands on them, I'll wring their fucking neck.'

Peter laid a hand on his arm. 'Come on now, mate. We can sort this out.' His tone was calm, soothing. 'I'll help you fix it.' He indicated the other men in the group. 'We'll all help. Won't we, lads?'

There was a murmur of assent.

'There's a chandlery in Beaumaris – they're sure to stock fibreglass repair materials,' chipped in one tall man, with a mop of thick, dark hair. 'I'll measure up to see what we need. I'm free this afternoon so I can go and get everything.' His eyes met Elin's and he gave her a consoling smile.

Elin had seen him at Catrin's before. He was from Pentraeth, a friend of Derfel's, although she couldn't remember his name. Was it Harry? He'd seemed nice enough, actually bothering to say hello, unlike some of the ignorant louts Derfel mixed with.

'We need to shift the vessels towards the groyne – every time the tide comes in, the water's going to seep in a bit more.'

Elin looked round and recognised the squat, balding man speaking as Hugh Roberts, the local butcher and another of the boat owners. She wasn't keen on him. Mam, who'd been a vegetarian for years, had had a run-in with him some months earlier when she discovered he was planning to sell kangaroo meat in his shop.

'Bad enough killing the poor things that are reared here let alone introducing more creatures from overseas,' she'd yelled at Roberts across his counter. 'What next? Will you be rounding up stray dogs?'

There had been a rumble of approval from the handful of people in the queue. One woman had even handed back the chops she was about to pay for in disgust, declaring she'd boycott the shop if he went ahead with the idea. Ironic really, Mam had later remarked when recounting the event to Nain, that the woman felt it was okay to tuck into the little lambs that she saw year-round frolicking in the fields. Nonetheless, Roberts had reluctantly bowed to public pressure and shelved the venture. But Catrin had told Elin she'd overheard him telling Derfel, 'That bitch has cost me. I could've made a killing there.'

Elin noticed Roberts giving her a sly sideways glance. He looked away again just as quickly.

'The holes need to be patched temporarily with some leak sealant putty so we can get them afloat, then they can be moved onto the beach to do a proper job.' He pursed his lips. 'I've got some in the shed at home – I'll go and get it now, then we can make a start. Davy, can you bring your tractor to tow them up the beach once they're plugged?'

Davy Jenkins, whose farm overlooked the bay, nodded. '*Dim problem o gwbl.*'

Ianto turned to Elin. 'Any news on Jac?'

She shook her head. 'Nothing. Poor Delyth's in a really bad way.'

'Huh. Maybe she should've kept him in then.'

All eyes swivelled to land on Hugh Roberts. The man gave a dismissive shrug of his shoulders. 'I mean, the lad's not safe to be out alone at the best of times, never mind in the middle of a raging storm. Bloody irresponsible, if you ask me.'

Everyone exchanged uncomfortable glances.

'That's pretty harsh,' chipped in Ianto, narrowing his eyes as he addressed Roberts. 'It's not like he's a little kid. He knows the area. And Delyth's a good mam. It's not easy for her.'

Roberts's jaw tightened. He rolled his eyes, making an odd sort of tutting noise under his breath but said no more. Everyone turned their attention back to the boats, but the atmosphere felt suddenly even more tense.

It turned out that four of the five grounded vessels had sustained damage. Derfel owned a launching dolly and though Davy Jenkins was ready with his tractor, moving the boats would take several hours and the tide was creeping in all the time, plus daylight would be running out early. They needed to get a move on.

Elin made her excuses and continued on her way, anger building inside her as she thought about what Hugh Roberts had said. What a vile little man he really was. She couldn't believe anyone could be so callous.

Arriving home, Elin had tried to sleep, but was too restless, despite being exhausted. At least she'd warmed through now. All she could think of was Mam. There was a horrible knot tightening deep in her chest, a heavy, overwhelming sensation. But though she needed some sort of release, Elin felt too wrung out to cry. After an hour of tossing and turning, she went back down to watch from the living room window as the men, now shadowy figures through the dim outside, continued to work like Trojans. Nain had returned earlier after spending the best part of the day with Delyth, then taken herself straight off to bed: for half an hour, she'd said, but it had been almost two now. Nerys had been uncommunicative when Elin got home, and eventually retreated to their room, where she lay on her bed, curled up like a snail into its shell, her face to the wall. The shocking aftermath of the storm had left an awful, empty atmosphere in the house.

Elin went through to the kitchen to make tea. She saw Mam's favourite *World's Best Mum* mug, the one Nerys bought her for Mother's Day, as she opened the cupboard and a further wave of misery engulfed her. She thought fleetingly of poor Jac, whom she didn't doubt had met with the same fate that had befallen her mother. Her eyes travelled to the clock on the wall, realising that only twenty-four hours earlier, he was safely at home with Delyth, while Mam had been upstairs, her music playing as she got ready for her date. Filling the house with her energy and laughter. The thought that everything could change so quickly terrified Elin. What if something happened to Nain? What would become of her and Nerys? What if . . .

A sudden knock at the front door made her start. She opened it, to find Ianto on the doorstep. In one hand, and with an old rag wrapped around the thing, he was holding some sort of metal rod, about a foot and a half in length, with a blob of blue paint at one end. Ianto looked washed out, his face pinched and grave.

'Is your nain home, cariad?'

'She's having a lie-down. Come in, she should be up soon.'

Ianto's jaw twitched as he entered. He seemed uncomfortable, still gripping the metal implement.

Elin glanced down at the object in his thick hands. It looked like one of those things people use to take wheels off cars. Maybe he'd been using it while they moved the boats or something. 'I'm making a *panad*, d'you want one?'

'I won't stay, thanks all the same. I've left Gel in the house and he'll be wanting out.' A lump moved up and down in his throat. 'D'you think you could see if your nain's awake, please? I just need a quick word.'

A creak from above told them she was up. '*Pwy sydd yna*?' she said. 'Who is it, El?'

‘It’s me, Mrs Owen,’ Ianto called.

‘Oh, hang on. I’ll be there now.’ Nain appeared at the top of the stairs, looking a little dishevelled. She came down into the living room, offered them both a half-hearted smile, then lowered herself into her armchair, exhaling as though it was a real effort.

Everything about Ianto seemed to tighten, making Elin wonder what this was all about.

‘Any news?’ Nain ventured, studying the man’s pained expression.

Ianto puffed out his cheeks. ‘I found this.’ Nodding slightly, he held up the metal rod. ‘On the sand, not far from the boats. It’s—it’s from Meinir’s car.’

‘*Meinir’s*? Are you sure?’ Nain leaned forward to take a closer look.

‘It’s the paint, see. No idea why, but whoever owned the Ka before her sprayed the end with touch-up paint, same colour as the car. I recognised it straight away. I changed the front wheel for her a few months ago, when she had a flat.’ Ianto’s face folded into a worried frown. ‘Some of the lads . . . well, they thought it might have been what was used to bash the boats.’

Elin felt as though she’d been punched. The very suggestion that her mam could have been involved in something so malicious was unthinkable – even more so that anyone could believe that of her.

‘*What*?’ Nain’s mouth fell open. ‘*Iesu mawr*. Meinir would never do a thing like that. You know as well as I do—’

Ianto raised a palm. ‘I know, I know. And I didn’t mention it was Mein’s, like. But I thought you should know what they’re saying – it’s sure to come out where the brace came from. I’ll have to hand it over to the police and I s’pose they’ll trace it back to her car.’

Nain clutched at her head with both hands. 'Why would it be lying on the ground like that? D'you think someone pinched it out of her boot? I s'pose it's not impossible it was used to hit the boats. Maybe someone else took it out of the car. It makes no sense.'

Ianto shrugged. 'Nope. And without Mein here to tell us exactly what went on, we're unlikely to find out.' There was a beat of uncomfortable silence, before he added, 'I expect the police'll be able to establish if it was used, though. You know, with their forensic people and that. I'm sure, you know . . .'

Elin noticed Ianto's eyes flicker as he spoke this last line. Surely *he* couldn't believe Mam capable of vandalism? She might be rather headstrong, but she was never aggressive or violent, even if she'd had a drink or two.

Nain didn't appear to have noticed him falter. 'Well, get it to the police then, and they'll be able to rule it out. It's sure to come out it was Meinir's and I won't have people spreading lies about her. Especially when she's not here to defend herself.' She seemed agitated now, shaking her head. 'I'm more baffled why it was taken out of her car. The police never said anything while they were here.'

'They probably weren't aware, to be fair.' Ianto smiled tightly. 'Anyway, thought I ought to tell you. I'll get it straight to the coppers now.'

He paused briefly in the doorway, as if about to say something else but thinking better of it, before heading slowly back out into the dusk. He looked beaten-down, disillusioned.

Elin felt a wave of despair wash over her. If Ianto, of all people, could think that of her mam, everyone else would believe it, too. The Owens would become pariahs by default, guilty by association.

Nain stared after him for a moment, then seemed to shake off her anger.

'Storm in a teacup, I'm sure.' She lifted her eyes to meet Elin's, forcing her lips into what passed for a smile. 'Shall we have that *panad* then, cariad? Let's see if we can't coax a cup into your sister, and a sandwich, too. She can't survive on fresh air.'

Chapter 10

NOW – Earlier on Wednesday 5th April 2023

Cai

Mercifully Dr Baden had come down with food poisoning, and by mid-morning it was announced that the afternoon's lecture had been cancelled. The cheap-and-not-so-cheerful fish paste sandwiches were no doubt responsible – food lying around uncovered and unrefrigerated for hours was a certified breeding ground for bacteria. Cai felt slightly guilty for his sense of relief, but aside from the artefacts that were on display, the course had proved pretty heavy-going, not helped by the older man's crusty delivery of information. Cai had learned a little, but not nearly as much as he'd hoped.

Having a few hours to kill, Cai decided to walk into the nearest village to catch the bus into Bangor, then another to Anglesey, to visit Nerys. It would take him a couple of hours to get there, but he'd promised Elin he'd make the effort if he was able. Besides, he felt pretty sorry for Nerys with everything she'd had going on the last few months. She would probably be glad of a visitor. Some of the other lads staying at the hostel declared cheerfully that they were going to find a decent pub and get slowly pissed. But Cai declined the offer to join them. Apart from checking on Elin's sister, he was keen to have another look at where the forthcoming dig at Traeth Coch was going to take place. It had been on his mind ever since he first researched the area, and Cai's excitement about his plans becoming reality was building.

He tried to call Elin again from the bus, but the mobile reception in the area was woeful. Less than one bar on his phone. He had intended to contact Nerys, tell her he was popping over. But she'd be in, he was sure of it. Even if she wasn't home though, it would be a day out, and he could just spend longer doing a recce of the area, refreshing his memory of the bits he wanted to focus on. Maybe grab a bite to eat in The Old Boathouse restaurant or The Quay. It was better than being stuck in that hostel – and he certainly wasn't up for getting drunk. He'd be travelling home the following day and didn't fancy nursing a hangover on the train. Even though they'd only been apart a few days, he missed Elin. Cai hoped she'd been coping okay with her broken foot. He was so glad she'd be coming with him to Traeth Coch next month. While they both loved Birmingham, from the wistful way she'd begun recently to recount tales of her childhood, he knew she was growing homesick. She'd been quite down for a while after her nain died. The change of scenery would do her good – and besides, he loved the place. Maybe they'd settle there eventually. Have a family of their own. He was in for the long haul.

Though he'd never told her as much, Elin reminded him so much of his mum. Not in looks, but the way she was. Warm; bright and funny. Affectionate. She made him feel safe, loved – something that had been missing in his life for so long before he'd met her, especially with the way his dad had more or less shut down after his mum died. The fact that Elin had lost her own mam, too, had forged an instant connection between them. She understood the days when he was down, the birthdays and Christmases; that empty, gnawing feeling that would grip him sometimes, the feeling something was missing. He could cry in her arms and never feel judged. She got it – got *him* – completely. And Cai felt Elin's pain, the days when the memory of Meinir's disappearance hung over her like a dark shadow, when she didn't want to talk and retreated into herself for a while. At least he'd been able to say goodbye to his mum, tell her how much he loved her. Neither Elin nor Nerys had had the bittersweet comfort of that closure. It was cruel. Never-ending.

The weather had been unforgiving since he'd arrived in Caernarfon, but though the air was still cool and the sky that familiar washed-out grey, the constant drizzle of the last couple of days had finally abated. Cai alighted the bus at Bangor bus station and had to run like hell to catch the 62, its engine already grumbling, about to head for the Britannia Bridge and the A5025 towards Amlwch. It would have meant another half-hour's wait if he'd missed it. The doors swished closed behind him as the vehicle pulled away immediately in a haze of diesel fumes. He flopped into a seat near the back, relishing the warmth beneath him. There were only six or seven other passengers, although from having made the journey so often in the past, he knew the bus would start to fill by the time they got to Menai Bridge.

Reaching into the outer pocket of his padded combat jacket, he felt around for his phone to try Elin again.

Cai sat up suddenly. Frantically, he checked the other side but it wasn't there. *Shit.* It must have fallen out when he'd made his dash for the bus. That'd teach him not to zip up his pocket.

Elin was forever telling him off about it. And it was a newish handset to boot. He let out an involuntary groan.

'Everything all right, cariad?' The elderly lady to his right turned to look at him.

'It's fine, thanks. Just, I think I dropped my phone when I was running for the bus. So stupid.'

'*Aw bechod*. Maybe someone'll hand it in at the depot. They've got a lost property office there.'

'Oh right, thanks. I'll have a look when I go back later.' He blew out a long, frustrated breath.

'D'you want to use mine?' The old woman had begun to rummage through her handbag. 'It's in here somewhere.'

Cai screwed up his face. 'That's very kind of you, but I don't actually know any of the numbers – they're just saved as contacts. Makes you realise how much we rely on these things, eh?'

The lady put down her bag. She looked up and smiled, a little sadly. 'I know. I've got the number for my doctor's surgery on a scrap of paper in my purse, but that's about it. But I still remember all the important ones from years ago. The ones that no one's there to answer any more.' She looked away, and Cai thought she gave a little sniff. He felt awkward then, concerned his words had unintentionally stirred an unhappy memory. Maybe he should try distracting her.

'Are you from the island?'

'Me? Oh yes, born and bred. You're not, are you?' She tipped her head knowingly. 'Can't detect any hint of the gog.'

He grinned at this reference to his accent, thinking of Elin's pronounced Welsh lilt. 'No. Well, I was born near Conwy, and my mum was from Anglesey originally, but my parents moved to Manchester when I was four.'

'So what brings you here then, all on your own?'

Cai glanced out of the window, at the lush fields peppered with sheep and cattle stretching far and wide beyond the hedgerows, the huge expanse of sky. It was so far removed from their home in the city, and yet it made his heart soar. He understood why his mum had often spoken of it so wistfully, and why Elin had begun to pine for it all. The more he thought about it, the more resolved he felt to find a home for them both here.

'My partner, Elin, is from Traeth Coch. She's stuck at home in the Midlands with a broken foot but I've been up here for a few days with work, so I'm just going to pay her sister a visit.'

'Traeth Coch, you say?' She sat up. 'I'm in Benllech now myself, in a retirement flat. But I was brought up a stone's throw away, in Pentraeth. I know plenty of people from round there.'

'You may have known Elin's nain, then. Hannah Owen?'

The old woman leaned towards him eagerly. 'Of course! She was in my big sister's year at school. But she wasn't Owen then. Jones, she used to be, before she married. A real head-turner in her day.' Her face clouded. 'I was sad to hear she'd passed, but maybe it was a blessing under the circumstances. She hadn't been good for a long time, had she? Terrible, losing her daughter how she did. And to never really know what happened, either.' She shook her head. 'Impossible to get over a thing like that properly. You'd want answers. Understandable that it sent her a little . . . well, you know. Sounded as if she was pointing the finger at everyone by the end.' She arched an eyebrow.

Cai pulled back, studying her with interest. 'Oh, really? Elin said she'd been saying all sorts, but I didn't know she'd actually been accusing people. I imagine dementia affects everyone differently.'

The old lady drew closer, lowering her voice. 'I think it was what happened that led to the dementia, personally. Meinir was a nice girl but a touch, well . . . flighty, I s'pose they'd have called it in my day. There were rumours it was some man she'd been out with did away with her – and there were a few of them to choose from, mind.' She pulled a face.

Cai chewed his lip. Elin had told him some people had been less than charitable about Meinir's tangled love life. But he was still curious to know what the rumour-mongers had been saying. 'I understood she'd drowned – there was a bad storm, wasn't there?'

'Everyone assumed that at first. The inquest ruled an open verdict – they never found her body, as I'm sure you know. But it was all very odd. You heard about young Jac Parry, did you?'

Cai had a vague recollection of the name. 'Was that the lad that drowned the same night?'

She nodded, leaning towards him conspiratorially. 'I knew someone who worked in the hospital. She let it slip that the pathologist suspected Jac could've been choked before he was thrown into the sea. They couldn't prove anything a hundred per cent. His body had been in the water too long, poor soul. But of course, it set everyone to thinking that maybe he'd been helped on his way. And the fact Meinir went missing the same night seemed like too much of a coincidence.'

The old woman's face was alight now. Cai regarded her sceptically. He understood what Elin had said scathingly about rumours and gossip being rife in the community.

'So people thought someone might've killed them both, is that what you're saying?'

'Exactly. That storm covered up a multitude of sins, if you ask me.' She clasped her hands across her stomach and sat back in her seat. 'No wonder really, that Hannah became so suspicious of everyone. I mean, you would be, wouldn't you? Especially when there were a few who might've wished Meinir harm.'

'But why?'

She shrugged. 'Men. Present company excepted, I'm sure – but lots of them don't like being brushed off. And Meinir was always the one doing the brushing off, let me tell you. The old male pride thing, isn't it?'

‘I thought the saying went “hell hath no fury like a woman”. . .’

The old woman laughed. ‘Ah, but when it comes to the really nasty stuff – not always, I grant you – but nine times out of ten there’s a man behind it, isn’t there?’

Cai tried to think of a witty response. But when he considered what she was saying, he couldn’t argue. It gave him a peculiar feeling in the pit of his stomach.

Maybe Meinir’s death hadn’t been an accident at all.

Chapter 11

NOW – Wednesday 5th April 2023

Birmingham

Elin

A cold feeling began to build from somewhere deep within Elin's core. Why would the police want to speak to her? It suddenly hit her. Something awful had happened to Nerys. She fought against the invisible hand constricting her throat, praying that her worst fears were unfounded; that the reason for their visit was something innocuous. But the officers' grave demeanour told her otherwise. And she'd been here before, hadn't she? The night Mam went missing was engraved on her memory, fresh and terrible, as if it were only yesterday. With trembling fingers, she slid back the chain and opened the door properly, then stepped aside for them to enter.

The pair refused the offer of a seat, standing awkwardly

in Elin's living room, each clutching their caps in both hands like footballers protecting themselves before a free kick. Elin lowered herself shakily onto the settee and studied their solemn faces.

'Wh—what's happened?' Elin looked from one to the other, the feeling of dread increasing.

Sergeant Chowdhury gave an odd little cough, unable to look Elin in the eye. 'I'm very sorry, but we're here to notify you of something that occurred in Anglesey in the early hours of this morning.'

Elin clapped a hand to her mouth, emitting a sob. She felt sick.

'Oh God.' It was as she'd feared. Nerys was gone. The poor girl had been all alone for far too long, struggling to cope after losing Nain, and now Elin would never be able to make it up to her.

The woman continued to speak but Elin had tuned out. All she could think about was how she had let Nerys down; how she could never forgive herself for being so utterly self-obsessed in the cosy little bubble she'd created with Cai. And now it was too late to put things right.

Sergeant Chowdhury had been talking all the while, but to Elin it had just been white noise as her mind turned everything over: the desperation poor Nerys must have felt, the sense of abandonment.

'Unfortunately, there were no witnesses.' The police woman cleared her throat. 'And the driver of the vehicle hasn't come forward.'

Elin lifted her head sharply, her stomach roiling. 'What—sorry, what vehicle?' *Oh Christ*. 'What's actually happened to Nerys?'

The officers threw one another a look of confusion. 'Who is Nerys?'

'My sister?'

'Miss Owen, we don't know anything about your sister. I don't think you could've heard what I said initially. This is in relation to your partner, Cai Rowlands? You are registered as his next of kin.' Sergeant Chowdhury exhaled deeply, her brow furrowing. 'Mr Rowlands was involved in a hit-and-run accident. I'm very sorry to have to tell you, he was pronounced dead at the scene.'

Elin felt as though someone had knocked all the breath from her lungs. At once it was like she had been propelled from her body and was floating somewhere above the room, in a weirdly altered state of consciousness. The police officers faded into the background for a moment, her vision blurring, any sound muffled. This wasn't real. This couldn't be happening.

With a jolt she was back in the room, crouching forward where she sat as though bracing for an explosion, her hands over her ears. A deafening keening sound filled her whole head.

Elin became suddenly aware that the sound was coming from her.

*

'El, have you ever really thought about what happens to us when we die?'

They'd been lying in bed one Sunday morning the previous June. Elin had been scrolling absently through her phone as Cai – wearing only boxer shorts, his bare, muscular legs stretched out over the covers – pored over the paperback he'd been reading for the last couple of days. He lay the open book face down beside him and turned to her, propping himself up on one elbow.

'I mean, d'you ever wonder whether it's just like a light going out, or if part of us carries on in some way? You know, the continuation of the soul or whatever they call it.'

That stopped her in her tracks. Elin set her phone on the bedside cabinet, tilting her face to look at him. His expression wasn't haunted or maudlin, just thoughtful, the kind of look she'd seen on his face when scrutinising fragments of pottery or a half-buried mosaic floor. It was that same slightly detached curiosity, as if death were simply another question to be examined. But there was something else, a small flicker in his eyes that made her wonder if there might be more to it. Cai was usually so pragmatic about everything – his musing over a subject like this felt alien.

A sudden bolt of panic shot through Elin. She sat up straighter. 'You're not . . . you're not ill or anything, are you?'

Cai threw back his head and laughed. 'No! Not as far as I'm aware.'

Her shoulders dropped. She let out the breath she'd been holding in. 'Then what the hell have you been reading?' Elin glanced down at the cover of his book. *All That Remains: A Life in Death*. Her brow furrowed as she looked back at his face. 'Is it something in there?'

'No, not really,' he replied. 'Just . . . I don't know, something set me thinking.'

Cai trusted facts and things he could actually touch and measure; he dismissed ghost stories with amusement and practical theories. He believed in history because it left solid, tangible evidence behind. Even though he'd lost his mum at a young age, he'd never vocalised thoughts about an afterlife. The question felt out of place coming from him and it had wrong-footed her. Elin pondered for a moment.

'I don't know,' she said eventually. 'I s'pose . . . I hope it's not just, well, *nothing*.'

He nodded, as if that were a perfectly reasonable response. His brow knitted slightly. 'D'you find the idea frightening at all?'

She hesitated. 'I try not to think about it, to be honest. But sometimes, yes. Not of being dead, exactly. More how it's going to happen. And the thought of leaving unfinished business. Leaving people I love behind.'

Cai was quiet for a moment, his warm fingers absently tracing a pattern along her arm now. 'If anything ever *did* happen to me,' he said, in that same steady tone, 'I'd want you to be happy, you know.'

Elin's chest tightened. She leaned back against the headboard, frowning at him. 'That's a horrible thing to say on a Sunday morning.'

'I'm serious,' he continued, his face earnest now. 'I wouldn't want you . . . you, know, stuck in limbo. Pining, or missing out on anything because of me. You should enjoy every day. As if it's your last, and all that. I mean, we never know what's round the corner. Tomorrow isn't guaranteed for any of us, right?'

She stared at him, a spark of anger rising to mask her underlying fear.

'Bloody pack it in, will you? You're not dying,' she said. But as she spoke, she could feel the quaver in her voice.

'I know,' he said. The hint of a smile played on his lips now. 'I'm not planning to, anyway. Occupational hazards aside. I mean, I could easily fall into a big hole, never to be seen again—'

'That's not even funny.' She gave him a mock punch on the arm, but she meant it. The conversation was giving rise to a feeling of horrible unease inside her. Cai leaving her wasn't something she ever wanted to contemplate.

'It *is* mildly amusing,' he responded, with a grin.

'It is *not*,' she insisted. Something twisted in her stomach. 'For God's sake, why are you going on like this all of a sudden? Just stop.'

He reached up to brush a strand of hair away from her face, his expression softening.

'Because it's important,' he said quietly. 'And because no one usually talks about these things until it's too late. I mean, if anything *should* happen to me, and I'm not saying it will, but . . .'

The sudden solemnity in his voice made her throat constrict. She wanted to dismiss it, to bat the suggestion away and make a joke of it all, but his words had provoked an unwelcome, unpalatable train of thought.

'I could never just replace you,' she said in a small voice.

'I didn't say *replace*. I said be happy. There's a difference.'

Elin looked away, blinking back tears. 'Cai, I really don't like this.'

Cai let out a soft, familiar laugh then, easing some of the tension that had crept in. 'Okay.' He cleared his throat. 'Let me rephrase that.'

She glanced back at him warily.

'If anything ever happens to me,' he continued, 'you are definitely allowed to find happiness with someone else.'

'That's not better.'

'It is,' he insisted. 'There's just one condition.'

She narrowed her eyes. 'Oh, is there now?'

'Yes.' His grin widened, mischief finally breaking through the seriousness. 'They can't be too good looking.'

Despite herself, a small, reluctant smile twitched on Elin's lips. '*Too good looking*?'

'Yep. Or too ripped. I don't want everyone saying you've had an upgrade.'

'You're an idiot,' she muttered, though the tightness in her chest had begun to loosen.

His eyebrows danced playfully. 'But a loveable one, I hope.'

Elin sighed, rolling her eyes, but she wriggled down to nestle closer beside him, placing her hand over his bare chest as if to reassure herself his heart was still beating. 'Loveable for a thousand reasons. Exasperating for a thousand more.' She paused for a second. 'And for the record, you're not allowed to die.'

'Noted,' he replied, dropping a kiss onto her head. 'I'll do my best not to.'

She huffed, but was grateful for the way his hand found hers, their fingers interlocking naturally as they always did. Elin held onto him a little more tightly than usual. No matter what Cai said, she could never find happiness with anyone else.

Not ever.

Chapter 12

NOW – Wednesday 5th April 2023

Birmingham

Elin

It transpired that, having travelled by bus to Traeth Coch earlier that day, Cai had walked up the narrow, winding lane leading from the beach, the one less inhabited than where Ianto's cottage was. The one where Delyth Parry used to live. He must have been heading to Pentraeth, to catch the bus back to Bangor. There was no street lighting nor any pavement. From what Sergeant Chowdhury said, the police who'd been called to the site of the accident theorised that the driver of the vehicle was probably travelling far too quickly for such a restricted, twisty road and hadn't seen Cai until it was too late, then panicked and fled the scene.

Sergeant Chowdhury told Elin in a careful voice that, from the information passed on by the Bangor *Heddlu*, Cai had been killed outright, with no chance that he would have suffered. But how could they know that? Were they just trying to spare her feelings further? All Elin could think was that *she* was the one who had sent him there, *she* had asked him to visit Nerys – whom, she'd discovered subsequently, wasn't even at home. It was almost impossible to take in the idea that her journey back to Anglesey would now end with her having to identify Cai's body lying on some cold slab.

PC Walker made Elin a cup of tea, but she had no interest in drinking it. Both police officers were kind and sympathetic, offering to contact family or friends on Elin's behalf, so that she wouldn't be alone. When she said there was no one, they exchanged concerned glances. They even suggested contacting someone from the local church. Elin wasn't religious and she certainly didn't want a stranger with her. She only wanted Cai. Apart from the searing pain in her gut and the feelings of complete despair, the reality that he wasn't coming back filled her with a strange kind of panic. And now she didn't even have Nerys to turn to.

Eventually, at Elin's insistence that she wanted to leave for Wales immediately, Sergeant Chowdhury made a couple of calls and arranged for a cab to take her there. She explained to Elin gently that they were liaising with the *Heddlu* in Bangor. Though she was sorry that they would be unable to accompany Elin on her journey, someone would be there to meet her at Ysbyty Gwynedd upon her arrival, she said. They would put her in touch with Brake, an organisation that offered support to the families of the victims of road traffic accidents.

Everything felt unreal to Elin. It was like being in a weird, distorted bubble; a nightmarish out-of-body experience. The very fact that she'd already packed for the train journey the next day made it seem almost as though this had all been pre-ordained. She stared out of the taxi window into the darkness, acid-yellow neon blurring the blue-black sky as they zipped along the M6, not really registering how much time had elapsed or even whereabouts they were. She was numb, hollowed out. Her whole life had been decimated.

Cai had been her rock. She remembered how he'd been the one shining light in the dark days after Nain's funeral. A beautiful distraction.

'I feel guilty going on about it when you're so sad, but I've got such a positive feeling about this,' he'd told her, as they walked hand in hand across the sands the day before they returned to Birmingham.

Elin hadn't vocalised her feelings, but she really didn't want to leave. They'd been back to Traeth Coch several times since she'd moved away, but losing Nain had made her realise how much she missed home. The thought of getting in the car and turning her back on it once more had opened a huge, gaping hole somewhere inside her.

Cai had stopped at the edge of the lane, pointing to the area above the beach, concealed behind dense, unkempt hedgerows.

'I can't explain why exactly, but I'm really drawn to that particular spot. Just think, El.' He'd turned her to face him, his dark eyes alight. 'This could be a real breakthrough if it's a decent hoard. It's so unspoilt up here, I bet there're potential dig sites all over the island. When – and I'm certain it's when, not *if* – we find something, we could get funding to set up a small visitors' centre or a dedicated museum. We could move here permanently.' He'd tilted her chin towards him. 'Find a nice little cottage to rent, even buy somewhere eventually. You'd like that, wouldn't you?'

Elin had leaned into him, allowing him to wrap her in his arms, the thought of coming back home with the man she loved lifting her spirits for the first time in weeks. It was all she could have asked for. *He* was all she could have asked for.

And now he was gone. Elin couldn't remember ever feeling so empty, so utterly lost. Any sense of purpose she'd had, any hope for the future, snatched away in the blink of an eye. Or to be more accurate, in the seconds it took one cowardly person to commit an act of unforgiveable recklessness. Cai, her beautiful, caring Cai. How was she going to go on without him?

Chapter 13

TEN YEARS EARLIER – October 2013

Elin

Over the coming weeks, the daily trek to see Delyth became almost obligatory. It was nearly a fortnight since the storm and Elin was in an odd kind of limbo, still reeling from the certainty that Mam had been swept away. It was like being on autopilot now, each time she plodded begrudgingly alongside Nain at low tide across the bay come rain or shine, trying not to dwell on the reasons for their visit. It felt as though they had worn a path straight to Delyth's door. But once inside, the atmosphere was even bleaker than in their own home, and though Nain did her best to buoy Delyth up, it felt futile.

As usual, Nain wanted to stay and keep Delyth company for an hour or two, but Elin was anxious to get back to Nerys. Her sister was still in denial and had hardly left the house, clinging to the vain hope that Mam would eventually reappear. She hadn't wanted to visit Delyth with them at all; maybe, Elin suspected, because it would just reinforce what everyone else now seemed to be resigned to. That, like Jac, her mother wasn't ever coming home.

Nain had stopped trying to coax Nerys out, saying that everyone dealt with things in their own way. But Elin was worried about her. She'd found her obsessively tidying and cleaning Mam's room, which had always been chaotic – garments on hangers decorating the wardrobe door and dado rail; make-up and perfume littering the sticky glass top of the dressing table, with more clothes – piled, not folded – on the stool. The bed unmade. The wastepaper basket overflowing. Shoes discarded higgledy-piggledy beneath the window. CDs scattered across the floor. Nerys certainly hadn't inherited her neat gene from their mother.

'Leave her be,' Nain had told Elin gently, after Elin was left in tears when Nerys had snapped the previous day that she wanted it all nice for Mam when she got back and to mind her own bloody business. It was so unlike Nerys, who was usually so even-tempered and rational.

'It's her way of coping. She'll come to terms with it in time.'

Elin hated seeing her like that. The situation with Mam was bad enough, without her sister turning into a stranger. Everything had been turned upside down. Elin missed her mother. So much. But although she was the younger of the two and it broke her heart, she could see there was little likelihood of Mam ever returning. All she could do was be there for her sister and hope that Nerys would eventually accept their loss for what it was, so that she could grieve properly and start to move on.

The tide was out, so Elin slowly made her way back across the sand. The boats that had been damaged had all been repaired now, though Derfel had chosen to store the *Sali-Mai* in a boatyard until the spring. Catrin had told Elin how he was almost obsessed with finding the perpetrator, possibly because of the boat's association with his dead wife. She said he watched the sailing vessels every night after dark for evidence of anyone up to no good. It was pointless, Catrin said. Whoever it had been wasn't likely to do it again, not now everyone knew.

As she walked into the cottage, Elin could hear sobbing from upstairs. Painful, heart-rending. She made her way up to Mam's bedroom and tentatively pushed open the door to find Nerys sitting at the end of the bed, her head in her hands. She lifted her tear-streaked face to meet Elin's. Her eyes were raw.

'She's not coming back, is she?'

Elin choked back tears of her own. She sat beside Nerys and wrapped her arms around her. There was no need for words as they clung to one another, each releasing the overwhelming sense of grief that had been weighing them down. Elin buried her head in Nerys's shoulder for a moment, then sniffed. The sour whiff of grease and something like stale bedsheets was all too evident. Elin pulled away a little. It was surely better to be honest.

'*Eew*. I'm not being funny, but d'you think you could do with washing your hair and changing your clothes? You really need to look after yourself, you know.'

Nerys looked down at herself, forcing a wan smile. 'Sorry. Didn't realise I was offending your nostrils.'

Elin gave a short laugh, blotting at her eyes with her cuff. 'Shall I run you a nice hot bath with some of those salts I got for Christmas? Nain'll be back soon, I'll get the kettle on.'

Chapter 14

TEN YEARS EARLIER – October 2013

Elin

Three weeks had passed since the night of the storm.

The news spread quickly. Jac Parry's body had been found, washed up on a rocky outcrop jutting from the waters near Penmon Point, a stone's throw from Trwyn Du lighthouse. Bloated and tangled in ribbons of seaweed, he was taken straight to Glan Clwyd hospital so that a postmortem could be carried out.

The weather had been glorious: a clear, early autumn day. Not the sort of day when you'd expect such awful news to be imparted. A sombre-faced Ianto had called round to tell them what he'd heard on the grapevine. Nain, with Elin in tow, had insisted on going straight round to see poor Delyth in her dilapidated *bwthyn* on the other side of the bay. She seemed to have made supporting Delyth her main focus, taking her soups and stews and cakes, making sure she felt the support of the community.

'To keep her strength up,' Nain had said. 'There's not a picking on the poor girl anyway, she'll waste away.' Elin quickly realised that, though Nain's motives were genuinely altruistic, focusing on someone else's needs was also providing her with a distraction. Something to block out the pain and hopelessness of the last few weeks.

'That woman's had nothing but bad luck,' she'd told Elin and Nerys. 'Everyone needs to rally round, let her know we're all here for her.'

Elin found it a little ironic, given their own tragic position. But at least they had each other – and she liked Delyth, and Jac had been sweet. He was an innocent soul; harmless, always smiling. Just like a little boy. It was so strange, the way both he and Mam appeared to have been swept away on the same night. There had been plenty of storms in the past: she'd never heard of anyone local being lost before in such circumstances. She'd run it through her head, over and over again, wondering if the pair of them had been together for some reason. Now she supposed no one would ever know.

*

'The final decision is obviously yours, Mrs Parry but it may be distressing for you to view Jac.'

A plain-clothes policewoman had already been at the house when they arrived and was attempting to discuss the situation with Delyth as gently as possible. The officer, who introduced herself as DS Bowen, looked really uncomfortable, and Elin actually felt rather sorry for her.

'Three weeks in the water can affect someone's appearance pretty badly. There's no need for a formal identification as we can establish it from DNA and the description of Jac's clothes.'

Delyth sat weeping in her battered armchair, her head dropped to her chest. Elin slipped an arm awkwardly around her frail shoulder as Nain went to make yet more tea. They seemed to have drunk so much of the stuff over the last few weeks that Elin felt awash, but she had come to realise that this was how a lot of old people coped in a crisis: they reached for the kettle.

Though emotionally drained herself, part of Elin felt that it must in some way be a relief for Delyth. It had been a hellish twenty-five days, the not knowing for certain, and still their own nightmare continued. How people coped with having loved ones missing for years, she couldn't even begin to imagine. She wondered if there would ever be an end to it.

'Then I won't,' Delyth sniffed. 'I don't want my last memory of my beautiful boy to be overshadowed by what he's become. Nor do I want anyone else gawping at him. He'd have hated it.'

Nain was back in the room and standing beside Delyth now, two mothers united in their grief. She shook her head, clearing her throat.

'I'd feel just the same. Give the lad his dignity.' From the look in Nain's eyes, Elin suspected this was just as much about how she would feel had it been Mam they'd found. Elin couldn't bear to think of Mam, always so particular about her appearance, ravaged by the water and the passage of time, not to mention the marine life which may have been feasting on her. It was horrible.

Nain drew herself to her full height, no hint of tears, her chin tilted upwards.

But Elin knew that her grandmother had been crying in private: she'd heard her downstairs a few times during the night over the interminable past weeks, sobbing quietly. Talking to herself, even. Mauve rings circled her eyes and she was paler than Elin had ever seen her. She wondered if Nain had slept at all and worried what the grief was doing to her. Nain had always been robust but wasn't young: it terrified Elin to think that the stress of it all could lead her to an early grave.

DS Bowen seemed hesitant as she hovered just inside the doorway, clutching her bag with both hands in front of her. 'The postmortem will take place later today, but we'll notify you when, erm . . . when Jac can be released, so you can make arrangements for his funeral.'

Delyth nodded slowly, tears continuing to spill silently down her cheeks. She dabbed at her raw eyes with a ragged tissue. 'And how long do you think that might take?'

'I can't really say at this stage. Hopefully it'll only be a few days or so. Depending on the findings,' she added hastily.

'Findings? The boy drowned, what else do they need to know?' Nain regarded the woman with narrowed eyes.

Delyth jerked her head up, her face suddenly anxious. She wiped a hand across her cheeks. 'Is this the way it usually works?'

'Even though the sea is quite cold and bodies don't deteriorate as quickly in salt water, it can be more challenging to establish the exact cause of death when someone's been submerged for a long period of time.' The sergeant chewed her lip. 'There'll probably be more in-depth tests carried out, so they'll have to wait for results on those to confirm things.'

'What things? Is there something you're not telling me?' Delyth turned to Nain, a look of panic crossing her face. Nain clasped her hand reassuringly, raising her eyebrows to DS Bowen in a silent question.

'No, no. Just preparing you in case there's a delay, that's all.' The officer smiled shakily. She began to edge towards the door. 'Once again, can I say how sorry I am for your loss. I'm afraid I need to get back to the station, but we'll be in touch soon.'

She nodded in Nain's direction, then made what seemed like a hasty exit. Casting a look at Elin, Nain excused herself, saying she'd see the woman out. Through the badly-sealed window, Elin overheard snatches of their conversation. Not all of it, but enough to grasp that there was some possibility of foul play. Whether certain injuries had been sustained ante- or post-mortem, or something.

It left the uncomfortable thought hanging that there was possibly more to Jac's demise than anyone had originally suspected.

Chapter 15

NOW – Wednesday 5th April 2023

Elin

The two police officers who accompanied her back from Ysbyty Gwynedd had finally gone. Elin's mind was reeling from the visit to the mortuary. The shocking sight of Cai's body stretched out on the hospital gurney had made her legs buckle. Someone had lifted her up and helped her into a chair, brought her a plastic cup of water. She was so disorientated, she had no idea who it was. The officers had been faceless; nothing about them had registered with her properly.

Nerys was in a ward only a stone's throw from where she'd been brought, yet the thought of seeing her sister at the moment was too much. How Elin would have loved to fall into her arms and sob her heart out. But from everything the nurse from the Hergest Unit she'd spoken to had said, Nerys was uncommunicative and confused. Seeing Elin distraught was unlikely to be helpful for her – and would probably make Elin herself feel even more desolate, if that were possible. Besides, it was very late. She might feel differently tomorrow.

Back at Nain's cottage, Elin felt utterly lost and alone. It had been harrowing, worse than anything she'd ever experienced, but there was no one here to share it with, no one to comfort her. Heavy, bone-deep exhaustion crept over her, but none of the beds were made up. Opening the linen closet, she breathed in the familiar, if now slightly musty, scent of the age-yellowed bedding, neatly stacked on the slatted shelves, sharp creases engraved into the pillow cases. She closed her eyes and stood for a moment, remembering with a deep ache in her chest being tucked tightly between smooth, crisp sheets, always ironed with care. With pride. The comforting weight of the coarse blanket with its satin border cool against her chin, the candlewick counterpane folded back and hanging down to the midnight-blue sisal carpet which covered the whole of the upstairs. Finding a thoughtfully inserted hot water bottle when she climbed into bed, warming her feet on cold winter nights. When was the last time she'd slipped into a bed like that? No one seemed to bother with such touches these days, did they? Most people felt it was time wasted, a pointless exercise. A hastily shaken duvet over a crumpled fitted sheet sufficed – and she was as guilty of it as anyone. But Nain was from that era when everything was about maintaining standards; about routine and the reassurance it brought. Even after they'd lost Mam, she'd still tried to carry on, preserving some sort of normality for Nerys and Elin's sakes. Elin realised with a crushing pang that routine was what she now craved most; everything was completely out of kilter. While a certain amount of spontaneity was good, refreshing even, for the most part those tiny, seemingly inconsequential actions always made her feel safe, grounded her.

How she wished she could block it all out; turn back the clock to when she was a child. Her whole life had been flipped on its head. What she wouldn't give to be transported back to that time now, to be a girl again with no worries or regrets. To live completely in the present, curl into a bed made up for her, the comfort of the cat stretched out lazily at her feet; to sleep like the dead and wake to the waft of breakfast frying, a cup of hot, sweet tea at her bedside. To hear Mam singing along to her music in the kitchen below. To have someone absolve her of any responsibilities: to take care of her. To wipe out the memories that, right now, brought her nothing but pain.

What was that saying, that thing about being better to have loved and lost than never having loved at all? Whoever dreamt that one up had obviously never found themselves in her predicament. The emptiness, the sense of hopelessness, was like nothing she'd ever experienced before. It felt as though a piece of her was missing, a vital part without which she couldn't function.

She had been so full of joy when she'd first moved to Birmingham. The sense of excitement at having Cai all to herself: no friends or family to compete with. Just the two of them in a place that was new to her, the promise of a bright future mapped out for them. A future which had been smashed to smithereens in one careless, cruel moment. She'd relived that knock at the door over and over, the grave faces of the police officers who had brought the news. Her stomach lurched at the thought of it now.

Elin hadn't been in a good place when Cai had come along. She'd been eight months into a relationship with Tom Buckley, the lad she'd thought she was going to settle down with, only to turn up at the pub one evening to find he had been playing away – 'for the last two of those months,' the heavily made-up girl wrapped around him had declared smugly. Despite his grovelling pleas and assurances that it had meant nothing, that

Elin was the one he really wanted to be with, she had kicked him into touch there and then.

'You're welcome to him and his tiny little dick,' she had said to the girl, loud enough for everyone to hear, turning on her heel and marching straight out of The Quay, her head held high. It had hurt, but she wasn't going to be taken for a fool.

She'd controlled the tears until she was far enough away from the pub to be out of sight, then had run across the quayside and past the shingle beach, up the track and back to the sanctuary of Nain's cottage, the two windows an orange glow against the dusk, a wisp of smoke climbing from the chimney.

'If he's done it once, he'll do it again, *bach*,' Nain had told her, stroking her hair gently as Elin had sobbed, kneeling on the rug beside Nain's favourite armchair with her head in her grandmother's lap. 'Don't you ever let anyone do that to you, cariad. You are worth so much more. Plenty more fish.'

And Elin had looked into the fire and felt suddenly comforted. Nain always had a way of making things feel better.

'You are an old witch, Mam,' she remembered her mother saying with an affectionate smile, on more than one occasion. Perhaps she was.

*

Less than six weeks since the break-up with Tom Buckley, Elin was still moping. But not for Tom so much as for the loss of a relationship with someone. As far as Buckley went, she was glad she'd seen him for what he really was; since the insult she'd thrown at him that night in The Quay, he had shown an even more unpleasant side to his character by plaguing her with increasingly abusive texts. She'd just deleted them initially, but eventually she'd blocked his number. Then the prank calls had started on the house phone – the usual: deep breathing, drawn-out silences intended to intimidate. He'd started hanging around the café where she was working, making a nuisance of himself. Elin was actually beginning to feel unnerved. In the end, Ianto had stepped in and warned him to stay away from her or he'd get the police involved. It seemed to do the trick – Ianto said he'd looked genuinely worried, and apologised, saying it had only been a bit of fun. What a spineless prick. Shortly afterwards, Tom took a job as a dock worker in Holyhead and moved to the other side of the island. Elin was hugely relieved that he had gone. But she still missed being with someone. Nerys seemed happy enough on her own, but being in a long-term relationship was something Elin had always wanted. She felt at a loose end.

She recalled how she had stood, disinterestedly, with pad and pencil, waiting to take Cai's breakfast order, and that of his clearly hungover friend, whose tawny head was resting, face down, on folded arms.

'What d'you recommend?' Cai had asked, pretending to pore over the menu but with his attention clearly on her the whole time. She hadn't seen him before and he clearly wasn't local – she'd detected the hint of a Mancunian accent.

Elin threw an eye-roll at Catrin, who had been watching this interchange, grinning at her from behind the counter. 'The buttermilk pancakes are always good. As long as you don't have a gluten allergy.'

He shook his head, the corners of his mouth lifting. 'I'll trust your judgement. Make that two stacks then, please, and a pot of tea for one.' He glanced down at his companion, who raised his head for just long enough to smile weakly, before dropping it back to the table, groaning. 'Better bring this one some strong black coffee. He's been a silly boy.'

A silly boy. She'd suppressed a smile, thinking that would've been exactly how Nain would have described the lad. But then she noticed Cai's Morrissey T-shirt, remembering the lyrics from one of the singer's hits, about someone called Hector. *Ah*. She felt a pang of nostalgia, Mam's voice singing along to 'Every Day is Like Sunday' playing through her head.

And it was as simple as that. The way he'd held her gaze as he lifted his warm brown eyes towards her, the way his hand had lingered on the menu as he passed it back. The way his smile had lit up his face. She'd had no intention of starting to see anyone else quite so soon. Rebound things were doomed to failure, that's what Nain had always said. But she'd let him have her mobile number before he left anyway, not really expecting him to call, and being surprised but quietly pleased when he texted later that same day to ask her on a date.

Catrin, who had been with her boyfriend, Rhys, for over a year, seemed even more excited than Elin. 'He was definitely keen, El. And so much nicer than that scumbag Tom Buckley. I always knew you could do better.'

And she really couldn't have done any better if she'd tried.

Chapter 16

NOW – Thursday 6th April 2023

Elin

The sky was bruised black the following morning, a downpour inevitable. Elin had barely slept. She sat on the settee near the cottage window, her leg propped on Nain's old stool, staring angrily at the clunky boot encasing her foot. The plastic was scuffed, the Velcro straps starting to fray. She had begun to loathe the thing.

Her foot: her *stupid* frigging foot. If it hadn't been for that, for her own carelessness, she'd have travelled here with Cai and this unthinkable, vile thing would never have happened. Beyond the window she could hear the old, familiar rhythm of the waves, a dog barking excitedly across the beach, and the intermittent sound of gulls screeching, carrying on as usual, oblivious to the fact that one precious life had been extinguished and another hollowed out completely. She wanted to throw something.

Cai should be here. The thought hit her like a sledgehammer. He'd be putting the kettle on, opening and closing cupboard doors, sheepishly poking his head through the doorway to ask where stuff was kept, even though he'd asked the same question a hundred times before. He'd have been complaining about the draught, about the way the wind found every gap in the windows and the walls. Cuddling up to her on the settee, saying it was the best way to keep warm.

If only she could rewind the clock. Just a few hours would have done it. He'd have found his way unhindered back to Birmingham where Elin had been waiting for him. Back from the course, telling her everything in his usual, chatty way while she sat on the edge of the bath and they shared a bottle of wine. Telling her how much he'd missed her. How Dr Baden's droning on had driven him up the wall; how, unfortunately, he hadn't managed to get to Traeth Coch, but that he was really looking forward to starting the dig next month.

Instead, he would never be in either place ever again.

Elin kept picturing the quiet, narrow lane that led from the beach. She and Nerys had walked it a thousand times as children; had climbed the embankment to look for blackberries, Nain calling after them to '*Gwyliwch*! Slow down, be careful.' Now she saw it differently: a car cornering too fast on a slippery road; a perilous blind bend. A death trap. Cai had been a body on wet tarmac by the time anyone found him. Try as she might, Elin couldn't block out the terrible image.

The back door opened with a familiar groan. Elin tensed, realising suddenly that she'd forgotten to lock it. Her stomach dropped as she recalled the sound of Cai's step that would often follow when they'd been to stay, the soft thud as he kicked off his shoes. Instead, it was Catrin's voice, low and tentative, calling her name.

Catrin and Rhys came through from the kitchen bringing

with them the faint smell of diesel and freshly cut hay. Rhys hovered by the door, tall and broad, a blue beanie hat in his hands, eyes fixed on the floor. Catrin crossed the room in three strides, stopping short a few feet away, as if unsure what kind of reception she would receive.

Elin stared up at her, the pain clearly showing in her eyes.

'Oh, El,' said Catrin, and then her face crumpled. 'Oh, cariad.'

Elin nodded, just once. What was there to say?

Catrin lowered herself into the armchair opposite her, close enough that Elin could see her tear-filled eyes, the faint crease between her brows that had deepened over the years. She'd grown her hair. As a teen, Catrin had always kept her dark locks in an urchin cut, but now they fell past her shoulders in waves, a few well-placed highlights softening her face. She looked sophisticated, grown up. Married life seemed to suit her. Rhys busied himself with making hot drinks, the building sound of the kettle drowning out his movements.

'I'm so sorry.' Catrin bit her lip. 'I should have been here sooner. I should've . . .' She broke off, putting a hand to her mouth. 'I'm sorry I've been so useless lately. At messaging and stuff. It's just the farm's been mad since Rhys's dad retired. Everything's gone wrong at once.'

Elin watched Catrin's hands twist together in her lap. She felt oddly detached, as though this were all happening to someone else. As though, if she pinched herself, she'd wake back in her bed in the flat and it would all have been a horrible nightmare.

But immediately the thought popped into her head.

'Why didn't you let me know about Nerys?' she blurted out suddenly. The question sounded more like an accusation.

Catrin blinked, taken aback. 'Let you know what?'

'That she was ill. That she was . . .' Elin swallowed. 'In hospital.'

Catrin's mouth fell open. 'Hospital? El, I didn't know. I swear. I thought she was just keeping herself to herself more since—since your nain.' Her voice softened. 'Rhi mentioned she'd been struggling, like, but I didn't realise it was that bad. I'm so sorry.'

The room seemed to sway. Elin gripped the arm of the chair, her knuckles whitening. The knowledge was torturing her. Cai had come here only because she'd asked him to. She had stayed behind in Birmingham because of her foot, because the train would have been too awkward; because there would be plenty of time later on. There was always time, until there wasn't.

'He never even saw her,' Elin said, as much to herself as to Catrin. Saying it aloud made it feel even more brutal. 'He came here, to Traeth Coch, to see Nerys, all because I asked him to. And she wasn't even here.'

Catrin got up then. She came and sat beside her, placing a hand on Elin's own. Her touch was warm, soft.

'Oh, El,' she said again. 'None of this is on you.'

Elin didn't answer. Her stomach churned, blame prodding her from every angle.

Rhys had been listening from the doorway. He cleared his throat. 'We can help,' he said quietly. 'With whatever needs doing. You know, phone calls, paperwork and everything.' He drew in a breath. 'And the funeral, when you're ready.'

'You'll want it here, won't you, El?' Catrin scanned her face. 'Near home.'

Elin turned to look through the window, to the miles of open sky, to the pewter-grey waters which stretched all around them; sitting between, the dark green wall that was Pentraeth Forest. Cai had come to love this place, almost as much as she did. Even on days such as this, with the waves choppy and the heavens ready to open. This was where they would have settled. Where they belonged.

'Yes,' she said, her voice a pitiful croak. 'Here.'

Catrin slipped an arm around her shoulder. 'You won't be on your own, doll,' she said, with a fierce protectiveness that surprised but touched Elin. 'Not now. Not again.'

Again. The word was a grim reminder of how lonely she'd been after losing Mam, with Nerys wrapped up in her own grief and their nain trying to soldier on as though it was business as usual, not wanting to talk about Mam in case it upset either of them. She'd confided in Catrin, who, having lost her own mother, understood. But somehow it was worse this time, back home but with Mam long gone, Nain, too; Nerys locked in a place in her own head. And now Cai, lost to a lane he'd been walking along to get back to the main road. To get back, eventually, to her. Elin felt suddenly, acutely, how fragile and transient everyone's existence really was.

Outside, a plump pigeon alighted on the gate post. It was carrying a tuft of something in its beak, no doubt building a nest somewhere close by. Preparing for the future, something Elin had no interest in any more. She stared into the distance, watching absently as the bird wrestled a loose twig from the front hedge and took flight once more. Eventually she allowed herself to lean into Catrin's embrace.

Rhys came through carrying two steaming mugs of tea, pausing to smile awkwardly at Elin and his wife. He placed the drinks beside them on the little table, then went to the window, peering out across the bay. After a few moments, he broke the silence.

'I was on the phone to Davy Jenkins first thing.' He scratched his head, turning to look at the pair. 'He was saying someone'd had a go at the boats last night. Holes in the hulls, like before.'

Catrin's arm remained tightly around Elin. She sat up anxiously. 'What? Was the *Sali-Mai* damaged? Does Dad know?'

'I'm not sure. But it's weird that, don't you think?'

'Weird how?'

He turned back to her, throwing a glance at Elin. 'Oh, nothing. Just . . . well, last time something really bad happened too, didn't it? The night when . . .' He stopped mid-sentence, his eyes flickering.

Catrin flashed him a warning look. 'It's a horrible coincidence, that's all. It was a long time ago.'

Rhys's eyebrows shot up briefly, though he said nothing. But the implication was there and it wasn't lost on Elin. When Mam disappeared, those boats had been vandalised. And now the same thing had happened the night Cai was killed.

A horrible coincidence indeed.

Chapter 17

NOW – Thursday 6th April 2023

Elin

With Catrin and Rhys gone, Elin was left to brood once again; on the past as well as the present. She reflected, with a stab of regret, on her own shortcomings. It had been Nerys who had shouldered everything alone when Elin swanned off to Birmingham five summers ago; who'd had to forego any social life or chance of a relationship as she looked after Nain until she was beyond the point of being cared for at home. Though Nerys had said nothing herself, Catrin told Elin when she came home on one occasion that Nerys had stopped accepting invitations to join in with anything, even barbecues the pub was laying on, or local live music events which she would usually have attended. 'Sorry, I can't – Nain's a bit out of sorts at the moment.' That had become her stock excuse. No wonder she'd finished up so depressed.

The signs had long been there with Nain: before Elin had left, even. The way she'd started to call her Meinir occasionally; and not in that way that was a mere slip of the tongue, a habit. As though she really thought she *was* Meinir. Of course, Elin knew how much she resembled her mother, and as she grew older the likeness was ever more apparent. Maybe it had triggered something in Nain. Mam's loss had affected them all deeply, but Nain buried her feelings, tried to carry on as normal. Thinking back, she was probably concerned about maintaining a brave front for Elin and Nerys, always trying to be strong for them.

Nain would sometimes talk to Elin as though she should remember certain things: things that had clearly happened to Mam when she was young. But then latterly came the paranoia, which had been more troubling. This idea that someone was coming into the cottage when they were out, moving things about. Taking stuff, even. A throwback, maybe, to when Mam used to bring casual acquaintances back to their cottage.

'I always told you not to bring them back here,' she'd muttered one day, convinced that Elin was Meinir and one of the men she'd become involved with was letting himself in for some reason.

Mam's string of casual male friends had been a bone of contention between her and Nain. Elin remembered overhearing an argument between them once, after Mam let a man she'd only been on one date with sleep over on the couch.

'Unless you're planning on settling down with one of them, you should keep the buggers at arm's length,' Nain had said angrily. 'You don't know who you're letting in and you've got the girls to think about.'

She'd had a point, to be fair. Mam had always been quite laid-back about things, and though Elin had never been in any doubt that she adored her and Nerys, in hindsight, sometimes their mother hadn't made the best choices. Elin wondered briefly now if it was one of those wrong choices that had led to her demise. But Nain had been down that route and almost sent herself mad with her obsession – the police had been satisfied that it was an accident. Elin reflected, too, on what Rhys had told them about the boats being damaged again. Maybe it was all just a coincidence. These things usually turned out to have a rational explanation, didn't they? It wasn't helping her state of mind to start imagining things that might not even have happened.

Nain's confusion would fluctuate; some days she'd seemed fine, like her old self. But on those days when she became muddled, a darkness seemed to come over her. She would mumble to herself, meander around the house aimlessly. After Elin had left home, Nerys had told her that Nain had started to throw wild accusations at people, although Elin hadn't mentioned this to Cai. 'Especially since one day she'd turned round and asked Nerys who the hell the lad was that Elin had taken up with and what did she actually know about him. It wasn't who her grandmother really was, and even if it was part of some sort of mental decline, she didn't want Cai to feel uncomfortable around her.' Elin wondered now if her leaving home had accelerated things, but didn't want to dwell on the thought. She felt bad enough without that additional guilt trip.

Of course, Elin had visited when she could, yes; sent cards and flowers and commiserated over the phone. But she hadn't been nearly as present as she should have been, she was all too aware of that. Nerys had been the one stuck at home, never complaining, soldiering on through it all. Cleaning up the daily mess, shopping, cooking; up all night and on pins when their grandmother had begun to wander and couldn't be left unsupervised for a moment. She'd dealt with the aftermath of Nain going into the nursing home, juggling the financial difficulties; ensuring she received the benefits she needed, the proper medical care.

A while before Nain went into the home, Nerys had had to cut her hours in the shop with Bethan, a role she'd been offered not long after Mam went missing. Bethan needed a helping hand, but though she could have filled the position with a click of her fingers, she'd given the job to Nerys to give her a focus. Elin was grateful to Bethan, who had always been a good and loyal friend to Mam. At least Nerys had someone to look out for her now Elin wasn't around.

Elin recalled one telephone conversation she'd had with her sister some months earlier, before Nain died. She could picture Nerys on the stool under the stairs, wild-haired and wild-eyed, worry-picking at the callous on her index finger as always, while relating her most recent visit to the care home.

'Bloody shocking it is, seeing some of those poor old souls who've got no one to speak up for them. I can't believe how they're treated, shoved in a corner in an armchair with a plastic cover, or propped up in bed with nothing to do all day but stare at the walls. No wonder half of them finish up doolally, even if they're not to begin with.'

Elin had smiled to herself, knowing Nerys would make it her business to take some of the 'poor old souls' under her own wing and make their lives that little bit brighter. It was just who she was: a mother hen with no chicks to care for. She'd pour her energy into looking out for those who needed a surrogate relative, standing up to the scariest of nurses if she felt they weren't doing their duty. Funny – and slightly sad – that she was always ready to speak out quite forcefully on behalf of others and yet almost reticent when it came to herself.

Her sister was seriously unwell. Nain had been gone almost five months; she'd spent almost two years in the home before her death. It had all clearly taken its toll on poor Nerys. Elin couldn't believe she'd been so ignorant of the strain she'd been under. She'd honestly believed that Nerys had turned a corner; that things were slowly getting better, not worse.

The sky was a dismal grey as Elin arrived at Ysbyty Gwynedd, the snow-capped mountains of Snowdonia rising behind it in the distance. Her stomach turned over as she looked up once more at the characterless, flat-roofed building, ominous dirty clouds hanging above it like smoke released from a crematorium chimney. She hated hospitals at the best of times, but only last night she'd been brought here and driven to the rear, where the mortuary was situated in a separate building. The pungent, cloying smell of the morgue, a cross between bleach and something she couldn't define, still lingered in her nostrils. The smell of death. It made her feel nauseous.

Elin had barely slept. Maybe she should have tried to go back to bed for a while, but she desperately needed to see Nerys now. Today's taxi driver had been cheerful and friendly, but soon stopped trying to make conversation as he was met with her curt, monosyllabic responses. He dropped her at the hospital's main entrance, casting her a concerned look as she eased herself out of the car.

'Follow up for your foot, is it? Hope it all goes well.'

Elin forced a tepid smile and thanked him. She hadn't meant to seem rude.

Owing to the foot and the cumbersome boot, it felt like a mission to reach the Hergest Unit. She limped round the back of the main hospital following a block paved route and through a more pleasant green space lined with trees. She was eventually met with the sight of a round, brick-built structure with multiple peaks and troughs to its deeply sloping tiled roof. The canopied entrance had a circle of trees planted in the centre of the turning circle before it and felt much less impersonal than the main hospital. From the reception, she followed the corridors until she reached the glass door to the ward where Nerys was staying. Taking a deep breath in anticipation, she entered.

Having explained who she was to the staff nurse, Elin waited for a moment to be shown to Nerys's bedside. She was led over to where Nerys sat slumped in an armchair next to the bed. Seeing her sister brought a sob to Elin's throat. The woman rubbed Elin's shoulder gently. 'She's quite heavily medicated at the moment, owing to the paranoia and hysteria she was displaying when she was first admitted, so you may find her appearance a little . . . well, distressing. Doctor's aiming to reduce the dose over the next week or two and see how she copes.'

'Paranoia? Why? What was she actually saying, then?' An unpleasant, slightly sick sensation rose in Elin's chest. What did her sister have to be paranoid about? She'd been under the impression Nerys had just worked herself into the ground and then overwhelming grief had taken hold. Just as Elin felt now. Was this simply an unusual adjunct to the bereavement?

The nurse squeezed a sympathetic smile. 'I understand you both lost your mother in upsetting circumstances some years ago. I'm very sorry for your loss.'

Elin could have said that she was reeling from a far more recent loss; that right now, losing her mother felt like a distant memory and the least of things she needed commiseration for. She thought again of Cai, lying so cold, so still, in another part of the hospital and swallowed down the hard lump which threatened to choke her. But she said nothing, simply nodded and allowed the woman to proceed.

'Your sister seemed to have got it into her head that someone must have killed your mum and that the same person has been creeping into your family home in recent weeks, with the intention of attacking or killing Nerys, too.' The nurse grimaced. 'She'd attempted to barricade herself into the house on a few occasions prior to her admission, actually called the emergency services several times in a really confused state.' She paused. 'The police went round a couple of times, but there was no evidence of anyone, nor of an attempted break-in. Doctor was telling us he'd heard the recording of the most recent telephone conversation Nerys had with the operator.' She chewed the inside of her cheek. 'It was after the call she made last week that mental health services were called to the house and they suggested admitting her. We were told she didn't make any objection.'

Elin suspected Nerys hadn't been in any fit state to either agree or object to anything. She was shocked to see the amount of weight that had dropped off her sister since she'd last seen her at Nain's funeral in January. She remembered how thin she'd become after Mam disappeared – Nerys was naturally curvy, but it had taken years for her to fill out again. It was obviously how stress affected her: some people ate for comfort, others lost their appetite completely. Nerys had been so focused on caring for their grandmother and anyone else who needed support, she appeared to have stopped looking after herself at all.

She was barely able to raise her head, let alone hold a conversation, though she'd managed a brief, weak smile as her gaze landed on Elin when she approached the huge armchair which made her look even tinier and more fragile than she was.

*

Elin was still struggling to regain her composure when they were approached by a young, slimly-built and rather twitchy-looking man, who introduced himself as Dr Bianchi, the consultant psychiatrist. The nurse nodded at him and returned to her station. He smiled hesitantly as he hovered beside Elin, glancing at Nerys and then back at her.

'I wonder, could I have a quick word?' He beckoned with his head towards the nurses' station.

Elin left her coat on Nerys's bed and followed him into the small, windowless office near the ward entrance. He closed the door behind her, spreading a hand to bid her sit. She already felt churned up by everything the nurse had said, and wondered what else she was going to learn. Lowering herself onto the chair, Elin looked up at the doctor apprehensively. He appeared flustered, as though he had some bad news to share.

After a moment, he sat down himself behind the desk facing her, the corners of his mouth lifting unconvincingly. 'I wanted to give you a brief update about your sister's condition. So, I've just been in a meeting with some of my colleagues. We've been monitoring Nerys quite closely. Originally it was thought that her fragile mental state was owing to paranoid delusions, possibly brought about by the nervous exhaustion and depression she'd had following your grandmother's death.' He paused for breath, his eyes wobbling slightly. 'We now believe she is also suffering from dissociative amnesia.'

Elin sat up straighter now. She stared at him. 'You mean she's lost her memory?'

'No, not entirely. Although there do appear to be huge recent gaps. But it's the cause of the memory loss that concerns me.'

He dipped his head slightly, elbows resting on the desktop now, his long fingers steepled. 'These things can often be attributed to some sort of trauma. Extreme stress causes high levels of cortisol to be released by the adrenal glands, which can disrupt the brain's ability to store lived experiences. Things usually return to normal eventually, but it can take time. Memories as they return can be fragmented, and it's obviously very distressing for the patient – and of course, their loved ones.'

A cold feeling trickled down Elin's spine. She leaned forward. 'So you're saying you think Nerys has been through some kind of traumatic experience which caused her brain to sort of shut down?'

Dr Bianchi nodded. 'That's it in a nutshell. We're keeping her under close observation and trying to calm her with the medication, but she will probably need intensive psychotherapy to address the underlying trauma and help her recover lost memories. I suspect it's going to take a while, I'm afraid.'

'And you think there's possibly more to it than losing Nain? I mean, all the stuff the nurse was saying, about the phone calls Nerys had been making to the police?'

Dr Bianchi drew in a breath. He leaned back in his chair. 'I think it's *unlikely* for a bereavement to provoke such an extreme reaction, yes. However, the fact that you both lost your mother at a relatively young age and Nerys was effectively alone – well, it could have compounded things, I suppose. We have to keep an open mind. But probing Nerys at the moment could do more harm than good. She needs to recall things in her own time, when she's emotionally stronger and ready to cope.'

He continued to speak for what seemed like hours, advising Elin on the best way she could help support Nerys. Elin was finding it hard to absorb all the information. The anti-anxiety drugs and sedatives they were using, the types of therapy that were generally helpful in such cases. It was all too much to take in at once.

Elin returned to the ward eventually, her mind reeling. She sat beside her sister for almost an hour, rambling inanely as she held her hand. Dr Bianchi had advised her to keep the conversation light, so though it wasn't easy, she'd tried her best to talk about positive things, reminiscing about happier times when they were children. But Nerys simply stared into space, her eyes glazed, locked in a drug-induced stupor. Elin felt utterly wretched. It would be pointless and probably unwise to tell her about Cai; pointless trying to talk about anything of any real importance. Nerys was away with the fairies somewhere. Elin was oddly envious. How nice it would be right now to have no memory of anything, to drift through life without a care in the world. Although the thought pulled her up sharply: she knew how horrified Nain would have been at her thinking this way. She was being completely selfish. Nerys hadn't chosen this. She'd become seriously unwell as a result of something that had happened to her. And for Elin to forget about Cai and all that he'd meant to her would be unforgiveable. She needed to give herself a shake.

As the nurse came to say it was time for Elin to go so that her sister could rest, Nerys seemed to gain a sudden moment of clarity. She sat up sharply, clutching Elin's hand tighter as if trying to stop her from leaving.

''S not safe in Traeth Coch, El.' Her voice was slurred, a hoarse whisper, but the sudden urgency in her widened eyes was alarming. 'Something very wrong there. Be careful.'

What if, as Dr Bianchi suspected, Nerys's breakdown and subsequent amnesia had been brought about by something other than losing Nain?

Rhys's remark about the damage to the boats had already set the cogs turning in her mind, though she'd tried to persuade herself he must be wrong. Was it possible there actually *was* a connection between Mam's disappearance and Cai's death? She tried to push the thought down, but all the way home a feeling of dread started to build.

What if it really wasn't safe back in her old home?

Chapter 18

NOW – Thursday 6th April 2023

Elin

Bethan was sitting outside the house in her Fiat 500 when Elin returned home from the hospital. She'd been unwell when they buried Nain and unable to attend the funeral, so hadn't seen Elin for more than a year. Seeing her approaching, Bethan became instantly emotional as she climbed from the car and came to wrap Elin in a tight hug.

'Oh, cariad, you're having such a time of it, aren't you? I heard about Cai. Just horrific. I'm so, so sorry.' Bethan stood back to hold her at arm's length. '*Duw*, you are so like your mammy.' Tears welled in her eyes, and she brushed them away with one hand, forcing a smile.

Elin felt drained and numb. She nodded mutely. It felt as if everything was crushing her suddenly, the whole world closing in. She didn't really want to see anyone; she just wanted to crawl under a duvet, try to sleep and block it all out. She couldn't think straight. As she glanced about at the sea, the gulls coasting on the breeze with outstretched wings, the peaceful, familiar surroundings that she'd yearned for when back in the Midlands, Nerys's assertion that danger might be lurking seemed suddenly absurd. Maybe it *was* just that: the overwhelming grief and nervous exhaustion had combined to bring about her current state, her fragmented memory and confusion. Poor Nerys.

Bethan looked up at the house and back to Elin. 'Shall we go inside, have a *panad*?'

Elin was too tired to protest. She led the way heavily up the path, fumbling in her purse for the key. Libby appeared in the upstairs window next door and raised a hand to wave. It was too much effort to return the gesture, but Bethan acted on her behalf.

'Come on, let's get inside quick before we're collared,' Bethan said in a low voice. 'Too many bloody do-gooders round here.'

Once inside, Elin sank wearily onto the settee, as Bethan went to put the kettle on. She looked over at the sideboard where the framed photo of the four of them sat: her, Nerys, Nain and Mam, laughing as always. The picture was taken when Elin was about twelve. It captured a happy, carefree moment, snapped by Ianto outside the front of the house one glorious summer. A time before events beyond their control had torn their little family apart. But as her eyes scanned the image, Elin noticed a crack running right across the glass.

Elin frowned. She remembered picking up the picture and gazing at it through her tears shortly after the police brought her home last night. She felt sure it had been intact then. Although, she'd been in quite a state – maybe she just hadn't really been focusing properly and didn't notice. Given everything that had happened to them all since, the broken glass almost seemed fitting now.

Bethan came back into the living room. She glanced at Nain's old armchair and purposefully ensconced herself in the one opposite, as though to use it would be disrespectful. She seemed suddenly awkward, as if now they were both inside she didn't quite know what to say.

'How was Nerys today? I went over to the hospital on Sunday, but I haven't managed to go back yet. Things have been . . . well, mad, for want of a better word. Mam took a nasty fall last week – and I'm short-handed in the shop now too, see . . .' Bethan broke off, clearly realising this might sound indelicate.

Unsmiling, Elin raised her eyes to look at her. She let out a heavy sigh. 'She's not good. Some sort of amnesia, which they think has been caused by trauma. It might just be the culmination of everything with Nain, although they're not sure at the moment. But the doctor said it could take quite a while before she gets back to normal.'

Bethan shook her head slightly. 'I should've seen it coming, I suppose. It was so odd, though – I really thought she'd turned a corner after your nain . . .' she screwed up her face apologetically. 'I don't know, maybe she'd been bottling it all up, putting on a front. She'd been really distracted recently in the shop, and then called in sick about ten days or so before everything finally went – well, pear-shaped. I think it all started with that horrible business with Nyten – you know, the cat that she got recently? She probably wasn't in a great place anyway and everything seemed to spiral after that.'

Elin studied her quizzically. She remembered Nerys talking about the little cat and her muttering something over the phone about taking her to the vet, but couldn't recall the details. If she was honest, at the time, she'd been too focused on her stupid pasta sauce and had one ear on *Eastenders*. The blunt truth was that she hadn't shown enough interest. 'Why – what happened exactly? She said she'd had to take her to the vet, but she didn't really elaborate.'

Elin felt a sharp prick of conscience. She shouldn't need to be asking these questions. She should have asked Nerys at the time. She'd been horribly self-absorbed lately, hadn't she?

Bethan pursed her lips. 'Maybe she just didn't want to worry you. Nerys was convinced – *adamant* – someone had come into the garden and attacked the cat while she was in the house.'

Elin put a hand to her mouth. 'Round here? That's shocking. Did the cat – was it okay?'

'It was awful at the time – a ruptured spleen, poor little thing. Blunt force trauma injury, that's how the vet put it. At first he said someone might have kicked her, then decided it could've been a fox or something, picking her up and slamming her into the ground, but Nerys wasn't having any of it.' Bethan grimaced, arching a sceptical eyebrow. 'The seed had been planted and she was certain then that she'd been attacked by a human. Thankfully Nyten didn't need the splenectomy in the end, but they had to keep her in for a few days to monitor her. She seems fine now though, thank God. It's been a few weeks. Pricey little do at the vet's, but thankfully Nerys had taken out pet insurance when she got her. I've got the cat staying with me at the moment – she's an absolute sweetie. Nerys had her home for a while, but then out of the blue, she decided she was worried about her being here, in case anything else happened. I didn't quiz her. She obviously wasn't in a good place and I was happy to have Nyten.'

'So I'm guessing *you* don't think someone attacked her, then?' Elin sat back, observing Bethan for a moment with a frown.

Bethan sighed, her shoulders slumping. 'I mean, it's not impossible, I s'pose. But Nerys'd got so twitchy about everything, you know? I think she'd been looking for things that weren't really there. Your nain, bless her, was on at her all the time about all sorts and well . . .' She lowered her gaze. 'I think after she passed, Nerys had actually started to believe her.'

Elin let out a long breath. Poor Nerys. She must have been trapped in a nightmare inside her own head for some time. Maybe it was what had happened to the cat that had been the final straw. She felt grateful that the hospital was taking care of her and keeping her medicated. Elin suddenly wished someone would medicate *her*, knock her out for a while. She realised she was in no fit state herself to look after her sister. Not now. The conversation with Bethan had distracted her momentarily, but the memory of what had happened to Cai suddenly resurged and the same terrible sense of hopelessness washed over her again. She wanted – *needed* – to cry, scream, hit something. After sobbing uncontrollably for hours when she'd seen him in the mortuary, it was as if a rock was stuck somewhere deep inside herself now creating a barrier, and the tears simply wouldn't come.

'Oh *Christ*.' She leaned forward suddenly, clutching her head with both hands. 'What a horrible, shitty world we live in.'

Bethan had just started to say something, when they were interrupted by a tentative knock at the window. They both looked up to see Libby peering in at them. She gave a small wave of her hand, smiling uncertainly.

'Oh for God's sake,' Bethan muttered from the side of her mouth. 'It's Mary bloody Poppins. She probably means well, but she can be a bit of a pain in the arse.'

Elin remained seated, looking on while Bethan went to answer the door, adopting a cheery but firm tone as she stood on the threshold. 'Hello. We're just having a chat here. Everything okay, is it?'

Libby craned her neck to look past her. 'I just came to see how Elin is. We heard about poor Cai . . .' she broke off, her face a picture of sympathy. 'I—I've brought a card.'

She held out an envelope which Bethan accepted, nodding politely. 'Elin just needs a little time, you know. But thank you. For the card.'

Before the woman had a chance to say anything else, Bethan had closed the door. She leaned back against it briefly, blowing out her cheeks.

Elin watched through the window as Libby, looking slightly affronted, turned and retreated down the path. She paused at the gate to glance back at the house, then disappeared behind the hedge towards her own garden.

Bethan crossed the room to hand over the card.

Elin placed it beside her on the settee, no enthusiasm to open it. 'That was kind,' she said emptily. 'She was here, actually – in the house the other day – she answered the phone when I tried to get hold of Nerys; told me she was in hospital.'

Bethan's eyebrows shot up in obvious alarm. 'You mean you didn't know? Didn't you get my voicemail?'

Elin shook her head slowly. 'No. The first I'd heard of it was when I spoke to Libby.'

'Oh *Duw*, but I left you a message.' Bethan looked mortified. She pulled her mobile from her jacket pocket and began scrolling through, then handed it to Elin. 'See? I rang you the day she was admitted but it went straight to your answer machine.' She let out a sigh. 'I did wonder why you hadn't called me back. I thought perhaps you were away or something. I'm so sorry, cariad.' She grimaced. 'I've been so busy, but I should've followed it up. I just assumed . . .'

Elin stared at Bethan's call log. She had indeed rung her; the duration had been almost two minutes. How the hell had she missed it? Then she remembered – she'd been at the hospital that day for a follow up about her foot – she could never get a signal in there. And her voicemail alerts didn't always come through, anyway.

She picked up her own phone and pressed the provider's voicemail service. '*You have five new messages and ten saved messages.*' She flicked through, listening and then deleting the unnecessary spam ones. And there, in the middle of them all, was Bethan's. Elin's stomach turned over. What an absolute fuck up.

Bethan studied her, the hint of a frown creasing her brow. 'How come Libby was in the house, anyway?'

'I think Nain gave her a spare key – she offered to feed Llwyd – you know, our old cat, when we went to the Eisteddfod in Llangollen for the weekend a few years ago. She'd been watering the plants, she said,' Elin mused half-heartedly. 'Why's she a pain? I always thought she seemed okay.'

Bethan glanced back to where Libby had just been standing. She cleared her throat. 'I'll make that tea. Oh, it's probably just me, making something out of nothing. A story for another day.'

*

Bethan

Bethan lingered at the end of the track for a moment, her hand on the car door, the taste of brine on her tongue. From the lane where the Owens' cottage perched, she could see the beach beneath and the wet sand spread out in wavy ribbons, the tide moving back and forth as it edged out; a gentle, soothing motion. But there had been no soothing Elin, nor could Bethan imagine there would be for a long while. It had been heartbreaking to see the poor girl. She'd stared at nothing, her grief palpable. Bethan had left her unwillingly, promising that she'd call again soon. She hated leaving her alone like that. And she was kicking herself for mentioning that thing with Libby – Elin had more than enough to worry her right now.

As she reached for the handle, Bethan's thoughts crowded her mind. Cai's death and its impact on poor Elin sat heaviest of all: the blunt, shocking cruelty of a hit-and-run on a lane she herself had wandered up many a time. Though she hadn't known the lad that well, it was heartbreaking to think that someone so young, who should have had a whole lifetime ahead of them, could be snuffed out like that in an instant. Nerys had always said what a kind, decent lad he was. Then there was Nerys herself, a shadow of the girl she knew, hollow-eyed and vacant in her hospital bed. Bethan wasn't the maternal type but the feelings she had for Nerys were as near to motherly as she could muster, and it had really upset Bethan to see her like that. She couldn't get her head round it – she had honestly thought Nerys had turned a corner, was starting to feel more positive. It was so odd.

On top of it all there was her own mother, proud and stubborn, insisting her recent fall was 'nothing' while Bethan agonised over her bruised cheek and leaving her alone with the treacherously steep stairs of her little terraced house. She needed to go there next, check the fridge supplies; make sure Mam had her personal alarm handy, her phone charged. Maybe it was time to look into sheltered accommodation, put the house on the market. Her stomach clenched at the thought. She had a perpetual mental to-do list to tick off; it seemed to be growing by the day.

'Bethan! *Ti'n iawn?*'

Bethan started, the deep voice interrupting her thoughts like a balloon bursting. She spun round to find Hugh Roberts standing a little too close, the butcher's ruddy-cheeked confidence intact despite the divorce gossip that was still circulating. He hadn't come out of that one well – forced to part with a substantial amount to cushion the blow for his now ex-wife, after revelations of unreasonable behaviour and downright nastiness. No surprise to anyone who knew him – he'd been an unpleasant child and had grown into an even more odious adult.

Roberts smiled broadly, as if they were old friends. As if he'd forgotten about her humiliating him in front of his customers that day only weeks ago. About how she'd left him and everyone else present in no doubt as to her opinion of the shoddy way he'd treated Nerys. The thought made Bethan bristle.

'Hugh,' she said, trying to keep her tone neutral.

'I thought that was your car,' he went on, glancing at the cottage to his right, then back at her face. 'What're you up to these days? Keeping busy?'

'Busy' was an understatement that she had neither the energy nor the inclination to unpack. She blew out her cheeks. 'Always. I'm in rather a rush, actually,' she said, making a show of unlocking the car door.

'Well, before you go,' he said, 'I wondered if you'd fancy coming out for a meal.' He puffed out his chest, getting into his stride. 'There's that new place in Menai Bridge – proper home-cooked food, not the crap they serve straight from a microwave. I know the proprietor. He'll find us a good table.'

The man's front was unbelievable. Bethan watched his blubbery lips as they formed words, felt the old prickle of irritation. The thought of his mean-spiritedness towards Nerys. A couple of bloody pies was never going to make up for the way he'd behaved over that thing with his stupid van. She remembered, too, Meinir telling her how he'd been with her after she'd challenged him about selling kangaroo meat, of all things, in his shop. Meinir had been livid. Bethan recalled how he'd made it sound like *she* was the difficult one; how he'd made horrible, spiteful comments and tried to turn people against her. Lovely, feisty Meinir, with her fierce sense of right and wrong. The memory hardened Bethan's resolve.

'No,' she said flatly. 'I'm not interested, thank you very much.'

His smile faltered. 'Oh. Right. I thought maybe . . .'

'You thought wrong,' Bethan said, more abrupt than she might normally have been, but not sorry. 'I've got a lot on.'

Roberts ran a finger under his collar. 'Huh. I s'pose the offers are pouring in, are they?' he muttered, his cheeks flushing more than ever as the charm peeled away. He stepped back, affronted, and for a moment they regarded each other, a wall of hostility filling the space between them.

Bethan got into the car without another word. As she pulled away, she caught sight of him in the rear-view mirror, standing rigid, watching her go. The image of his stony, cold-eyed expression sat uneasily with her all the way back to Beaumaris, sending a shudder through her.

Though there was no way on earth she'd have accepted his invitation, she had a niggling feeling that Hugh Roberts was a man who could readily bear a grudge.

Chapter 19

BEFORE – February 2021

Nerys

Though the signs had been there for some years, Nain's mental confusion had grown progressively worse. Nerys had seen it initially in the way she had begun to repeat herself; leave drawers open, forget to close the front door behind her. Dress herself in odd combinations of clothes that she would never normally have worn. She would pick up and then quickly abandon her knitting, seemingly restless and unable to focus on the task. All small, relatively insignificant things, that when put together started to make Nerys uneasy.

One day Nerys had asked her where the can opener was, to which she'd responded deadpan, 'In the fridge, of course'. It was obvious that something wasn't right.

Latterly her grandmother began to develop obsessive behaviour. She dwelled more and more on the past: particularly about what had happened to her daughter. Nerys couldn't pinpoint what, if anything, had triggered it.

'I keep thinking about that wheel brace from your mammy's car.' Nain's words had come out of the blue one afternoon as she stood, her gaze fixed on something through the living room window.

Nerys had been re-reading *Rachel's Holiday*. She looked up from her book. 'What about it?'

'Something very odd about it, that's what. The police never did explain it to us. I don't think they knew themselves. I wonder . . .' But then she had shaken her head as if she'd said too much, though her eyes were narrowed, her lips pursed.

Nerys had dismissed it at the time. Nain's rambling was getting worse and Nerys wondered if much of what was happening to her was the result of bottling up her feelings around Mam's disappearance for so long. It was desperately sad.'

The old lady became increasingly paranoid, considering every man in the area as a potential murderer. At first, she'd been convinced that Hugh Roberts, the local butcher, held a grudge against Mam, as she'd had a run-in with the man in his shop once. Then, for a long while, it had been Derfel. The fact that his boat had sustained damage; the fact he was so ready to accept the idea that Mam had been behind the vandalism. At one point, Nain even suggested that he was the one who'd attacked the boats, to deflect attention from himself. Nain had called the police several times, asking why they weren't looking into Derfel's activities on the night of the storm. Unusually, he hadn't been seen in The Quay that evening, which was unlike him – so where the hell was he? – she'd demanded to know. Everyone knew he had it in for Mam, she said. She was sure he'd had something to do with her disappearance. Thankfully the police were understanding and tried to placate her with assurances, that though they had already spoken to Derfel, they would certainly look into her concerns. But Nerys worried that Nain's phone calls would start to annoy them if they persisted. Once she'd got the bee in her bonnet about Derfel out of her system, she quickly became fixated on his friend, Harry Edwards. He was a local electrician, and a quiet, unassuming man. It was becoming ludicrous – and embarrassing.

Nain's finger-pointing at Derfel had really upset Catrin, especially as she was Elin's oldest friend. Nerys had apologised on Nain's behalf, explaining gently to her that her grandmother wasn't well, that the dementia was at the root of everything. That lately she was imagining things disappearing from the house: silly things that no burglar would have wanted. She'd even accused Peter of breaking into their rickety old garden shed and stealing some of Taid's rusty tools, which was completely ridiculous. Peter, who had never done anything but show them kindness, who'd gone out of his way to help whenever they'd had DIY problems that would have cost them a fortune to get a tradesman to fix. Nain had stood in the back garden one afternoon, shaking with rage as she yelled at him over the fence, saying she'd make sure everyone knew what he'd done. What he really was. Nerys felt so awkward about it all, but as ever he'd been reasonable and understanding.

'Don't worry. My dad had Alzheimer's. I know how it can affect people, make them all irrational and suspicious. I've got a hide like a rhinoceros,' Peter had joked. But it still left an uncomfortable atmosphere, and Nerys found it hard to look him and Libby in the eye after that. Despite Peter's joviality, she was sure he'd been offended. It must have felt like a kick in the teeth after everything he'd done for them over the years.

As far as the wheel brace was concerned, the police had ruled out the possibility of it being used to inflict the holes in the boats immediately – it had been made with something much wider, they'd said, plus there were no traces of anything from the boats on its metal surface. No one had a theory as to why it had been removed from the car. But Nerys was sure there must have been a rational explanation, even if Nain had become fixated on it.

There was no evidence that anything sinister had taken Mam from them, but the only way Nain seemed able to reason it all through now was to apportion blame. For years, she'd talked very little about what had happened, but it had clearly all been festering in her mind and the dementia had brought everything to the fore. There were days when she was more rational, but these were fewer and further between. Nerys had become frightened to fall asleep, after she woke in the early hours one night to discover the front door wide open, a chill filtering through the whole house. She'd run outside to find Nain in her nightdress and slippers, wandering up the lane towards The Quay, ranting that if the police weren't going to look for her daughter's killer, she would flush him out herself. The commotion had woken people and lights were coming on in the houses along the quayside.

Nerys felt sick, heartbroken about it all, but she knew the time had come for Nain to go into somewhere secure. She had her little job at Bethan's shop in Beaumaris, so couldn't be at home all the time, and Nain clearly wasn't safe to be left alone any more.

Bethan reassured her it was for the best. 'I know it's hard, cariad,' she'd said, tipping her head to one side as she regarded Nerys with a consoling smile. 'I had an old auntie went the same way. Your nain's safety is your priority – she could leave something on the stove, start a fire. Or what if you got home one day and she'd gone missing? I mean, with all the cliffs around the bay and everything . . .' she grimaced. 'It doesn't bear thinking about.'

Nerys knew she was right. But it didn't make her feel any better about it. She'd phoned Elin to discuss her concerns, but the ball had been left firmly in her own court.

'I'm not there to see how bad she's got,' Elin had said. 'But obviously if you think she could be a danger to herself, maybe you're right. The doctors will be able to advise you better, but ultimately it's your call.'

It was noncommittal, not exactly the thumbs up of support Nerys had hoped for. Nor an offer of coming straight home to see what, if anything, she could do to help. Nerys loved her sister, but a tiny part of her resented the fact that she'd been left to make all the decisions while Elin was far enough away in her little cocoon with Cai for it all to wash over her. Since Elin had moved to Birmingham, a chasm had opened up between them and it made Nerys sad. It had been almost four months now since Elin had been home and she rarely called: if Nerys wanted to speak to her, *she* was the one who always had to pick up the phone. Sometimes it would be nice to have a sounding board, another person to share the load.

Chapter 20

BEFORE – February 2022

Nerys

It was Wednesday. It had been almost a year since Nain had gone into the nursing home, but although Nerys always made the journey to Llangefni to visit her in the afternoons, her days off felt lonely. When she'd woken that morning, the silence in the cottage had been overwhelming. She showered, had a light breakfast, then made *cawl* from the various vegetables she had in the fridge. After picking up a loaf from the Spar in Pentraeth, she began the trek to see Delyth Parry to take her some of the soup as Nain had always done. Delyth was unwell: rumours were that she'd been diagnosed with an incurable blood condition, but had refused the more invasive treatment suggested by the hospital. The district nurse visited regularly and she was being monitored, but Delyth was forgetful and apparently not taking the medication she'd been prescribed. It felt as if she was allowing herself to slowly slip away.

After the downpour the night before, the lane leading to Delyth's cottage was waterlogged. It had become a familiar route that Nerys, Elin and Nain had trodden countless times in the years since Jac's death, a regular mission of mercy. Nerys took it slowly, heaving her boots one at a time as they were sucked down by the mud, taking care not to drop the plastic carrier bag containing the pot of soup and the bread. The wind blew into her face as the sea rushed behind her, the clang of a buoy's bell ringing somewhere in the distance.

Delyth's place was huddled towards the bottom of the lane, the lower part of its walls dark with damp, sandbags piled along them. A couple of old tin buckets sat either side of the entrance. The new front door Ianto had hung still looked out of place, its pale, new wood against the old grey stone, but it was solid. Proof of someone wanting to help. Of kindness.

Delyth opened up before Nerys had even knocked. She looked smaller and thinner than ever, as if the house was slowly swallowing her. Her cardigan hung off her shoulders, the bones at her wrists were frail as a tiny bird's.

'Oh, *helo*.' Delyth seemed startled, craning her neck to look past Nerys's shoulder. 'Did—did you see anyone else on your way over?' Her eyes were wide, anxious-looking.

'No,' Nerys said brightly. 'It's just me.'

The woman ushered Nerys inside, casting about once more before closing the door behind her.

Delyth's little *bwthyn* had been improved substantially since she'd lost Jac. Owing to everything that had happened lately with Nain, Nerys hadn't been for a while. She knew that people from the community had rallied round Delyth initially, but wondered if over time their support had gradually waned. Nerys needn't have worried. She was pleasantly surprised by the freshly painted walls; what she knew to be Peter's careful brushwork smoothing over years of water marks. Sturdy shelves that Ianto had put up since her last visit displayed Delyth's mam's crockery. Smart, recessed spotlights had been mounted along the low beams of the ceiling by Harry Edwards, Derfel's friend, making the little sitting room more welcoming. There was a new rug in front of the range, donated by a woman from Pentraeth, plus hard-wearing blue Ikea slipcovers that she'd no longer needed covering the old chairs, and someone had clearly washed and ironed the curtains. Sitting under the window, a dehumidifier, bought with the collection Peter and Libby had organised at the church, hummed. It was helping a little, but the deep-rooted damp still seeped through, leaving an odd, musty taste in the mouth. Libby's influence was evident in the tidy surfaces and well-organised pantry; the glass vase on the sideboard held a mixed bunch of supermarket flowers that had begun to wilt.

But despite her more comfortable surroundings, Delyth herself was more dishevelled than ever. Though almost ten years had passed since Jac's death, it was clear that the loss weighed on her every bit as heavily. It was acknowledged by everyone in the community that whenever they called by to see Delyth, her son's name inevitably crept into the conversation at some point and her eyes would glaze, before she'd go off at a tangent, reflecting, as she always did, on what had actually befallen Jac that terrible night.

Delyth seemed unhappy today, agitated. More confused than usual. Every little sound made her jump: the whistle of the kettle, a crow squawking, the wind rattling the latch on the door. It was as though she were scared of her own shadow. She perched nervously on the edge of her armchair instead of sitting back.

'They're out there somewhere,' she said, wringing her hands. She looked slightly manic. 'At night, mainly. I still hear them.'

'Who?' Nerys asked wearily. Delyth had repeated the same thing so many times over the years. No matter what anyone said, she couldn't be deterred from her line of thinking and it seemed to have got worse, rather than better.

Delyth's eyes darted about. She lowered her voice. 'You know who.'

For a moment, Delyth seemed to lose herself then, her gaze drifting to the far wall where Jac's old school photograph hung. He smiled out from it, a picture of innocence and good humour, his then tawny hair blown sideways, his blue eyes bright. The storm that had taken him and Mam had left its mark on them all. Nerys still remembered the sound of the wind that night, the way the sea had roared like it had a grievance. She couldn't bear to think of it.

'Jac'll be back soon,' Delyth said, brightening suddenly. She gave a small, hopeful nod. 'He said he wouldn't be long.'

Seeing Delyth's optimistic smile, her widened eyes, Nerys's heart went out to her. 'Oh, Delyth . . .'

But just as quickly, Delyth began shaking her head, as if brushing this last thought away. Her face clouded again. She pushed herself out of the chair and hurried to the window, peering round the curtain, her breath fogging the glass.

'I'm not mad,' she said. 'Nor stupid. I know what I heard back then. What that police woman said.' Her voice dropped. 'Your nain spoke to her. *She* knew.'

Nerys thought of Nain as she was now, crumpling into herself in the nursing home, the past slipping its moorings. A shadow of her grandmother as she'd been all those years ago – capable, keen-eyed, proud. That policewoman had spoken out of turn, she'd told her and Elin angrily that day. She'd had no business mentioning the tests on Jac's body, especially not when Delyth was clearly so fragile. And it was all standard procedure, apparently – they had to investigate any injuries to the body in case anything iffy had gone on. The inquest had ruled that it was just a tragic accident. But the officer's careless words all those years ago had burrowed into Delyth's mind and never left.

This again. It was becoming an obsession with Delyth, this

idea that Jac's death had been something more. That it wasn't a tragic accident at all. Maybe it was Delyth's way of coping with everything, rather than blaming herself for allowing him out alone that night with the weather the way it had been.

Nerys let out a long breath. 'The coroner said it was an accident,' she said quietly.

'Well, they would say that, wouldn't they?' Delyth replied, a sudden hardness to her tone. She turned back, and for the briefest second the confusion seemed to clear. She looked straight at Nerys, her gaze steady now and startlingly lucid. 'I found his Spider-Man torch, you know. Poking out from under the hedge.' She waved a hand towards the door. 'In the lane, not far from home. He'd been on the road back. So how did he end up in the sea?'

Something turned in Nerys's gut. 'Did you—did you tell the police?'

Delyth's eyes flashed with anger. 'They didn't believe me, said he must have dropped it on his way to The Quay, not on the way back. But he loved that torch and he was so careful with it, he'd have made damn sure he was holding it the whole time. He hated walking up here in the dark.' She shook her head, her hands balling into fists. 'I'm his mam, I can feel it. Someone took him from me. And whoever did for my poor boy keeps coming back. They say that, don't they? Killers always return to the scene of the crime. They're out there somewhere. Always.'

Nerys crossed the room and took Delyth's tiny hands in her own. They were cold and dry, the skin paper-thin.

'No one's out there,' Nerys said gently. 'You're upsetting yourself and it's not good for you.'

Delyth's mouth twitched, as if she might smile, but the moment passed. She pulled her hands free and sank back into the chair, exhausted. 'Let's have a *panad*, shall we. Then I'm going to take a nap. I'm so tired all of a sudden.'

Nerys left, dragged down by a heavy, troubled feeling. Later she would wonder if it was some sort of premonition.

*

The news came a few days later, delivered by the postman. He'd tapped on Nerys's door, an apologetic look on his face. The district nurse had found Delyth in her armchair early that morning, last night's half-eaten sandwich on the table beside her, he'd heard. She had choked, apparently. Tragic. He hoped it was quick, he'd said. It didn't sound like the peaceful end Delyth deserved.

Nerys sat on the edge of the settee and stared at the wall where the light reflecting from the morning sky shimmered faintly. The news about Delyth had shocked and saddened her at first. But her misery had quickly been replaced with something else, something she wasn't sure she ought to be feeling: a sense of relief. An end to poor Delyth's perpetual torment, to her grief. And then the disconcerting thought of what the little woman had said crept into her mind, her absolute certainty that someone was hanging around her house. That the same someone had taken Jac.

Maybe Delyth should have been in sheltered housing, somewhere she'd have felt safe, even if there was nothing substantial behind her anxiety. Maybe Nerys herself ought to have done something to help, to sort arrangements for her. After all, Delyth had no one.

Later, in Bethan's little shop in Beaumaris, the bell over the door chimed as Nerys walked in. Bethan looked up from the till, her features arranging into a sad, sympathetic smile.

'I just heard about Delyth,' said Bethan, coming round from behind the counter to slip an arm around her. 'I'm so sorry, cariad. I know you and your nain spent a lot of time with her over the years.'

Nerys nodded. The shop smelled of her favourite sea salt and sage reed diffuser, but it failed to lift her spirits. She leaned into Bethan, everything spilling out before she could stop herself. About the last visit to Delyth. The way the woman had looked at her; the way she'd spoken with such conviction, such fear.

'I feel awful. I keep thinking I should've done something to help.'

Bethan rubbed her shoulder. 'What more could you have done? Poor Delyth was ill – in body and mind.'

'She was all over the place. It was like she couldn't hold a thought.' Nerys recalled how agitated Delyth had seemed. The memory made her stomach clench now. 'Maybe she should've been somewhere – you know, a home or something?'

'But that'd be down to the authorities, not you,' Bethan said quietly. She cocked her head, studying Nerys's anguished face. 'You looked out for her, took her food. Kept her company.'

'But I hadn't been for ages. And she was so thin,' said Nerys, her voice cracking. 'And so alone.'

'She wasn't alone,' said Bethan firmly. 'Not really. And even if she'd been surrounded by people day and night, it wouldn't have changed anything. Losing a child does that.' She paused, her eyes glistening. 'After Jac, her life was never going to be the same. No one could cushion that blow, cariad, no matter how hard they tried.'

Nerys swallowed. She thought of Ianto's door and the shelves he'd built for Delyth, her new furnishings; Peter's paintwork, Libby's cleaning and casseroles. The modern, if slightly incongruous, lighting that Harry Edwards had installed. Of Nain's help and comfort over the years. Of the donated dehumidifier droning away at the damp. All those small, human efforts against a mother's grief that would never ease.

When she left the shop later, Nerys took a walk down to the sea front. She skimmed a few pebbles and watched as they skipped on the surface of the water. Mam had loved to do that; count how many times she could get a stone to bounce before it disappeared beneath the waves. The early evening light rippled across the water, and for a moment the sea looked almost kind. Serene. Nerys knew better: she hadn't even paddled since the night of the storm, nor would she ever again. She stood and stared at it emptily, thinking of Delyth, at peace at last.

But what if Delyth had been right? What if there really *had* been something unnatural about Jac's death? The thought of what the little woman had said about the torch had begun to play on her mind.

Why *would* it have been found close to his home if he was washed out to sea?

She pushed the thought down. It was pointless going over old ground. Delyth had driven herself to an early grave with the worry – it was common knowledge that stress could bring on all sorts of illnesses, mental and physical. And the last thing Nerys needed was to become unwell.

She had Nain to think about.

Chapter 21

TEN YEARS EARLIER – October 2013

The night of the storm

Jac

Jac had seen enough now.

As he'd hoped, there were endless forks of lightning, bright white against the ebony of the sky. It had been captivating at first, observing from the warmth and safety of the pub. Nearly as good as the firework display Mam had taken him to once, years ago. Though he loved the sparkling colours, he hadn't liked the bangs when he was little, and she'd had to take him straight home when he started to scream. People were staring at him, she'd said, and though it wasn't kind of them, it was probably best they left. People still stared at him now sometimes – but only those who didn't know him. Even if he looked young for his twenty-five years, it made him cross when they spoke to him as if he were still a child. Mam said they didn't intend to be mean; they were just *ignorant*. He'd liked that word: it was a good one. He would use it now and then if anyone was particularly rude.

It was the best view now, looking out towards the sea through the picture window, the cresting waves lighting up each time a bolt bounced off the horizon. Between flashes, he'd waited for the thunder, pressing an ear to the cold glass to hear it properly. The people sitting at the table under the window didn't appear to mind when he'd wriggled between them and knelt on the bench to watch. They seemed to find it funny for some reason.

But soon Jac became bored. Mam had said they could watch a film before bed. He wanted to see the *Harry Potter* DVD she'd bought from the charity shop. He'd enjoyed the last one. And Mam had bought a bag of toffee popcorn and a big bottle of cola to share, too. It was still raining quite hard, but he had his pac-a-mac. He would change into his pyjamas as soon as he got home, anyway. Remembering to say 'excuse me' this time as he clambered back across the bench, Jac slipped the waterproof on over his jacket, said goodbye to the people standing by the bar and the fruit machine, and went out into the night, pulling up his hood before venturing from the pub's doorway. He felt in his pocket for the small torch he'd brought out with him. His Spider-Man torch. It might even give him superpowers, Mam had said. She always told him to be careful he didn't tread in anything nasty when he was coming back up the lane in the dark – some people weren't that fussy about picking up after their dogs.

Conscious of the incoming tide – Mam had always impressed upon him how quickly it could change – Jac kept well to the side of the bay as he headed across the wet ridge of sand and towards the footpath which led back to their cottage. The lane would be waterlogged for sure: he hoped the rain wasn't getting into the house again – they often had water dripping through the slates when there was a downpour, and Mam had to leave buckets and bowls everywhere. They'd even been flooded a couple of times in the past, and that had been worse.

He pointed the beam of the torch forwards and kept his eyes trained on the ground, as Mam had instructed, taking purposeful strides, his eyes never deviating from his route. Even with the pac-a-mac, he was getting soaked: he could feel icy water leeching through the seams and trickling down his torso and it was making him shiver. Lightning flashed again somewhere to his left, followed by a deep, ominous rumble. The storm didn't feel like fun any more. He cast the torch about briefly – there was nobody else around. Normally he wouldn't have minded, even in the dark, but suddenly the ghostly, black-toothed face of Gwrach y Rhibyn, the vengeful witch foretelling death that Mam had read to him about, popped into his mind and he felt unnerved. Although, he would be home in just a few minutes now: the thought spurred him on and he began to step up his pace. He'd reached the bottom of the lane. He needed to be extra careful here about where he put his feet. Sand gave way to mud, and Jac had to lift one trainer at a time as they were sucked into it. Suddenly, something caught his attention a short way ahead. Jac stopped, screwing up his eyes as he played the beam of the flashlight upwards for a moment. It looked like someone bent over, struggling to drag something heavy up the lane.

Maybe he could help. Whoever it was would be getting *very* wet, moving so slowly as they were. Unless their raincoat was much better than his.

'*Hel-o?*'

As Jac called out tentatively, the person froze; dropped whatever they had been trying to move. Recognising the face under the direct rays of the torch, Jac's mouth broke into a smile. He swiped at the water running from his hood and down the bridge of his nose.

'I didn't know it was you. D'you want a hand?' He began to move more quickly to meet them. But as he grew closer, his eyes dropped, the flashlight landing on what was being dragged along in the mud. He stared up at the person uncomprehendingly, his initial confusion turning to cold fear as he realised something was very wrong. Jac backed away suddenly, not sure what he should do. But there was no time to decide on any course of action before he was being pursued, away from the path to home, away from safety, back towards the shingle beach and the ever-nearing tide.

Terrified, Jac dropped the torch and began to run blindly, stumbling across the sand at the perimeter of the bay towards the upturned boats on the far bank, throwing a look back over his shoulder and almost tripping over his feet in his haste. He screamed, the sound of it echoing in his eardrums. But there was no one to hear him. No one to come to his aid. This was much worse than any fears he'd had about Gwrach y Rhibyn. Much, much worse than the creepy creaking of the floorboards in his room at night and the wind whistling through the window pane.

Without warning, gloved fingers clapped heavily across his mouth from behind as a muscular arm gripped him tightly around the neck, slamming him to the floor. The hand over his mouth moved swiftly to the back of his head, forcing his face into the ground. Though Jac tried desperately to prise the arm away, he simply didn't have the physical strength.

The crook of the elbow around his throat squeezed tighter and tighter, the hand pushing ever harder against his skull as it held him down. Sand filled Jac's mouth and nostrils as he gasped painfully for breath, all the while thinking about his mam and how cross she'd be if he didn't come home soon.

Until everything went black and Jac knew no more.

Chapter 22

BEFORE – February 2023

Nerys

Nain was gone.

Since the funeral, Nerys had been on her own in the house for almost six weeks, and even at work, the days seemed interminable, overshadowed by the dread of going back to an empty house filled with so many memories. The trips to the nursing home, as well as the long hours spent in the shop, had kept her focused for nearly two years. But now, closing the door behind her as she returned home in the evenings had an odd sense of finality about it. The bitter realisation that her grandmother would never be coming back and that this was her lot.

Even at the end, Nain had always recognised her, thankfully. Nerys had dreaded the day she would visit and be met with a blank expression – or worse still, hostility. It was Elin who seemed to confuse Nain on the odd occasion she'd visited, but

Nerys supposed that was understandable. The older she got, the more Elin looked like Mam. Nerys had even found herself staring at her once or twice. It was slightly unsettling, if she was honest.

But though Nain was always happy to see Nerys, her grandmother's erratic behaviour had persisted. On some occasions she'd be calm, a little vacant, but on others she would grasp Nerys's hands earnestly in hers; beg her to listen to what she was saying. Nerys had always tried to mollify Nain, to persuade her that it was all in her head: that Mam had been swept away by the storm. That no one was to blame.

Nain had ranted so often that Nerys learned to switch off to it in the end. But one thing Nain had said, a remark on one of her more lucid days as she'd watched out of the window all those months earlier, had sown a seed of doubt in Nerys's own mind.

'Look at him,' she'd hissed angrily, her hands gripping the windowsill. 'He collars everyone, makes it his business to seem like he's everyone's friend. But I know better. I've *seen* things. And I'm not the only one. I've learned stuff that'd make your hair curl, let me tell you.'

Nerys had peered outside, wondering who she was referring to. One of the orderlies, his broad back to them, was loading something into a van. Whether Nain was talking about him or confusing the man with someone else, Nerys couldn't be sure. But the remark resonated with her for some reason. She studied the man for a moment, the way he carried himself. From behind, he looked remarkably like Peter.

Her grandmother had broken off then, her butterfly mind easily distracted by something, as had become the norm. She'd begun to ramble about a completely unrelated subject, never revealing what hair-curling anecdotes had been shared with her. Nerys had let it go, hadn't questioned her, assuming that her grandmother's failing, muddled memory was playing cruel tricks on her.

But now, all by herself in the house and with time on her hands, Nerys had started to wonder. Whether Nain's suspicions were unfounded and rooted in her dementia – or whether there might be some truth in what she had said. It was a disturbing thought.

Initially reluctant, realising things were unlikely to improve on their own, Nerys had eventually succumbed to the GP's proposal of antidepressants. 'Just to lift you out of the doldrums, calm your anxiety,' the woman had suggested kindly. Nerys knew she needed something to help her cope with everything going round her head. There seemed to be a permanent cloud of doom hanging over her and it was showing no signs of shifting.

After a couple of weeks of unpleasant side effects, Nerys was beginning to feel slightly better. More human again. Though she still had moments of sadness when she thought about Nain, she wasn't dwelling on her negative thoughts as much. Her spirits were definitely lifting a little. She wondered why she had been so resistant to taking the medication before. She wouldn't hesitate in future.

Getting a little rescue cat had felt a good solution for the loneliness. Given she worked four days a week in Bethan's shop, she didn't think it would be fair to have a dog. They could pine if left alone. But cats were more independent, slept a lot. When she and Elin were growing up, they'd adopted a stray, Llwyd. Well, Mam had. He was only a scrawny kitten when she'd found him cowering behind the dustbins at the back of Bethan's shop, but had grown into a handsome, blue-grey brute with the loudest purr Nerys had ever heard. Llwyd, always so present in the house, had disappeared at the ripe old age of nineteen: probably taken himself off somewhere to die, Nain suspected. But it had broken Nerys's and Elin's hearts; Nain's too, especially as

Mam had loved him so much. Consequently, Nain would never entertain the idea of having another cat, saying it was just too upsetting when anything happened to them.

But now the time felt right. Nerys had contacted the local cat rescue near Bodffordd, and Bethan had accompanied her to choose a suitable feline companion. Nerys was drawn to Nyten, a small brown-and-white female, instantly. She was vocal and friendly, standing on her hind legs to stretch up and be stroked. The lady from the rescue wasn't sure how old she was, only that she'd already had at least one litter of kittens. She'd been found, scraggy and dishevelled, wandering the streets looking for scraps some six weeks earlier.

'We think someone probably dumped her,' she told them. 'Too many people have cats and don't get them neutered, then they can't cope. God knows what became of her kittens.' She shook her head sadly. 'So irresponsible.'

Nerys had scooped Nyten into her arms, the need to protect this little creature suddenly overwhelming. 'Poor baby,' she'd whispered. 'I'll take care of you now.'

February was coming to a close. A week had passed since Nyten's arrival and she was settling in well. Nerys was outside putting rubbish into the bin, when a flash of white in her peripheral vision caught her attention. She turned to see Libby peering over the fence. Nerys greeted her with a smile. It was funny, how alike Libby and Peter looked, the pair of them with such bright white hair.

'Like a bloody pair of ageing Midwich Cuckoos,' Bethan had remarked one day, as they'd seen the pair approaching across the beach, arm in arm. Nerys had winced. It seemed quite mean.

'Morning, Nerys. You've got a new cat, I see.' Libby tipped her head toward the house.

The wind was blowing Nerys's curls into her face. Pushing them back, she turned to see Nyten watching through the kitchen window, her mouth opening in a silent *miaow*. Seeing her little face, Nerys felt a rush of affection.

'Yeah. I've called her Nyten. She's a rescue, really sweet nature.'

'That's nice. Company for you.'

Nerys nodded, slightly wistfully. 'Thought it was time – you know . . .'

'Of course.' Libby gave her a sympathetic smile. She paused. 'Is she . . . will she be a house cat?'

'I'm keeping her in just now, but once she's settled, I'll let her come out here,' she said, gesturing towards the garden. 'See what she wants to do. It's pretty safe, even if she goes round the front. There're only one or two cars in the lane, and they can't go very fast.'

Libby pursed her lips, seemingly considering this for a moment. 'I believe females don't tend to wander like the males anyway, do they?'

'So I've heard.' Nerys smiled.

Libby looked as if she were about to say something else, then a noise from her own house distracted her. Her head whipped round. Peter was standing in their open doorway, his eyebrows raised in an unspoken question.

'Better go. We normally have a coffee about now.' She shot Nerys a quick smile. 'See you again.'

'Yeah. See you.' Nerys watched for a moment as Libby hurried back into the house, closing the door behind her.

Chapter 23

BEFORE – March 2023

Nerys

More than three weeks had passed since Nerys had brought Nyten home and it had been the best decision she could have made. The little cat was affectionate and gentle. She loved to curl up on Nerys's lap in the evenings, or lie at her feet as she slept. Nerys had kept her indoors for the first week or so, and then allowed her to explore the back garden under close supervision, a little longer each day. Nyten seemed happy to stay within the confines of the space and showed no inclination to roam. The garden was well sheltered and on warmer days, Nyten favoured the far corner beside Taid's old shed. She had flattened an area of the shrubbery, where she would curl and soak up the sun. Whenever Nerys called her in, she would come trotting happily to greet her with a soft *miaow*. It was so lovely to have company, someone to take care of again.

The post arrived as Nerys descended the stairs that morning, dumped through the slot in the front door and landing with a slap onto the mat. Nerys was running late. She gathered the letters up as she walked to the kitchen to make tea, flicking through them hurriedly. Most were for her – bills, a flyer for a yoga class in Benllech she'd never attend. There was a letter for Nain from a local hospice charity she used to donate to, which sent a pang of misery through her – she thought everyone had been notified. But one official-looking envelope made her pause.

It was addressed to Peter. The typed address was one she didn't recognise, somewhere in Leicester. But through this, a line had been put diagonally and beside it, another written. This in turn had been scribbled out so that it was illegible. Someone had added next door's address beneath in scrawled, barely legible handwriting. The reason the postman had put it through the wrong door, clearly. The return address on the back was for a legal firm; again, in Leicester.

Nerys frowned, then shrugged, slipping the letter into her bag. She'd drop it round later. Peter was usually out and about, and if not, she'd give it to Libby – she often saw her pottering round the garden. But Nyten chose that moment to rub round her legs, purring and licking her bare ankles so that it tickled. Nerys laughed, scooped her up, and forgot all about the envelope.

Though Nain's death had hit her hard, after a few weeks on the antidepressants, Nerys was slowly starting to get back into the rhythm of life. Her grandmother's care had dominated her own existence for years, even after the old lady had gone into the nursing home. Nerys had felt so guilty about it, had worried constantly whether she was being properly looked after. It was as if the rest of her own life was permanently on hold.

But Bethan reminded her gently that she'd done everything possible for Nain, that she needed to focus on herself now. Let her hair down, get out and socialise more. Maybe find someone to settle down with. That she could feel proud of the unselfish way she'd always put her grandmother first and that she needed to move on.

'You don't want to finish up like me, cariad,' she'd warned. 'I love my mam to bits, but caring for her on top of running the business has pretty much been a nail in the coffin of every relationship I've had since – well, since The Bastard.' Bethan's face hardened automatically whenever there was any mention of her adulterous ex. 'I can't be arsed any more, if I'm honest. It's too much like hard work trying to juggle it all. And I'm too set in my ways now, anyway. I've got too used to my own company. Not sure I could share my home with a man again.'

The town, and therefore the shop, had been busy. It was the Easter holiday, and a few days' fine weather had brought tourists flocking to the coast. The till had been ringing at a steady pace throughout the day, and Bethan was in a buoyant mood, telling Nerys she could finish an hour early as she'd worked so hard.

As Nerys was about to leave that afternoon, Bethan pressed an envelope into her hand. 'A little bonus for you, cariad,' she told her, with a wink. 'Get yourself something nice. There's a sale on in that boutique up the road. They've got some fab tops in the window – go and have a look before they close.'

Nerys smiled, thanking her with a hug. Bethan paid her pretty well anyway and had always been flexible if she needed to take time off here and there. She was lucky, she realised, to get on so well with her boss. Grateful that her mam's lovely friend had become her own.

She wandered up the high street in the direction of the clothes shop, the air still cool but blue skies and sunlight reminding her that warmer weather was on its way. Coming towards her was a tall, thirtyish man with shaggy brown hair, his hands in his pockets. He seemed to slow down as he grew nearer, clearly appraising her, his face lighting with a shy smile as their eyes locked for a moment. Nerys smiled back. As they passed one another, she threw a glance over her shoulder, only to see that he had done the same. The man grinned, and Nerys felt her cheeks warm. She turned back, continuing on her way.

But suddenly her heart felt lifted. Maybe Bethan was right. Maybe she *could* find love with someone. Maybe life could finally be taking a turn for the better.

It was an exciting thought.

Chapter 24

BEFORE – March 2023

Nerys

Nerys clutched the paper carrier bag containing the blouse she'd chosen, feeling quietly pleased. It had looked nice when she'd tried it on in the shop – flattered her figure. It was the sort of thing she'd have felt confident in, should she ever be asked on a date. She dropped her handbag onto the settee, stooping to fuss Nyten who'd come running to greet her. But as she went to open the back door to let Nyten out, her mood darkened at once. The key was lying on the floor beneath, the door unlocked.

Nerys stopped, the carrier still hooked over her wrist, and frowned. She must have forgotten to lock it, maybe knocked it out as she passed, she'd been in such a hurry earlier. She'd been late that morning, distracted. That explained it. Traeth Coch was quiet, safe: the sort of place where people left doors on the latch. Out of holiday season, everyone knew everyone. Even so, unease prickled at her as she glanced about.

The kitchen looked almost the same as she'd left it. Almost. Nerys caught her breath. She could have sworn that the small pile of post on the counter had been disturbed – shifted, rifled through – and then, as if in haste, subtly rearranged. Not quite right. Not quite wrong. She stared at it, her heart thudding, trying to decide whether the disorder existed anywhere except in her own mind.

You're imagining it, she told herself. But still she went cautiously through all the rooms, checking for any other signs of disturbance. Everything *looked* normal. She made tea, put down food for Nyten; tried to shake the thought. She was being silly. Why would anyone come in to poke through her mail and nothing else?

Then Nerys remembered the letter addressed to Peter.

Her handbag lay on the settee where she'd dumped it. She rooted inside and pulled out the envelope. It was ridiculous, she knew that, but the letter felt heavier somehow, weighty with significance. The flap wasn't glued down properly. She hesitated, a hot bloom of guilt spreading through her chest. But she couldn't resist taking a look.

Nerys's eyes skimmed the page, and she had to sit down, re-reading in disbelief. *Seven thousand pounds*. A penalty imposed for malicious damage to a neighbour's property that was supposed to have been settled out of court. Payment outstanding. Interest accruing. A warning of further legal action and a possible court summons if the fine wasn't settled immediately.

She stared at the words until they blurred. Peter? Cheerful, pleasant Peter, who painted their fence and fixed things with a smile, offered help wherever it was needed in the community? It didn't fit. Nothing in her experience of him matched the cold, legal severity of the letter. The kind of person who was capable of something like *that*.

Nerys scanned the contents once more, suddenly noticing the date beneath the letterhead. She frowned. It had been issued in July 2009. She'd heard of mail going astray occasionally and not reaching the intended recipient for years. Maybe the debt had been settled now. Maybe, for whatever reason, the letter had been forwarded in error. But still . . .

Shaken, she shoved the page back into the envelope, her fingers clumsy. Nerys wrote *not known at this address* across the front, the lie making her wince, and then, without allowing herself time to reconsider, she grabbed her coat and walked the hundred or so yards to the postbox near The Old Boathouse. The soft thud of the envelope dropping inside told her there was no going back. The deed was done.

On her way back, Nerys's breath caught in her throat as she saw Libby coming down the path towards her. Nerys's whole body tightened. She felt awkward now and prayed it didn't show in her face.

'Hi, Nerys,' said Libby. 'Lovely evening, isn't it?' The woman smiled amicably, the way she always did, but her eyes flickered, her thoughts clearly elsewhere. While Peter was often walking around the locality doing one thing or another, it was unusual to see Libby out on her own. Nerys cast about surreptitiously, but there was no sign of him.

'It is,' she replied, groaning inwardly. Her voice sounded artificially bright, too high-pitched in her own head. Nerys considered, for the briefest moment, saying something – asking if everything was all right. But she couldn't bring herself to mention the letter. It would be better to carry on as before. Before she'd discovered Peter's uncomfortable secret.

A horn sounded suddenly from the path in front of the cottages. Nerys looked round, her eyes landing on Peter's old

Ford Mondeo rolling slowly down the track. He was waiting for Libby.

Libby tipped her head towards the car. 'Oh, that'll be him,' she said, already turning away. 'We're going for a bite to eat in Beaumaris. Best not keep him.'

Libby hurried off, and Nerys watched as she climbed into the passenger seat. They both waved as the car pulled away, leaving an oddly ominous silence in its wake, with only the sibilant rush of the sea whispering beyond the wall.

Nerys stood there for a moment, the unease building from somewhere deep within her. She had done the sensible thing, she told herself. The correct thing. And yet, as she went back inside and locked the door carefully behind her, Nain's words echoed in her mind: *I've seen things*.

Had she? Perhaps it had been the dementia talking again – or maybe Nain really *had* known something unpleasant about Peter.

Nerys couldn't shake the feeling that she herself now knew something she wasn't meant to – and that choosing to turn a blind eye might not necessarily be the best course of action.

Chapter 25

NOW – Earlier on Wednesday 5th April 2023

Cai

After several attempts, Cai gave up knocking on Nerys's door and it was, unusually, locked. He peered through into the living room and had even been round the back, in case she was in the kitchen with the radio blaring or something, but since the rear door was also bolted, there was clearly no one in. It was approaching 1.30 p.m., so he decided to head for The Quay to get a sandwich and a coffee before taking a walk to re-acquaint himself with the proposed dig site. Coming back down the path from the cottage, he noticed Peter, the Owens' neighbour, approaching across the sand. Cai raised a hand in greeting.

'A'right, young man. How are you?' Peter smiled genially as he approached. He was wearing wellingtons and carrying a plastic bucket.

'I'm good, thanks.' Cai eyed the man's gloved hands. 'What've you been up to?'

Peter held the bucket aloft. 'Scraped a few mussels off the rocks for dinner – Libby makes a nice sauce with 'em. What brings you up here, then? You on your own?'

'I've been working in Caernarfon for a few days. Yeah, Elin's back in Brum. I just popped over to see Nerys, but she seems to be out.'

Peter's brow creased into a frown. 'Haven't seen much of her at all since Mrs Owen passed, to be honest. Can't be easy for her, young woman on her own like that.'

'Ah. I was going to knock on your door actually, ask if you'd seen her.' Cai felt rather guilty. After all, he'd been the one to ask Elin to leave Traeth Coch. He hadn't thought about the predicament it might land Nerys in once anything happened to their nain.

Peter shook his head. 'Libby's been round to check on her a few times, but she don't seem to want company. Not easy to help someone if they don't want to be helped, is it?'

'No, I guess not.'

Peter's gaze drifted suddenly towards the Owens's cottage. His eyes narrowed. Cai glanced back over his shoulder to see a glimmer of movement in the upstairs bedroom.

He turned back to Peter. 'Hey, did you just clock somebody up there? Maybe she's hiding, if she doesn't want to see anyone.'

Peter rolled his shoulders. 'I thought at first I might've, but I reckon it was just a breeze moving the curtain – bloody draughty these old places. I've had to put sealant all round the windows in ours.' He gave Cai a brief grin. 'Well, better get these indoors. I'd shake your hand, but . . .' he indicated the bucket. 'If I see Nerys, I'll tell her you called by.'

'Thanks. I'm sure Elin will have spoken to her, but no doubt we'll be seeing her in a few weeks anyway, when I start the dig.'

Peter's expression shifted. He put down the pail to lean on the front wall of his cottage, clearly more interested in hearing about Cai's plans than discussing Nerys. 'Oh yeah, I remember you mentioning it a while ago. Still going ahead, all that, is it?'

'Absolutely. I've been gearing up for it for ages now.'

'They found a load of ancient stuff here, ooh – over a century ago, didn't they? Where you gonna be digging, then?'

Cai turned and waved a hand towards Castell Mawr, the huge limestone mound overlooking the bay's northern shore. 'The Scandinavian artefacts were found somewhere over there. So I'm planning on focusing my efforts on the other side – you know that narrow lane that winds up towards Pentraeth?'

Peter nodded, casting a look across the beach. 'And you've got the go-ahead, have you? Don't want to upset the local landowners.' He gave a short bark of laughter.

Cai grinned. 'Oh yeah, that's the first hurdle before you even make plans for something like this. The fine could be pretty hefty otherwise. I've secured funding through Cadw – you know, the Welsh equivalent of English Heritage? And I got permission from the farmer whose land borders the lane, so it's all above board. A couple of my old uni mates'll be joining me, and Elin's going to muck in when she can. I'm awaiting confirmation from a few other volunteers, but we're good to make a start already.'

Peter scratched his head. 'And you really think you'll find stuff? I mean, if there's been a dig here in the past, you'd've thought they'd have looked into where the most likely spot'd be.'

'Oh, definitely. With the Viking connection, the whole area's a potential hotbed of undiscovered loot – archaeologically speaking, I mean.' Cai smiled. 'If you've got a few hours to spare, you're welcome to join us when we get underway.'

'Ah thanks, but I've got plenty to keep me busy. It's so true – now I'm retired, don't know how I ever found time to go to work! I'll ask about if you like though, see if anyone else might be interested.' Peter picked up his bucket again, gripping the handle with both hands. 'Anyway, I'll be seeing you. Mind how you go.'

Cai tapped his temple in a sort of salute and started towards the pub. Hearing voices behind him after only a few yards, he glanced back to see a tall man with dark hair had collared Peter by his gate now, and the bucket had been set down once more. Cai smiled to himself. Those mussels were never going to get to Libby at this rate.

Disappointingly, though the pub was fairly busy, there was no one in that he recognised. Rhiannon wasn't working and there was no sign of Ianto, though Cai knew he often called in on his lunch break if he was close by. Cai liked Ianto. He was an easy-going sort of bloke, the kind who put you at ease. Cai had hoped to ask him about what the old lady on the bus had been saying, about Meinir's disappearance. He wondered whether Nerys or even Elin had ever considered the possibility that there had been something more sinister behind it than the storm and sheer bad luck. Elin had never said anything hinting at it before. Maybe she'd tried to blot it out – and with the absence of a body, how could anything ever be proved? He could imagine the anguish she must have felt if rumours like that had been circulating. Giving voice to the idea herself might have made an already unbearable loss even worse for her and her family.

Cai found a seat near the window. From one of the capacious inside pockets of his jacket, he took out the book he'd brought with him about the local area and its history. He worked his way through a cheese salad crusty baguette while he read, then ordered an Americano. He had almost finished his coffee when his attention was drawn by the door swinging open. Ianto breezed in, shook the rainwater from his waxed jacket and looked around. As his eyes landed on Cai, he broke into a grin and strode across to greet him.

'*Sut mae*! Pissing down out there it is – came out of nowhere. I was going to go to Holyhead but decided against it.'

Cai's eyes travelled to the window to see rain bouncing off the tables outside. He groaned inwardly. He'd been so engrossed in the book that he hadn't noticed.

Ianto cast about again, clearly expecting to see Elin. 'Where's your other half, then?'

'Back in Birmingham with a broken foot.' Cai grimaced. 'I've been working in Caernarfon – came over to see Nerys, but she's not home.'

Everything about Ianto seemed to tighten. 'You haven't heard, then?'

'Heard what?'

'Nerys was taken into hospital a few days ago. She's not been good for a while, but it all sort of came to a head last week.'

Cai put down his cup. 'Oh God. I'd no idea.' He felt his stomach plummet. 'We've been quite, well, preoccupied lately. I feel awful now. Is she okay?'

Ianto winced, lowering his voice. 'It's a bad do. Mental health, poor girl.' He ran a hand across his beard. 'I'm going to see her at the weekend – I've just had a lot on this week.'

'Where is she? Ysbyty Gwynedd?'

Ianto nodded. He transferred his weight awkwardly from one foot to the other, then glanced towards the bar. 'I'm getting a pint in, d'you want one?'

Cai hesitated. He hadn't intended to drink anything, but he wasn't going anywhere in that weather. And besides, he wanted to talk to Ianto, find out more about what had gone on with Nerys. He wondered why Peter hadn't mentioned it. Maybe he wasn't aware.

*

Afternoon had given way to early evening. Cai had stayed far longer in The Quay than he'd intended to, but at least the deluge had abated. His conversation with Ianto had given him food for thought. It seemed that since her nain had died, Nerys had developed some sort of paranoia. But the odd thing was that it all tied in with what the old woman on the bus had been telling him. Ianto, however, curled his lip sceptically.

'She's a good girl, Nerys. But I think she got a little carried away, if I'm honest. Maybe it was her grandmother putting ideas in her head. I mean, Mrs Owen did get pretty confused towards the end, to be fair.' He shook his head sadly. 'It was pretty tough on Nerys, all those months of to-ing and fro-ing to that care home. I know she felt awful guilty about putting her in there. And she went every day, you know, even when she'd been working in the shop. Nerys took her death very badly. I think everything just got on top of her in the end.'

Cai gulped down the miserable little knot that had lodged in his throat. He really felt for Nerys; it seemed a poor excuse to say the pandemic had turned everything on its head. She'd had a raw deal, stuck there alone without any moral support for so long. Although it was true that he and Elin hadn't been able to travel back to Anglesey for some months due to the regulations, and after the restrictions had been lifted, they had, for want of a better expression, got out of the habit. He was always so busy with his own work and Elin was absorbed in hers. As time passed, the distance it had created had become emotional as much as physical between Elin and her sister. He knew that Elin regretted it, but life had got in the way, as it so often could. Hopefully they could make amends now – the dig would mean they'd both be close and able to support Nerys, help her get back to health. They needed to make it up to her.

Chapter 26

NOW – Thursday 4th May 2023

Elin

Elin glanced at the bedside clock dispassionately. It was 12.10 p.m.; even though she hadn't been asleep for a good chunk of that time, she'd been in bed well over twelve hours. But there was little point in getting up. She rolled over and stared at the empty bed where Nerys should have been. Her heart lurched. She'd visited her sister in the hospital numerous times now since returning to Traeth Coch four weeks ago and there had been no obvious improvement.

Everything Dr Bianchi had said and the way Nerys had behaved that first time she saw her still prodded at her. She wondered if Nerys would ever recover sufficiently to be able to explain her fears – or whether they could all be attributed to her grief and there really was nothing rational behind them at all.

Elin heaved out a weary breath. She sat up and dragged

herself from the bed. At the very least, she ought to get up and open the curtains. Nain would have been appalled.

'Duw anwyl – we only keep the curtains closed during the day if there's been a death in the family.'

She remembered her grandmother scolding her on several occasions, when she'd had a lie in after a few too many ciders with Catrin. Nain would sweep into the room, flinging wide the thin bedroom curtains and making Elin groan as she screwed up her eyes against the sudden glare and the pounding of her head.

'Chop chop, you'll sleep your life away at this rate.' This was Nain's mantra throughout Elin's wayward later teen years, always accompanied by a clap of the hands.

Although, there had been a death, hadn't there? But even if a fortnight had passed since Cai's funeral, for Elin, nothing had moved on. Because it was still difficult for her to get about, Cai's ashes had kindly been delivered by the funeral director, but the sight of the biodegradable green container inside the hessian bag that the man handed over and the substantial weight of it in her hands had reduced her to a sobbing wreck. The knowledge that this was all that remained of the man she loved, seven pounds of gritty grey dust, had almost destroyed her. Constantly seeing the pot was too painful and Elin had stored it away at the back of her old wardrobe. Though she knew she would have to deal with it eventually, maybe scatter the contents or arrange to have them interred somewhere, it felt far too soon. If she didn't have to look at it, she could almost pretend it wasn't there at all.

Elin was still on sick leave. The pain of loss, she'd found, was physical as well as emotional – even more so than when Mam disappeared. Her limbs ached and there was a constant knot in her chest and stomach. The idea of returning to work was inconceivable – sounding endlessly enthusiastic and putting on her best telephone voice to persuade people to buy into things. Managing clients' accounts and responding to inquiries.

Some days it was bad enough even when she was fully well. But right now, concentrating on anything other than trying to wade through the day was impossible.

Elin's foot had pretty much healed and spring was bringing longer days, the flowers coming into bloom. Birds were starting to build their nests. It was a season that would normally lift her mood, imbue her with a sense of eager anticipation. But no matter the weather, Elin could see nothing but grey. It was like being enveloped by a suffocating, toxic cloud, as though time had stood still the moment Cai had left the world. As though all the colour had been drained from everything.

Working from home in Birmingham meant Elin hadn't really forged any proper relationships with people there, and even within Cai's circle of friends, she had never felt fully at ease. They were nice enough, but all die-hard archaeology boffins, and she often felt out of her depth and ignorant trying to make conversation. One of them, Rajesh, had contacted her to give his condolences and to explain, rather awkwardly, that the decision had been made to postpone the dig at Traeth Coch until the following year, saying the volunteers Cai had rallied all had other projects they could become involved in. 'We talked it over and everyone agreed it wouldn't seem right, going ahead without Cai. It was – well, it was sort of his baby, wasn't it?'

And it was true: the whole thing had grown from Cai's vision and drive. But Elin didn't care about the dig any more. She didn't care about anything.

Thankfully, since Cai's mum had been from the island, his father had shown no objection to the funeral being held in Anglesey, and as promised, Catrin and Rhys had rallied round to help Elin organise everything. The whole thing had felt unreal to Elin, who'd drifted through the no-man's-land of the fortnight building up to the day of the service in a state of tearful confusion and emptiness.

Cai's dad had put in an appearance for the service, but hadn't stuck around. His new, much younger wife was in the second trimester of her pregnancy and he needed to be there for her, apparently. Elin had only met the man once before and found him distant and lacking in emotion. Cai must definitely have taken after his mum.

'Obviously I don't expect you to vacate immediately,' he had told Elin shortly before his departure. 'But the flat'll have to be sold. Of course, I'll give you plenty of time so you can move all your stuff out. I'm sure you'd much rather be up here with your own family anyway, wouldn't you?'

It had felt like a body blow, the realisation that she had no rights regarding the little home she and Cai had built together in Birmingham, even if she didn't intend to return there to live. Nerys was still unfit to be discharged from the hospital, Bethan was busy with the shop, and although Catrin did her best to come round whenever she could, she lived almost half an hour's drive away – and now had the additional stress of her in-laws moving in with her and Rhys for a few weeks, while they had an extension built in their retirement bungalow. Elin was utterly, completely alone.

*

Elin had barely set foot downstairs when there was a knock at the front door. She ignored it initially. She didn't want to see anyone right now. Apart from anything else, she was aware she looked a complete mess. She hadn't brushed her hair or cleaned her teeth for a couple of days, and had slept in the same pyjamas for over a week. But whoever it was clearly wasn't going away. Eventually a face appeared at the window, hands cupped around it to peer through the glass, and Elin saw the navy uniform.

She blew out a long breath and got up to answer the door.

A young woman with tied back, curly auburn hair showing from beneath her cap, held up a police badge with one hand. Her mouth curved tentatively upwards.

'Um, Elin Owen?'

Elin felt her pulse jumping in her throat. Her thoughts immediately went to Nerys. Surely not more bad news. She felt suddenly nauseous, her hand gripping the door jamb.

'Yes? What is it?'

'So sorry to bother you. I'm WPC Llinos Lloyd.'

The officer put away her ID and bent down to pick something up. Elin's eyes travelled to the brown, lidded cardboard container, about the size of a shoe box, at her feet.

The woman straightened, smiling apologetically. 'I've come to deliver this. I wonder – could I come in for a moment? I just need a signature.'

Elin's heart rate slowed gradually. So the girl wasn't the bearer of further ill tidings. She stepped back, allowing her to enter.

'I'm so sorry, but somehow these got overlooked. We should have returned them sooner.'

Llinos held out the container hesitantly. 'These are the rest of Mr Rowlands' effects. I'm afraid there was, um, a mix-up – they got separated from the other things.'

Elin stared at the box for a moment before accepting it. She'd thought that the clear refuse sack that Cai's jacket, jeans, shoes, underwear and sweater had been bundled into had been everything. The wallet she'd bought him the previous Christmas. She'd asked the fresh-faced policeman who handed it over if they had Cai's phone, but he'd responded saying they hadn't found one. Maybe it had been flung far away into the bushes, when the car . . .? She'd tried to shake the thought. What use was it now, anyway? Cai hadn't had it that long and there were no photos on there. All of their more recent pictures were on her own mobile – he'd downloaded everything from his old one before disposing of the handset.

The forensics people had taken samples from Cai's clothes. The only potentially useful thing they'd discovered, Elin had learned, was a microscopic paint transfer onto his jeans from the impact with the vehicle. But being black, it could have come from any number of cars – finding a match was extremely unlikely. A minute fragment of plastic, thought to have broken off the headlamp, had been sent for analysis but the absence of any unique markings made it impossible to identify the make and model conclusively. Although, they had been able to establish that the vehicle hadn't been a SUV or a truck but something smaller, with a shallower profile, from the fact the injuries he'd sustained had been to the lower extremities. Elin hadn't wanted to think about any of it. She just couldn't fathom how anyone could have driven away from the scene without a backward glance. It was callous beyond belief.

Cai's bag at the hostel had contained one change of clothes, a plastic bag with his dirty laundry, and a washbag, and that had all been sent on via a courier. Her mind had been so full at the time that she hadn't considered there might be anything else missing.

'Thank you,' she said slowly. 'Does this happen often? People's stuff getting misplaced, I mean?'

Llinos looked uncomfortable. 'Now and again, unfortunately. Sometimes people are in a hurry and don't inventory things properly. It's not very good, I know. But sooner or later the mistake's usually rectified.'

Elin nodded, smiling tightly. She wondered how many other people's loved ones had unclaimed items sitting on a shelf in a police station somewhere. Maybe even important things, things of immeasurable sentimental value.

Llinos turned to leave. 'Oh sorry, do you have any form of ID, please? Just for my records, you understand – I don't want to get my knuckles rapped.' She gave Elin a nervous grimace.

Elin placed the box on the side table. She cast about for her handbag, then flicked through her purse for her driving licence. She handed it over, one eye on the box, wondering what they'd forgotten to give her earlier.

Llinos looked at the licence, then up to Elin's face, before giving it back, tipping her head slightly as she studied Elin's unkempt appearance with evident concern.

'Thank you, that's all fine. Again, apologies for the delay. And can I say how sorry I am for your loss.'

Elin's throat tightened. 'Thank you,' she responded, her voice quavering.

She closed the door behind the young woman and paused for a moment, before crossing the room to lift the lid off the box. On the top was a leaflet offering support for bereaved relatives of road traffic accidents. She set it to one side, before sifting through an assortment of clear, sealed bags. A small one containing Cai's watch, which had belonged to his maternal grandfather, jumped out at her. How had she not missed that? It was far too big for her, but she took it out and slipped it onto her wrist anyway, stroking the scratched glass.

In another was a well-thumbed paperback about the history of Traeth Coch and the surrounding area. A squashed A5 notebook, a leaky Bic biro. She flicked through the little book, but there appeared to be nothing other than scribblings about artefacts, dates and such. He must have been using it to take notes about the exhibits from the course. A smaller bag contained the usual things she'd have expected to find in his pockets. Scrunched up, unused tissues. A bus ticket. A packet of chewing gum. A lottery scratchcard, which had clearly yielded nothing.

An old clay pipe – that was just the sort of thing Cai would have been excited by – he'd have found it on a walk somewhere, no doubt. He could never resist poking around in soil. But the other thing . . .

It was one of those Swiss Army Knives. She couldn't remember Cai owning one, unless they'd been given out at the course he'd been on for some reason. She frowned, turning the object in her hands. There was something engraved along the handle. A name – one she recognised.

But what was it doing among Cai's possessions?

Chapter 27

NOW – Friday 5th May 2023

Elin

Bethan called round that afternoon, saying she'd decided to take a half day.

'Well, it's my shop, isn't it? My prerogative to have a jolly once in a while if I feel like it.' But Elin could see from the slant of her eyes that Bethan was concerned about her. Bethan had mentioned that her mum had some sort of bug, and Elin felt rather guilty that she felt the need to run around after her, too. But she hadn't the energy to protest. She sat in the living room, staring into space as Bethan busied herself, folding clothes that Elin had left draped over the chairs and taking empty cups and glasses into the kitchen. She heard Bethan swear and remembered the overflowing bin that she'd had no motivation to empty. It was probably stinking out the room but Elin had grown accustomed to it. Everything felt like too much of an effort.

Bethan reappeared moments later with two steaming mugs and a plate of sandwiches, which she set down on the little side table next to Elin. Bethan picked up her own tea and stood awkwardly by the window, glancing through it and back to Elin.

'So how are you? Really?' Bethan's brow furrowed into a frown. 'I'm worried you're not looking after yourself. Are you even eating?'

'I'm not hungry.' Elin's voice caught in her throat. She thought about her predicament, about how pointless everything felt without Cai. About how it would have been a welcome release to fall asleep and never wake up again. 'My whole world has been blown apart.' Admitting her feelings aloud wasn't easy. She dipped her chin, avoiding eye contact. 'I still can't take it all in. It's like living in a permanent nightmare. And seeing Nerys like that every time I go . . .'

She let out a long breath, squeezing her eyes shut for a moment as she recalled the last soul-destroying visit to her sister. No response to the gentlest of questions, no reaction to Elin's attempts to remind her of joyful past experiences. It was like sitting with a shadow of Nerys, an empty shell. The awful ache in Elin's chest intensified. Instead of helping her work through it, talking about her situation was making her feel even worse.

She turned back to Bethan, desperate for something to distract her, then remembered the knife.

'Oh, a girl from the police called round yesterday. She brought Cai's jacket and a couple of other things. But I found this in the pocket.' Elin got up stiffly and went to the drawer in the sideboard where she'd put the Swiss Army Knife, handing it over to Bethan.

Bethan peered at the thing, flicking out the various implements from the handle.

'Neat bit of kit.' Screwing up her eyes to read the inscription, she lifted her face towards Elin, her lower lip pushed forward. 'Harry Edwards? What was Cai doing with this?'

Elin shrugged. 'I've no idea. I didn't think Cai even knew him.'

'Maybe he got talking to him once. He always was a friendly chap, your Cai.'

Bethan smiled sadly, handed the knife back. 'Ask Harry – I'm sure he'll be able to tell you. I'd ask him for you, but I'm trying to avoid him at the moment, to be honest.' She grimaced slightly.

'Oh? Why?' Elin studied her with mild interest.

'Well, he asked me out a couple of weeks ago. Came into the shop and said he'd been wanting to ask me for a while. Right out of the blue. I felt really awkward. He's a nice enough guy and everything, but not a lot going on up there, if you know what I mean.' She tapped her head with her fingers. 'So I made an excuse. Stupid really, but I actually hid in a doorway, last time I spotted him in town. Still feel sort of – well, uncomfortable about it.'

Elin raised an eyebrow. 'Oh dear.' She couldn't imagine Bethan feeling awkward around anyone. 'I'll ask him myself when I see him, then. I don't feel much like going out at the moment, though.'

'He had a thing for your mam once too, you know.'

Elin widened her eyes. 'Did he?'

'Yep. Mein said he pestered her for a while, but she really wasn't interested. Kept sending her flowers. She had to be quite blunt with him in the end, as he just wasn't getting the message. Like I said, he's rather slow on the uptake, bless him.' Bethan screwed up her nose. 'He got over it soon enough, but I think he was gutted at the time.'

Elin was surprised. She had no memory of Mam mentioning Harry Edwards. Maybe it had happened when she was small.

'Hey – changing the subject, guess who I saw in town the other day?' Bethan's eyebrows twitched. 'That bloody Tom Buckley.'

Elin's breath caught in her throat at the mention of her ex.

It had been so long since she'd even thought of Buckley – she'd done her best to block him from her memory after the way he'd behaved towards her. She could still picture the hateful way he had stared at her that last time she'd seen him, hear the bitterness in his voice.

She swallowed. 'Where was he?'

'Going into the Liverpool Arms at about midday with a couple of other lads, all in their work scruffs – I spotted him when I nipped out for a sandwich. Funny, I thought he worked in Holyhead – maybe he's got another job now. He turned round and gave me a filthy look. Haven't laid eyes on him in years – not since before you moved away. I remember the hassle you had with him – like he had a frigging vendetta against you, wasn't it? Horrible little shit.'

Elin shuddered. 'Tell me about it. He made my life hell for a while. I was so glad when he left.'

'I think a lot of people were. He managed to upset half the community when he lived in Traeth Coch. One of those who could start an argument in an empty room.' Bethan narrowed her eyes.

Elin had seen Buckley only once after she'd moved away, about three years earlier, when she'd been home to visit Nain. He was passing through, just coming out of The Quay, and he'd stopped to stare at her for a moment, then made some loud comment to his mate about her being up herself and not belonging there any more. And then a more direct remark aimed straight at Elin herself.

'His mam still lives locally – her health's not great,' Bethan went on. 'Don't think she goes out much these days. Nice enough woman. You'd wonder how she could've produced such a nasty piece of work.'

Elin remembered Mrs Buckley. The woman had always been pleasant towards her, even after she and Tom split up. It couldn't have been nice for her, knowing her son had such a vicious streak. How did the saying go? You can choose your friends, but you can't choose your family. Elin was certain no one, given the choice, would want someone like Tom Buckley as a son.

She paused. The sudden creak of next door's gate reminded her of something else. 'Oh – a while back, you were going to tell me something about Libby. What was it?'

Bethan's eyes flickered, her attention somewhere in the middle distance suddenly. She looked as if, on reflection, she'd spoken out of turn, and was hoping Elin had forgotten what she'd said.

'It was nothing, really. I shouldn't have mentioned it.'

Elin sat up a little straighter. 'Well, there must've been *something*. Just tell me.'

Bethan exhaled through her nose, as though bracing for a revelation.

'*Ugh*. Look, I was probably overreacting, you know me. And it's not that I think she's *bad*. Libby's . . . well, she's one of *those* people. A bit drippy. Kind on the surface. Always volunteering, always offering help before anyone's even asked. But sometimes . . .' she hesitated. 'Sometimes I get the impression she crosses lines she doesn't seem to realise are there.'

Elin rubbed at her face. Bethan *could* be quite melodramatic at times. 'What d'you mean – what sort of lines?'

Bethan sat down, smoothing her skirt nervously. 'A couple of weeks before Nerys's breakdown, I popped round to drop off some copies of old photos she'd asked for – pictures of your mam and me when we were at school. But Libby answered the door. Said Nerys was "resting" and it wasn't a good idea to disturb her.'

Elin frowned. 'And she wouldn't let you in?'

Bethan shook her head. 'She obviously didn't intend to. But

I wasn't about to be fobbed off. I sort of eased my way through the door. But then I realised Libby was already inside the house. Not just in the hallway, not dropping something off. I mean *properly* in the house. Cleaning out the larder cupboard, like she bloody lived here. She had Nerys's mail stacked on the counter – opened. All of it.'

Elin stiffened. 'Opened? Maybe she was just, I don't know, helping?' Even as she said the word, Elin realised it sounded lame.

The muscles in Bethan's cheeks twitched. 'That's what she said. *Helping*. But she'd taken it upon herself to sort through Nerys's bills, tidy out the drawers. Like she was being paid to run her frigging life for her.'

Elin widened her eyes. 'She never mentioned any of that.'

Bethan leaned forward. 'No, I bet she didn't. I think Libby's one of those people who does things with a sweet smile, and then you'd feel ungrateful if you questioned it. But there was something sort of off about her reaction. When she realised I wasn't comfortable, she got, well . . . prickly. Not angry, exactly. Just laying it on. Saying how much Nerys was struggling and no one else seemed to be stepping up. As if she was having a dig at me for not doing my bit.'

Elin's jaw tightened. 'So you think she's been . . . what? Worming her way in so that she could poke around in Nerys's affairs?'

Bethan nodded uneasily. 'I get the impression Libby likes being needed. Too much for my liking. And when someone's vulnerable, like Nerys was . . . It's a good opportunity to wade right in.'

There was an uncomfortable beat of silence as Elin digested this. She'd always thought of Libby as being well-meaning, benign. The idea that she had been interfering rather than helping rankled with her.

'Like I said, I might've got the wrong end of the stick. But it just put my back up,' Bethan resumed eventually. 'Because the way she was talking that day . . .' She lowered her voice, as if worried someone might be listening in to their conversation. 'It felt to me like she thought she was the only one who had the right to be here. You know, to be looking after Nerys and taking charge of everything.'

A burst of indignation surged through Elin, the implications turning in her mind. Why would Libby want to control what was happening in Nerys's life? She'd always thought of the woman as being quite meek and a little inept, if anything. It didn't seem to ring true.

A sudden clatter sounded from somewhere beyond the kitchen, startling them both.

'*Mam bach*. What the hell was that?' Bethan leapt up and hurried through to investigate.

Elin continued to sit, musing on what Bethan had been saying. Maybe she was being overly suspicious, but the idea that Libby *had* been trying to take over made her uncomfortable. Poor Nerys wouldn't be able to shed any light on anything at the moment. Elin would need to speak to Libby, but not now. Not yet. She had too much else going round her head.

'It was just Peter.' Bethan rolled her eyes as she returned. 'Filling up his bloody garden-waste bin. He'd knocked their bird-table over somehow.'

'Oh.' Elin sat back in her seat, staring into space. Peter loved his garden ornaments. She remembered looking out of Mam's bedroom window once to see him angrily chasing Llwyd across his lawn when the cat had rubbed past one of his small resin gnomes and knocked it over. Llwyd had scrambled frantically over the fence, his fur on end, tail fluffed out like a huge bottle brush. It had seemed like an overreaction to her – the gnome wasn't broken, after all. Mam had laughed; said Llwyd had just used up one of his nine lives. Peter obviously wasn't a cat person, she'd remarked. Libby had told Nain so once, too. Maybe he felt protective of the birds – or maybe just didn't like them peeing in his immaculate herbaceous borders.

Lots of people were funny about cats.

Chapter 28

BEFORE – March 2023

Nerys

Nyten's arrival at the cottage had given Nerys a new sense of purpose. And to be fair, in addition to the usual dust, there was now a fine layer of cat hair settling on the various surfaces that couldn't be ignored. She thought of what Nain would have said, how she'd have told her to pull her socks up. Her grandmother couldn't bear fluff and spent hours cleaning up after Llwyd, shooing him off her chair and attacking the seat with a lint roller.

'*Nefi blw*! How can one animal leave so much bloody fur everywhere?'

The memory brought a smile to Nerys's face. Everything needed a good clean, so Nerys decided to dust and push the vacuum round. Nyten clearly wasn't a fan of the noise, and shot upstairs to hide under the wardrobe.

Nerys wiped the kitchen surfaces, mopped the floor, then looked out into the garden and groaned. The grass was overgrown, riddled with dandelions and thick with clover, but even if she couldn't face tackling the borders yet, giving it a good haircut would make it look more presentable. It was a fine day – if she left it, there was the danger they'd have rain again and she'd have to put it off even longer. Besides, Peter had cut it for them in the past, and she wanted to do it before he felt the need to offer. She didn't like accepting help unless it was absolutely necessary; she was quite capable of mowing the grass herself.

The door to Taid's old shed was warped and a nightmare to open, but she needed to get the lawnmower out. After wrestling with the rusty padlock which Nain had insisted on using, she eventually managed to manoeuvre the door open by lifting and lowering the thing a couple of inches at a time. If she'd dragged it along the ground, she was worried the rotting wood might disintegrate and there would be no door at all. It was exhausting – how Nain could've thought anyone had been pinching things from there was ridiculous. No burglar in their right mind would have gone to such lengths for a few tatty old tools. She plugged in the mower through the kitchen window and ploughed up and down for a few minutes, then stood back. Not perfect, but a bloody sight better than it had been. She replaced the machine, then began the arduous task of closing the door again. It hardly seemed worth the effort, as the mower was probably the only thing in there worth nicking. But Nain had been emphatic – it was Taid's shed and she'd been determined to protect its contents, so Nerys steeled herself and, with supreme effort, heaved it shut once more.

After pegging out the washing, Nerys sat down to an early lunch and then allowed herself a few minutes to sit and admire her polished surfaces. Pleased with her progress, she went upstairs to clean the bathroom. Opening the window to shake out the bath mat, she caught a strong whiff of smoke. She pushed the window wide to see flames flickering inside next door's garden incinerator bin, Peter feeding the thing with branches and cuttings he had been trimming from their shrubs. Thick, acrid fumes billowed out, carried on the wind right in the direction of her clean washing. Nerys was incensed.

Dropping the bath mat, she ran downstairs, grabbed her laundry basket and flung open the back door, the smoke immediately catching the back of her throat.

'Peter, my washing is going to stink,' she shouted angrily. It was too late. Looking up, she saw her clean laundry swaying on the line, white sheets and pillowcases being slowly peppered with soot. The air had a metallic, chemical bite. There was something else being burned: something that had no place in a garden fire. Household rubbish.

Nerys began yanking the almost dry bedding and towels from the washing line and stuffing them into the basket. Realising it would all have to be rewashed, she dropped everything and marched to the fence, heart banging with the sudden, helpless fury of it. 'For God's sake. You could've let me know so I could take my washing down first.'

On the other side, flames licked lazily from the metal barrel. Peter stood with his hands behind his back, like a site official overseeing a civic improvement. He was wearing wellingtons, his straight, white hair poking from beneath a beige bucket hat. Turning to look at Nerys, he flashed her the faint, vacant smile of someone lost in thought.

'Afternoon, Nerys,' he said pleasantly. Her eyes travelled to a pile of rags, old plimsoles and several plastic containers at his feet. Peter tried to push it aside with one boot, as if disassociating himself from it.

'Hey, that's not garden waste,' she said, pointing. 'You can't burn that. Look at all the smoke – what the hell are you playing at?

He peered upwards, squinting, as if noticing the grey haze surrounding him for the first time. 'Oh dear. Is it bothering you?'

She could taste bitter flecks of ash in the air. 'It reeks,' she said. 'And apart from being completely inconsiderate burning stuff during the day, getting rid of your unwanted things like that's illegal.'

Peter tutted and shuffled closer to the fence. 'Is it? Oh, I hadn't realised.' He glanced at the lawn where Nerys's laundry had spilled from the upturned basket, at the dark speckles sprinkled across her sheets. 'Oh dear. It *has* ruined your washing, hasn't it? Sorry about that. Terrible shame.'

Had she detected a hint of glee? His tone implied no real contrition. Nerys waited for him to reach for the hose, or the metal lid of the incinerator. He did neither. Instead, he picked up a long, thin branch and began to prod at the burning rubbish, sending up a fresh belch of smoke that wafted over the fence and straight into Nerys's face, making her cough.

Furious at his apparent lack of concern, she jabbed a finger towards the fire. 'Put it out, please,' she hissed. '*Now.*'

Peter raised his palms, as if admitting defeat. 'Of course, of course. No need to get upset.' His eyes slid past her, taking in her garden with evident disapproval: the overgrown borders, the weeds creeping through the paving. 'I'll let it die down.'

She stared at him, then at the flames that showed no sign of dying down at all. 'If you don't put it out right away, I'll report you,' she said, surprising herself with how assertive her voice sounded.

Something flickered, briefly, in his expression. Then the smile returned, conciliatory now. 'There's no need for that,' he said. 'I wasn't thinking, that's all. I didn't do it on purpose. I don't want to fall out with anyone.'

Nerys turned away before he could say anything else, scooped up the washing and stomped back towards the house. Behind her, the fire continued to crackle, a trail of smoke seeming to follow her.

The smell clung stubbornly to the bed linen, but after a third rinse, it seemed finally dispelled. It was too late in the day now though, the air outside damp with sea mist, so she draped everything over the clothes horse instead.

When she went back outside to the dustbin later, the metal incinerator drum was gone. So was the smoke. Peter's garden looked immaculate, swept clean, as if nothing had happened.

But just as Nerys was about to close the door, through their open kitchen window, she overheard him speaking to Libby, his voice carrying across the fence on the soft breeze. He was laughing, the tone low and smug; saying something about some neighbours letting the side down, and about how certain people needed reminding that they didn't own the air.

Nerys went back inside, her jaw clenched. She had no doubt that the fire had sparked something else, and – not that she'd have wanted it – that Peter might not be inclined to offer her any help in future.

*

Arriving home from work the following day, Nerys bristled at the sight of Peter's distinctive white hair at her front door as she pulled up at the end of the track. The memory of the incident with the incinerator had dominated her thoughts the night before and clouded her day. She'd mentioned it to Bethan, who had rolled her eyes.

'Silly old sod,' she'd said. 'But then, he's from that generation, isn't he? I expect his wife does all the washing in their house. He probably had no idea what a nuisance he was being. I wouldn't let it get to you.'

But Nerys *was* letting it get to her. It wasn't nice to think someone living next door could be so unreasonable, especially now she was there on her own. She waited in the car for a moment, hoping that he would go away. But he turned and, seeing her, lifted a hand to wave, smiling a little uncertainly. Nerys drew in a breath as she got out and walked towards the cottage, wondering what he wanted.

Peter scratched the back of his head awkwardly with one hand. In the other, he was holding a blue-and-white gift bag.

'Hello, Nerys. I just wanted to apologise. About yesterday. It was thoughtless of me and I felt bad afterwards. I hope you won't hold it against me. I should've thought, you know, about your washing. Libby gave me a proper telling off when I told her.' He studied her face, his brow knitting earnestly. 'Anyway, I hope you'll accept this and let bygones be bygones. I don't want to fall out with anyone – you and your family have always been such good neighbours.'

He handed over the bag, which Nerys accepted hesitantly. She peered inside to find a large box of chocolates.

'Oh. Thank you.' She looked back at his pleading face, his awkward body language, and in spite of herself, felt a little sorry for him. After all, he'd never stepped out of line before, and they'd always got on in the past.

'It's okay. But please don't go lighting any more fires when I've got my washing out, will you?'

Peter's expression brightened. 'Absolutely not. And thank you. For being so understanding.'

Nerys nodded, watching as he made his way down the path and back into his own house. She felt a little better. At least he'd acknowledged he was in the wrong.

Chapter 29

NOW – Saturday 6th May 2023

Elin

Elin had a fitful night. On top of everything else, she was now worrying about the Swiss Army Knife. A jumble of thoughts turned through her head constantly: was there some sinister significance to it being found among Cai's belongings? More and more, she had begun to dwell on what had actually happened to Cai that night. She kept coming back to what Rhys had said about the sabotaged boats. It had only happened twice in a decade – and on both of those occasions, someone had died. The suggestion that there could be a connection was genuinely disturbing.

It had just turned 3 a.m. and Elin felt exhausted and jittery. Eventually, she got up to make herself a cup of chamomile tea, hoping it might help her sleep. Maybe she could listen to a light-hearted podcast for a while, try to fill her head with something to drown out her thoughts.

As she began to descend the stairs, Elin thought she heard a soft click from below. She stopped in her tracks, her pulse quickening as she peered cautiously over the banister. Through the archway, she could see the glow of the kitchen light. She had switched it off before going to bed, she was certain.

Elin froze. Was there somebody down there? Should she go back upstairs, ring the police? She strained to listen for a moment, but there was no evidence of any further sound other than her own blood pounding in her ears. She tiptoed back up to her room, retrieved her mobile from the bedside table and curled her hand around it tightly, her fingers ready to press for the emergency services. Slightly reassured by having the means to contact someone, Elin tentatively returned to the landing, all her senses on alert once more.

Nothing. Slowly, hesitantly, she made her way down the stairs and walked towards the kitchen, looking constantly from left to right, then back over her shoulder. Everything *seemed* normal; nothing appeared to have been disturbed. Both the kitchen and the living room were empty.

She went straight to the back door and tried the handle. It was locked. Secure. But the room felt cool, as though a recent draught had passed through. Elin cast about anxiously, then realised that the pantry door was ajar. She obviously hadn't closed it properly.

Elin closed the walk-in cupboard and turned her back to it, expelling the air from her lungs. Her eyes scanned the kitchen surfaces once more, her heart rate gradually slowing. There was no one here. The key sat on the worktop next to the back door, where she always left it. Everything looked as she expected it to. Maybe she *had* left the light on – after all, she'd been going around in a daze for weeks now. She boiled the kettle, made herself the herbal tea and climbed the stairs back to bed. With one ear still listening out for anything unusual and an earbud pushed into the other, she lay down and pressed play on Daisy May Cooper's entertaining podcast on her phone. Soon she had drifted off from sheer exhaustion.

*

By the following morning, in broad daylight, the idea that someone could have been moving around downstairs seemed even more improbable. It was most likely to do with her own state of mind, already feeling jumpy and now anxious about Harry Edwards's knife to boot. She was letting her imagination run away with her.

Elin took the knife from the bedside drawer and turned it over in her hands, examining every millimetre of the thing as if it might suddenly reveal some momentous clue. It was odd, the knowledge that Cai must have held it in his hands. She thought about what Bethan had said – that Harry Edwards had been slightly fixated on her mam. She wasn't sure whether to feel unsettled or amused by this news. But she really needed to speak to the man to find out what Cai was doing with his knife.

It suddenly occurred to Elin that Derfel would probably have Harry's phone number. She decided to call Catrin, see if she could ask him for her.

'El? Everything okay?' Her friend sounded breathless as she picked up, as though in the middle of something.

'Oh, you know.' Elin paused. 'You busy?'

'Just changing the beds. Hold on.' There was the muffled thump of footsteps, the sound of a door closing. 'That's better. Can't talk for long, I'm going for lunch with Rhys's mam while his dad helps him out with some machinery on the farm.'

'Catrin, d'you know if your dad has a contact number for Harry Edwards at all?'

Catrin paused. 'Harry? Erm, he might've done a while back,

but I think . . . well, I'm pretty sure he deleted his number. They sort of fell out.'

'Fell out? Why?'

Elin heard her let out a breath. 'It was a few months ago. They were on a night out. Dad had one too many, as he does. Picked a fight with some bloke in a bar in Bangor. Harry tried to break it up and got caught in the crossfire – a broken nose and two black eyes for his trouble. Said he couldn't hack Dad's behaviour any more and he pretty much severed ties after that.'

'Oh God. Not good, then.'

'No, not good at all. They'd been mates for years. I think Dad tried to make it up with him once he'd sobered up, but Harry'd obviously had enough. I don't really blame him, to be honest.' A crackling sound came down the line. 'What did you want with him, anyway? Are you after an electrician?'

'No, nothing like that. It's just that the police brought back some more of Cai's stuff yesterday and Harry's Swiss Army Knife must have been in one of his pockets. I just wondered why he had it and if Harry could shed any light.'

'Really? That's funny. Maybe Cai borrowed it or something? You know, if he was looking for bits and bobs, like he used to. Scraping mud off coins, or whatever.'

'Maybe. Probably nothing. I'm just curious about it, that's all.'

'Yeah, probably nothing.' The distant sound of a female voice calling Catrin's name came from somewhere in the background. 'Sorry, doll, gotta go. I'm being summoned. See you soon. Ta-ra.'

'Ta-ra. Have fun.'

Elin hung up. She'd have to wait, then. But a phone call wasn't what she really wanted, anyway. It would be better to speak to Harry face to face, ideally. She tried to put the thought out of her mind for the time being.

*

It was worse when Elin was all alone for a day or so, overthinking constantly and with nothing to distract her. Bethan's mam's virus hadn't improved much since the previous Monday, so she'd been rushed off her feet juggling visiting the old lady and running the shop. Catrin, who had been a real brick and checked in with her regularly, despite having to keep Rhys and his coworkers on the farm fed and watered, had been busy entertaining her in-laws for the past few days.

Sunday had been a particularly bad day. Cai had been there, at her bedside, speaking softly into her ear, telling her to wake up. Elin had opened her eyes, a half-smile on her face, expecting to find a coffee beside the bed and Cai looking down at her, tapping his watch playfully as he feigned disapproval at the lateness of the hour, telling her she was wasting the day.

But Elin was all alone, the bedroom empty. The house silent. That image of Cai, as real as it had seemed, had all been in her mind. And as the vicious, unbearable memory of what had happened hit her with fresh, searing anger and pain, she pulled the covers over her head, curled into a ball and screamed.

*

Catrin

Catrin felt helpless. It was wearing her down, trying to constantly juggle coming over to Elin's nain's place and returning to the farm to help her husband and entertain her in-laws. She'd tried to persuade Elin to come and stay with her and Rhys – they had plenty of room even with his parents there – but Elin refused to even leave the house. Trying to get the girl to eat anything was almost impossible. She remembered Elin telling her about how Nerys had been in the aftermath of Meinir's disappearance. Elin had coped better then – but this felt like a carbon copy of how loss had affected her sister. Worse, even.

She'd been over briefly on the Monday, but Tuesday was Rhys's regular night out with the lads, and his mam and dad were catching up with some old friends, so Catrin had stayed longer than usual. This evening had been particularly bad. Elin's grief was coming in waves. It was clearly omnipresent, although some days it had begun to seem more subdued, rolling quietly and with some degree of control. On this occasion, it had reached another roaring, angry crescendo. Catrin had ordered a veggie pizza in the hope of tempting Elin with something she knew she enjoyed, but it remained untouched in the open box on the kitchen table.

'I wish—I wish I wasn't here any more,' Elin had blurted out suddenly, raising her face to look at Catrin. 'I want him back so much it hurts. Right here.' She'd thumped at her chest with a fist. 'It's like a part of me died with him. I just can't believe I'll never see him again. I feel like I've got nothing left worth living for.'

After staring unseeingly at the pizza for over half an hour, Elin had stumbled from the kitchen and was now curled up on the settee, her knees drawn up. She sat clutching one of Cai's old jumpers to her, clinging to it as though to relinquish it would rip his memory from her forever.

The room was half-lit by a strange, ethereal light seeping through the window, the sun melting into a pool of amber over the sea beyond as dusk approached. Elin's eyes were red and raw, from sheer exhaustion as much as tears. She pressed her face into the sweater and a series of painful sobs escaped her lips.

Catrin stood quietly in the doorway, unsure whether to speak. She felt useless; nothing she said or did made poor Elin feel any better. She was worried that Elin was slowly sinking into a pit of despair she'd eventually be incapable of clawing her way out of. She'd already tentatively suggested medication, but that hadn't gone down well at all. It was like treading on eggshells.

Catrin took a few steps forward and leaned over her friend, stroking Elin's hair away from her face. 'You've been stuck in here for bloody ages,' she said gently. 'Even if you can't face food, you really should drink something. I've brought some flavoured water, if you don't want tea.'

Elin shook her head, burying her face in the fabric. She drew in a deep breath and sobbed again.

'It still smells of him. I keep thinking if I hold on long enough, he might just . . . I don't know, come back. That I'll suddenly wake up and it'll all have been a horrible, sick dream.'

Catrin stooped and knelt beside her. 'I know. I know it feels impossible right now. But you're not betraying him by allowing yourself to carry on. To start living properly again. Cai wouldn't have wanted this for you. If he could see you now, he'd be so worried.'

Elin finally lifted her head, her hollow eyes searching Catrin's face. 'I don't ever want to forget him.'

Her voice was small, like that of a frightened child, bringing a lump to Catrin's throat.

'Oh El, you never will.' She hesitated, then drew in a breath. 'Listen. There's something I want to suggest.' There was a weighty pause as Catrin considered the prudence of what she was about to say. 'Rhys's cousin Aaron's a kind of tech wiz. He's working for this new company in Liverpool and . . . Have you heard of *grief holograms*?'

Elin frowned. 'I read something about them once – remind me how they work.'

Catrin screwed up her nose. 'They're AI-generated things – life-size holograms you can interact with, built from actual recordings of people who have died – voice notes, videos, messages and that. But they're designed to help people cope with grief, not to make them pretend someone's still alive.' She spoke softly, tilting her face to look at Elin. 'They don't talk unless you want them to. They just . . . let you say stuff you never got to say. Or hear things they already shared with you, in moments you need it most.'

Elin's hands tightened around the sweater. 'I don't know if that would help or not. It's a weird thought.'

Catrin shook her head. 'That's okay. I just thought I'd mention it as an option. It's usually really expensive, but Aaron could easily get it for you for next to nothing. Mull it over. You don't have to decide now. I just don't want you to feel like you're alone in all this.' She sighed. 'It doesn't mean you love someone any less because you start to move on with your own life, you know. There are ways to cope with loss without it consuming you.'

A silence settled as Elin considered this. Catrin rose to sit on the settee and wrapped an arm around her.

Elin leaned her head against Catrin's shoulder, trembling. 'I just miss him, Cat. So, so much.'

'I know. And you're allowed to, of course you are. It's only natural. You just need to take things one day at a time. I know it doesn't feel like it right now, but the pain will lessen, I promise.'

*

Elin

Elin stared at the wall, suddenly picturing Cai standing in front of her once more: talking, smiling. His eyes dancing with life. Would it be such a bad thing, giving this grief-hologram idea a try? The room remained quiet, the only noise from within the slow, rhythmic ticking of the clock. Beyond the window, the wind murmured around the walls, the soft susurration of the sea in the distance. Repetitive, familiar sounds that had lately begun to feel almost claustrophobic. But for the first time in weeks, Elin felt a glimmer of something. Not of hope, exactly – but the vague notion that there might actually be something worth getting out of bed for now.

*

Elin thought long and hard about what Catrin had said. She remembered reading an article about these 'ghost-bots' or whatever they were, before Nain died. She'd wondered fleetingly what it would've been like to have a hologram of Mam, then dismissed the idea as being in bad taste. She suspected Nain would have been horrified by it all, too. And although the memory of Mam's loss still saddened her, Elin had had years to come to terms with her grief and it was no longer so raw. Best to let sleeping dogs lie, as they say.

But she'd mentioned the bereavement avatar idea to Cai anyway, interested to hear his views. He had grimaced dubiously. '*Best left well alone, if you ask me,*' he had said. In his opinion, a thing like that could prolong someone's grief rather than alleviate it; prevent them from moving on.

Although, Elin couldn't move on, could she? It was as if she'd been crawling through wet cement for weeks, unable to function: watching the world go by but no longer a part of it. Existing rather than living. She craved the oblivion of sleep, praying to see Cai in her dreams, only to wake over and over to her horrible reality and feel the pain of his loss anew. Maybe, in spite of what Cai had thought, she had nothing to lose by giving it a go.

Elin wanted to understand the concept better. Opening her laptop, she googled: '*How does a grief avatar work?*'

There was a lot of information, much of it over Elin's head. The general gist was that artificial intelligence is used to analyse a dead person's digital presence: like Catrin had said, using their photos, audio and video recordings, text messages and so on, in order to gain an accurate understanding of their personality, mannerisms and how they would have spoken. The AI is then trained to replicate this. It even uses voice-cloning technology, taking old conversations to generate new ones. From different clips of video footage and photographs, an interactive, full-sized 3D image is created and played via a 'hologram box', often small enough to sit on a desktop.

It all sounded mind-boggling, this idea of AI creating what amounted to a digital, interactive ghost. Elin wanted to weigh up the pros and cons. She typed '*grief tech first-hand experiences*' into the search bar next, then began to trawl through the seemingly endless amount of information, listening to people describing their own personal anecdotes.

'*I feel so much less alone now*,' enthused one woman.

'*I chat to my partner for a while most days now. It helps me to feel we're still connected*,' declared another.

'*It's amazing how much it's helped me to cope with my grief*,' a young, vibrant-looking woman with shining eyes spoke out from the screen. '*I hit rock bottom. But I can get on with the business of living my life now. It's like I don't have to let go until I feel ready to. And if that's never, then it's fine*.'

The final video clip had helped sway her decision, especially after reading a thought-provoking comment from one bereavement counsellor: '*At the end of the day, the question is whether someone draws comfort from interacting with a digital version of their lost loved one. What right has anyone else to dictate how someone navigates their way through grief?*'

Snapping the laptop lid shut, Elin paused for a moment, before picking up her phone with a new sense of purpose. She clicked on Catrin's WhatsApp profile, then tapped in a message.

Have decided the grief-bot thing might be worth a try. Please ask Aaron if he can create one for me xx

Chapter 30

BEFORE – March 2023

Nerys

It was a Wednesday, Nerys's day off. She had made it a regular routine now, using the time to clean the house and trying to keep on top of things. But today she wanted to begin sorting through some of Nain's stuff – a job she'd been putting off far too long. The cat rescue was having a car boot sale to raise funds. Somehow it didn't feel as bad parting with things if they were going to help the sanctuary – she was sure Nain would have approved. Nerys had checked on Nyten several times, but the cat was clearly quite happy sleeping peacefully in the garden. Content that she wasn't going to wander, Nerys continued with her tasks for the best part of the afternoon.

Nerys finished washing up after a well-earned cup of tea and a slice of carrot cake, and went to call Nyten indoors. She pushed open the back door with one elbow, still drying her hands on a tea towel, and stepped out onto the paving slabs beyond the back door. The late afternoon air was cooling, carrying with it the faint smell of petrichor mingled with the usual seaweed and salt, implying rain was on its way. She scanned the garden automatically, ignoring the weeds, but taking in the lavender, the fiery orange abundance of Nain's crocosmia that had spread the full length of the border, before her eyes caught on the small, familiar brown-and-white shape near the far corner.

'*Nyten*, *ty'd yma*.'

Nerys called the cat, but she failed to stir.

Nerys's voice wavered as a chill spread through her. 'Nyten?'

The cat lay on her side, legs tucked in awkwardly, her tail motionless. For a moment Nerys could only stare, the world narrowing to a deafening ringing in her ears. She dropped the tea towel and raced across the grass, kneeling so fast her knees thudded into the ground.

Nyten blinked up at her, pupils dilated. When Nerys reached out, the cat flinched.

'Oh, Nyten *bach* . . .' Nerys's voice fractured in her throat. She slid her hands beneath Nyten as gently as she could, but the cat gave a small, sharp yowl. Nerys had never heard Nyten make that sound before.

Something was wrong. Terribly wrong.

With trembling fingertips, Nerys examined her. There were no cuts, no blood; no evidence of flying fur to indicate a fight with another cat. But the way she resisted Nerys's touch confirmed a definite, unnatural tenderness along her side. Nerys looked more closely, noticing a small amount of soil and grit trapped in Nyten's fur. Though she had no idea what had happened, the little cat's laboured breathing and inability to stand told Nerys that this was an emergency.

Her whole body shook with fear as she gathered Nyten carefully to her chest, feeling the cat's shallow, frightened breaths against her own. 'We're going to get you to the vet's,' she whispered, though her voice barely held together. 'I've got you, *pwtyn*. I've got you.'

*

The road down to Traeth Coch twisted like a slalom, narrow and steep, the hedges tall on either side above the old stone walls. Nerys drove from habit, her hands light on the wheel of the Aygo, though her heart felt anything but light. Her thoughts were a million miles away. The sea was hidden from view until the last bend, but her window was open a little and she could smell the salt air, mingling with a waft of woodsmoke from somewhere below.

Nyten should have been in her carrier on the passenger seat, miaowing in her thin, pitiful voice. Instead, there was only the hollow, intermittent rattle of the seatbelt buckle and the vet's words on repeat in her head: '*Suspected ruptured spleen. Is it possible someone could have kicked her?*' The grave tone. The way they'd taken Nyten from her arms too quickly and whisked her away, the frightening speed, confirming this was a critical situation. Tears pricked Nerys's eyes as she thought of her sweet little cat. Nyten was in good hands, she knew – but surgery, if it was needed, could be risky.

The vet's suggestion that someone could have inflicted this on her was unthinkable. Nyten had never strayed from the garden, never got into fights. Nerys pictured the little cat's favourite spot, the suntrap in the corner behind the cottage where she could always be found. Her stomach rolled as she thought again of Nyten's limp body in her arms as she'd lowered her gently into the carrier, praying that the next time she held her wouldn't be the last.

Nerys's mobile started ringing from the back seat.

The sound startled her. It was inordinately loud in the small car, too sudden. *But it might be news about Nyten . . .* She flicked a glance in the mirror, then twisted in her seat, reaching back with one hand, her eyes leaving the road for just a second.

That was all it took. The Aygo drifted over the unmarked centre of the road. Headlights flashed in her peripheral vision. A horn blasted, loud and furious, and Nerys's eyes snapped forward just in time to see a white van hurtling towards her, its brakes squealing. The van swerved uphill, tyres skidding, and scraped along the low wall with a grinding shriek that echoed through her whole head.

Nerys wrenched the wheel back, slamming on her brakes. Her heart was hammering so hard she thought she might black out. She pulled into the turning for the caravan park, trembling hands still gripping the steering wheel, and sat there for a moment, breathing in rapid, shallow gulps. The phone had stopped ringing.

Eventually, she got out of the car, legs unsteady, and leaned against the bonnet. The van jerked to a stop behind her. The driver's door flew open and Nerys's stomach turned over as Hugh Roberts climbed out.

Of course, it would have to be him. Broad and red-faced, his white, blood-smeared apron still on beneath his jacket, as if it were an integral part of him. Nerys hadn't seen him up close in a long while, but he hadn't altered much. He had less hair, but still the same bloated cheeks; the neck like that of a prize bull. She remembered all too well the way Mam's face had hardened whenever his name was mentioned; the way Nain had refused ever to set foot in his shop again.

'I'm so sorry,' Nerys said, fighting back tears. 'I didn't see you. I mean, I did, but my phone . . .'

Roberts didn't let her finish. He jabbed a finger towards the side of the van, where a long grey scrape cut through the white paintwork, bare metal exposed beneath it.

'You stupid little – look at that,' he growled. 'Look what you've done.'

'I'm so sorry,' Nerys said again. She had begun to shiver, despite the mild temperature. 'It was my fault. I wasn't paying attention.' *Oh God*. She shouldn't have mentioned the phone. What was she *thinking*?

'*You weren't paying attention*?' His voice rose, the tendons in his neck bulging. 'You shouldn't be on the fucking road. That's my livelihood you nearly wrote off. I can't drive around like that.' He waved a hand towards the van. 'And I can't afford to take time off while the thing is in the garage, can I? There aren't enough hours in the bloody day as it is. You think the carcases butcher themselves?'

She shook her head, mute now, shame and fear overwhelming her. The wall behind him now bore a ragged-edged cavity where a sizeable chunk of stone had been torn away. Nerys replayed the sound of the impact again, over and over, and felt sick.

'I'll pay for the damage,' she said eventually. 'Of course I will. Just, please . . .'

Roberts stepped closer, much closer than felt comfortable. She could smell raw meat on him, making her recoil. His eyes were dark with anger. With venom.

'You will indeed,' he snarled. 'And it won't be cheap.'

Nerys's heart sank at the thought of how costly the repair might be. She had a horrible feeling that with everything going on lately, her insurance had lapsed. She needed to check it right away.

For a moment she thought he might say more, might lash out at her, even; do something worse than shout. Nain's cottage felt suddenly very far away, the road uncomfortably deserted. Nerys found herself backing away, gradually edging towards her own open car door.

Roberts regarded her with obvious contempt, his nostrils flaring, hands balled into fists at his sides. 'I know where you live. I'll be in touch, you can count on it.'

Then, abruptly, he turned away, muttering under his breath. Climbing back into his van, he slammed the door and pulled out with a roar of the engine, spraying grit as he went.

Nerys stood there long after he'd gone, the wind blowing into her face. Though she'd taken deep breaths in an attempt to calm her nerves, when she finally got back into the car, she was still shaking from head to toe. As she drove the rest of the way down to the beach, Nerys felt increasingly anxious. *Shit*. Hugh Roberts knew where she lived all right. And he wasn't a man to be crossed.

Poor little Nyten's life hanging in the balance. Her nain gone. Her mam gone. Elin so far away.

And now this.

By the time the cottage came into view, Nerys had the sickening sense that the accident was only the start. That there was worse to come.

Chapter 31

NOW – Earlier on Wednesday 5th April 2023

Cai

A damp chill enveloped Cai as he reached the narrow lane that snaked beyond the beach. The rain was only a mist now – fine, drifting droplets that clung to his wavy hair and sat like tiny glass beads on the fabric of his jacket – but the air still carried the briny, metallic tang of the earlier downpour. He'd have to try to ring Elin to tell her about Nerys – maybe there'd be a payphone somewhere on the main road he could use. Although he would certainly enquire, he wasn't very hopeful that his phone would have been handed in at the bus depot. Thankfully, it was insured and he'd be able to get another when he got back to Birmingham. He could have kicked himself for being so careless.

After Ianto left the pub, Cai had thought more about their conversation and then suddenly remembered the movement he'd seen in the upstairs window of Nerys's cottage. Maybe he'd imagined it.

Cai screwed up his eyes as they adjusted to the prematurely settling gloom. He felt a twinge of exhilaration. This was the area he planned to excavate next month: the swathe of land above him, between the beach and farmland, was bordered by tall, unkempt hedgerows and was well concealed from the road below. He'd left it far too late in the day to see much: he'd wanted one more look at the terrain before deciding exactly where he and his team should focus their efforts. But even just walking across it would give him a sense of the place; he felt it in his bones.

He'd been here a few times before. But tonight, the lane felt different somehow. Heavy. Expectant. He felt oddly uneasy as he turned off and began to climb from the road towards the scrubland concealed by the overgrown foliage to his right. He felt something beneath his foot in the long grass. Thinking it was perhaps a stone, he kicked at it, only to see a flash of red. Stooping to pick the item up, Cai saw what it was: a Swiss Army Knife. Well used too, by the looks of it. He remembered his dad having one. He shrugged, supposed that other people must come this way from time to time. There seemed to be an inscription of some sort on the side, but it was difficult to make out in the dim. He'd have a proper look later, hand it in at the pub next time he was up, in case someone was looking for it. Slipping the knife into his pocket, he continued, deeper into the undergrowth.

As he pushed his way through the heather and gorse, sudden movement ahead drew Cai's attention. He stopped in his tracks. A hunched figure was squatting in the waterlogged soil on the rise a few yards ahead, the area he'd felt in his gut would be a prime dig location. The yellow beam of a torch, lying at the person's side, fanned out across the ground in front of them.

For the briefest moment, Cai assumed it was a dog walker; that maybe they'd dropped something.

His first instinct was to offer help. He looked around for evidence of a dog, but could see none. Peering through the shadows at the ground where the person was crouching, his curiosity deepened. Cai's heart quickened – maybe they'd found something – one of the elusive artefacts he himself hoped to uncover. It would only confirm his own suspicions: that there was something of real importance to be discovered here. The dog walker might just have helped to pinpoint exactly where his team needed to focus.

What a fortuitous moment to have come across them.

Chapter 32

NOW – Wednesday 10th May 2023

Elin

Catrin had been on the phone first thing, sounding apologetic. She wasn't coming today, she'd said, as she had to take her mother-in-law to the shopping outlet in Ellesmere Port. But she was checking in to make sure Elin was okay and assured her she'd ring again in the evening. She had contacted Aaron regarding the grief-bot and he was already working on it, she said. In order to obtain the best, most realistic avatar, it would take a week or so to incorporate the various recordings and videos that Elin had forwarded. Aaron had explained that in order to synchronise everything and for the AI to learn to mimic Cai's mannerisms and the tone of his voice accurately, fine-tuning might take a few days longer, although he'd told Catrin that he would endeavour to finish it as quickly as possible.

Elin felt restless. The idea of Cai's hologram and how she

would actually react to it filled her with both apprehension and excitement. Though she didn't want to build it up in case it wasn't all she'd hoped for, an image of how it might look kept creeping into her thoughts. She tried to occupy her mind with morning TV, but gave up and went back to bed for an hour, as she'd slept badly. The constant drum of rain against the window sent her back to sleep quite quickly, and she awoke to see that it was gone two o'clock. Not that it mattered: she wasn't going anywhere.

The earlier shower had passed, the pale afternoon sun glinting now off the wet grass. Elin stepped outside to breathe in the sweet air. Seeing Libby come into the garden, Elin remembered what Bethan had told her. There hadn't really been an appropriate time to broach the subject before now and, moreover, she hadn't felt inclined, but after her nap she was feeling a little stronger, less dead-headed. She really should seize the opportunity to say something. Elin crossed the lawn and stood on her side of the low wooden fence, folding her arms as she watched Libby on the other side, her white head dipped, pruning a potted rosemary bush. She looked up to see Elin, startled by her sudden appearance.

'Oh, you made me jump! Everything okay?'

Elin took a breath as she studied her neighbour. It was better to get everything out in the open, surely. 'Have you got a minute?'

Libby wiped her hands on her gardening apron, forcing a bright smile that didn't quite reach her eyes. 'Of course, love. Has something happened?'

Elin hesitated. She didn't want a heated confrontation. At the same time, she needed some transparency. She wanted to give Libby the benefit of the doubt but if there was anything in Bethan's suspicions, she needed to know. 'Look, I feel a bit awkward about this. But Bethan was telling me a few things the other day. She mentioned what you'd been doing before I came home, while Nerys hasn't been well and since she's been in hospital.'

Libby's smile faltered. She straightened, bristling. 'Ah, I see.'

Elin observed Libby for some hint of guilt, but her face was unreadable. There was a long, uncomfortable pause, before Elin finally spoke again. 'Bethan said you'd been coming into the house a lot. Sorting cupboards. Opening Nerys's mail. Doing . . . a lot more than watering the plants.'

Libby took a step backwards, looking genuinely shocked. 'Elin, I wasn't trying to hide anything. I thought you knew – about Nerys, I mean. I thought . . .'

Elin tried to keep her expression neutral, though her pulse had quickened. 'Well, I didn't. And I need to understand why you thought it was your job to do all that.'

Libby put down her secateurs, gripping the fence as if anchoring herself. She let out a deep, weary sigh. 'Because she was drowning, Elin. She'd been steadily going under for quite a while. And no one else seemed to see it.'

Elin blinked, taken aback by the intensity of the woman's tone. She thought of Nerys, of the things she must have been holding back when they'd spoken on the phone over the last few months. Of the ominous pauses when it seemed she was going to say something, but then thought better of it. From everything that had happened since, Elin knew now that there had been much more going on than she'd realised. Why hadn't she read between the lines?

'Well, yes. She was grieving for Nain. We *knew* she was struggling, but . . .'

Libby smiled sadly. 'Not just grieving. Sinking. After your grandmother went into the home, Nerys kept saying the house felt "wrong". I assumed she meant it felt too big, too quiet. She confided in me when your nain's memory started failing, but I'd recognised it myself, anyway. I cared for my great aunt when she had dementia. You learn the signs.' Libby shook her head. 'I think when your nain finally passed away, it sent Nerys into a state of real confusion. She'd had all this responsibility and suddenly she was all alone with hours to fill and didn't know what to do. So she did nothing.'

Elin swallowed hard. Though everything Libby was saying made sense, she was still on the defensive. 'And you thought that meant you should start rooting through her cupboards?'

'I was worried about her. I went round to see if there was anything I could do. She got really upset, Elin. Told me she couldn't find half her things. Important things. Medication. The doctor had prescribed her antidepressants after your nain died – they weren't going to work if she wasn't taking them.' Libby looked away sheepishly.

Elin winced. Nerys hadn't told her about the antidepressants. Had she wanted her to think she was coping, that everything was fine? It made her feel even worse, to think that Nerys felt unable to talk to her about it all – and that she hadn't read between the lines when they'd spoken over the phone. She wondered now, a slow sinking feeling in her gut, whether that last call had been Nerys trying to reach out to her, hoping Elin would pick up on her desperation without having to spell it out. That an invitation to come to Birmingham for a few days might have felt like a lifeline to her. 'There were several letters about council tax arrears,' Libby went on. 'She told me she thought she'd paid the bills, but I checked and she hadn't even opened a lot of them. She was ashamed – and she was getting frightened, but didn't want to admit it because she thought it made her seem weak.'

There was a slight tremor in Libby's voice now. It could have been from emotion, or equally from guilt. Elin studied Libby with narrowed eyes as the woman continued to speak.

'When I went in the day Bethan called round, days' worth of

washing up was piled up in the kitchen and there was stuff on the floor all around the bin. Who was going to sort it out? Not Nerys, not with the state she was in. And as for me opening the mail . . .' She gestured helplessly. 'The envelopes were already open. I just sorted them out. Put the ones that mattered on top. Tried to get some kind of order there. I didn't read anything private, honestly. Just the bills.'

Elin looked down at her hands, torn. Her voice was hesitant as she wrestled with this explanation. 'Bethan thought you were taking over. Acting like you knew better than the rest of us.'

Libby flinched visibly, hurt flashing across her face. 'I never thought I knew better. I just thought someone should care for her the way your nain did. You know yourself, she was such a capable lady. She used to deal with everything – Nerys had never needed to worry about anything before. When your grandmother became unwell and when she eventually went into the care home, Nerys lost that anchor.' Her voice softened. 'I wasn't trying to replace her. I just didn't want Nerys coming home to chaos. Not when she was grieving and barely holding it together.'

Elin looked up, her eyes searching Libby's face. Was her expression one of earnest sincerity, or was the woman just being patronising? She felt a sudden burst of anger. 'Why didn't you say any of this to me before? I mean, you could've got my number somehow – Nerys would've had it in her phone.'

'Because you had your own grief to deal with. Even more so now.' Libby dropped her gaze. 'And I didn't want to sound like I was criticising anyone, you know, laying blame.' There was an awkward pause. 'I wasn't trying to poke my nose in. Truly, all I wanted to do was help. I just couldn't watch the poor girl slip through the cracks like that.'

A long silence stretched between them. A robin landed on the fence suddenly, hopped once, then darted away. Elin stared after it unseeingly. The more she thought about Libby's lame explanation, the more irate she became. Her own grief for Cai's loss was recent and no excuse: and the pain she and Nerys shared over Nain was all the more reason to keep her informed. Much of her frustration was aimed at herself, for not supporting Nerys in the way that she should have. But if she'd had any idea at all of the state she was in, Elin would have been there like a shot, and maybe things would never have spiralled the way they had. Libby had clearly been in the thick of it and more aware than most just how much Nerys was struggling. What right did she have to step in and then decide to keep everything from her? What if things had got so bad that Nerys had attempted to take her own life?

Elin's eyes settled on Libby once more. 'Well, in spite of all your so-called help, my sister did fall through the cracks, didn't she? Maybe if you'd bothered to keep me informed it would never have come to that. She needed me, Libby – and it seems to me you made a decision not to let me know and used the opportunity to nose through her stuff. That's pretty unforgiveable from where I'm standing. I don't know what you were playing at, but as far as I'm concerned you haven't helped at all.'

Libby opened her mouth to speak, but Elin was already marching back towards the house. If she stayed out there any longer, she might have said much more and this conversation was only adding to her stress levels. She needed to take a beat, consider it all properly when she'd calmed down.

*

As she crossed the lawn, a glimpse of bright blue, half-covered by the grass, caught Elin's eye. Stooping to get a closer look, she saw that it was a loop of wool, threaded through the end of a key she didn't recognise. Frowning, Elin picked it up and tried it in the lock of the back door. It turned perfectly. She shrugged. Maybe Nerys had had an extra one cut, for some reason. She glanced back towards the Fowlers' garden, but Libby had already retreated into the house.

Elin took the key inside, locking the door behind her. Living in Birmingham, it was something she did automatically now.

Maybe it made good sense in the twenty-first century, wherever you lived.

Chapter 33

BEFORE – March 2023

Nerys

The cottage was ominously quiet, in the way it only ever seemed to be when something had gone wrong. Nerys lay on the settee, where she'd slept fitfully the night before under the throw, the sound of Nain's old clock ticking from the wall, steady and loud, reminding her even more how alone she was. She stared at the ceiling, a hollow feeling in her gut.

When she finally pushed herself to get up, it was with the anxious feeling that the day would bring further upset. Her first thought was for Nyten. She called the vet's, praying that no news must mean good news.

'She's critical but stable,' came the response from the surgery. 'We're keeping her comfortable and she's still on the drip. If there's any change, we'll let you know.'

Nerys made tea. She couldn't face breakfast. Carrying her

mug back into the living room, she decided she couldn't face going into work, either.

She rang Bethan, apologising, telling her about Nyten, the vet's suspicion that someone may have harmed her, and that she'd barely slept. Feeling embarrassed about her carelessness, she didn't mention the bump with Hugh Roberts, although the repercussions of that were very much at the front of her mind, too.

Bethan was, as ever, understanding. 'You get yourself back to bed, cariad. I can manage. Keep me posted about Nyten. That's just awful if someone has done that to her. You take care now, and I'll see you soon. *Sws mawr*.'

Nerys's relief at not having to leave the house was short-lived. She'd finished her tea, then taken a long bath, hoping the hot water would ease away some of the tension and enable her to catch up on some sleep. She managed a couple of hours, then decided she needed to give herself a shake and do something constructive to keep her mind occupied.

Coming back downstairs at around noon, Nerys immediately spotted an envelope lying on the mat inside the front door, white and official-looking. Her chest tightened as she saw the butcher's personalised 'bull's head' logo over the seal. She stood barefoot on the cold flagstone floor for a long moment, before bending to pick it up. She didn't need to open it to know what it was. Hugh Roberts had been true to his word.

The paper rustled as she opened it out. The figure stared back at her. It seemed an extortionate amount for the actual damage done. *Nine hundred pounds*. Her stomach dropped. She thought of the moment on the hill the day before, the stupid, ordinary sound of her phone ringing from the back seat of the Aygo. Why couldn't she just have ignored it? One ill-judged glance, a heartbeat of lost concentration. Then the horn, the glare of lights; Hugh Roberts's van veering across the lane and that awful ear-splitting screech . . .

She folded the bill back up and held it for a moment, drawing in a breath. The next thought came like a physical blow. *The insurance.*

Nerys dropped into the armchair opposite her nain's and stared at the sagging, empty seat cushion. She could see Nain there as she'd been before the dementia took hold, arms folded, mouth pursed in that familiar half-frown. *Meddwl, hogan. Think, girl.* Her grandmother's voice rang in her ears. Nerys hadn't renewed the policy, she knew that now. Somewhere between funeral arrangements and empty evenings and the slow, grinding ache of being left to pick up the pieces of her miserable life, she had simply . . . forgotten.

'I can't pay this,' she said aloud, casting her eyes to the ceiling.

Her first instinct was to cry, but the tears refused to come. Instead, she sat staring at the piece of paper, the panic starting to build. She'd mentioned her phone, too – what if Roberts reported her? She couldn't afford a fine and points on her licence on top of it all. If she didn't cough up, she had a horrible feeling that the man was quite capable of making things very unpleasant for her.

There was only one person she could ask, and the thought made her cheeks burn.

She rang Bethan from the armchair, her palms sweating as she gripped the phone. Bethan answered on the second ring, brisk as ever, the shop bell tinkling faintly in the background. She clearly thought Nerys was ringing to update her about Nyten.

'Nerys, any news?'

It all spilled out then – her stupid dip in concentration, the accident, the size of Roberts's repair quote, the lapsed insurance. She hated how small her voice sounded, how pathetic, as though she were confessing to something shameful. She half-expected Bethan to sigh, to say it was too much.

Instead, Bethan swore, raucous and heartfelt.

'That frigging *arsehole*,' she growled. 'It would have to be him, wouldn't it? But don't worry, cariad.' Bethan's voice was firm, reassuring. 'I'll sort it. I'll go and see him myself. I'm shutting up shop early anyway, as I've got to take Mam to the doctor's. I can do it on the way home. Just pay me back when you can.'

Nerys blinked back tears. 'Thank you so, so much. Of course, I'll let you have it all back,' she said quickly. 'A few quid at a time. I just—I didn't know who else to ask right now.'

The relief was so overwhelming it felt like a balloon deflating rapidly inside her. Nerys thanked Bethan over and over, the guilt at having to ask her sitting like a stone in her chest, but Bethan waved it away and told her to go and have a *panad* or take a walk, and to call the vet's again.

'They're probably too busy to keep ringing you with updates every five minutes. Doesn't hurt to give them a prod.'

After the call ended, Nerys sat very still for a moment, staring out of the window. She imagined Bethan marching into Hugh Roberts's shop, a wad of cash in her handbag, her jaw set. The thought brought the glimmer of a smile to her lips.

It had just turned four o'clock, when Bethan rang her back.

'Well, I paid the bugger,' she said, a hint of glee in her voice. 'In front of half the community. I think all the old dears must've just got their pensions and gone in to treat themselves this afternoon.'

Nerys closed her eyes, wincing a little at the realisation that everyone would now know what she'd done. She could picture the man behind his counter, giblet-spattered apron stretched over the cushion of his ample stomach, his voice loud and overly sure of itself. He wouldn't have appreciated Bethan approaching him at work.

'I counted it out for him, note by note. Oh, and I may have mentioned,' Bethan went on in a matter-of-fact tone, 'that he can't be that bloody hard up if his shop's as busy as it is. And that it wasn't very kind to hound a young woman who's recently lost her nain and nearly lost her cat.'

A sound escaped Nerys's throat, somewhere between a laugh and a sob.

'What—what did he say?'

'He didn't like it one bit,' Bethan snorted. 'But his customers seemed to.'

They chatted a while longer, Bethan reassuring her that Roberts had been well and truly left with egg on his very red face; that Nerys had nothing to worry about and she should just put it all behind her.

'And don't beat yourself up about bumping his bloody van, either,' Bethan told her firmly. 'Main thing is that no one was hurt. He'll get over it. You just focus on yourself. You've had so much going on – no wonder you weren't concentrating.'

Nerys let out a sigh. 'I just feel so bad asking you for help. If you could take half out of this month's pay and then the rest next time . . .'

'Pfft, don't be daft, it's not like you've left me short. Forget the money – but if you could do a couple of extra hours here and there when I need to see to Mam, I'd really appreciate it.'

Nerys said that of course she would; that if there was anything Bethan needed, she only had to ask.

When the call ended, Nerys went to the window. Sunlight was breaking through the cloud and casting a shimmering path across the water. For the first time since finding Nyten in the garden, since the altercation with Roberts, since that envelope landing on the mat, she felt able to exhale.

She was still scared. Nyten still wasn't out of the woods. Hugh Roberts would still look at her with that hard, contemptuous stare whenever their paths crossed.

But she wasn't alone. Even though Elin had moved away and she no longer had Nain or Mam, she always had Bethan.

Chapter 34

NOW – Wednesday 10th May 2023

Elin

Elin's hair clung to her face and neck, dampened by the persistent drizzle. Under the grey, soulless sky, she had trudged right across the beach to Benllech and back, trying to shake off the memory of her awkward earlier conversation with Libby. She hated an atmosphere, even if she knew she'd been right to question Libby about her behaviour. She would have to ring Bethan later, tell her what had been said. She was grateful that Bethan had shared her concerns about Libby. Bethan had been a good friend to Mam, and she'd always looked out for Nerys. But Elin wished she'd been less accusatory when she approached Libby. Their exchange had left an unpleasant aftertaste and it wasn't nice to feel she was on poor terms with her neighbours, especially as she was on her own in the house. She was torn, too, as to whether Libby had genuinely been trying to help Nerys. If she had, Elin had been pretty rude to her.

She was almost home when, passing beneath Castell Mawr, something drew her attention to the cliffs above. Shielding her eyes, Elin looked up. There, at the edge of the rock, loomed a hooded figure, apparently observing her. She couldn't tell whether it was a man or a woman. The moment her head tipped in its direction, whoever it was paused briefly, then withdrew sharply from sight. A chill crept over Elin's flesh. She stepped up her pace and was glad when she reached the track leading to the cottage. She didn't like the idea that someone had been watching her. It had unnerved her a little.

She was stamping sand from her trainers on the mat when she heard the creak of the gate. Turning sharply, she was relieved to see not a person in a hood but Ianto coming up the path, his beanie hat pulled low against a wind that dispersed the fine rain like the spray of a sprinkler. Pentraeth Forest's wall of pines loomed tall and sombre in the distance, the darkening sea edging ever closer to the shore. She'd stared out at that view so many times as a girl. Elin felt the familiar squeezing behind her ribs, the resurgence of memories of Mam and Nain compounding the relentless grief she felt for Cai's loss.

It had been months since she'd seen Ianto properly; even at Nain's funeral, the chapel had been too full and the air too thick with misery for anything beyond nods and murmured condolences. And though he had been at the service for Cai, she hadn't been in a fit state to speak to anyone, much less absorb anything that was said. Now he stood there, hands shoved into his coat pockets, eyes taking in the cottage wistfully as if remembering happier times.

'*Sut wyt ti?* Sorry to just roll up,' he said. 'I was passing, like.'

Elin studied his face. There were more lines now, a slight downturn to his mouth; wisps of greying hair were escaping from beneath the sides of his hat and woven through his beard. His brown eyes seemed to have lost their twinkle.

'You don't need an excuse,' she replied, though the words came out more curtly than she intended. She led him inside, told him to take a seat, before going into the kitchen herself, where the kettle had been kept warm on the range from earlier. Nerys's Cath Kidston mug hung from the wooden tree on the worktop, an unsightly chip in the glaze on one side. It must have happened when Nerys knocked it over that day. Elin sighed, turning it so that the chip wasn't showing. She would have to try and find her a new one.

'So how are things?' Ianto called from the living room. It was an unnecessary question, the answer plain and painful.

Elin brought the tea and sat opposite him, conscious of his sad eyes straying to Nain's empty chair. She wondered if Ianto was lonely. Gel had died over three years earlier and he still hadn't got another dog. '*Irreplaceable*.' She remembered Nerys telling her what he'd said; that his grief had been heart-rending. Elin's theory that he'd been keen on her mam had quickly been squashed years ago by Nain, who'd told her he'd long held a candle for Bethan but that nothing had ever come of it.

'Stubborn buggers, the pair of them,' she'd said. Two lonely people. It seemed such a shame.

They made small talk at first, the obligatory dissection of the weather, their jobs; anything and everything to avoid the elephant in the room. Elin felt the conversation skirt around her loss without touching it, as if the mention of Cai's name would bring the walls crashing in around them. Eventually, she brought up the subject of Nerys, pleased to learn that Ianto had visited her a couple of times, even if not for a week or so.

'Has there been any improvement?' he asked. 'It's awful to see her like that. I feel so bad that I haven't been able to go more often. I did pop in here from time to time after your nain but . . . well, you know how it is, I'm sure.'

Elin sighed, acutely conscious of her own failings. 'She's still in a bad way,' she said, absently watching a curl of steam rise from Ianto's mug. 'The doctor thinks she's got a type of trauma-based amnesia – although she's so doped up at the moment, it's hard to get much of anything out of her. When Nain died, it all . . . well, I suppose it was obvious. It all fell apart. Apparently Libby was helping her before things reached crisis point. Shopping, tidying up and stuff. Checking in on her.' She cleared her throat, picturing Libby's stunned face as she'd ranted at her.

Ianto nodded, his gaze narrowing, mouth setting into a thin line.

'Bethan was suspicious about her motives,' Elin went on. 'She suggested Libby might not be doing it all out of the kindness of her heart.' Elin could hear the edge in her voice now, the memory of her own angry words ringing in her head. 'I felt I had to confront Libby, but I'm feeling pretty uncomfortable about it all now. She looked hurt. I think she probably was.'

'Maybe,' Ianto said. He stared at his tea but wasn't drinking it, his eyes wobbling. 'But Bethan's pretty astute. Nothing wrong with asking a few questions, you know. I mean, how well do you know that woman really? And her husband's a funny bugger, if you ask me.'

Something in his tone and the curl of his lip snatched her attention. 'You don't like them, do you?' she blurted out. 'Libby and Peter, I mean.'

The muscles in his cheeks twitched, his focus drifting to the window and the rolling waves beyond. 'I'm not . . . I'm unsure about them,' he said at last. 'That's all I'll say.'

Elin waited, but he chewed his lip, his eyes dropping. She cocked her head, seeing the tension in his face. 'Come on, you must have your reasons.'

'There were the damaged boats,' he admitted, after a moment. 'A bloody savage attack, whoever did it, and we never did find out. The night of the storm . . . the one that took your mam and young Jac.' He swallowed. 'Oh, good old Peter was there as usual, wanting to help with the repairs. But I'd clocked him hovering around earlier. I reckon he'd been eyeing them up. It dawned on me when I thought about it afterwards. And *her*' – he tipped his head in the direction of the Fowlers' home – 'whenever she's out, she's like his bloody shadow.' Ianto's jaw clenched. 'I've had my suspicions about a few other things besides. For a long time. But suspicions aren't proof.'

Proof. The word sat between them, heavy and baleful. And there it was again: the mention of the boats. A cold feeling prickled along Elin's arms. She wrapped her hands a little tighter around the warm curve of her mug, leaning forward uneasily.

'What other things?'

'Well, someone keyed Derfel's van a couple of months ago, for a start. Not just one quick line, really went to town on it; obscenities all over the bonnet, down both sides. He had to have a respray.'

Elin widened her eyes. 'And you think one of *them* might've done it? But why?'

Ianto blew out a long breath. 'There'd been a bit of aggro in the pub. Peter and Libby were at the bar and Peter started arguing with Rhiannon, said she'd short-changed him. ''Course, her dad came in, didn't he. You know what Derfel can be like when he's had a few. He was ready to land one on Peter – a couple of us had to step in and pull him back. Libby was screaming like a banshee at Derfel. She looked like she wanted to kill the man.'

'Christ. And *had* Rhiannon given him the wrong change? I mean, did Peter have good reason to be annoyed?'

Ianto shrugged. 'It was pennies, even if she had. And she

wouldn't have done it on purpose, you know that. A real fuss about nothing. But it was the aggressive way Peter was speaking to her, the look on his face. It was like a mask had slipped.' He chewed the inside of his cheek. 'It made me even more convinced there could be a whole other side to him – and not a very nice one. And his wife certainly wasn't behaving like the little mouse I'd always thought she was.'

Elin shuddered. 'So did Derfel do anything? About the damage to his van?'

'*Naddo.*' Ianto rolled his eyes. 'He was pretty dismissive, which I found bizarre. Claimed it was probably kids. He does upset a lot of people, to be fair. Maybe he'd already been expecting some sort of payback for something. He got a mate to do the paint job, said it needed sprucing up anyway. Peter shook his hand the next day, explained it away by saying he'd not been feeling too well; said no hard feelings and everything. It seemed to be forgotten just like that.' He snapped his fingers.

'I think Derfel's . . . well, shot to hell with the drink these days if I'm honest. Probably didn't remember the half of it. But I won't forget the look in that man's eyes in a hurry and I think Rhi's quite wary of him now too, even though he apologised afterwards. She packed in her job not long after that – said she'd had enough of dealing with awkward punters. Works for some cleaning company in Bangor now.'

'I haven't seen Rhi properly in ages. She's still living at home, isn't she?'

'Yep. I feel sorry for the girl.' Ianto pushed out his lower lip. 'Can't be much fun, especially now Catrin's moved out. But I think she feels responsible for her dad. He's going to drink himself into an early grave the way he carries on.'

There was an uncomfortable pause. Ianto drew in a breath. He spoke more softly now. 'Changing the subject, I saw Cai that afternoon, you know – just before he died.'

Elin stared at him. Something turned over in her stomach. 'What? Where? Did you speak to him?'

'In The Quay. We were chatting a good while. He'd called round to see Nerys, he didn't know she was in hospital, like. He seemed pretty cut up about it. Mentioned he'd been speaking to Peter earlier.' He tipped his head towards the window. 'Outside the cottage.'

Elin's breath caught in her throat. She pictured Cai leaning against the gate, hair flopping around his face, explaining something expressively with his hands as he always did.

'He'd caught the bus over from Caernarfon,' Ianto continued. 'Lost his phone on the way, he reckoned. That's why you couldn't reach each other.' He met her gaze then, his brown eyes steady. 'I left the pub before him – had a job on, like. He said he was waiting for the rain to stop, then going to take a walk to look at the proposed dig site before getting the early evening bus back.'

Elin thought for a moment. 'Ianto, do you have any idea what Cai was doing with Harry Edwards's knife? It's one of those Swiss Army ones – I found it in Cai's jacket pocket when the police sent some of his stuff back. I think they must've missed it.'

Ianto frowned. 'Harry's? Not a clue. I wasn't aware they even knew one another.'

'Oh, I just wondered if he might've mentioned it. If you see him, tell him I've got it, will you?'

'I can take it if you like. I'll probably see him in The Quay at some point – he calls in for a game of darts quite often.'

Elin thought for a moment. 'Would you ask him to come and see me? I'm just curious. I'd like to ask him myself.'

Ianto shrugged. '*Chwarae teg*. I'll tell him to pop round.' He ran a hand over his beard. 'Funny, that. I'm sure Harry'll be able to clear it up.'

She nodded mutely, the terrible gnawing feeling returning to her chest as she thought again of Cai's final hours. So Ianto was possibly the last person ever to speak to him, but not to see him. And whoever had been behind the wheel of that car had never come forward, nor were they likely to now. The knowledge was eating away at her. She suddenly felt the need to steer the conversation towards something else, something less painful. What would Ianto think of the grief-bot idea, she wondered? Should she mention it? But he was older, less technologically minded. It might even freak him out. Elin bit her lip and resolved not to say anything in case he didn't approve. She was fairly sure Nain would have thought she'd lost her mind.

Ianto finished his tea, which by now must have been stone cold, and rose to leave. Elin saw him to the door. As she opened it, she saw Peter approaching, close to the gate. He raised a hand tentatively to wave. Elin smiled tightly and returned the gesture, but without enthusiasm. Ianto glanced over his shoulder and, seeing Peter, turned back to Elin with a roll of his eyes.

'I just wondered, and I don't want to be insensitive, but what's going to happen about Cai's dig?' Ianto studied her face. 'Do you have any say in it? Only he was so keen – seems a shame to cancel it.'

Elin had thought long and hard about it. And it was true: it had been Cai's dream to excavate that area above the lane. Initially, she couldn't stomach the idea of setting foot near the place where he'd died. But although it was still painful, she knew he'd have wanted the dig to go ahead. She was going to have to set aside her own feelings, be strong for him.

'I've got contact details for a couple of his mates. It may not be quite as quickly as originally planned, and I know they weren't keen to do anything for a while, but I'm going to encourage them to go ahead as soon as possible. To do it in Cai's memory.'

Ianto nodded, smiling sadly. 'That seems a fitting tribute. He was a fine young man. And he'd be proud of you, I'm sure.'

He left Elin with a lump in her throat. She really hoped Cai would have been proud. It was the one thing she could still actually do for him: ensure his carefully-laid plans were fulfilled.

*

With Ianto gone, Elin was alone with her thoughts once more. She was really anxious now to find out about the knife. Perhaps Cai *had* borrowed it – but she couldn't recall him ever mentioning it. She wondered too about what Ianto had told her about Peter and Libby, but then remembered Nain saying some years back that Peter, who'd told them he'd been a carpenter himself before he retired, had mended old Sion Morgan's gate for him free of charge after someone kicked it in, doing Ianto out of the job in the process. He'd probably done other things too – he was always lending people a hand. Maybe there was some deep-rooted resentment there which had coloured Ianto's judgement. After all, even if she was still feeling ambivalent about Libby's actions, Peter and Libby had been so helpful to them in the past – and so kind to Delyth after Jac died. The thing in the pub had been an isolated incident – and everyone had their off days. Christ, she knew herself how she'd almost bitten the head off a couple of customers when things were getting to her at work. Even in telesales, things could be incredibly frustrating at times.

Thinking about it now, it sounded like Ianto was making something out of nothing.

Chapter 35

NOW – Thursday 11th May 2023

Elin

Ianto called by again briefly the next morning, to let Elin know he'd just found out that Harry Edwards was in Corfu for a week's holiday with his brother. He said he'd tell Harry about the knife when he got back, as he didn't have his personal mobile number. He'd managed to find his business contact details, but it had gone straight to an out-of-office voicemail message.

Elin felt deflated. She was sure there must be some mundane explanation for the knife being in Cai's possession, but she was still keen to speak to Harry. She didn't know the man well, but he'd always seemed friendly and easy-going. It was a shame, really, that Bethan wasn't interested in him. She needed to see Nerys again; she was clinging to the hope that with each visit, her sister's condition would improve slightly. That even through the fog of medication, maybe Elin's own presence would help to raise Nerys's spirits, with the knowledge that there would be someone to come home to now; that Nerys wouldn't feel so alone. That her memory would be restored and hopefully it would have been caused by nothing more than the trauma of her grief. Elin had to keep going, keep trying. All they had now was each other. She hoped that by talking to her sister about home, about familiar things and shared memories, that something would eventually shift in Nerys's consciousness. That she would come back to her.

*

When Elin arrived at the Hergest Unit, Nerys hardly looked at her. Her sister's face, once so open and bright, had softened into something barely recognisable, her mouth slack, her dull gaze slipping past Elin as she sat beside the bed, as though she were just another object in the room. There was a plastic cup of water on the bedside table, untouched. A television droned from behind the drawn curtain of the bay opposite; some daytime programme Elin doubted anyone was watching.

She would have loved to talk openly, pour her heart out about everything that had happened; about Cai. Ask Nerys whether she thought she was doing the right thing, agreeing to an artificial, digital version of him being created. But she remembered Dr Bianchi's advice, knowing she could share nothing that might agitate her sister in any way. Best to stick to small talk for the time being.

Elin's heart was heavy. Her run-of-the-mill questions went unanswered, making Elin wonder if Nerys was absorbing anything she was saying at all. Whether she even knew who she was – or whether she'd actually registered she was there. It was only when Elin mentioned their mam that something in Nerys seemed to alter.

'I was looking out at the boats yesterday,' ventured Elin, unsure whether she ought to talk about Mam or not. She stopped short of mentioning the more recently inflicted damage. 'It made me think about her, somehow. About how she'd been that last night. Happy. Full of life, as usual.'

Nerys's eyes widened then, a brief flash of lucidity. For a moment, the sister Elin knew so well was back. 'Did it?' she asked, turning to look at Elin properly for the first time that day.

Elin leaned forwards, her heart giving a small, painful lurch. 'Yes,' she said softly, praying this could be some sort of breakthrough. 'I always think of her when I'm home.'

Nerys watched her for a few seconds. She shook her head a fraction. 'No,' she said. 'Not like that. Not just . . . reminiscing.'

Elin frowned. 'What d'you mean?'

Nerys's fingers curled around the bedsheets. This sudden glimpse of clarity in her eyes had already begun to waver, but it was as if something inside her was fighting to stay focused. 'Have you ever really thought about it properly?' she asked. 'About what happened to her?'

A chill crept up Elin's spine then. 'She was lost during the storm. A horrible accident,' she replied, hoping to mollify her. 'You know that. How unpredictable the tide round the bay can be, and—'

'But what about Jac Parry?' Nerys cut in abruptly. 'Delyth always thought there was more to it.' Her eyes darted now, as if something else was stirring in her memory.

Elin swallowed. 'I remember. Poor Delyth.'

'She found Jac's torch, the one he'd had with him that night. Did you know that? Halfway up the lane. How could it have got there?'

Elin felt a ripple of discomfort. She hadn't known. The memory of Mam's wheel brace turning up as it did surged to the front of her mind suddenly. It had never been made clear why it had been taken from the car. In fact, the police had said very little about it. Maybe it had been easier for them. One tragedy wrapped up neatly by another, both conveniently explained away by the storm.

Nerys leaned back, the bedding still bunched in her fists. 'Everyone said the sea took them,' she mumbled, her eyes beginning to glaze. 'Easy, wasn't it? Just blaming the sea.'

She began to ramble incoherently suddenly, retreating again into the stupor she'd displayed when Elin first arrived. By the time Elin rose to leave, Nerys's eyes were blank and staring out at nothing once more. She didn't look at her; didn't even flinch as Elin planted a kiss on her cheek.

Elin hobbled from the ward with a heavy heart. As she made her way back to the main hospital building, she glanced back briefly at the Hergest Unit, wondering how long it would be before Nerys was well enough to leave the place. Right now, it felt as if it was going to be a long job.

*

The water was calm when the taxi dropped Elin back outside Nain's cottage, its familiarly deceptive stillness stretching out under the grey sky. Elin stood on the track in front of the sea wall for a long time, watching the horizon unseeingly as the tide crept in. Though it wasn't a good memory, she tried to retrieve the version of the past she had always hung onto: the storm that night, the wild wind, the angry waves. The terrible tragedy of it all; the cruelty of nature.

Elin wrapped her arms around herself, her coat flapping against the breeze. For the first time, she'd begun to consider Nerys's question without dismissing it out of hand. Initially she'd tried to convince herself that it was just the illness speaking. That her sister's mind, muddled and strained, had twisted the past into something considerably darker than it really was. It would have been so much better, so much *easier* to believe that.

But the urgency in Nerys's voice wormed its way through her thoughts now, insistent and unsettling.

'*Have you ever really thought about it properly?*'

Though she knew that Nain had become irrationally fixated with the idea there was more to Meinir's disappearance than met the eye, she had completely dismissed it, sure that it was the dementia talking.

'She's getting worse,' Nerys had bemoaned over the phone one day, shortly before Nain went into the home. 'I can't seem to pacify her any more. She got quite angry earlier when I suggested she should see the doctor. Said I was the one with the problem if I just blithely accept the police's explanation for everything.' A sigh came down the line. 'I found this bit of paper – she'd been making a list of people she suspected. Really bizarre. I'm worried she'll do something silly sooner or later.'

Elin had always suspected that the demise of both Mam and Jac had been connected in some way: that maybe they'd been together when a freak wave had swept them out to sea. Mam would certainly have looked out for Jac if she'd seen him out on his own. But the news about Jac's torch niggled her. And once Nerys's suggestion had taken hold, she couldn't shake the thought. *Had* there been some terrible trauma that had caused her sister's illness – and was it possible that it was in some way linked to their mother and Jac?

It was as if the seed of something malign had begun to germinate in Elin's brain.

On Friday, the day after her previous visit, Elin had gone to see Nerys again, but it was as though the shutters had gone down once more. Dr Bianchi had called Elin into a side room and suggested gently that perhaps she should stay away for a while, until her sister was a little better. That the last visit had seemed to have set her back. It saddened Elin not to be able to see her sister, but she couldn't bear the thought that her presence might impede Nerys's progress. Maybe a few days would make all the difference.

Still the memory of what Nerys had implied filled her with discomfort. Had the police looked into Mam's disappearance as diligently as they might? What if it really hadn't been an accident? And how would anyone ever know, with any evidence long gone? It must be too late to revisit the investigation now, surely. But the thought that another human being could have been responsible for her mother's death had sent Elin into turmoil. With everything else going on, it was too much to bear.

Back at home that evening, Elin's thoughts were a mess. Everything felt wrong, her grief and anxiety eating away at her. There was no one she could talk to, not properly. Catrin had Rhys and her in-laws to worry about; Bethan had her mam and the shop. Ianto was nice, kind – but somehow she didn't feel able to tell him everything that was getting to her. Maybe *she* needed to speak to a doctor or something. Someone she didn't know personally.

Elin sat for a while, the TV on, but was too restless to focus on anything. It was only nine thirty, but above all, she knew she needed to sleep. Hopefully the tiredness had caught up with her and she would manage a few hours; feel more rational in the morning. She made herself chamomile tea and was about to take it up to bed, when the house phone buzzed. Putting down the cup on the sideboard, Elin picked up the receiver on the fourth ring.

'*Helo*?'

From the other end came a deathly silence. Elin paused, her pulse quickening. 'Who's that?'

Someone began breathing. Heavily, oppressively. Clearly meaning to instil fear. Elin held her breath, finding herself inexplicably unable to move. A sudden peal of deep, muffled laughter came down the line, before the call ended abruptly, leaving Elin standing rigidly at the foot of the stairs, her heart pounding in her ears.

She stood for a moment staring at the phone, waiting to see if the caller would try again. But it remained silent. And then her anxiety was replaced with a sudden flash of anger. Wasn't this exactly what Tom Buckley used to do, after she'd blocked his number on her mobile? He must have heard what had happened if his mam was still local – learning about Elin's predicament would probably have filled him with more than a little schadenfreude. Quickly, she dialled 1471 – but the number had been withheld. Elin ripped the line cord from the wall. She would leave it disconnected from now on. Anyone who really needed to contact her could do so via her mobile.

Picking up her tea, she checked the front door before climbing the stairs to bed. Though she did feel a little shaken, if Buckley intended to scare her, she was determined not to give him the satisfaction. Somehow her indignation won over her nerves and eventually she fell into the deepest sleep she'd had for days.

*

Elin rang Catrin on Saturday morning to tell her about the hoax call. Her friend was in agreement that it was definitely the kind of thing that Tom Buckley might have done. She'd reminded Elin how, the last time, her nain had got hold of a whistle from somewhere and blown it loudly down the phone. The calls had stopped immediately after that. The pair recalled with amusement Nain's evident satisfaction in inflicting some sort of discomfort on Tom, dusting off her hands and commenting she hoped his sore ear would give him food for thought. It was quite a sweet revenge.

Catrin had popped her head in for an hour in the afternoon, but had been on pins about getting back, telling her that Rhys's mam would be spring cleaning her house if left alone for too long. The woman was a proper neat-freak, Catrin had said, and she was mortified at the prospect of her seeing all the stuff she'd hastily shoved into cupboards and drawers before her in-laws had arrived. She assured Elin they'd be leaving for a fortnight's holiday in the Algarve on Thursday ('*I'll be putting the flags out*,' she'd breathed), and she'd have more time after that. Plus, with a bit of luck, Aaron might have the grief-bot sorted by then.

Elin stumbled her way through the weekend. Whether it was a good idea or not, the thought of Cai's hologram was giving her something to cling to. With so much time spent alone, she had watched countless videos of other bereaved people and seen clips from the holograms that had been developed for them. There had been no negative feedback from any of the people involved, only the assertion that the experience was helping them to work through their grief. Elin held onto the hope that it would be the same for her. Though she still had no appetite, she had begun to eat a little and was forcing herself to take a daily shower, reminding herself how ashamed she'd have been at the idea of Cai seeing her looking such a mess.

Outside, the breeze was keen, jostling the foliage and making the fence creak and groan. A typically windy Anglesey day. Elin had just finished a reasonable portion of scrambled eggs for lunch and was standing at the sink, absently watching two blue tits pecking at the swaying feeder she had filled with peanuts that had probably been in the cupboard far too long. The birds didn't seem to mind.

There was a sudden rap at the front door. She quickly rinsed her plate and went through into the living room. As she opened the door, she was met first by a cool gust of sea air, followed by a woman she didn't recognise.

The woman's long, greying hair was scraped back untidily into a bun, her raincoat too thin for the harsh north-easterly breeze. She looked dishevelled, as though she had travelled a long way, or slept in her clothes. Her eyes were dark and almost haunted-looking, her mouth set in a line that suggested both anxiety and determination.

'So sorry,' the woman said, her accent unmistakeably Spanish. 'I hope I'm not disturbing you, but it's important. I'm looking for someone. Her name's Fliss. Fliss Michaels?'

Elin felt the familiar tightening in her chest, the way anything unexpected seemed capable of undoing her at the moment. She couldn't even listen to the radio without anything remotely associated with Cai invoking a sudden burst of emotion. Only yesterday she had been reduced to a sobbing wreck by the opening bars of Radiohead's 'No Alarms and No Surprises'. Seeing someone else looking so anguished brought all her own misery to the fore.

She shook her head. 'I'm afraid I don't recognise the name.' In spite of herself, she pushed the door a little wider. Nain and Mam had always encouraged her to be hospitable, hadn't they? And Cai – he would have wanted to help . . . 'But please, come in for a bit. That wind's chilly. You look like you could do with warming up.'

The woman hesitated, then stepped inside, glancing around the low-ceilinged living room with its yellowing walls and Nain's faded curtains. She didn't take off her coat. Elin noticed how her hands fiddled constantly with the strap of her bag, twisting it until the worn leather creaked.

'My name is Valeria,' the woman said. 'I'm sorry to just turn up like this. I've been asking everyone. I don't know what else to do.'

Elin gestured to an armchair and went to put on the kettle, before sitting opposite her on the settee. From here she could see the woman properly: the scuffed court shoes, the ragged cuffs of her mac, exhaustion and worry etched into her clearly once beautiful face. It struck Elin, with a stab of empathy, how life wore people down.

Valeria took a breath, as if about to impart something she

found difficult. From her handbag, she produced an old, creased photograph, which she handed to Elin.

'Fliss was my partner. My life partner. We lived together in Seville.' She smiled briefly, though her eyes remained sad. 'We argued. About nothing important.' She let out a sigh. 'Well, about everything. She came here, years ago, to see her sister and her brother-in-law. Libby and Peter. Your neighbours.'

Elin nodded slowly. The name Fliss stirred something vaguely in the depths of her consciousness, like a shape glimpsed through fog. She stared at the photo. It was of two laughing women, their arms wrapped around each other: a much younger version of Valeria, long, dark curls framing striking bone structure and huge brown eyes and a handsome, strong-jawed woman with short fair hair, who was obviously Fliss.

'They didn't approve of us,' Valeria went on, taking the photo as Elin handed it back. 'You know, of two women being together. But Fliss wanted to see her younger sister. She said it would only be for a short visit.' Her eyes scanned the picture. 'But she never came home.'

The kettle began to sing on the stove. Elin excused herself while she went to fill the teapot, then returned moments later with two mugs. She handed one to Valeria, who nodded gratefully. The woman's voice filled the room as she continued.

'A week after Fliss was meant to return, I received a text from her. Just a text!' Valeria's jaw clenched. 'She said she had been thinking for a long time. That she did not have feelings for me any more and she wanted to end things. That she was going to Canada, to be with an old girlfriend, Jen. She told me to keep her belongings, or give them away. Whatever. That she wanted a fresh start.'

Elin felt a chill that had nothing to do with the wind creeping under the door. A *text*, she thought. That seemed impersonal at the very least. Callous was probably closer to it.

'I was very angry,' Valeria said. 'We had parted badly and I felt humiliated. I did not reply. I did not call. I threw her things away.' She stared down at her hands. 'I met someone else. That ended too.'

Outside, a gull cried, the sound mournful and lonely. Elin thought of Cai's old sweater still lying on her bed: of the way she could never bring herself to dispose of it. Of all his possessions back in Birmingham, that sooner or later she would have to deal with, and how painful it was going to be. Maybe things between Valeria and Fliss had been really acrimonious. But she waited for the woman to explain, rather than asking.

'Then, a few months ago,' Valeria continued, 'a wedding invitation arrived. Addressed to us both. From Jen. She had signed it from herself and her fiancée.' Valeria looked up, her eyes bright now with something like anger. 'There was an address and phone number on the card, so I called Jen and she said she had not seen Fliss for almost twenty years.'

An uneasy silence settled between them. Elin became acutely aware of the ticking clock on the wall, the one Nain had wound every Sunday without fail. The atmosphere was intense, Valeria's face wrought with frustration, but Elin could think of nothing that might reassure her. It sounded to her as if perhaps Fliss didn't want to be found – and this was surely something Valeria wouldn't want to hear.

'I've been knocking on doors, asking lots of people,' said Valeria. 'No one seems to remember her. Peter and Libby were . . . polite. But cool. They said Fliss went back to Spain. They said they never heard from her again.' She spread her hands helplessly. 'Fliss had visited Anglesey once before. She'd told me how beautiful this place was. I thought maybe she'd stayed. Somewhere on the island.'

Elin searched her memory, feeling guilty for how little it yielded. A woman standing by the gate, perhaps. A brief nod, a 'hello' exchanged years ago when she was much younger and probably impatient to be elsewhere. 'I think I *do* remember her,' she said at last. 'Sort of. Or at least, I remember a lady staying with Peter and Libby when they first moved in. But I was only a kid – I never spoke to her properly. Just in passing. I'm afraid I don't know where she went.'

Valeria closed her eyes for a moment, as if absorbing this information resignedly. When she opened them again, they appeared glassy. 'Thank you for your time. And the tea,' she said wearily, putting down her empty mug on the side table. She fished in her coat pocket and produced a small white card, placing it next to the mug, then tapping it with her long fingers. 'My number. Just in case. I will keep looking, but I am losing hope. If I find nothing . . . I may have to go to the police.'

Elin wasn't sure what to say. Though she felt sorry for the woman, she found the intensity of her mood discomforting and was actually glad that she was leaving. She rose to show her out. 'Sorry I couldn't be more help. I really hope you find her.'

Valeria dipped her chin, smiling tightly. The wind tugged at her coat as she stepped back onto the path, the restless sea stretching out behind her, white waves leaving a trace of creamy foam as they left the shore. The woman paused, as if about to say something more, then shook her head and turned away.

Elin watched until Valeria was just a small, stooped figure against the grey, rocky sweep of the beach. Only then did she close the door, leaning her forehead against the wood for a moment. She *had* remembered something, but it was all quite hazy. Nain and Mam remarking with raised eyebrows on the arguments next door. But Peter and Libby were always so pleasant. Maybe Fliss had been hard to get along with.

The cottage felt heavier somehow, as though it had absorbed yet another unanswered question; another loss with no resolution. Elin's visitor had left her feeling more troubled than she already was.

Chapter 36

NOW – Friday 19th May 2023

Elin

When Catrin called on Friday to say that Aaron had put the finishing touches to the hologram package and that she'd be round with it later, Elin felt an odd, slightly conflicted frisson of excitement. The news of the arrival of the machine had pushed her other worries from her mind. It was almost as though, if she could just see Cai once more, things would be resolved. She kept trying to persuade herself she was being irrational in her fears about Mam and Jac. That, like Nerys, her grief and her inability to sleep without vivid, torturous dreams, was playing tricks on her fragile mind, distorting her view on reality.

With the reality of seeing the grief-bot imminent, Elin allowed herself to succumb to the daydreams she'd been attempting to push down. She tried to picture the hologram: what it would look like, how it would sound. What she herself should say.

Whether it would really feel as though Cai were in the room with her – or whether the whole thing would be a big letdown.

Catrin arrived in the late afternoon. Though the sun had yet to go down, she closed the curtains, leaving the living room fully dark, except for the pale blue glow from the desktop projector – the 'holo-box', as Aaron called it. Elin stared at the thing for a long time. It was a strange thought, that this little device contained a kind of gateway to Cai. Well, maybe not a gateway – but a means to see his face once more, hear his voice. She drew in a breath as she sat beside Catrin on the settee, reaching for her hand.

'Well, this is it then.'

Catrin squeezed an uncertain smile. 'Yep. This is it.'

She had placed the box on the small side table. It buzzed softly, beads of light twinkling across the display like neon over an urban sky.

Catrin studied Elin, her brow knitting. 'I'm sure this must all feel a bit daunting for you. You don't have to turn it on yet if you don't want to, you know. There's no rush.' A bead of sweat trickled from her forehead and she swatted it away. It occurred to Elin then that Catrin was equally apprehensive about what they were about to see.

Elin shook her head, her face tight, resolute though her stomach fluttered with nerves.

'No. If I wait, I'll lose my bottle.' She tapped the final confirmation into the keyboard, holding her breath.

They both looked on as a shimmering form gathered in the air. The 3D image glitched, resolved gradually, then sharpened. Almost instantaneously, a full-height figure materialised before them. It stood casually, shirt sleeves pushed halfway up, one leg crossed in front of the other, hands in the pockets of its torn jeans. The head tilted slightly at that angle she knew so well. Elin's heart began to race.

Cai's familiar, warm voice suddenly came through the speakers. 'El?'

Elin let out an involuntary cry. Not from fear or shock – more a sense of relief so intense it almost hurt. Reflexively, she put out an arm, her fingers quivering.

'Cai. Oh, God. You sound . . .' Her voice cracked as she studied the incredible likeness before her, so real she felt she could reach out and touch it. 'I—I almost thought I'd forgotten your voice. How could I have thought that?'

The hologram gave her a brief, wistful smile, the way Cai used to when he was trying not to cry. Those times when he'd spoken of his mum and how much her loss had affected him. 'I should hope not – I left a hell of a lot of messages over the years, remember? You always said I talked too much.'

Elin laughed uncertainly, wanting desperately to believe Cai was actually here with her once more. Her eyes swept from his head to his feet and back, as she tentatively allowed herself to bask in the illusion. She turned to Catrin, her eyes shining. 'This is so weird. But it's sort of comforting. And I really did say that.'

Catrin forced a small smile, though her eyes still darted with unease as she watched Elin. She spoke quietly, a hint of caution in her voice. 'It's built from things he recorded, El. That's all.'

But Elin barely heard her. She was watching Cai's face, drinking in every detail she thought she'd lost forever. She stretched out a hand once more. 'I've missed you so much. I'd give anything just to have you here with me again.' She leaned forward, tears blurring her vision now. 'We never got to say goodbye,' she said, the words choking her. 'I didn't . . . there was so much I wanted—'

The hologram flickered. Cai's outline blurred, his face stretching momentarily, like a reflection rippling in a pool. Elin realised in horror that the image was fading away.

'No!' she cried out, panic surging through her. 'No, don't go—'

The holo-box hummed, more loudly and persistently. Cai's mouth moved, but the words lagged, echoing oddly; a recording played at half-speed. His eyes had lost focus.

'I'm here he said, or something like it. Or maybe she imagined it.

Then the light collapsed in on itself, shrinking to a speck of white before vanishing entirely. The space where he had been was suddenly just air again: empty, a vacuum. Elin stared at it, her mouth gaping.

Catrin was beside her in an instant. She placed a hand on her arm. 'El, I'm so sorry. It wasn't meant to fizzle out like that. Aaron said the projection should hold quite a while, but—'

'Get him to fix it,' Elin said, her voice ragged. '*Please*. I just need to see Cai again. I need more time with him.'

'I will,' Catrin promised, rubbing her back gently. 'We'll try it again as soon as we can. I'll send the box back to Aaron by express delivery first thing tomorrow. He should have it by Sunday.'

Elin forced a smile, though the motion felt mechanical, her mind still whirring with the intensity of the experience. Catrin's brow was creased with concern. She shrugged on her coat with another mumbled apology, gave Elin a quick squeeze and a hesitant nod of reassurance, then retrieved the holo-box and headed for the door. It felt as though she couldn't leave fast enough. Maybe the whole thing had unsettled her.

Once she had finally gone, the cottage fell into silence again.

She sat motionless, her heart still fluttering, and realised that beneath the ache – beneath that vast, omnipresent void that had filled her chest for weeks – there was something else now. A thin, fragile wisp of lightness. Of hope. How glad she was that she had agreed to try the grief-hologram. She had *seen* Cai. Heard him say her name. And once Aaron had sorted things out, she'd be able to see him again. For the first time since the accident, it felt as though she had something to look forward to. Even if it wasn't real.

On impulse, she stood, pulled on her jacket and trainers, and stepped outside. She breathed in the clean, briny air, drinking in the ozone until it made her giddy.

The beach stretched wide, wet sand glistening beneath the gold-streaked sky. The tide was slowly receding, waves inching calmly in and then creeping out. Elin looked about. The pub car park was full and the buzz of a crowd outside carried across the bay, but right now she didn't want to be around people. She wanted to be alone with the thoughts tumbling through her head, to try to make some sense of what she was feeling. Rather than heading towards The Quay, at the end of the path from the cottage, she turned left and began to make her way towards Castell Mawr. Elin walked robotically, the rhythm of her steps gradually quieting her mind. She imagined Cai beside her, hands in his pockets; telling her to be careful, to watch her feet on the slippery stones. Crouching with sudden excitement when he spotted a fossil. The dull ache was still there in Elin's chest, but it was no longer draining every ounce of strength from her. No longer crushing the air from her lungs.

At the foot of the huge limestone mound, Elin stood for a while in the semi-darkness, staring out at the water as the pale moon began to rise against the gradually dimming sky. As she climbed back up the track towards the cottage, she spotted Libby approaching from the opposite direction, her neighbour's slow, slightly pigeon-toed gait unmistakeable even at a distance. Elin's stomach tightened. She couldn't face talking with anyone, let alone Libby, right now. Libby raised a hand to wave and Elin dropped her gaze sharply, before stepping up her pace. Hurriedly, she ducked inside, shutting the door quickly behind her, her heart pounding as though she'd just escaped something dangerous.

Inside, the cottage felt empty again. Lonely.

Elin remained there for a long moment, staring at the spot where Cai's hologram had appeared. Then she reached for her phone and called a cab.

*

As usual, the Hergest Unit smelled of disinfectant and stewed tea. Nerys was already in bed, but though it was late, no one objected to Elin entering the ward, the nurse on the reception desk offering her a warm smile. Enough time had elapsed since her last visit, and they couldn't expect her to stay away forever. Her sister lay propped against pillows, eyes heavy, hair unkempt. A glimmer of recognition lit her face as Elin approached, though her responses were slow and dull. No attempt to engage verbally. But at least she was reacting to things Elin was saying again, nodding intermittently; even smiling a little as if Elin's words registered with her. That was progress, wasn't it? Elin remembered what Dr Bianchi had said about keeping things light. She sat beside Nerys's bed and talked about the improving weather, about how much she'd missed the sea while she was in Birmingham; about nothing in particular. After last time, she knew to avoid making any mention of Mam, despite the fact that Nerys's words still haunted her. Though she still hadn't broken the news of Cai's death, Elin was desperate to tell her about the amazing hologram: the way he'd looked, the way his voice had sounded. But she couldn't; she knew that. Nerys still looked too thin, too frail; as though one wrong word might shatter her completely. This was a conversation for another day.

Instead, Elin fished for something else to fill the silence. 'Oh, I saw Libby earlier.'

Nerys's eyes seemed to focus instantly. She straightened, her knuckles growing white around the bedcovers. 'Libby?' Her response was sharp, staccato.

'Yes,' said Elin, confused by this sudden change in her. 'She was on the path coming up to the cottage.'

Nerys shook her head, her breathing faster now. 'No. No, you mustn't . . .' Her voice wavered. 'She shouldn't be there.'

Elin leaned forward, alarmed. 'Nerys? It's all right. She was just heading home.'

But Nerys was no longer listening, her gaze fixed somewhere beyond the room, her head wobbling as fear flickered across her face.

Elin reached for her sister's hand, her own heart sinking. The paranoia had clearly been subdued by the medication, nothing more. The hope she'd allowed herself that Nerys may have been improving was suddenly very small indeed.

*

Back at the cottage, Elin sat in the half-light, staring emptily at Nain's old chair. The atmosphere in the room seemed to have changed somehow, the memory of the grief-bot still hanging in the air. But she couldn't shake the thought of Nerys's troubled expression as she'd left the ward. What had made her sister react in that way? Could there have been something else – something other than losing Nain and the inevitable subsequent grief – that had driven her into such a debilitating state of anxiety? Could Nain's paranoia have triggered Nerys's own – or was there more to it?

Nerys's words on that last visit still kept turning through her mind.

'*Have you ever really thought about it properly*?'

Was there more to Mam's disappearance than she'd always

believed? If the police hadn't managed to uncover anything a decade ago, how the hell would she ever find out now?

The people who'd been in The Quay that night had all been spoken to, that much she knew. Ianto had mentioned a man called Griff, who had come to meet Mam in the pub, but Rhiannon said Mam had left well before him. Later on, an old acquaintance of Griff's had come in unexpectedly; they'd had a couple more drinks, and then left together once the downpour had abated – the acquaintance had joked that he'd timed it just right for a lift home, as he deposited his empty glass on the bar.

Elin sprang to her feet suddenly. What about the other man – the one Mam originally planned to meet that night in Moelfre? Had they ever questioned him? And if not, how the hell would they even trace him now? All Mam had said was that she'd met him when he came into Bethan's shop one day. Elin couldn't even remember his name. It may have been clutching at straws, but maybe – just *maybe* – Mam had written his number in her address book. If Elin saw the name, it might jog her memory.

She made her way upstairs and turned on Mam's bedroom light, catching her breath as her eyes took in the painfully familiar surroundings.

It was always a strange feeling, being in Mam's room. Even when Elin had been living at home, as time passed, she rarely went inside. It felt like a shrine; a constant reminder of Mam's absence, salt rubbed into a wound. Nerys had kept the room tidy – something it had never been when Mam was here. Nothing had been thrown away; even now, her clothes and shoes remained. Her make-up, trinkets. The wastepaper basket lined with a fresh, empty bag, ready for use. Almost as if, in spite of everything, Nerys had always clung to the hope of her breezing back in one day.

But from what she'd said to Elin, any hope Nerys might once

have had, had been replaced by something else. Something dark and unthinkable.

Elin went straight to the bedside drawer where she knew Mam had kept her little address book. She lifted out a pink gauze lavender bag, pressed it to her nose. The scent was still there, faint but definite. And right beneath it, next to a handful of loose change, a cellophane-wrapped pack of tissues and a half-empty tube of hand cream, was the book.

Elin sat on the bed and started to leaf through the staggered index with trembling fingers. She began at '*A*', working through alphabetically and methodically, her finger tracing every name, every address and phone number. She wasn't sure Mam had ever mentioned the man's surname – or whether she'd even known it. Such had been Elin's mother's love life: impulsive and erratic.

There were the usual contacts Elin would have expected to find: home, Bethan, Ianto. The hair salon. A handful of old school friends, plus several men's names – some familiar, some not – that Mam had put a line through; clearly people she'd wanted to consign to the past. She'd even added comments next to some of them. Elin raised an eyebrow at someone she'd labelled '*Octopus*' in red capitals.

'*Dipso Derfel*'. That one made Elin cringe.

She was surprised to find Harry Edwards under '*H*', crossed out with one line written next to it: '*H for Harassment*'. It didn't fit with how she herself had always thought of the man – but then, she was of a different generation, wasn't she? Perhaps he was a different kettle of fish if he took a romantic interest in someone. The thought made her slightly uncomfortable.

Elin got to the end and was about to give up hope when, as she flipped the last page, a slip of paper fell to the floor. She stooped to pick it up, turning it the right way round to read the almost illegible handwriting. It wasn't Mam's.

'*Will Roundtree.*'

A name, followed by a string of hurriedly scribbled digits.

That was it. That was *him*. Will. It came to Elin like a zap of electricity from somewhere in the recesses of her brain. Her heart quickened. *An actual phone number*. She would take this to the police the next morning, ask them to check if they'd ever spoken to the man.

In the aftermath of the storm, Elin had never considered that, much like Jac Parry's, Mam's departure was anything other than a tragic accident. She herself had only been fifteen, after all. She'd never questioned anything; never even wondered about her mother's date that evening. When Mam saw Ianto in The Quay the night she'd disappeared, she'd told him the date had turned out to be a non-starter, and that had been that. It was nothing new where Mam was concerned.

But what if he'd been an angry sort, someone who didn't take kindly to rejection?

Elin's stomach twisted at the idea that this Will Roundtree could have followed Mam back to Traeth Coch, quietly seething that she had thrown him over. Was it possible he might have harmed her? It was something she needed to find out.

Chapter 37

NOW – Saturday 20th May 2023

Elin

At nine o'clock the following morning, with the scrap of paper she'd found bearing the name and phone number tucked safely into her purse, Elin had taken a taxi to the nearest *Gorsaf Heddlu*, the police station in Bangor. It was becoming a bind, having to call for a cab every time she needed to go anywhere, not to mention costly. The swelling in her foot had diminished considerably now; although it hadn't completely healed, she had finally ditched the boot and was impatient to begin driving again. Another day or so should do it.

Elin felt wrung out, her eyes felt gritty from lack of sleep. She'd already announced herself and had been waiting for about twenty minutes for someone to talk to her. Now she was growing impatient. Eventually she'd risen from the uncomfortably hard plastic seat in the waiting area and approached the desk again.

The balding sergeant who'd just appeared on the reception desk looked up at her, his brow knitting. His chin was dark with stubble and he looked weary, as though he'd already done a full day's work and wanted to go home.

'What can I do for you?' It almost came out as a sigh. He didn't sound as if his heart was in doing anything at all.

'My name's Elin Owen. I told your colleague earlier – I was hoping to speak to someone who was involved with my mam's disappearance in October 2013,' Elin explained. 'Her name was Meinir Owen. She was believed to have drowned in Traeth Coch, on Anglesey. I think I may have found something that was overlooked at the time.'

The man puffed out his cheeks. 'D'you have any idea who the officers working the case were?'

'No, I'm afraid not.' She paused. 'Look, the thing is this—'

The officer raised a hand. 'Hold on. Let me see if I can find someone who can help you. Have a seat.'

'No thanks, I'd rather stand. That chair's sending my backside to sleep.'

The man raised an eyebrow, but said nothing. Turning his back for a moment, he made a phone call, although his voice was too quiet for Elin to hear what was being said. He seemed to be nodding slowly. Putting his hand over the mouthpiece, he swivelled round to address her briefly.

'Was this the same night a young lad drowned?'

Elin nodded. Her heart quickened. Maybe the person he was talking to was familiar with the case. The man went back to his phone call while she waited, hopeful that someone would come and speak to her.

The sergeant ended the call. He came back to the desk, giving her a tight smile. Elin studied his face optimistically.

'The main officer in charge of the investigation has sadly since passed away. But it seems the case was closed.' He cleared his throat. 'The young man that drowned – the verdict was accidental death. And I'm very sorry, but if someone has been missing over seven years, they are officially declared deceased.'

Elin shook her head vigorously. 'No, you've misunderstood. I'm not disputing that my mam is dead. What I wanted to show someone is the name and phone number of a man she was seeing the night she disappeared – I'm pretty sure he was never mentioned. I thought maybe . . .'

The man's face softened, but his tone had become infuriatingly patronising. 'Listen, Miss Owen, the case was closed for a reason. I remember that storm myself – shocking night, it was. But the investigation was thorough and it does sound as if your poor mam was as much a victim to it as that unfortunate young lad.' He dropped his eyes and began to shuffle some paperwork, as if to imply without saying as much that he'd finished dealing with her.

Anger started to rise in Elin. The officer glanced up at her in an almost pitying way, clearly thinking she was either not very bright or neurotic. Her nerves were frayed now and she was weary to the bone; something inside her snapped. The fury and exasperation in her voice were undisguised.

'For God's sake, aren't you at least going to ring the number I've found? Get him in for questioning?'

'On what grounds?' The sergeant's expression had grown suddenly stern. 'And anyway, I'm sure our officers would have spoken to this person during the original investigation. They'd have had the good sense to question anyone with a connection to your mother. It's standard procedure when someone has disappeared. Please don't try to tell us how to do our job.'

Elin was shaking. Her cheeks burned with rage. She could quite happily have thrown a punch over the counter.

'Well, the people on the case didn't do it very fucking well, did they?' Elin yelled into the man's face. 'Otherwise they'd have found my poor mam.'

The sergeant put down his paperwork and drew himself up, glaring at her. His voice became officious and hard. 'We don't tolerate foul language or being verbally abused in here. I'm going to have to ask you to leave. Either that, or I'll find you a nice quiet cell until you calm down.'

Elin said no more. Her heart thudding with rage and frustration, she turned on her heel and pushed her way through the swinging doors and back out onto the street. She stood for several minutes, taking deep breaths to pacify herself, before eventually flagging down another cab.

Arriving home later, Elin had calmed down and begun to think more rationally. She realised, reluctantly, that the sergeant had probably been right – Will Roundtree would most likely have been eliminated from the police's enquiries at the time of the original investigation. She had been clutching at straws, wound herself up unnecessarily and very nearly got herself arrested.

What a complete waste of a taxi fare that had been.

Chapter 38

BEFORE – March 2023

Nerys

Since Bethan had paid him, there had thankfully been no repercussions after Nerys's uncomfortable set-to with Hugh Roberts. But given the horrible way he'd reacted, she'd been careful to avoid the man. His behaviour had made her put things into perspective and look at other people in a different light. Peter, for one. Unlike Roberts, he'd never done her any harm. Nerys was glad now that she'd decided to keep schtum about the solicitor's letter. She didn't know the circumstances – and it just didn't tie in with the Peter she had come to know. The more she thought about it, the more she wondered whether it could all have arisen from a misunderstanding or a wrongful accusation. These things happened, didn't they? People were accused of things, then evidence would come to light years later and there would have to be a public apology. It wasn't even impossible it could have been a case of mistaken identity.

That Tuesday had been a very long day in the shop, and Nerys was so glad she could lie in for an hour or so the next morning. As she closed the front door behind her, all she wanted to do was have supper, watch some mindless telly and get an early night. Her relief at having Nyten home was dampened by the constant worry that someone had actually deliberately hurt the little cat. Nerys felt mean, but was keeping her in the house for the time being. Thankfully, since her misadventure, Nyten didn't seem too keen to go outside anyway.

Nerys washed up after eating, and had just sat down on the settee beside Nyten with a cup of tea, when there was a sharp rap at the front door. The curtains were already closed and she couldn't see who was calling on her. Warily, she went to answer it, opening it only a fraction and peering through the gap.

On her doorstep stood Hugh Roberts. He looked oddly sheepish, an expression she'd never seen on his puffed up face before. What the hell did he want now? Every muscle in her body clenched.

'Yes?' Her voice was terse. She glanced down to see he was holding out something in the flat of both hands, wrapped in a plastic bag.

The man cleared his throat. 'I just wanted – my mam thought – you might like these.' He thrust the bag forward, his cheeks flushing beneath the glow of the door lantern. Nerys stared through the aperture, her eyes narrowing in suspicion.

'What are they?'

Roberts squirmed. 'Look, it's a couple of pies, that's all. Vegetarian ones. We've started stocking them in the shop lately. I'm right in thinking you don't eat meat?'

Nerys nodded. She opened the door wider and took the bag hesitantly, taking care to keep it level, and peeled back the plastic to examine the contents. Inside were four glossy-crusted pies, decorated with pastry leaves, each a generous size for one person.

'Oh. *Diolch*.' She wasn't sure what to say.

The high colour in Roberts's cheeks had subsided slightly. 'Two are mushroom, potato and onion, and the others are butternut squash and leek. Pretty good, considering there's no meat in them.' He offered her a tight smile. 'I thought after . . . about, well, about that business with the van. Mam said I always overreact to stuff. I'd had a shit day and that was the final straw. You know how it can be.' He grimaced. 'Anyway – um . . .' Roberts seemed lost for words, fidgeting a little where he stood. He scratched the back of his head, his eyes not meeting hers.

Nerys stared up at him, slightly bemused. It was as if the man had had some sort of personality transplant. Although, it didn't alter the fact that Bethan had had to fork out £900 for the damage to his van on her behalf. She wondered whether he was genuinely sorry or just trying to sweeten her up after the disgust about his callous attitude expressed by some of his customers. She'd heard through the grapevine that it had begun to affect his business. Nain had always said his mam was a wily old soul – she'd obviously told him it was a good idea to have Nerys on side. But whatever his motive, it was better than having to fear bumping into him whenever she was out and about. It wasn't nice, feeling the constant need to avoid someone.

Nerys managed a smile. 'Well, they sound very nice. I'll look forward to trying them.'

Roberts nodded, his mouth curving upwards in a slightly self-satisfied way, as though confident now his mission had been successful. 'I'll let you get on, then. Let me know what you think of the pies. I'll be ordering more if people like them. *Nos dawch*.'

'*Nos dawch*.' Nerys closed the door behind him and stood for a moment, not knowing quite how she should feel. A sudden grin tugged at her lips at the memory of Roberts's unwonted awkwardness. It must have really pained him, having to apologise – even if it had been in a roundabout way.

Now there was a first.

Nerys put the pies into the fridge, then settled back down to watch TV with Nyten curled into her lap. She would have to tell Bethan about Roberts. She wondered what she'd make of it all.

Wednesday morning began with a fresh breeze ruffling the cottage, a sound Nerys was happiest hearing from beneath the warmth of the duvet. She stood at the living room window, hands wrapped around a mug of tea, and watched as fluffy clouds were swept across the lightening sky. Her nain had loved this hour; had called it the quiet edge of the day, before reality set in and the daily slog began.

Nerys told herself she was only going to sort a little at a time, only do what needed to be done. There was no rush. The cottage was still thick with Nain's presence – her preferred lavender polish, the faintly medicinal scent of the hand cream she'd always used and that Nerys had now adopted. Drawers remained stuffed too full because, though Nain was a natural hoarder, throwing things away had felt like a kind of betrayal. Months had passed since she'd been laid to rest, yet the rooms still resisted being emptied, as though they were waiting for the old woman to shuffle back in from her morning walk across the beach with some new tale to share.

Nerys heaved a battered cardboard box down from her grandmother's bedroom, setting it on the rug by Nain's armchair. Charity, recycling, keep: she knelt beside the chair and began to make neat piles on the floor, trying to be practical and to remain detached; trying not to feel as though she were discarding things that had obviously meant enough to Nain that she'd stored them carefully away. About how her own day off was supposed to be a rest day, rather than a reckoning.

This particular box had been heavier than she'd expected. Inside were gloves and folded scarves, old Georgette Heyer novels. A school photo of Mam, its glass cracked. A small brown teddy bear, the stuffing spilling out of one foot, waiting to be repaired. At the bottom was a bundle of envelopes, secured with a faded blue ribbon. Nerys hesitated. Letters had a way of revealing the past, and she'd learned lately how unsettling that could be.

She untied the ribbon anyway and began to slowly leaf through the pile.

Most of the envelopes bore her nain's slightly shaky hand in some form. There were Christmas cards that had never been sent, old bank statements; paid bills with dates scribbled across the front. But another made her pause.

Though she couldn't explain why, her stomach tightened before she even picked it up. The envelope was yellowed, the corners dog-eared, addressed in block capitals to their home but with no named addressee.

Nerys rose to sit in Nain's chair, the springs creaking beneath her, and turned the envelope over as if it might bite. She thought immediately of the solicitor's letter that had arrived days earlier by mistake, pushed through her own letterbox addressed to Peter with a redirection scrawled across the front. She'd persuaded herself it was nothing, some old business that had no bearing on the man who waved cheerfully over the hedge and offered help free of charge to anyone who needed it. She had said nothing to anyone.

The thin paper inside the envelope trembled slightly as she unfolded it. The handwriting was slightly unsteady, though the letters were capitalised and clear enough.

Nerys's eyes widened in horror as she began to read.

Chapter 39

NOW – Monday 22nd May 2023

Elin

Elin had spent Sunday bitterly regretting her visit to the *Gorsaf Heddlu* in Bangor. But it was pointless dwelling on it: though she now felt a little foolish, she told herself it had been something she needed to get out of her system. She thought of something Nain had said once: 'Learn from your mistakes, but don't waste energy beating yourself up about them. Life's too short'. It seemed like good advice.

She was counting down the days until Aaron had repaired the holo-box, but until then she needed to do something constructive, rather than moping about. It was futile, going over and over what had happened to Mam in her mind, too. The best thing she could do was to get out of the house for a while. Away from Traeth Coch.

Though it was probably woefully inadequate, Elin had been thinking she'd like to take Nerys a little gift when she next visited. Her sister had always loved knick-knacks – Elin couldn't do much else for her at the moment, but at least it would be a gesture of sorts. And hopefully a distraction from Nerys's troubled frame of mind.

Bethan's shop was a veritable emporium and there was sure to be something Elin could find for Nerys. Something that would demonstrate how sorry she was for not having been there for her, without having to say much else. Something that might lift her spirits a little. Though she hadn't driven for weeks, she'd decided to risk it. If she was careful, she should be fine – she'd take Nerys's little red Toyota Aygo, which probably needed a run anyway after sitting idle in the lane for so long.

Arriving in Beaumaris, Elin parked round the corner from Bethan's shop and sat for a moment with the engine ticking, her hands resting on the wheel. It was a clear day and busy, almost lunchtime. She caught the waft of fish and chips as she climbed from the car, remembering with a pang sharing a bag of chips on the pier with Cai the previous spring. Cai had laughed at her indignation when a gull swooped in to lift a beak-full of chips from the paper in her lap. He'd bought her an ice cream later; '*to cushion the blow*,' he'd teased.

He should have been with her now. She recalled him pulling a face as she'd stopped to look at the painted driftwood hearts in Bethan's window, playfully mocking her for liking them. '*Soppy*,' he'd called them. But he'd thrust a paper bag at her when they got home, having bought one when she wasn't looking. She could still picture the unmistakeable look of love in his eyes as he'd handed it over. The memory landed, bittersweet, bringing a lump to her throat.

Inside, the shop was warm; cluttered, but in a nice way, and humming with the low radio Bethan always kept behind the counter. Bethan looked up and smiled, the lines around her eyes creasing into something kind but slightly worried.

'Hello, you. Everything okay?'

Elin nodded, squeezing a small smile as she cast about. 'I needed to get out for a while.' She let out a long breath. 'It's been ages since I've been here.'

'I know. I remember Cai . . .' Bethan broke off awkwardly. She studied Elin for a moment, her head cocked. 'Did you just want a chat or can I tempt you with something? Would you like a *panad* while you're here?'

Elin shook her head. 'No, I'm fine thanks.' She dropped her gaze for a moment.

'I'm looking for something small – just a token for now. Something for Nerys. To show her I'm thinking of her.'

Bethan's lips curved upwards. 'Aww that's a lovely idea.' Her eyes roamed the shelves of bric-a-brac. 'Well, take your pick – mates' rates and all that.' She nodded towards a display in the far corner. 'Got some lovely hand-painted pottery, just in.'

Elin wandered, touching watercolour prints, glazed bowls and floaty, printed scarves, until she found a small ceramic dish decorated with quirky little cats. It seemed the right size: useful, pretty – the sort of thing her sister would love. She imagined Nerys's hands, the careful way she always held things, and felt the heat of shame rise again at the thought of how alone she must have felt and the mental anguish she had been through. Bethan wrapped the dish in tissue paper, saying that it was a sound choice, something Nerys would definitely appreciate once she was better. Her eyes lingered on Elin's face as if she was still worried about her and she gave her hand a gentle squeeze as she was about to leave.

'It's good to see you out and about, cariad. You look after yourself now.'

Elin followed the coast road home, the more twisty but scenic route. The sea glistened in her peripheral vision, soon opening out into the Menai Strait, gulls circling the tall masts of boats moored along its banks. She'd missed this. She'd missed her homeland. If only Cai were here now; if only Nerys were well again. Tears pricked her eyes once more.

Arriving back in Traeth Coch, she pulled up on the track outside the cottage, the afternoon light glinting from the windows. The building looked sad, somehow. She felt Nain's absence even more keenly now; Nerys's, too. On top of everything else, it wasn't nice, being here all alone and feeling as though she'd provoked hostility from her neighbour. Maybe she needed to clear the air with Libby, even if she didn't really feel like apologising. Elin decided to tap on the door before going home. She lifted the wrapped dish from the passenger seat, took a breath and opened the gate to Libby and Peter's cottage, rehearsing what she would say: '*Just wanted to say I don't want any ill feeling. I'm not myself right now. Can we draw a line under everything?*'

Her neighbours' garden was neat as ever, the soil evenly turned, the rhododendrons in full bloom. As Elin walked up the path, she glanced toward the front window and stopped.

Through the net curtain, she could see Libby, sitting in her armchair, shoulders rounded. Peter's bulk loomed over her, close enough that his shadow swallowed her face. His mouth was moving in an exaggerated fashion, lips peeled back to show his teeth, and though Elin couldn't hear him through the glass, something in his posture made her stomach roil. He lifted an arm; not fully, but enough, and Elin saw Libby shrink back, her chin ducking as if expecting the blow.

Elin gasped. Nerys's gift, which she'd almost forgotten about, nearly slipped from her hands, but she caught it just in time. Peter turned his head sharply then, as if he'd sensed her, and his eyes found her through the window. For a fraction of a second his expression remained unchecked, ugly and vicious, before it smoothed itself into something more palatable.

Elin stepped back, her heart hammering, and turned away quickly. She stumbled down the path, aware of his eyes still on her, her neck prickling. By the time she reached her own gate she felt faintly sick, the salty air catching her throat.

Once inside, she sank into the settee. Everyone thought Peter was solid, helpful. The man who fixed fences and mowed lawns. She thought of Ianto's lowered, anxious voice; telling her about the incident with Rhiannon in the pub. Peter needed watching, he'd implied, and she'd dismissed his warning too readily. She pressed her palms flat against the cushions and drew in a breath to calm herself.

Maybe things in Swift Cabin weren't as harmonious as she'd always believed.

Chapter 40

NOW – Tuesday 23rd May 2023

Elin

Morning came, the sky cobalt blue and cloudless, the kind of Anglesey day that Elin had often pined for on grey, fume-filled days in Birmingham. She had slept badly and turned over to feel an uncomfortable knot in her chest. In her dreams, she'd seen Cai through a crowd and had been running, trying to reach him, but all the time he moved further and further into the distance. She'd woken abruptly in the early hours, her face wet with tears. But now the memory of what she'd witnessed the previous afternoon resurged and her whole body grew taut.

Elin switched on her phone, checking for messages. There was just the one, from Catrin, asking how she was doing. She thought about explaining what had happened with Peter. But no, it wasn't something she wanted to share over a message. She responded with a *meh* emoji, and a one-liner to say she'd call her later. She made her way downstairs to make tea, then sat in the living room, staring up at the window. Though she still wanted to clear the air with Libby, the thought of what she'd seen was clouding her mind. She had no desire to see Peter and resolved to wait until he was safely out of the way.

Elin needed air, needed a walk to clear her head. Pulling on her coat, she forced herself to step outside and stood for a moment, staring out at the expanse of sand gleaming at low tide. As usual, several anchored boats sat skew-whiff along the seam at the periphery of the rockier end of the beach, making her wonder whether they had been repaired after the latest attack. What on earth would motivate anyone to do a thing like that? Some people were really twisted.

She had just locked the door when she turned to see Peter, appearing at the end of the lane. Elin caught her breath, her heart quickening. He was walking up from the beach with his spade in his hand. He lifted it in greeting, smiling as if everything was perfectly normal. As if she hadn't witnessed something she shouldn't have.

'Elin,' he said. 'Got a minute?'

She hesitated, her fist tightening around her keys. He came closer than felt necessary, stopping just inside her gate. She noticed how his eyes kept searching her face, the lightness of his tone covering an underlying uncertainty.

'I just wanted to clear something up,' he said, giving an odd, unnatural little laugh. 'You must've got the wrong end of the stick yesterday. What you saw, it wasn't what it looked like.'

Elin's mouth felt dry. 'Oh? What was it, then?'

He waved a hand. 'I was just demonstrating something. Libby's got a touch of arthritis – her shoulder's been playing up. I was showing her an exercise. I made a joke of it, that's all. Bad timing, you looking in when you did.' He smiled again, but his eyes remained cold.

Elin remembered Libby cowering, the way the woman's body had folded inwards. She drew herself up slightly. 'It didn't look like she was finding it very funny from where I was standing.'

Peter's jaw clenched, just for a second. 'Libby's a bit sensitive,' he said. 'You know that, I'm sure. I'd hate for there to be . . . a misunderstanding.' His gaze narrowed, and Elin felt the weight of it, heavy and almost threatening.

Something knotted in her chest. 'Right,' she said. 'I should get on.'

He stood there a moment longer than was comfortable, then stepped back. 'Of course,' he said, squeezing another smile. 'Don't forget, if you ever need us, you know where we are. Any time.'

Elin watched as he retreated into his own garden and disappeared into the house. Abandoning the idea of a walk, she went back inside and closed the door, leaning against it as her pulse thudded.

The cottage was eerily quiet now. Elin felt uncomfortably exposed. She took out her phone with hands that shook and went straight to her recent messages and Catrin's name. She pressed the phone icon and willed her friend to pick up.

'Hiya, doll.' Catrin's response was breezy. 'Everything okay?'

'Um not really. Can you come round?' Elin responded, trying to keep her voice steady. 'Now, if you're not too busy.'

Catrin paused. 'Erm, Aaron hasn't quite finished with the hologram, but . . .'

'No; no, it's not that. Could you come over anyway? I— there's something I want to talk to you about and I'd rather not do it by text.'

'Oh. Yeah, I've just got a couple of things to do here, then I'll be on my way.'

'*Diolch*. See you soon.'

As she hung up, Elin blew out a long breath. She glanced

towards the window, her stomach plummeting. If Libby *was* in an abusive relationship, the last thing the woman needed was to feel isolated. Maybe she and Catrin should go round, talk to her. Offer her some support.

It was the least she could do.

Chapter 41

BEFORE – March 2023

Nerys

Nerys couldn't take it in. The letter was, in no uncertain terms, a complete character assassination on their neighbour. Unless both had been hoaxes, or from some crank with an irrational grudge against Peter, this time she couldn't just ignore it. One letter, sent years ago, she could have dismissed as a clerical error. But a second – expressing a similar message – from a completely different source? Her mind whirred as her eyes moved over the page once more.

> HELLO, I AM WRITING TO WARN YOU ABOUT YOUR NEIGHBOUR, PETER FOWLER. HE IS A SNEAKY, MALICIOUS INDIVIDUAL WHO CAN'T BE TRUSTED. HE SMASHED MY WINDOW AND SLASHED MY CAR'S TYRES FOR NO REASON. HE POISONED FISH IN A

POND BELONGING TO ANOTHER PERSON IN OUR COMMUNITY. HE HAS MADE MY LIFE, AND THAT OF OTHERS, HELL AND I'VE NO DOUBT HE WILL DO THE SAME TO SOMEONE ELSE. HE CAN'T BE ALLOWED TO GET AWAY WITH IT ANY MORE. PEOPLE NEED TO KNOW WHAT SORT OF MAN HE IS. I KNOW WHERE HE LIVES NOW SO I'M MAKING IT MY BUSINESS TO WARN YOU. DON'T BE TAKEN IN BY THE GOOD NEIGHBOUR ACT. A SMILING ASSASSIN, THAT'S WHAT HE IS.

That was all. No signature, no address. Just the words, shouting earnestly from the page as if they were desperately trying to reach someone. She peered at the postmark on the envelope. Though it was faint, she was able to make out that it had been mailed locally. But Peter and Libby had moved from the Midlands, hadn't they? It made no sense.

Nerys stared at the letter until the room seemed to swim around her. The roar of the wind outside was louder now, or perhaps she was only hearing it differently, every gust edged with threat. Her nain's agitated voice rose unbidden in her mind, low and insistent.

'That Peter isn't right, I'm telling you. Dw i wedi gweld e. *I've been watching him. Smiles like butter wouldn't melt, but there's a knife underneath.'*

Nain's words rang in her ears.

Nerys had nodded then, soothed her with what she now saw as patronising reassurances. She'd blamed the disease. Dementia could make enemies out of shadows; everyone knew that. She had dismissed it all, gently but firmly, the way you might dismiss a child frightened by a bad dream.

Now her skin prickled with the memory of it.

She thought of Peter's benign face, the proud tidiness of his garden; Libby's fluting laugh when they chatted over the fence.

And then she remembered that day he'd been burning rubbish, the snarky comments about neighbours letting the side down that she'd overheard. Had she been too ready to accept his apology – and had it even been genuine? She thought of how easily people could put on a front; how things were not always as they seemed. Even with Nain gone and Elin so far away, living alone had never troubled her before – not in this way. She was surrounded by a caring community. This was home, warm and safe.

Wasn't it?

Nerys clumsily folded the letter again and slipped it back into the envelope. Her nain had kept it. Not forgotten it in the fog of her failing memory, but tucked it away, saved it, as though the thing might be some sort of safeguard in the future.

Outside, a gull shrieked suddenly. The piercing sound seemed amplified, echoing from the chimney and making Nerys cover her ears.

She didn't know what to do. Whether to tell Bethan, or Elin, or even the police. Although it might potentially open a whole can of worms – and she was here, all alone, with Peter living only a few feet away. Nerys felt terrible now, having patronised poor Nain and chosen to ignore her words when there had clearly been actual reasoning behind them. But what was it that her grandmother had seen Peter doing?

Nerys imagined him forcing something – a door, a window; testing the weak points of someone else's house. Or something more spiteful and calculated: poisoning a garden, cutting through wires, loosening tiles so that they would slip later without warning. The kind of harm that would allow someone to walk away whistling, while chaos bloomed behind them.

Her nain had lived long enough to recognise that kind of inner malice. She had known hardship and grief, survived the loss of her husband and then her beloved daughter. She'd watched neighbours turn on each other over petty squabbles and imagined slights. She knew that people could hide behind smiles and pleasantries.

Nerys gathered the letter and the rest of the bundle together, holding them against her chest for a moment. Her head was spinning. The atmosphere in the cottage felt suddenly different, as if it had long been an unwilling harbour of secrets it was finally ready to reveal.

Nerys wished fiercely now that Nain was still there to ask. Even confused, even raving, she had clearly known things. She *had* been watching.

And now, it seemed, so would Nerys have to be.

Chapter 42

NOW – Tuesday 23rd May 2023

Traeth Coch

Elin

'So you think Peter was going to hit her?' Catrin looked appalled. 'Fuck.'

Elin nodded, her face grim. 'I mean, what the hell should I do? I didn't actually see him *do* anything – but it was that horrible look on his face more than anything. It made my skin crawl.'

Catrin shuddered. 'I know he was verbally aggressive with Rhi in the pub once. Didn't think he could be violent, though.'

They sat on the settee, mugs of coffee gripped in their hands, both looking towards the window. The view was the same as ever: boats bobbing, people going about their business, gulls wheeling as they always did. As if nothing had changed. Elin watched the water shift from pewter to iron grey and back under a sky that seemed unable to decide how to behave. The rocky perimeter of the beach stretched away below the path, the sand beyond darkened by the recent high tide, choppy waves easing back.

How she wished Cai was there. The thought came like a punch to the gut. He would have known what to do, what to say. He'd always been steady; always fair and rational in his point of view. Elin felt hot tears rush to her eyes and mopped at them with her free hand.

Catrin watched her for a moment, looking suddenly uncomfortable. Her gaze settled on the object wrapped in paper on the sideboard. She gave a small cough. 'Is that the present you got Nerys?' she asked. 'I know you said you were going to get something for her.'

Elin nodded. She cleared her throat. 'Yeah. I found it at Bethan's place. It's a dish, decorated with cats. She loves anything like that.'

She put down her mug and rose to pick up the package. Bethan had wrapped it expertly, brown paper folded neatly around the tissue paper within, twine tied in a careful bow. Through the wrapper she could feel the small bowl. The thought of handing it over to Nerys had given her a little lift. But what she had seen last night and her earlier exchange with Peter had obliterated any brief sense of lightness. She turned to Catrin. 'Will you come with me? To speak to Libby?'

Catrin nodded. ''Course. I'll be interested to hear what she's got to say about it.'

Elin tipped her head in next door's direction. 'As soon as he goes out, we'll go round.'

They waited, the room charged with anxious energy, until the slam of the neighbours' door was heard. Elin jumped to her feet, to see the back of Peter's white head disappearing through the gate. They watched as he plodded down the track. The moment he turned right towards The Quay, Elin felt her pulse quicken.

'Come on, let's go,' she said.

They hurried out of the front door and up the path to the neighbouring cottage. The place looked the same as ever from the outside: the blue door with the little swifts' nest peering from the portico, the potted bay trees flanking the entrance. But in Elin's mind it had taken on a sinister aspect, as though it were putting on a front. Elin knocked and felt, absurdly, as if daring to cross the threshold could be potentially perilous.

Libby opened the door almost at once. She summoned a brittle smile.

'Elin. Catrin. Come in, come in.' She stood back, hands fluttering awkwardly, then clapped them together as if she was catching a ball.

Inside, the air smelled faintly of polish. Elin noticed how tidy everything was. Too tidy, perhaps. Maybe Libby was rather obsessive about housework, about having everything orderly. Maybe it was the one thing she had control over in her life. The thought made Elin feel suddenly guilty.

'I was coming to see you yesterday,' Elin said, her hands clasped in front of her a little self-consciously. Though she knew Peter wasn't likely to return immediately, her focus was constantly drawn to the window. 'Just to say sorry. For ranting at you before.'

Libby's eyes widened. 'Oh. There's no need. I mean, I realise you were upset. I know you're going through a lot at the moment . . .'

'I thought—' Elin began, then stopped. She pictured the raised arm she'd seen through the window the day before, Peter's twisted face, Libby's bowed head. The memory made her stomach lurch. But how was she going to broach the subject? She turned to her friend, her eyes imploring.

Catrin cleared her throat. 'Elin was telling me – she saw Peter yesterday, through the window,' she said, her voice hesitant. 'Standing over you.'

Libby laughed. It was an unnatural, nervous sound. 'Oh, *that*. Honestly. You mustn't worry.' She stood beside her gleaming sideboard, absently pushing the ornaments back from the edge. 'He was just showing me an exercise. For my shoulder. It's the arthritis – it's been playing me up a lot lately. He'd been reading up about it.'

Elin watched Libby's hands as she spoke, fiddling now with the buttons on her cardigan. The woman's eyes seemed to oscillate. The response had sounded rehearsed, coached. She scrutinised Libby's body language, noticing something travelling up and down in her throat.

'Libby, he had his hand lifted above you,' Elin said quietly.

'And then he put it down,' Libby said. The response was sharp, defensive. 'Oh, he's always waving about when he speaks. He gets a bit carried away sometimes.' She smiled again, less broadly this time. 'Honestly, I'd tell you if there was anything to tell.'

Elin thought of what Ianto had said, about there being a dark side to Peter. She wanted to believe Libby. She wanted it all to be a horrible misunderstanding. But she wasn't convinced.

At once, Libby shifted the conversation, to talk first about a fete the church were organising, then asking Catrin how things were on the farm. It was clear she wasn't going to be pressed further on the matter they really wanted to discuss, when Libby announced that she didn't want to be rude, but she had jobs she needed to get on with.

Elin and Catrin realised they had been gradually steered back towards the front door. When they stepped back outside, the breeze was colder. They stood on the path for a moment, neither of them speaking, the roar of the tide and the keen wind smothering any other sound.

Catrin blew out her cheeks. She turned to look at Elin. 'I don't buy it.'

'Neither do I,' Elin responded. 'But what can we do?'

Movement below them on the sand drew Elin's attention suddenly. She turned to see Peter's distinctive white hair as he strode back across the beach, eyes fixed straight ahead. Reaching the end of the path, he looked up. His gaze slid over Catrin, then landed on Elin, flat and cold.

'Come on,' said Elin hastily. 'Let's get back inside.'

They hurried back into the cottage, shutting the door behind them. Through the window, Elin saw Peter pause at his gate, just briefly, staring up at her window before continuing into his own house. A shudder passed through her. It felt as if something had been set in motion and she didn't want to contemplate what it might be.

Chapter 43

NOW – Wednesday 24th May 2023

Bethan

Bethan had driven to work early that morning. It was only 6.45 a.m. and the main road descending into Beaumaris was deserted, many of the pastel-painted terraced houses with their curtains still closed. But she had so much to do: an extra couple of hours before opening would make all the difference. She'd been restless, woken just after five o'clock worrying about her mam and Elin, among other things, and thought she might as well make the most of the time as she was already up.

Somehow Bethan sensed something was wrong before she fully understood what it was.

The side street where she always parked had seemed ominously quiet, even for that time of morning: gulls silently lining the rooftops like sentries, the pier stretching emptily behind her. She slowed as she turned the corner, keys already in her hand, her mind still on stock she needed to reorder and a framed print she'd promised to wrap for a lady who was calling to collect it later.

Then she saw the shopfront.

For a moment, she was confused, her brain refusing to make sense of it. The window looked odd. Darker than it should have been, the reflection of the street fractured into jagged shapes. She took another step, then another, her stomach tightening as the reality came into focus.

Broken glass. Everywhere.

The nautical-themed display she'd arranged so carefully the previous afternoon lay buried under ice-like shards, the early morning sunlight glinting off them. A blue-and-white striped ceramic bowl had tipped onto its side, miraculously unbroken, and was surrounded by glittering debris. The bell on the door hung still, as if holding its breath.

Bethan stopped dead on the pavement. She became suddenly aware of her own heartbeat thrumming in her ears, loud and uneven. Who could have done this? Someone had stood here, right outside, and hurled something with enough force to shatter the expanse of lovingly polished glass that people always peered through as they admired the contents of her little shop.

She pushed the door open cautiously. The crunch underfoot made her flinch. Inside, the space felt cold, the sea-salt smell of the outdoors permeating the air, overriding the usual fragrance of reed-diffusers and the oils she would often burn. On the floor near the centre of the shop lay a dull terracotta brick, a solid, unwelcome intruder, incongruous among the quirky figurines and balsa wood sailing boats.

She bent down, hands trembling as she carefully picked fragments from the surface of a little calico cat dressed as a pirate. And then her eyes landed on the square of paper. It was wrapped tightly around the brick with a brittle rubber band, one word written in thick, angry black strokes. Bethan stared at it, heat rushing to her face, then draining away just as fast. The shop felt suddenly exposed, the wide empty window like an unblinking eye glaring back at her.

Her first instinct was to rush back outside, scan up and down the street, as if the perpetrator might still be there, watching gleefully from behind a parked car or secreted in a doorway. But the road looked the same as it always did – peaceful, indifferent, carrying on as if nothing had happened.

Bethan straightened slowly. The keys slipped from her hand and clattered onto the tiles, the sound making her jump. She stood there amid the broken glass, the brick at her feet, the cold realisation of what had happened leaching into her bones.

This wasn't an accident. And it wasn't a random attack.

It was aimed at her.

*

Bethan managed to restore some sort of order before the glazier arrived. She swept up the glass, picking up items and brushing them off carefully. Astonishingly, a hand-painted cup and saucer set were the only true casualties. She stood aimlessly in the doorway of her shop long after the man had finished, the smell of sealant still hanging in the air. The replacement pane looked wrong somehow – too clean, too shiny – even more than usual. Like it was pretending nothing had happened. On the ledge beneath it, a few glittering shards clung stubbornly to the frame, catching the light.

She picked up the brick and turned it over in her hands again. It was heavy, as she'd have expected, ordinary in every way except for the scrap of paper still bound to it with the thick rubber band. The ugly word scrawled across it seemed to throb when she looked at it, angry and pointed. *Whore*.

She'd felt too embarrassed to share this particular fact with the operative from the insurance company that she'd spoken to over the phone, but the presence of the thrown brick was sufficient for them not to quibble. An act of vandalism, the woman had confirmed, commiserating. Self-evident.

But this was clearly not an act of mindless vandalism. Bethan knew, that for whatever reason, she had been singled out.

Across the road, the café door swung shut as Glan, the owner, went back inside, leaving Bethan alone with her thoughts. Glan's CCTV covered the length of the pavement outside Bethan's premises and those which flanked it, and on his small monitor, they'd rewound the grainy footage again and again. Bethan kept picturing those same few chilling seconds playing out: the hooded figure emerging from the darkness of the side street she always parked in, its arm swinging, the glass exploding. And then, that pause. The furtive glance around. As if checking whether anyone was watching.

After her visit to Elin, she hadn't slept much anyway, but now fatigue overwhelmed Bethan: a heavy, bone-deep weariness. Beaumaris had always felt safe to her – a bustling place of vibrant shops and familiar, friendly faces, where she knew who liked which scented candles and who always asked about her mam. Now the street felt altered, tainted by what had happened. Every doorway looked capable of hiding someone. Every passer-by was a potential suspect.

Was it someone she knew? A disgruntled customer she'd refused a refund to? Maybe even those kids she'd suspected of shoplifting the other week and frog-marched out of the door? Someone who resented her shop, her presence here; her name on the sign?

Or could it have been someone whose advances she'd rejected? The thought sent a slow shiver through her. Hugh Roberts, standing by her car at Traeth Coch that day, his face hardening, his pride dented. She wanted to believe it had been meant for someone else entirely, an error of location or identity. No, this felt too considered. *That word*. It was no mistake. For someone to do such a thing, they'd have made sure they were hitting the right target.

Bethan locked up early, the sound of the key far too loud in the quiet of the afternoon. As she walked away, her eyes scanning the street once more, she felt an unsettling certainty creep through her: whoever had thrown the brick hadn't just wanted to break the window.

They had wanted her to know she was hated.

Chapter 44

NOW – Wednesday 24th May 2023

Elin

It had been a torturous night. Everything that had been happening ricocheted through Elin's brain: the holo-bot, the uncomfortable situation with Peter and Libby; Nerys's agitation. The gulls had begun to shatter the silence now, their amplifying cackles telling her the rest of the bay would soon be waking.

Eventually Elin got up to make herself coffee. She opened the living room curtains to a dove-grey sky, the sea choppy and restless. Peter and Libby were walking down the track towards the beach, arm in arm. From behind, they looked like a pair of bookends, each with their short, straight white hair, not much difference in height. She saw Libby turn to say something to Peter and they both laughed. The sight unsettled Elin somehow.

She curled into an armchair and stared at the space where Cai's hologram had stood, almost willing it to materialise again.

Closing her eyes for a moment, Elin spoke to Cai in her head. *Give me a sign*, she pleaded. *Something to let me know you're still around.* She thought about the conversation they'd had all those months ago. Cai musing about the continuation of the soul. More than anything in the world, she wished it were actually true. But having seen no real evidence of it, now, more than ever, she was desperate to see the grief-bot again. How she wished Cai were here to offer his calm, rational advice; to give her another perspective on everything that was going on. Would he have believed Peter? Had she misconstrued what she'd seen?

Scrolling through her phone, she pored repeatedly over old messages she and Cai had exchanged, looking for patterns in his style of speech that could have been used to create the artificial version of him. Right now, she didn't care if it wasn't real: in any guise, it was so much better than not seeing him at all. She kept waiting for a text to come though from Catrin. She didn't want to pester her, but hoped that Aaron had finally got the box back to her. Finally, she succumbed to her impulses and tapped out a couple of lines, then waited anxiously for a response. Elin kept checking; the message had delivered, but frustratingly her words remained unread.

The morning dragged. Elin forced herself to take a shower, checking her phone again the second she'd stepped out. Her heart gave an odd little leap. Catrin had texted to say she would be on her way in the next half-hour or so.

Elin sat on the settee, legs tucked beneath her, the soft afternoon light spilling through the window, as she waited with butterflies in her stomach for her friend to arrive. When Catrin stepped inside, it felt as if the cottage took in a breath, as if the building itself was now in anticipation of what she was bringing. She cradled the box like something precious and alive.

'There you go, he's finally fixed it,' Catrin said, a little breathlessly. 'Aaron, I mean. He said he's replaced some component or other and recalibrated everything. Reckons it should be okay now.'

Elin nodded. She felt briefly unable to move. She stared at the holo-box, praying it wouldn't fail this time. The shattered image from last time still bounced round her head: Cai's face pixelating, his mouth frozen on his closing words. It had left her yearning for more.

Catrin set the box on the low table between them once again. Her hands lingered a moment, fingers splayed on the casing. 'You don't have to turn it on straight away.'

'I know. But . . .' Elin surprised herself by reaching forward immediately, touching the cool metal. It vibrated faintly but reassuringly under her palm. 'Thanks so much for bringing it back. It was good of Aaron to fix it so quickly.'

Catrin's lips curved upwards, but the smile wavered as her eyes landed on the box. 'He was fine about it – likes a challenge, he says. He's told me to ring later, let him know whether the thing holds out this time.' She paused, tipping her head towards the window. 'Anything more from next door?'

Elin shook her head. 'All quiet on the Western Front.' She sighed. 'Maybe it's me. Maybe I jumped to the wrong conclusion. I mean, I'm all over the place at the moment.'

Catrin arced an eyebrow. 'Well, I for one wasn't swallowing her story. You hear about these women, don't you? Victims of domestic abuse. They make all sorts of excuses for their partners, make out everything in the garden's rosy. It's kind of like they've been brainwashed.'

Elin felt her throat constrict, her stomach fluttering even more. She wondered again what Cai would have made of it all. Her eyes drifted to the holo-box now. Would it be possible to ask him questions? She craved that sense of connection, something to give her the feeling that a real part of him was actually coming through, even if it was all just an illusion.

Catrin watched her for a moment, then leaned in and pressed a kiss to Elin's hair. She smelled of the Daisy perfume she always wore; of coffee and the vague scent of the farm.

'You want to switch it on, don't you? I can stay – make us some tea if you like – or d'you want me to clear off and give you some privacy?'

Without knowing why, Elin felt suddenly panicked. 'Can you stay? Please? Don't worry about the tea for now.'

Catrin nodded. She offered her a small smile, then retreated slightly, seating herself in the old armchair opposite Nain's, looking on tentatively as Elin's eyes fixed upon the box, at her own warped hall-of-mirrors reflection across its surface.

Silence fell. Taking a breath, Elin activated the hologram.

Light flooded the space in front of it. Particles gathered, gradually knitting themselves into familiar lines again: the casual posture, the angle of the head. Cai stood in the middle of the room once again, looking just as he had on the previous occasion.

The sight of him made Elin dizzy.

'Hey, you,' Cai said, smiling. Hearing his voice brought her instant comfort. 'There you are.'

Tears blurred Elin's vision. She laughed, but in her own head it was an odd, jarring sound. 'Oh, my God. You're really back,' she said. She threw a glance at Catrin, feeling slightly foolish. Catrin nodded, returning a hesitant smile.

'I didn't know I'd gone anywhere,' Cai teased, familiar creases lifting the corner of his mouth. 'You look tired, El.'

She reached out, stopping just short of where his arm would be. Wanting to touch him, yet not wanting to shatter the image, spoil the moment. The air shimmered faintly in front of her fingers. 'The box broke last time,' she said. 'You—' Her voice quavered. 'You sort of cut out.'

'Well, I'm here now,' Cai said cheerfully. He shifted his

weight and rolled his neck a little, the movement so achingly recognisable it made her stomach flip. 'You had nothing to worry about.'

Elin inhaled, even though she knew there was nothing of him to smell. No hint of his aftershave, his spearmint chewing gum, the shampoo he always used. But for just a moment, the ache eased, like an overworked muscle finally unclenching.

She knew she couldn't tell him, not really. But she wanted to share the news that she was going to make sure the dig still went ahead. She wanted to make him proud. But as the words came out – as she told him she was going to contact Rajesh and encourage him to recall the volunteers they'd rounded up – the aura around the hologram seemed to darken.

Cai's gaze flicked past her. It was the smallest shift, almost indiscernible, but Elin noticed. His smile faltered. Something had changed.

'El, you mustn't do that. You need to leave here,' he said suddenly.

'What?' She turned, raising an eyebrow at Catrin for her reaction. Catrin shrugged, moved in her seat, pushing out her lower lip.

When she looked back, Cai was closer. Too close. Even though this was supposed to be the man she loved, an uneasiness crept over Elin. The projection's edges had become fuzzy, light bleeding through where it shouldn't.

'El,' he said again, and now there was something overlaying his voice. An authoritative tone, like something else taking over. 'Listen to me. Evil is closer than you think.'

Elin's heart began to race. She drew back a little. 'Cai? What are you trying to say?'

He lifted his hands, and they juddered, moving jerkily, like an automaton. His eyes, unblinking and unnaturally bright now, locked on hers. 'It wasn't an accident.'

A cold sensation shivered down Elin's spine. 'What d'you mean?'

The image guttered. Cai's face fragmented for a split second, then reassembled.

The room dimmed as the hologram briefly drew more power, light sparking around the edges. The box on the table emitted a high-pitched, nerve-jangling whine.

'El,' said Cai, urgency breaking through the distortion.

A sudden crack split the air. Cai's image fractured, his face splitting into overlapping squares of light and shadow. His mouth kept moving, though the words had dissolved into meaningless noise.

'*No*,' Elin cried. She stepped forward. 'Cai, stay. Please.'

'El . . . you have . . . to listen to me.'

She froze. This all sounded wrong – too intense for Cai's usually laid-back manner, too serious for any recording she could remember. 'Cai?'

The projection flickered again. Catrin sat up straighter, turning abruptly to Elin. Something like panic quivered in her eyes. 'I think maybe we should turn it off—'

The hologram resumed, more forcefully now. '*No*. Don't.' The timbre of the voice deepened suddenly as it addressed Elin once again. 'It was no accident, El.'

The room seemed to close in around them, a chill suffusing the air. Elin had begun to tremble. She darted another look at Catrin, whose face had darkened. 'What d'you mean? Why would you . . .?'

Catrin moved purposefully toward the device, her expression pinched and anxious. 'I'm sure this isn't part of the program. It shouldn't be talking like that – this isn't how grief-bots are supposed to work. Remember it's not really Cai talking, El.'

The hologram's eyes swerved towards her – too assertively, with an unnerving realism that made Catrin recoil in evident shock.

'Catrin, butt out.'

The tone was harsh, impatient, unlike anything Elin had ever heard from Cai's lips. Catrin clapped a hand to her mouth, her widened eyes betraying her fear.

Elin looked from her friend and back to the hologram. Gooseflesh rose along her arms. 'Cai, you're scaring me. You're scaring *us*.'

The projection turned its focus back to Elin, its face softening but in a way that felt forced. There was real desperation in the voice now. 'I'm sorry. I don't want to frighten you. But this is important. I may not have another chance and you really need to listen. And if you want proof it's really me talking, think about what you once told me. About Ivy Nettleton. El, you were right and I was wrong. They do exist—'

Elin gasped. She took a step back, throwing a panicked glance at Catrin. 'What? Why? Tell me . . .'

The voice began to distort, the image breaking up. 'El, please. You're not sa—'

The hologram raised a hand toward her, shuddering, stuttering through the static.

'Don't trust the—' The device emitted a sudden pop. The hologram spasmed, then collapsed into a cloud of overlapping pixels, like a completed jigsaw being broken apart once more. There followed an unnerving silence.

Elin stared at the empty air, trembling from head to foot. 'Catrin. What the hell was that?'

Catrin seemed unable to answer initially. She went shakily over to the device, checking its controls with fumbling hands. 'I don't know.' Catrin turned to look at Elin, her face chalk-white. 'But that wasn't Cai. And whatever it was – it wasn't supposed to happen.'

Elin's eyes remained fixed on the darkness where the hologram had stood, expectant, afraid, as if something might reappear at any second. But there was nothing: no sound, no light. Just an uncanny, ominous stillness. Her skin prickled. Because, no matter what Catrin said, it *had* been Cai.

She backed away from the table, her pulse pounding in her ears, and for the first time since Cai died, her grief receded, overridden by the unsettling certainty that he had tried to reach out and warn her about something from beyond the grave.

Overridden by fear.

Chapter 45

NOW – Wednesday 24th May 2023

Elin

Elin couldn't get Cai's words out of her head. She had never told anyone about her experience – and probably wouldn't have shared it with Cai, had it not been for the amount of wine they'd drunk that Halloween. They'd watched a rerun of *The Conjuring*, a film she'd always found creepy, and the subject had turned to the existence of ghosts – or lack of it. She'd wondered if Cai might have thought her fanciful. Cai loved his history, but he was down to earth, always looked for rational explanations for things. But she knew what she'd seen. And she never wanted to see it again.

Traeth Coch had a dark past, the very name a reminder of a bloody battle in which countless lives had been lost. But perhaps most unsettling, in more recent times, the cottage next door to theirs – now Swift Cabin, Peter and Libby's home – had been the site of a murder. Used as a holiday let in the 1940s, an ex-soldier, Albert Nettleton, had rented the cottage with his wife, the mentally unstable and controlling Ivy. Driven to breaking point by Ivy's jealous, irrational behaviour, Nettleton had finally snapped one day. He bludgeoned her to death with a hot iron and attempted to bury her in the sands. Unfortunately for him, he was disturbed when lights came on in a nearby house before he could finish the job properly he'd abandoned his task. The woman's barely concealed, lifeless body was discovered by two horse riders a couple of weeks later. Acquitted of murder owing to the circumstances, the long-suffering Nettleton was sentenced to five years' imprisonment for manslaughter.

The Owens's own cottage had been in the family for almost a century, and Elin and Nerys's grandfather had been a small boy when the killing took place. Murder on the island was an incredibly rare occurrence even now, but in the 1940s it had been unheard of. Nain recalled her husband telling her of people jumping onto the running boards of the vehicle carrying Nettleton to the court hearing in Llangefni, as though the poor man were some kind of circus freak.

'The murder house' – as the cottage had become known in the community – held a morbid fascination for locals and holidaymakers alike, and for years afterwards, people could often be seen hovering outside, gawping at the building as if expecting to see a re-enactment of the tragic event.

Nerys and Elin had learned of the murder when they were still in primary school. 'It brought the ghouls out in force,' Nain had growled, when they'd quizzed her about the incident.

'Your taid's father would always send them packing. It was horrible for poor Mrs Williams when she first moved in. Bad enough knowing someone had died like that in her house, let alone having silly buggers reminding her of the fact all the time.'

But one night years later as they sat beside the fire in the evening, in a lowered voice, Nain shared the tale of a ghostly apparition wandering outside the Min Y Don, the hotel at the end of the track which sat in the shadow of Castell Mawr. The ghost was a woman in white, whom many believed to be the restless spirit of the unfortunate Ivy. The hotel was long gone, demolished to make way for a block of smart holiday flats. But still the myth persisted. It had long been a dare the local children would impose on one another, to stand alone outside the building after dark. And one Elin wished she'd never accepted.

'I saw her,' she'd admitted to Cai. 'This fuzzy shape, hovering there in the doorway. But I saw her face clearly. It was like she looked right through me, these staring, wild eyes. Scared me so much I never spoke of it, almost like if I said it aloud it made it real – as if I might – I dunno, summon her up or something.'

Thankfully it never happened again. Over the years, Elin had tried to persuade herself that she'd simply been fired up by the other kids that night and imagined it. She had forced herself to look at the building many times since, but had never seen anything else unusual. But as an adult, having read accounts from other people who'd witnessed it too, she wondered if the apparition had indeed been real.

Cai had given her a squeeze, said he didn't doubt for a minute that she *thought* she'd seen something; that in the right conditions and the right moment, the mind could be persuaded of anything. That it was probably the way the light fell. How the human brain is programmed to see faces in everything – like people who think they've seen Jesus in a slice of toast. Elin had laughed it off. She wasn't going to argue. But however compelling Cai's rationale, nothing could entirely convince her that it had all been in her imagination. And now it seemed he was finally acknowledging that what she'd told him *was* true.

What was he so anxious to tell her? And who shouldn't she trust?

Chapter 46

NOW – Earlier on Wednesday 5th April 2023

Cai

Standing in the undergrowth above the lane, Cai continued to observe the figure crouching on the rise ahead of him for a moment. There was still no evidence of a dog. Cai glanced around, half expecting some great hairy brute to come bounding up from behind and taking him by surprise. He loved dogs, but wasn't keen on the thought of being knocked flying by some overenthusiastic Great Dane or something similar.

The person seemed very focused, the head turning this way and that, as they scanned the area of ground lit by the torch beam. Cai was intrigued to know what they, or perhaps their dog, had uncovered.

Then he noticed the spade. The disturbed earth. The long, narrow pit.

On the air, he caught the faint but distinct scent of the freshly turned, moist soil. Permeating through, Cai detected another smell: something sickly and repugnant. An unwelcome smell he'd come across in the past. Cai wrinkled his nose in distaste. He thought it about time to announce his presence, when something stopped him. For a little longer he looked on, trying to make sense of what he was seeing.

Maybe the person wasn't a dog walker who'd stumbled on something. Maybe someone else was interested in the area as a site of historical interest. After all, he wasn't the only archaeologist on the island and it was perfectly feasible that others had drawn the same conclusion as himself. But it seemed an odd coincidence that two of them would be here at precisely the same time, especially as the light was growing so dim. Not the ideal time to start searching . . .

The figure froze suddenly. A hood fell across the face, but Cai saw their shoulders tense. They had heard him. The beam of the torch picked out one gloved hand hovering over what looked like an exposed scrap of ragged turquoise fabric – fabric stretched over something solid beneath. Cai caught his breath, his heart beginning to race as the realisation of what he was witnessing slowly dawned.

The thought hit Cai suddenly: someone had known he was coming to excavate this place. And that same someone had come to remove what they'd hidden long ago, long before he'd ever been here; before he'd ever laid eyes on the land he planned to dig. It seemed unthinkable in such a peaceful, quiet location, but he felt certain that what he'd just seen was a shallow grave.

Slowly the figure straightened, turning to face him.

Cai's blood ran cold as immediately he recognised the hard, narrowed eyes meeting his own. 'Oh, hello . . . I . . . um. I didn't see you there . . .' he stammered, though he knew the lie was futile. His voice sounded weak and pathetic, smothered by the mizzle.

Gripped by fear, he stepped back unsteadily; once, twice. But as instinct suddenly kicked in, he turned and began to run for his life, the rush of adrenaline lending him the speed of a trained athlete.

Behind him came the sudden clatter of metal hitting the ground. The shovel being dropped. Heavy, purposeful footfall. A low, guttural curse carried on the air.

Cai scrambled frantically back down the embankment and began to sprint up the winding lane, desperate to reach the main road, his boots sliding on the wet ground as he tackled the incline, his breath coming in rapid, painful gasps. *Get to the road. Get to lights. Get someone to call the police.*

He heard the engine before he saw the car. The growl of an ignition ticking over, a rumble that reverberated through the quietness of the deserted lane. Headlights snapped on behind him, illuminating the rain-slick road in a wash of halogen-white.

Cai didn't dare look back; he couldn't. He pushed harder, his lungs burning, the roar of the engine building as the car gathered speed. He was nearing the road. Only fifty or so yards to go; forty now . . . The headlights surged closer, stretching his shadow across the tarmac.

The culprit had abandoned the grave.

And now they were heading straight for him.

Chapter 47

NOW – Thursday 25th May 2023

Elin

May was almost at an end and it was a gloriously clear morning. The tide was still right out, so Elin had made the most of the opportunity to get a long walk in, around the curve of the bay to Benllech and back, time to mull over the things going round her head and blow the cobwebs away. Walking helped, she found. Maybe it was the sea air and the miles of empty sand stretching before her, the closeness to nature. The feeling that she was an inconsequential dot and that her own problems, in the grand scheme of things, were not so very great. Or that was what she tried to tell herself.

She was just coming back past Castell Mawr, when ahead she spotted a familiar figure in the car park in front of The Old Boathouse, standing chatting to a woman with a shiny black bob. Slightly greyer than the last time she'd seen him and a little weightier, but still with a thick head of hair. And a glorious tan.

Harry Edwards was back.

Her heart quickened as she approached. Harry and the woman turned as she drew nearer, and Elin saw to her surprise that it was Rhiannon, Catrin's sister. She'd changed her hair – it suited her heart-shaped face. Elin hadn't seen her since Cai's funeral, and then only very briefly, as she'd had to leave straight after the service. Upon spotting her, Rhiannon looked a little emotional and hurried forward to give Elin a hug, which brought tears flooding to her eyes. The two of them stood in an awkward clinch for a moment before Rhiannon stepped back to hold her at arm's length, studying Elin's face with obvious concern.

'How are you, El? And how's Nerys? I had a quick chat with Catrin the other day, but she's always in such a bloody hurry. Never has time to fill me in on anything any more. We're like ships that pass in the night these days.'

'I'm getting by. Just taking one day at a time, you know.' Elin smiled tightly, blotting her eyes with her cuff. 'Nerys still isn't great, but at least she's reacting more to stuff now. I'm hoping she'll start picking up soon.'

Harry lingered close by, seemingly waiting for the right moment to speak. '*Helo*, Elin,' he beamed, extending a hand to shake her own. Despite the smile, something like uncertainty hovered in his eyes. He was staring at her, scanning her face warily, almost as if he'd seen a ghost.

'Long time no see. In spite of everything, you're looking well.'

She knew from the hollow eyes that greeted her in the mirror each morning that this was far from the truth, but returned a brief smile and nodded anyway. 'Thanks.'

'I was going to come and see you actually,' Harry went on. He ran his tongue along his lower lip. 'I saw Ianto last night – he tells me you've got something of mine?'

Elin drew in a breath. 'That's right. It's your knife. Well, it's got your name on it. It was in Cai's pocket.'

Harry frowned, running a hand over the top of his head. 'The Swiss Army Knife, Ianto was saying? Now there's a puzzle. I lost it – or should I say it went missing.' His eyes flickered a little. 'Must be . . . oh, at least ten years ago now, maybe?'

Elin tensed. Something knotted in her chest. 'So you didn't give it to Cai, then?'

He shook his head, pushing out his lower lip. 'Nope. Don't think I ever spoke to your Cai properly, not that I recall. Only really knew the lad to nod to, like.'

Elin glanced at Rhiannon, who shrugged. 'Maybe Cai found it somewhere. Maybe he was keeping it to give back to Harry when he saw him.'

Elin nodded. 'I guess so. Can't think of any other explanation, really.' She studied Harry's face with narrowed eyes, wondering if he was being entirely truthful. Cai definitely hadn't had the knife for any length of time or she would have seen it before, she was certain.

Harry looked slightly uncomfortable. 'Is it—would you mind if I had it back? Only it was a present, see. My mam bought it for me one birthday and had it engraved. I've got another one but it's the sentimental value, you know. Especially now she's no longer here.'

Elin nodded, watching his worried face with unease. 'Of course. Just come over to the house when you've got a minute.'

The worry seemed to evaporate then, the smile restored. '*Iawn*. I'll pop over later, then. Gotta go now.' He nodded to the pair of them, then strolled off towards his van, parked on the road near the post box.

Rhiannon's gaze followed him for a moment. She turned back to Elin. 'Well, I'd better be off too. Takes me a lot longer to get to work these days, now I'm not in The Quay.'

Elin suddenly remembered what Ianto had said about the incident with Peter. 'I hear you had a spot of bother in there?'

Rhiannon pulled a face, her eyes travelling in the direction of Peter and Libby's cottage. 'Yep. That man behaved like a total arsehole. I mean, he apologised afterwards and everything, but you know, someone accuses you of a thing like that and other people are going to start questioning you. I've never fiddled anyone out of anything in my life. Fuck knows where it came from. He was as nice as pie one minute, then started thumping on the bar saying he wasn't going to be treated like that. It was like a switch had flicked.' She shook her head. 'He's got a screw loose, if you ask me. And his wife's a bloody wet lettuce.'

Elin considered for a moment, the uncomfortable memory of Libby's hasty explanation for what she'd seen through their window that day replaying in her mind. 'Maybe it's living with him. Maybe she's . . . I dunno, brow beaten?'

Rhiannon nodded, looking thoughtful. 'You could be right there.'

'Still, don't suppose you really have to see them any more, do you?'

'Thankfully not. I don't drink in The Quay these days.' Rhiannon's face lit up. 'Got a fella now, he lives in Holyhead, so I get over there whenever I can.'

'Good for you. And your dad? How's he?'

Rhiannon rolled her eyes. 'He never changes. I mean, I'm still at home, like, do his washing and cook his dinner and stuff. But I realised I need to make a life for myself. It's actually done me some good, leaving the pub. Broadened my horizons, as they say.'

Rhiannon made her excuses as she was running late, gave Elin another hug, saying they'd have to catch up soon.

Elin waved as she drove away, then headed back to the cottage. She took a shower and got changed, then put on a load of washing. Not having had breakfast, she made herself a sort of brunch, a croissant with melted cheese and pickle, followed by an Americano accompanied by a piece of Victoria sponge that Catrin had brought over the other day. Carb overload, she'd thought at the time. But she actually enjoyed it – maybe the walk had done her good.

She had taken the coffee and cake into the living room on a tray, and had barely swallowed the last mouthful, when her eyes landed on a folded sheet of paper on the door mat. Elin squinted to see what it was. A flyer, probably. She hadn't noticed it earlier.

Setting down the tray on the floor in front of the settee, she went to pick up the leaflet. Opening it out, Elin's breath caught in her throat. A chill crept along her arms.

It was no flyer. In bold, black letters, there were just five typewritten words staring back at her.

YOU SHOULDN'T HAVE COME BACK

Was this some kind of sick joke?

Remembering what Cai's hologram had said, the similarity felt too close for comfort. Elin let the paper fall from her shaking hands. She rushed to the window, scanning the track, the beach beyond. It was high tide and there was no one she recognised close by; just a handful of people wandering casually towards The Old Boathouse and a postal worker emptying the contents of the letterbox into a mail sack.

But then she considered the wording once more. Could it actually be a jibe – a dig from someone who resented her returning after so long? Someone like her horrible ex, Tom Buckley, maybe. She thought of his narrowed eyes, the contemptuous sneer; the way he'd almost spat the words at her that last time she'd seen him outside the pub.

'Thinks she's a cut above now, this one,' he'd said to his

drinking companion, staring at Elin the whole time. '*Why don't you just fuck off back to Birmingham with your history nerd. You don't belong here any more.*'

She remembered the prank call the other week, and Bethan saying she'd seen Buckley in Beaumaris recently. It wouldn't surprise her in the slightest if he was behind this. After her initial shock and disbelief, anger flared in Elin now. Stooping to pick up the paper, she screwed it up into a ball and went into the kitchen, where she dropped it straight into the bin.

This was her home and no one, whoever they were, had the right to try to make her feel unwelcome.

She wasn't going anywhere.

Chapter 48

TEN YEARS EARLIER – October 2013

The night of the storm

Meinir

Meinir made an abrupt exit from The Quay, swearing under her breath. Looking up, she saw young Jac Parry approaching, wide-eyed, his face alight.

'*Sut mae*, Mein. Mam says there's going to be lightning later. I've come to watch out the window.' He waved his hand towards the pub.

Despite her foul mood, Meinir couldn't help but smile. Jac knew everyone, and everyone knew Jac. He must be twenty-five now, but looked all of twelve, he was so small and slight. People looked out for him – they all knew his mam, Delyth, had had it tough since the lad's father had left her. But in Meinir's opinion, she was better off without the man – he'd been a selfish prick. It would've been like looking after two adult children – at least Jac was nice-natured and amenable.

'Yes, and there'll be a lot of rain too.' She nodded, suppressing a grin as she noticed his old, mismatched trainers. He often seemed to do that, put on a shoe from one pair and one from another – Delyth had said she'd given up trying to tell him. 'Watch you stay inside until it's stopped – you don't want to catch a cold.'

'Yeah, Mam told me.' Beaming, he held up a bright red, rolled up pac-a-mac. 'She said to put this on.'

'Well, you make sure you don't lose it now.' Meinir ruffled his ever-tousled dark hair. 'Have fun, Jac, but be careful, won't you? See you.'

'Yeah. I'm always careful. Mam's told me. See you.'

She turned to watch for a moment as the lad disappeared into The Quay, then looked back out at the bay. As the clouds descended, any remaining daylight was being rapidly obliterated, the only illumination the single lantern above the pub door and the glow from within. Thunder rumbled in the distance; rain was finally beginning to fall now from the cloud-heavy skies, softly at first, but the minute she started to retreat from the building, the drops quickly grew fatter and soon it had become a torrent, as though someone above had just turned on an enormous tap.

'Shit,' she muttered, slipping off her jacket and pulling it up over her head like a canopy. Meinir made a dash for the car. She could sit inside to wait until the worst had passed, then head for home. She wasn't used to drinking spirits and the rum had gone to her head; she didn't dare risk driving, even if it was only a stone's throw – it'd be just her luck that someone would pull her over and whip out a breathalyser. Fumbling the key fob from her handbag, she opened the door and threw herself inside, shaking the drops from her jacket and hooking it over the back of the passenger seat next to her.

Meinir felt suddenly frozen. She turned on the engine and sat, shivering and damp, as she waited for the car's heater to kick in, watching the rain as it fell in sheets, sweeping down the windscreen. Listening to the constant drumming against the roof. Normally she loved a storm at sea – it was invigorating somehow, watching from the comfort of home as lightning bounced from the horizon, splitting the sky and igniting the water. But sitting in a metal box, she felt vulnerable – she'd heard stories of vehicles bursting into flames when their fuel tank had been struck. Not that likely, maybe, but the chance was always there.

Her view of everything outside was blurred and Meinir switched the wipers on to full pelt, peering out at the raging waves beyond, crashing onto the sand as they began to edge in towards the sea wall. Pale lights from across the bay smudged the surface of the water, the sky black and seemingly impenetrable. The masts of the boats anchored in the sand bowed; their sails, unleashed by the wind, flapped frenziedly, looking in danger of being torn clean away. Unsurprisingly, there wasn't a soul in sight now. Meinir sat for a few minutes, just staring out at the sea. The rain was showing no signs of abating: if anything, it was getting worse – much like her evening. Meinir groaned impatiently. How she wished she hadn't bothered going into The Quay at all – what a complete waste of time that had been. She wanted to get back to the cottage, have a cup of tea and a moan to Mam. See Nerys and Elin.

Now that she'd had time to calm down, she felt bad that she'd had a go at Griff. On reflection, he was just trying to defuse the situation. He was probably a perfectly nice guy. To be fair, he didn't know her from Adam – and the fact that she was arguing with someone so much younger wouldn't have put her in a good light. She should have risen above it. But Rhiannon's words had stung. Meinir really hoped she wasn't an embarrassment to her daughters – she'd never thought of it like that before. She questioned her own constant quest to find a man. Why did she need a partner to validate her as a person, anyway? And what kind of message was that conveying to her girls? She felt a surge of love as she thought of Nerys, her little home bird, always helpful, always trying so hard to please. And Elin, her little Mini-Me, in both looks and character. But better: so much better. They were daughters to be proud of.

Meinir had a sudden impulse to rush home, wrap both her girls in her arms, tell them that they were and always would be the most important thing in her life; that she'd give up on men completely if that's what they wanted. But the bloody rain was continuing to batter the car: she'd get drenched if she ventured out now. She would just have to stay put.

A sudden flicker of movement drew Meinir's attention to the swaying masts. As the car's wipers swished aside a huge arc of spray, she could just make out what looked like someone wearing a shapeless hooded cape, weaving between the moored vessels. The figure stopped abruptly, crouching beside one.

'Friggin' nutter,' she murmured to herself, shaking her head. Who in their right mind would be out there, faffing about doing God knows what on a night like this? Surely there was nothing that couldn't wait until the storm had passed? She sat forward in her seat, screwing up her eyes to see if it was anyone she recognised. But as she watched, the realisation of what she was witnessing sent a shockwave through her. The figure straightened, raising a bulky arm and bringing it down with force. They were taking a hammer to the hull of one of the boats.

Chapter 49

NOW – Friday 26th May 2023

Elin

As had become the norm, Elin had slept fitfully, tossing and turning for most of the night. Just as she was drifting off again, a noise from somewhere jolted her awake once more.

Elin sat bolt upright, her heart pounding, senses immediately on alert at the sound of an intermittent, impatient rattle, like someone attempting to open a long-stuck door. Though she was sure it was emanating from the back of the house, with the stillness of the night and the calm sea, any sound was being amplified and could just as easily have been coming from the room next door.

Climbing from her bed, Elin creaked open the door ultra slowly, ultra carefully, and tiptoed tentatively along the landing to Mam's old room. In the half-light, everything was in eerie monochrome. The door was ajar, as she'd left it the previous night. She padded across the floor and, taking care to keep to one side, peered down at the garden through the gap in the curtains.

Elin caught her breath.

The moon was full, washing the small lawn and Taid's old tool shed in an ethereal silver-white light. A broad, hooded figure, their back to her and shoulders hunched, was attempting to lever the shed door with what looked like a crowbar. But rather than forcing it open from the padlocked side, they appeared to be trying to prise the hinges off – albeit without much success, it seemed. A cold fear took hold of Elin. What the hell were they doing? She stood, rooted to the spot, adrenaline coursing through her. Should she stay and observe – or call the police?

Elin was about to go back for her phone when the person appeared to change tack, pausing suddenly and putting down the crowbar. They straightened for a moment as if resting, before producing a smaller tool from the pocket of their oversized coat. It looked as if they were now using a screwdriver or something to undo the triangular plates securing the hinges to the frame. Eventually, one of the metal plates sprung outwards. The action was repeated until both hinges had been loosened, creating a gap at the unlocked side of the door.

Elin drew back sharply as the intruder began to open the door a fraction, inch by inch, as though taking care not to crack the wood. Why anyone would go to such lengths to break into her grandfather's dilapidated shed was beyond Elin. But then, whoever it was bent down to pick up something at their feet. Elin screwed up her eyes and could make out that they were now holding a light-coloured carrier bag at arm's length, something bulging within. Not heavy, judging by the way it was being brandished in just one hand. Sliding the bag into the gap created by removing the hinges, the intruder shook out whatever was inside, withdrew the empty carrier and hurriedly forced the door shut. The fixings were expertly replaced and the door secured once more. It was bizarre.

After casting about for a moment, the figure disappeared stealthily into the shadows along the side of the house. Her heart hammering, Elin rushed back down the landing, hoping to catch a glimpse of them from her bedroom window. But looking frantically from left to right, she could see no one. It was as if they'd evaporated into the night.

Elin's first instinct was to contact the police. But then she thought back to her recent outburst in the station, and her heart sank. The sergeant on the desk that day would undoubtedly remember her and would more than likely have shared the information about her behaviour with his colleagues. She couldn't imagine they'd be very sympathetic – and they hadn't exactly been helpful with regard to her concerns about Mam's disappearance. She felt as though she'd shot herself in the foot. Although, from what she had witnessed, nothing appeared to have actually been removed from the shed. Would they even be interested if nothing had been stolen?

She went downstairs to check the doors and windows, peering fearfully outside in case the intruder was still lurking. But there was no sign of anyone. No sign that anything had happened at all. Eventually satisfied that everything was secure, she returned to her bed.

*

Sleep evaded Elin completely afterwards. She lay rigidly in bed, the thought that someone had broken into the shed in the way they had, eating away at her. She didn't dare venture outside to investigate, though her mind was constantly turning, trying to figure out what they might have deposited inside. A sick feeling was building in her stomach, remembering the way the bag had been held at a distance, as though it might contain something hazardous, or at the very least deeply unpleasant. But whatever it was, why had they targeted the old shed in her garden?

*

At first light, wrapped in her dressing gown and exhausted, Elin steeled herself and made her way into the garden, the key to the padlocked shed in her trembling hand. Crossing the dew-wet lawn, the moisture seeping through her slippers, she glanced about her for some clue that the intruder might have left to their identity, but could see nothing. Though she knew she needed to discover what had been left inside the shed, the mounting dread of what she might be presented with was making her feeling nauseous. Hesitantly, she unlocked the twisted, crumbling door. It had dropped at an angle and was stuck fast, the wood jammed against the slabs it sat on. Elin had to push and pull, lifting it above ground level before she was finally able to heave it open.

Elin sniffed. Something was out of place: a sickly, sweet scent mingling with the usual odours of creosote and oily rags. Then, looking down, her eyes landed on it.

A small grey bundle lay on the rotting wooden floor, its downy feathers squashed and ruffled. A young gull – too young maybe to have even flown the nest. Its little body was twisted unnaturally, as if someone had wrung it out, squeezed the life from it.

Elin recoiled in disgust. An awful coldness ran along her spine. Was this why such lengths had been taken to conceal the break-in to the shed – so that she wouldn't discover the body until it was completely rotten and putrid? To attract flies, maybe?

Or maybe someone knew that the door was so old and warped that it wouldn't open from the other side without making a din and alerting Elin to their presence. She backed out of the shed, one hand over her mouth, when a sudden squawk sounded from behind her.

Elin spun round to see another young gull, dishevelled and obviously disorientated, pottering across the lawn. A mass of twigs and feathers lay just beyond it, in front of the overgrown buxus bush. Had its nest been blown across the grass, having fallen from the chimney? There had definitely been one up there on several occasions over the years. But as she looked closer, it seemed that the remains of the nest lay beneath the shrub, and someone or something had dragged it out from where it had been constructed.

A sudden shriek split the air. The mother gull came like a white flash from the apex of the roof, its wings wide and furious, slicing the sky with raw, tangible rage. Elin gasped, cowering as the bird swooped, its angry claws skimming the crown of her head. The rush of air and the wild, panicked beating of its wings filled her ears, momentarily drowning out her thoughts.

Another dive, this time driving at her with its lethal beak. It rose and swooped savagely once more, taking a chunk of her hair as it attacked. She cried out in pain, raising her arms to protect her skull, her heart thudding against her ribs. The bird's cry was jagged, full of accusation, driven by the urge to defend her chick.

'It wasn't me! I didn't do it!' Elin yelled pointlessly as she fled in horror across the garden, eyes watering from the repeated onslaught and stench of fish. The gull circled above her, screeching relentlessly, clearly trying to steer her away from its one remaining offspring.

Someone had targeted her deliberately; had vandalised the nest in the mother's absence, knowing that the bird would return with a fierce maternal instinct to protect her young and attack anyone unfortunate enough to be close by. The cold certainty sank in her chest like a lead weight. Cai's prophetic words rang through her head. Someone out there wasn't to be trusted. Someone wanted to unnerve her, show her they meant business.

And as the gull wheeled and screamed overhead, she wondered what exactly that business was.

Chapter 50

NOW – Friday 26th May 2023

Elin

Elin had to get away from the house for a while. She hadn't dared risk going back to the shed to remove the dead chick, fearing a further attack from the mother. She showered, dressed and headed straight out. Waitrose café did cooked breakfasts: she'd call in there for a bite on her way to the bridge and pick up a couple of things, then make her way to Ysbyty Gwynedd. It had been a few days since she'd seen Nerys. Hopefully she'd be showing some signs of improvement. And she wanted to give her the little dish. She resolved not to say anything about the gull incident – it seemed likely that such news would do more harm than good at the moment.

The weather took a turn for the worse – and very quickly. The sky was quite clear as she'd driven away from Traeth Coch, but within minutes of leaving the supermarket, ominous dark clouds had begun to gather. As Elin crossed the bridge, the heavens opened and she had to turn the wipers onto full speed. She couldn't believe she had forgotten how rapidly things could change up here.

Cursing the fact that she'd neglected to bring an umbrella, she had to run as best she could from the hospital car park to the Hergest Unit, the carrier bag containing the wrapped dish clutched beneath her mac. Though the foot had healed, she still wasn't able to move as swiftly as before and everywhere was out in the open, with nowhere to take cover.

Elin dripped her way through the corridor, pushing her wet hair back from her face. Walking through the double doors, she wrinkled her nose at the familiar smell of the ward – an odour that always seemed to cling to her clothes long after she left. She hooked her sodden mac over the back of the vinyl chair by Nerys's bed, took the dish from the plastic bag and placed it on the side table. She glanced around at the other patients and their visitors, exchanging a smile of solidarity with a tired-looking woman sitting at the bedside of an elderly man, clutching his hand in her own as he stared far into the distance somewhere.

Outside, the rain continued to batter the hospital roof, though now she was indoors, the sound was somehow soothing. She sat down in the chair, smiling as Nerys turned to look at her.

'Hiya,' said Elin softly.

'Hiya,' Nerys replied, and there was the merest suggestion of a grin.

She looked different today. Not better exactly, but more alert. Her hair was brushed, her eyes clearer; she held Elin's gaze as she spoke instead of constantly drifting past her. She was propped up against her pillows, cardigan buttoned neatly, hands folded in her lap on top of the bedcovers.

'You're soaked.' Nerys tipped her head towards the door. 'It's hammering it down out there – listen to it.'

Elin blinked, surprised. Small talk. Normal talk. 'Nothing new there,' she said, glancing down at her damp jeans. She shivered a little.

'You should go and use the dryer in the loos – you'll catch a cold.'

'You sound just like Nain.'

'Yes, well, she always did give good advice. Not that we always listened. Oh God, your hair that time . . .'

Elin widened her eyes, grimacing at the memory. She'd asked Nerys to highlight her hair for her once, and had finished up with ridiculous, badger-like stripes. Nain had warned them beforehand that things like that were better left to the professionals, but of course, they'd carried on anyway. She'd still paid for Elin to go to the salon in Pentraeth to undo the damage though, saying she couldn't have her going round looking like that.

'Hope you've learned your lesson,' she'd said, her face stern. But there'd been a definite hint of mirth in her eyes as she'd handed over the cash.

They sat for a minute, the quiet moments between words less oppressive than they had been on previous visits. Elin felt a cautious optimism. She indicated the dish.

'Oh, I brought you something.'

Nerys's eyes travelled to the tissue paper wrapping. She looked surprised. 'What is it?'

'Open it and see.'

Elin watched as she picked up the package, her hands slightly shaky, and began to peel back the paper carefully. As the dish was revealed, she threw a look at Elin, a smile lighting her face.

'Oh, it's lovely. *Diolch*. Don't know what I've done to deserve this.'

Elin smiled back tentatively. 'You've been through a lot lately. Just wanted to cheer you up a bit, that's all.'

Nerys studied the dish for a moment. She pointed at one of the cats in the design. 'This one's a lot like my Nyten.' Her eyes welled. 'I do miss her. Have you met her yet?'

Elin shook her head. 'I'm looking forward to it. Bethan says she's lovely.'

'She is. I don't think Bethan will want to part with her when she has to come home.'

'I'll bet.' There was a pause. Elin thought of the reasons Nerys had given for wanting Bethan to look after the little cat and wondered if Nerys had remembered them. She cleared her throat. 'Anyway, how're you feeling?' she asked.

Nerys shrugged, placing the dish back on the table. 'Less foggy. They've changed the meds again. At least I can think without everything getting scrambled.' She hesitated, then grimaced. 'I know I haven't been . . . well, quite with it.'

'That's one way of putting it,' Elin said, attempting to keep things light.

Nerys screwed up her face. 'The stuff they pump you with in here – it's obviously designed to calm things down, keep you on an even keel. But there are big chunks up there that are still quite hazy—' She rapped her head with the heel of her hand. 'I mean, I remember some things that were going on, but not when they actually brought me into hospital. It's really frustrating.'

Elin studied Nerys's face, seeing the sister she knew and loved now, not the empty shell she had been visiting for all these weeks. Elin knew the time was right to share the news about Cai with her. Saying it aloud was going to be painful.

Elin's smile wobbled. Her eyes swivelled, landing on a magazine deposited on the locker next to the bed. She leaned over to pick it up, feigning interest in the cover. Nerys frowned. She knew her too well.

'What's wrong?' Nerys asked, drawing herself more upright. 'You look so sad all of a sudden.'

Elin drew in a breath. She had rehearsed this moment over and over, every time she'd driven across the Menai Bridge to the hospital, waiting for a time when Nerys was more like her old self and able to absorb what she was saying. She had told herself she would stay calm, be factual. But now the words stuck in her throat.

'Cai's dead,' she blurted out eventually. 'He was knocked down by a car and killed. Not far from home. In the lane going towards Pentraeth.'

Nerys stared at her uncomprehendingly. For a second Elin wondered if she'd misjudged everything, if this apparent clarity had just been an interlude; a blip. Then Nerys's face crumpled.

'Oh, El *bach*,' she said, opening her arms.

Elin folded into her embrace and allowed herself to be held, sobbing quietly. Nerys smelled faintly of medicated soap and starchy hospital linen. Elin hadn't realised how much she needed the contact until it was there, solid and comforting. She buried her face in Nerys's shoulder, the words she hadn't said to anyone else, not even Catrin, spilling out now: how unfair it all was, how she ached for Cai, for his company, the feel of his arms around her. The grief hologram and how unsettled it had left her; her increasing anxiety about the circumstances of his death. How lonely she felt. The fact that her whole future had been decimated and she could no longer see the point in anything.

Nerys murmured motherese comforts, rocking her slightly. Her own tears soaked into Elin's hair. 'I'm so sorry, El. And I'm sorry I've been in here and useless to you when you needed someone.'

Elin drew back, wiping a sleeve across her eyes. 'No. No, if anyone needs to be sorry, it's me. I'd no idea you'd been having such a terrible time of things. I've been a crap sister, not keeping in touch as much as I should. I should've realised you'd be struggling, should've been here to support you after Nain . . .'

She broke off, seeing a sudden shift in Nerys's expression.

'El,' she said, pulling back. Her hands tightened on Elin's arms. 'You have to listen to me. Because I've been trying so hard to remember stuff, but there's one thing that keeps coming into my mind.'

Elin frowned. 'What is it?'

'It's Peter and Libby next door,' Nerys said. Her voice dropped, the tone urgent. 'Everyone thinks they're harmless. The nice old man who fixes things with a smile. The sweet old woman who goes out of her way to help everyone. But I don't think they are. I really don't.'

A prickle of unease crept up Elin's spine. 'Nerys, I . . .'

'They were there – in the house, when the ambulance came to get me that day.'

Elin relaxed a little. 'I think they were just waiting with you until it turned up,' she said gently. 'They were worried about you. Libby said you were in a bad way—'

Nerys shook her head vehemently. 'I didn't want them there.' She cast her eyes skyward in frustration. 'It's all so muddled, El, but the feeling keeps coming back. There was something . . . I dunno, off about it all.' She reached out to grab Elin's hand. 'You do believe me, don't you, El? I'm getting better – I know it's not just my imagination.'

Elin nodded, smiling at Nerys as she returned the squeeze. 'Don't worry,' she soothed. 'It'll all come back soon, I'm sure. In the meantime, don't upset yourself.'

Nerys flopped back on her pillows, blowing out her cheeks. 'Maybe it's the bloody meds, messing with my brain. I wish I could remember more. But just be careful around them anyway, won't you, El? Promise? I mean, maybe I've got them all wrong. But it doesn't hurt to be cautious, does it?'

Elin promised that she would. She looked up at the clock, grimacing. 'Hey, I'd better go before they hoof me out. But I'll be back very soon. It's been so good to talk properly again. I've missed you very much, you know.'

Nerys tipped her head to one side, smiling sadly as she studied Elin's face. 'I've missed you, too, El *bach*. And I'm so, so sorry about Cai. You had a good one there.'

Elin couldn't speak. She nodded, smiling through tears that blurred her vision. She gave Nerys one last hug before picking up her mac and heading out of the ward.

All the way home, Elin thought about what Nerys had said. The warning to be cautious. Was she right? *Was* there something off about their neighbours? Maybe Nerys had also witnessed Peter being aggressive towards Libby, and something in her subconscious was trying to remind her. Elin hadn't wanted to mention what she'd seen, in case Nerys got more het up. It was as frustrating for Elin as it was for her sister that she couldn't remember everything, but Nerys seemed to be making great strides now. Elin didn't want her to get agitated in case she had a relapse. But the more she thought about it, the more feasible it seemed that Libby might indeed be a victim of domestic abuse. Catrin certainly thought so.

The way Libby always fell into step with Peter, the way she seemed never to stray far from him whenever they were out together; to echo his opinions, hang on his every word. The way she never mixed with anyone in the community unless he was in tow. The way she had been so quick to jump to his defence.

As if she was always scared of doing or saying anything that might upset him; as if she were acting under instruction. Under duress.

On the main road into Pentraeth, Elin slowed to obey the speed limit, glancing to her left as she passed the petrol station. Her breath caught in her throat. A tall, familiar figure, wearing blue workman's overalls, was climbing into the driver's seat of a parked van on the forecourt. Bulkier and with longer hair than she remembered – but it was definitely him. Tom Buckley.

The sight of him made her pulse jump uncomfortably. She didn't think he'd spotted her, but she couldn't be sure. He might have recognised Nerys's car. The van pulled out, turning left to head in the same direction as Elin, with only one car between them. All the way through Pentraeth, she kept glancing anxiously into her rear-view mirror, but thankfully at some point Tom's vehicle disappeared. He must have turned off. Elin exhaled deeply as she approached the slip road for home. She had enough to worry about without an encounter with Buckley.

The rain had stopped completely by the time Elin arrived back in Traeth Coch, the afternoon sun bathing the cottage in pale yellow light which glinted from the windows. Remembering the dead gull in the shed, her chest tightened. She would have to deal with it sooner or later, although the thought filled her with dread. But before she tackled it, she would need to change – her clothes were still slightly damp and she wanted another hot shower to warm her through.

Elin was in her bedroom and had barely had time to dress after showering, when there was a sharp rap at the front door. She finished buttoning up her cardigan as she hurried down to answer it.

Harry Edwards stood on the threshold, smiling tentatively. 'I hope s'okay to call now – I'm between jobs – got to head off to Amlwch to start a rewire on a property later this afternoon.'

Elin's stomach clenched. She had, after all, told him to come and collect his knife, but knowing that Cai had been in possession of the thing, she felt uneasy about being alone in the house with the man – even more so after the unnerving way Harry had stared at her the other day. The sooner she got rid of him, the better. She paused for a moment, then stepped back hesitantly for him to enter. 'No problem. Have a seat a minute – I'll go and get the knife for you now.'

She made her way upstairs, quickly fishing the knife out of her bedside drawer where she'd been keeping it, and returned within seconds. Coming back downstairs, she observed Harry for a moment where he sat, his face unsmiling, eyes trained on the sideboard. She followed the trajectory of his gaze and realised he was staring at the family photo.

The one with the cracked glass.

Elin drew in a breath as she rejoined him. She held out the knife with a slightly unsteady hand.

'There you go.' She studied his face for a reaction, but he looked genuinely puzzled.

Harry accepted the knife, gazing at it and running a finger over the inscription as if he couldn't quite believe it. He flicked open the various tools, his brow knitting.

'It's definitely mine. So weird though, after all this time. And it looks like someone's used it a lot. But thanks, I really appreciate you returning it.' His eyes lifted to meet hers and he smiled sadly. 'I was just looking at that picture of your mam. I realised I must've been staring when I saw you the other day – I'm sorry if it seemed rude. It's just you look so much like her, you know? Gave me a bit of a start.'

Elin felt the tension in her shoulders ease. 'Yes, everyone says so. I am my mother's daughter, after all.'

Harry gave a nervous little laugh. He glanced up at the clock, blowing out his cheeks. 'Well, better be off anyway – there are temporary roadworks near Dulas, so I need to allow more time.'

Elin showed him to the door. 'Where did you lose your knife, by the way?'

Harry's face clouded. 'Well, that's the thing. I'd left it on the bar in The Quay one afternoon. It was pretty quiet in the pub that day, too. I reckon someone just took it when I went to the loo. Never found out who.' The muscles in his cheeks twitched. 'You don't expect that sort of thing round here, do you?'

Elin shook her head slowly. But then, several things that she'd never expected to happen in their community seemed to have occurred recently. Nothing, she realised, could ever be taken for granted.

As Harry stood at the front door, she felt a sudden weight lifting. From his general demeanour and the way he spoke, Elin was 99 per cent satisfied that he meant her no harm. And his explanation for the disappearance of the knife seemed perfectly plausible.

A thought occurred suddenly. She didn't want to play the helpless female, but needs must. There was no harm in asking.

'Are you in a real rush? Only I'd be very grateful for a hand with something if you've got a minute.'

Harry looked a little surprised. 'Sure, *dim problem*.'

Elin led him back through the kitchen, explaining about the previous night and her predicament with the dead gull chick.

He screwed up his face. 'Eww. Sounds like someone's played a nasty practical joke on you. Not funny at all, though, and some lengths to go through, coming in the middle of the night like that.'

'I know. I need to dispose of it, but I'm pretty squeamish.' Elin grimaced. 'And I think the mother's probably still about but I'm worried she'll have another go if she sees me again.'

He arched an eyebrow. 'So you'd like me to play undertaker, is that it?'

Elin chewed her lip, feeling sheepish. 'I'm sorry to ask. But if you stay well away from where the nest is, hopefully she won't bother you.'

Harry grinned. 'Right. I take it there's a spade out there somewhere. Have you got a plastic bag or something?'

*

Elin waited in the living room, not wanting to watch Harry executing his grim task. Through the open kitchen window, she could hear the shove and scrape of the shed door being manoeuvred and covered her ears, bracing herself for the screeches of a furious bird. But within minutes, Harry had returned, brushing off his hands.

'All done. And the mother must've been elsewhere – no sign of her.'

Elin let out a long breath. '*Diolch*. I really appreciate it.'

'*Croeso*.' Harry smiled. Tipping his head towards the back door, he blew the fringe from his forehead with a jut of his lower lip. 'Hey, that shed's seen better days. I could ask Ianto to come and fix it up for you if you want. The door's hanging on by the skin of its teeth.'

Elin nodded. 'I know. But don't worry about it. I'll ask him myself when I see him.'

'Okay. Well, you take care, now. And if you have any more bother – with dead birds or anything else – I'm always happy to help.' He looked at her, suddenly serious, and she wondered if he was concerned by what had happened with the gull. It had definitely been intended to put the wind up her.

'Hey, did you ever have any more bother with that toerag Tom Buckley? I remember hearing he gave you a hard time after you split up. You don't think he could've had anything to do with it?'

'I hadn't seen Tom for years, but I think I clocked him in Pentraeth earlier,' Elin said slowly, a feeling of discomfort turning in her gut. The thought had occurred to her, though she'd dismissed it – the figure she'd seen last night had looked shorter than Tom. But it wasn't impossible he'd got one of his cronies to do it.

'Yes, he comes home now and then to visit his mam. He's

not here that often, but I've seen him in The Quay a couple of times.' Harry raised an eyebrow. 'Just a thought.'

She nodded. Clearly trying to curry favour, Tom *had* cut the lawn once for Nain when he and Elin had only been dating a short while. He'd have known about the state of the shed door. After the hoax call and the note that had been pushed through the letter box too, she wondered now if her resentful ex could have had something to do with all three events. Deliberately antagonising the gull seemed like the sort of spiteful stunt he might have pulled – or suggested. She felt the heat of anger rise in her. It would take more than a waster like Tom Buckley to terrorise her in her own home. He was a coward, that much she knew. She remembered how scared he'd been when Ianto threatened him with the police and was pretty sure he'd shit himself if they actually came to his door. All mouth and no trousers. She might ask Ianto to have another word if anything else happened.

'Thanks. You may well have something there – I'll bear it in mind. *Ta-ra*, then.'

Harry tapped his temple with two fingers. '*Ta-ra*. See you again.'

Elin watched through the window as he walked back down the lane. Peter was coming the opposite way and stopped him briefly. The two men exchanged a few words. Peter seemed to laugh and slapped Harry on the back good-naturedly, before carrying on back towards his gate.

So if Harry was telling the truth – and she strongly suspected he was – someone had stolen his knife.

But how did Cai get hold of it?

Chapter 51

TEN YEARS EARLIER – October 2013

The night of the storm

Meinir

Frantically, Meinir rummaged through her bag and pulled out her phone. She needed to call the police. With uncoordinated fingers – she may have been a little drunk – she keyed in her pin code – only for the screen to fade to black immediately. Why the hell hadn't she checked the charge earlier? She looked back out, scanning round for the figure, who had now moved on to the next craft. Again, they lifted the tool and brought it down hard against the side of the boat. The person looked from side to side, apparently checking they were safe to continue unobserved, then moved towards a third vessel.

Thankfully Meinir hadn't switched on her headlights – clearly whoever it was hadn't realised they'd been noticed. But though slightly woozy from the drink, she was still incensed: she couldn't sit back and allow such malicious vandalism to continue. There was no one else about and her stupid bloody phone had died, so she could neither call for help nor take photographs as evidence. She turned to look back at the pub. She'd undoubtedly get soaked, but she could make a run for it, bring help. Although if the person spotted her leaving the car, they'd have enough time to disappear before she could return – there was a winding, overgrown path not far behind where they were standing that led from the beach, with numerous offshoots which would provide ample places to hide. Or she could sneak up and confront the saboteur herself: if the bastard realised they'd been seen, they'd surely stop before any more damage was done. More than anything, she had a burning curiosity to see if the face concealed beneath the hood was one she knew. She could take the wheel brace from her boot in case things turned nasty.

Pleased with this idea and emboldened by the alcohol, her heart pounding with the adrenaline coursing through her, she decided on the latter plan. Pulling on her jacket once more, Meinir switched off the internal light in case it gave her away, before easing the car door open. In her attempt to remain unseen, she almost fell out. Keeping low to the ground and quietly cursing the grit digging into her hands and shins, she made her way round the back of the vehicle.

With one eye on the assailant, who had now moved on to a fourth boat, Meinir popped the boot open a fraction and slid her hand inside. Thankfully the howling wind and the roar of the waves drowned out any sound she had made. She groped around for the wheel brace, and feeling its cold but reassuring surface, eased it out, then pulled herself a little unsteadily to her feet, peering over the car to make sure the figure was still in sight. Yes, no sign of them moving on yet. She crouched down and began to inch her way across the car park, stifling a snort of laughter at the thought she must resemble a Cossack doing their traditional squatting dance. But the knowledge of what she was doing, plus the cold water seeping down her neck and through her clothes, was instantly sobering.

The wind whipped at her long hair, which she paused to push back from her face and out of her mouth with one hand, still gripping the wheel brace tightly in the other. Soon she had reached the far end of the car park which sloped down towards the shingle end of the beach. She was less than a hundred yards away from the damaged boats, close enough to get a better look. Although some distance from the pub now, with the light levels meagre and the moon a pitiful, cloud-veiled crescent, her eyes had begun to adjust to the dim. The perpetrator had their back to her, seemingly pausing and looking from left to right as if deciding what damage to inflict next. Meinir continued to move forward, still ducking low, until she could make out a pair of wellingtons jutting from beneath the dark folds of the cape. Lying next to them was a hefty bolt cutter. *What the hell?* Was the intention to cut through the chains anchoring the boats into the sand, set them adrift and let them sink?

Time to make her presence felt. Her heart thudding hard against her ribcage, Meinir gripped the wheel brace in both hands and drew herself up, reeling against the force of the gale. But before she could shout out, the figure wheeled round sharply, ceasing any movement as the head dropped, all focus evidently turned towards her.

The peaked hood of the cape slipped down; a gloved hand raised quickly to pull it back into place. But not before Meinir had glimpsed the shock of hair that had previously been covered. Timed to perfection, lightning flashed suddenly above, illuminating the whole sky for the briefest moment: just long enough for her to look upon the face of the individual.

Meinir froze. It was indeed a face she knew – and knew well.

The unblinking eyes narrowed, the expression in them unreadable. Fear flooded through Meinir as she stood, pinioned to the spot, not knowing now whether to stand her ground as she'd intended, or turn and flee. But all ideas of a confrontation on her terms, even the citizen's arrest that she'd considered only moments earlier (how could she have been so *stupid*?) evaporated in a heartbeat. She should have gone for help, brought a posse to back her up. Suddenly the damage to the boats seemed completely insignificant as she grasped the perilous position she had put herself in. The drink had dulled Meinir's reflexes: precious seconds passed before she saw she was being approached, and with surprising speed. Common sense prevailed now: she needed to get away – and fast. She cried out for help, but her voice was ragged and lost to the wind, with no hope of anyone having heard her. Her heart hammered, adrenaline coursing through her. The storm continued to rage, lightning ripping through the sky once again as the rain pelted her unrelentingly. Still wielding the wheel brace, she spun round in desperation, aiming to run back towards the pub, but the narrow heel of one of her boots sank into the wet sand between the pebbles. As she tried to dislodge it, she found herself flying forwards, losing her weapon along with traction as her hands went out instinctively to save herself. Briefly winded, her palms and knees smarting from the impact with the unforgiving shingle, Meinir tried to push herself up, twisting her face skywards in time to see the caped figure, just a few feet behind only moments ago, now towering over her, as the sheer horror of the situation dawned.

Before she had time to react, one thick arm reached from beneath the flapping fabric and struck out viciously with the hammer. Meinir felt the reverberation through her head, the dull, sickening crack caused by the impact echoing in her ears as her whole body convulsed. Her vision blurred; but not enough that she couldn't see what was coming.

The second vicious, life-extinguishing blow.

The blow that would send her into oblivion.

Head cocked to one side, Meinir's attacker stood for a moment, coolly observing her lifeless form, deliberating on the best course of action. The tide was moving in – the whole area as far as the sea wall would be under water within the next couple of hours. But the waves were rising angrily: it was far too risky to take the body out on a boat to dispose of it. Casting about until they were satisfied that still no one was in evidence, the mission to move Meinir began.

Chapter 52

NOW – Saturday 27th May 2023

Elin

The following morning, just wanting to hear a friendly voice, Elin rang Catrin. She filled her in about the dead gull chick, spotting Tom Buckley, Harry Edwards's knife, and more importantly, her visit to Nerys, wondering what her take on it all would be.

What Nerys had said had really shaken Elin. She had been torn, wrestling with Bethan's notion that Libby had been interfering and the woman's explanation about Nerys's predicament and her own desire to help. After all, Nerys had had no one – and Elin still flooded with guilt every time she thought of the state of turmoil her sister must have been in – and Bethan couldn't be blamed for not stepping up: she'd had the shop to run, her own elderly mam to take care of. She didn't have the time to take care of Nerys as well, even if she wanted to. At least Libby had been getting on top of the practical stuff, even if she hadn't been able to do anything about Nerys's fragile state of mind. Or so she'd thought.

But now Nerys's rationale was becoming more coherent, more plausible. Though initially Elin had put her sister's ramblings down to her mental health, what she'd said about their neighbours had sown a further seed of doubt. And now she was beginning to wonder if maybe Bethan had been right about Libby all along.

She thought back to when she'd phoned the house to speak to Nerys all those weeks ago, to how Libby had denied seeing Cai. Had she been telling the truth – or was she hiding something?

It was Nerys's opinion about the Fowlers that Catrin pounced on.

'So Nerys thinks there's something weird about their relationship too, does she?' Catrin's lilt came down the line, a hint of triumph in her tone.

'Well, she didn't say that exactly.' Elin was sitting, feet curled beside her on the settee, absently twirling a finger through her hair. 'Her memory's been affected by the meds and she's still a little slow, not as sharp as usual. It's like she's got some sort of mental block. But she's pretty adamant she didn't want them here – she said they'd been in the cottage that day she was taken into hospital. Seemed really het up about it.'

Elin could hear Catrin exhaling. 'Sounds like something must've gone on. Hopefully it'll all come back to her eventually. Hold on a sec.' There was a pause. Elin could hear Rhys's muffled voice in the background. 'Hey, Rhys just reminded me of something,' Catrin resumed. 'We were talking about it last night. You knew about Peter accusing Rhi in the pub, right?'

'Yeah. Ianto told me.'

'Peter was quick to come and apologise afterwards, to my dad and her. He'd been pretty nasty, from what she said. I'd popped round to see Rhi, so I was there when Peter came over. He was standing at the door and I was in the hallway, earwigging. He definitely wasn't sorry, you could tell. It was more like he was . . . I dunno, worried. He made some excuse about not being well. Didn't want to fall out with anyone, he said. And Libby was behind him, all anxious-looking. Anyway, I left Rhi to it, went into the kitchen. The window was open, and when they were going, I overheard Libby saying something to him about not wanting to have to move again. About thinking this had been a fresh start for them.'

Elin considered this. 'Sounds as if they might have left their last place under a cloud, then. Maybe he's got a history of being aggressive towards women.'

'I could well imagine it. Even more so now,' agreed Catrin. She paused, her tone suddenly serious. 'I'd keep your distance if I were you, El. Stay away from the pair of them. Especially being on your own there and that.'

'I'm *fine*.' Elin feigned an exasperated sigh, although she had begun to feel uncomfortable with Peter living so close. She'd started to watch out for him coming and going, timing leaving the house or even going out to the dustbin so that she wouldn't bump into him again.

'Like I said, you're always welcome to come and stay with us for a week or two,' Catrin went on.

'That's very kind, but I'm okay, honestly.' Elin glanced up at the clock. 'I better go. I'm going to go to the hospital again, I think. Will I see you tomorrow?'

'Aww I'm sorry, doll. We're off to Liverpool in the morning – staying with Aaron and his partner for one night. Ben's a scouse lad, he's really nice. Got us all tickets for a show – he works at the Liverpool Empire.' There was a beat of silence. 'Why don't you come along? I'm sure they wouldn't mind.'

Elin forced a laugh, though she felt slightly deflated. 'No, it's fine. Don't want to be a gooseberry.'

'Seriously, you'd be very welcome. Aaron was asking how you'd got on with the hologram.'

Elin's pulse gave a little jump. 'Did you tell him? About what happened?'

'Not exactly.'

She could hear Catrin shifting about. 'I mean, I did mention it'd conked out again, like. He seemed disappointed and I didn't like to ask him to fix it again just yet, he spent quite a while on it last time. And we don't really know what happened, do we?' Catrin spoke with a lowered voice.

'No,' agreed Elin. 'Apart from it scaring the bejesus out of us. I *know* it was Cai, just know it. It's really been playing on my mind.'

'Listen, El.' Catrin's voice was gentle but firm. 'It's just a computer program. These AI things . . . God knows how they actually work. If it's going to upset you, maybe better leaving well alone, eh?'

Elin could see there was no persuading her friend that anything other-worldly had happened. Either that, or it had unnerved her and she didn't want to admit it. She wasn't going to push it.

'Yeah, maybe you're right. For now, anyway. Perhaps I'll try it again at some point when all the teething troubles have been ironed out.'

Catrin didn't sound convinced. 'Yeah, maybe.'

Elin let out a long breath. 'Right, I'm off then. Have a great time in Liverpool and I'll see you when you get back.'

'See you, doll. Take care.'

She hung up, feeling a little crushed. Maybe Catrin was right and the hologram was best left well alone. Maybe at some point she and Cai had texted about the incident with Ivy's ghost and the grief-bot's narrative had picked up on it. But she definitely couldn't recall any such message.

But those words still kept going round her head. *It wasn't an accident*. The memory gave her a peculiar, uneasy sensation in her gut.

Nerys was actually out of bed, sitting in a chair chatting to one of the nurses who had been doing her observations. Her face lit up as Elin walked in.

'Back so soon! Glad to see you're not looking like a drowned rat today.'

This was much more like the Nerys of old. Elin grinned. The nurse flashed her a smile, then went to get another chair for her, before leaving them to talk.

'You're looking so much better,' Elin told Nerys as she sat down. 'What's happening with the meds? Are they reducing them all gradually?'

Nerys pursed her lips. 'I don't think so. They switched to a different type from what I can gather – and now it's in my system I'm sort of getting used to it. Hence feeling slightly more human. I think they'll start weaning me off it when they think I'm no longer in danger of relapsing. I've got to have "therapy" now, apparently.' She made air quotes with her hands and pulled a face.

'Well, that's no bad thing. The fact they're mentioning therapy must mean you're heading in the right direction. You were barely able to hold your head up a few weeks ago.'

Nerys dropped her eyes for a moment. 'I know,' she said. There was an awkward beat of silence. 'Oh, Bethan was here,' she said suddenly. 'After you left last night. Last time she came, I was still quite out of things. Awful, wasn't it. Her shop window getting broken like that.'

Elin's mouth gaped. 'What? What happened? I haven't heard from her for a while.'

Nerys leaned forwards. 'She got to work the other day and

someone had chucked a brick through the glass. Made a right mess, she said.' She lowered her voice. 'I think she suspects Hugh Roberts, but she's got no proof. The guy opposite has CCTV that covers the shop, but Bethan said you couldn't make out who it was from the footage.' She sighed. 'Sounds like the sort of thing Roberts might do, though. He's got one hell of a temper.'

'Poor Bethan.' Elin shook her head. 'Yeah, I never was keen on that man. Too full of himself by half.'

Nerys tipped her head, studying Elin's face. 'How are you doing, El? What are your plans now, now that—' She broke off, closing her eyes for a moment. 'I'm sorry, that must sound really insensitive. I just wondered if – hoped – you might be coming back here for good?'

Elin gave her a sad smile. 'If you'll have me. I mean, I did sort of desert you, to be fair. And I feel so bad about it. But I've really missed home. And now I've got nowhere else to go.'

'You've always got a home here, you know that. It's as much yours as mine.' Nerys reached out to press her hand. 'And God knows I'd rather not be there on my own when I get out of here.'

Her eyes flickered briefly, as though bringing something to mind.

Elin thought about what she'd seen through their neighbours' window. She wondered whether to mention it, given Nerys's anxiety about them. But maybe it might help to jog her memory.

'Nerys, have you ever wondered if Peter might be violent towards Libby?'

Nerys looked taken aback. 'Violent? Why? Has something happened?'

Elin proceeded to tell her, adding how Peter had behaved afterwards; the way he'd spoken to her and how it had left her feeling uncomfortable.

'It was the look on his face when he turned to the window. It made me go all cold.'

Nerys shuddered. 'Now you've said that, I remember hearing he was pretty nasty to Rhiannon. I thought at the time maybe he'd had an off day – it didn't seem like him, somehow.' She shook her head. 'Who knows what goes on behind closed doors, though. Maybe you're right. Maybe he keeps her in check by threatening her or whatever – she is pretty . . . I dunno, submissive around him, I s'pose. There's definitely something odd there. I still keep thinking . . .'

Nerys broke off suddenly. Her face had turned deathly pale, her eyes widening.

'Oh God. I've remembered something.' Nerys pressed a hand to her mouth. The words tumbled out in a rush now. 'That thing – the thing I found. In Nain's stuff. Just a few weeks ago.'

Elin recalled that earlier visit, Nerys breaking through her stupor to clutch at her sleeve, eyes wild, begging her to be careful. She swallowed. 'What thing?'

'A letter,' Nerys said, sitting forward. 'An *anonymous* letter. From someone who lived next door to Peter and Libby before they moved to Traeth Coch. It was in one of Nain's keepsake boxes, among a pile of letters.' She began to pick at her index finger, the way she always did when she was agitated. 'It was a warning. About him. About how malicious he is. How he seems to take pleasure in inflicting damage.'

Elin's mind pounced on the word *malicious*. She felt suddenly lightheaded. 'Why would Nain have kept that?'

'I don't know,' Nerys said, her eyes darting. 'But she'd said stuff about him to me before. I just thought it was the dementia talking. But maybe she really knew something. Maybe she saw something herself.' She leaned closer, her voice dropping to a whisper. 'I traced the address – went to see the neighbour.'

Elin widened her eyes. 'You did *what*? What happened?'

'He followed me.'

Elin's stomach contracted. 'Peter?'

'Yes. Yes, I think so.' Nerys tugged at her hair, rolling her eyes to the ceiling in evident frustration. '*Ohh*, it's so annoying. Everything's still jumbled up. I can't quite remember exactly . . . But he came round, that much I do know. I remember him standing there in the kitchen. Said he knew I'd been poking my nose in and told me if I said anything to anyone, I'd live to regret it.'

A chill ran through Elin despite the overheated ward. 'And their old neighbour? What happened there?'

Nerys shook her head. 'I still can't quite—it's all pretty hazy. Like a dream, when you can't quite recall the details. I just know I acted on the letter and it obviously wound him up.'

Elin opened her mouth to ask more: When? How? Why the hell hadn't she told anyone at the time?

A nurse appeared at the foot of the bed, her expression business-like.

'That's enough for today,' the nurse said, gently but firmly. 'Nerys, you're getting yourself worked up. It's time for your medication.'

'I'm fine,' Nerys protested. She grabbed Elin's hand. 'I need to think. But I'm sure there's more.'

'And *I'm* sure it's nothing that can't wait,' the nurse said, looking pointedly at Elin. 'Visiting time is over.'

Elin stood, her legs unsteady. 'I'll come back, I promise,' she said, leaning in to give Nerys a squeeze. 'Soon.'

Nerys nodded, but her eyes were filled with anxiety. 'Be careful, El,' she said. 'Please.'

The rain had eased to a fine mist by the time Elin drove back towards Traeth Coch. Ahead of her, beneath the huge, bleak expanse of sky, the sea lay slate-grey and calm. Too calm. The sort of calm which always seems to precede something turbulent.

As Elin turned down the lane, Nain's cottage came into view, with its familiar chimney and rounded stone. Though she would normally feel comforted by the sight of home, glimpsing Peter and Libby's car parked at the end of the track, her muscles tensed. The glow of the lamp through their curtains told her they were home. It only added to her discomfort.

Elin sat in Nerys's Aygo for several minutes. Her mind was reeling with everything. Cai's loss, the memory of her nain's steady, watchful presence in the house, replaced by the old lady's suspicion and anxiety in her later years. But above all now, Nerys's fear: paranoia, the doctors had labelled it. All part of her illness. Although Nerys had almost certainly been through a trauma of some sort, that much they had recognised. And what her sister had told her seemed to validate Elin's own niggling suspicions after her recent experiences.

Glancing up at Swift Cabin as she finally stepped out into the damp air, Elin couldn't shake the feeling that something had changed. That the very ground beneath her could no longer be trusted.

Keeping her eyes focused on her own front door, Elin marched up the path and turned the key in the lock. Only when it was safely bolted behind her did she feel able to exhale.

Chapter 53

NOW – Saturday 27th May 2023

Elin

Finally back in the cottage, Elin closed the curtains and sat on the settee for a moment, her mind flying. Remembering the anonymous letter that Nerys said she'd found among Nain's things, she wanted to see it for herself. And she wondered if there was anything else up there. Something that Nain had put away in case she needed it later. Something that Nerys had missed.

She climbed the stairs and poked her head into what was now Nerys's room – the room she herself was sleeping in and that they'd once shared. The faded rosebud curtains Nain had made still hung at the window. Even in her state of mental anguish, Nerys had left everything as orderly as ever, and Elin had taken care not to disturb any of her sister's belongings. She hadn't even unpacked her own suitcase properly.

There had been no reason to search the room – until now.

But a quick glance into the drawers revealed only neatly folded clothes, items stored on hangers in the cupboard pressed and ready to wear. The bare essentials in the way of toiletries sat on the dressing table. Paired shoes stacked in boxes in one corner. Nothing of any note.

She went into her grandmother's bedroom and paused for a moment before opening the wardrobe. The faint, familiar smell of baby powder and Nain's favourite rose eau-de-toilette still lingered on the clothes hanging there. On the top shelf was the Aran sweater that she'd knitted years ago for Mam. Tears sprang to Elin's eyes, remembering how soothing she'd always found the constant click of Nain's knitting needles. The jumpers and scarves she had made for so many people in the community over the years, never asking for a penny.

The bottom of the cupboard was crammed with boxes stacked on top of each other: shoes, hats. Knitting patterns, an assortment of wool and needles.

Miscellaneous – clearly marked in Nerys's handwriting. Far too many miscellaneous.

Elin blew out her cheeks, not knowing where to start. Taking a box at a time, she sorted through each, meticulously examining everything within. Owing to all the various pieces of paper to sift through, it was a painfully slow process. After almost two hours, she had gone carefully through all of the paperwork she'd discovered and found nothing of any significance. Feeling deflated, she put everything back as she had found it. She wasn't about to discard anything without Nerys's say-so.

Having had no supper, Elin decided she'd better make something. Stiff from kneeling for so long, she eased herself to her feet and was about to go downstairs, when she paused in the doorway of Mam's bedroom. Would Nain – or even Nerys – have put something in there instead? Nerys's jumbled memory still hadn't yielded everything and she must have stored that letter away somewhere. It certainly hadn't been in any of the boxes Elin had just gone through.

Elin took a breath as she entered the room. She went purposefully to the wardrobe and opened both doors, slowly separating the clothes on the rail, feeling inside any pockets. She checked every corner at the bottom where the shoes were laid out in pairs. Nothing. She began wistfully opening and closing drawers, lifting items to look beneath them, but everything was where she'd have expected it to be.

In the corner sat Mam's old portable CD player, the narrow pine shelves beside it crammed with discs. Elin scanned the edges, reading off some of the familiar titles. She felt a pang of nostalgia, the memory of Mam's melodic voice singing along to some of her favourite songs ringing in her head. But as her eyes travelled to the foot of the stack, Elin realised that those at the bottom were sitting on a small box.

Elin frowned. She couldn't slide it out without the whole lot tumbling out. One by one, she removed the discs, placing them carefully on the floor beside her, until she came to the rectangular cardboard container. It was around three inches deep, maybe eight long by six wide. The lid was embossed with a single pink rose. It looked as though it probably once contained stationery or something similar.

Elin wasn't sure what she was looking at when she lifted the lid. Broken bits of things; odd items that she was sure had no connection to Mam. A small, scruffy notebook. But there, tucked on the shelf behind where the box had been, was an envelope. No name, just Nain's cottage's address. Elin's heart quickened.

She had found the letter.

Sitting on the floor, she began to read.

Chapter 54

BEFORE – March 2023

Nerys

Nerys's mind was in overdrive. She was kicking herself now for not having taken down the phone number for the solicitor's firm in Leicester. But then again, the letter had been sent years earlier. Things might not be kept on file for that long – or the person dealing with it all might have retired.

How could she trace who'd sent the anonymous letter? It *must* have been a neighbour of Peter and Libby's – and from the postmark, it had been mailed somewhere on the island. Like the letter from the solicitor in Leicester, it had been sent over a decade ago. But she felt sure that the sender couldn't have been anyone in Traeth Coch. If Peter had been up to anything underhand, everyone in the community would have got to hear about it by now.

Nerys fished out her iPad and typed into the search bar:

How to find someone's address from fifteen years ago.

It came back with 192.com – People Finder. Nerys typed in Peter and Libby's names and waited.

To view full address, you need to subscribe.

She gritted her teeth when she realised she'd have to pay a fee to access the details, but entered her card number anyway.

And there they were: Peter and Liberty Fowler. An address in Leicester from twenty-two years ago. But then – and this was news to Nerys – another more recent, located in Mynydd Mechell, a small hamlet on the other side of Anglesey. There was only one way to find out if the person who sent the letter lived there. Taking care to lock all the doors and windows in the cottage, she headed for her car.

*

Nerys hadn't realised quite how tucked away Mynydd Mechell was. The Sat-Nav took her little car along winding, single-track lanes, hedges clawing at the doors as she slowed for other vehicles to pass, the sea long gone from sight. The address from the website had looked much closer on the screen – just another dot on the island map – though the hamlet felt withdrawn from the world, right in the back of beyond. But eventually she arrived.

Nerys held her breath for a moment as she pulled up in a lay-by, opposite a sagging stone cottage, its roof patched with mismatched, lichen encrusted slate. Next door stood the house Peter and Libby had once lived in. Seeing it unsettled her more than she'd expected. It was smaller than she'd imagined, hunched beneath a row of trees, its windows blank and dark. They had lived here. All those years ago. Not newly arrived retirees from the East Midlands; not strangers to the island at all.

They had lied.

The letter remained at the front of her mind as she crossed the road: the shaky, urgent handwriting, the damning accusations. *A smiling assassin.* That's how it had described Peter. Stronger words for the similar sentiment expressed by her nain.

Climbing from the car, Nerys had the odd sense of someone watching her, but looking around there was no one in evidence. It was probably the fact that the lane was so secluded, the trees wrapping around the little cluster of houses giving it an air of foreboding. Steeling herself, she pushed open the rickety iron gate to make her way up an uneven, overgrown path, then knocked on the neighbouring cottage's door. When it opened, she found herself looking at a woman in her late forties or early fifties, thin and drawn, with nervous, narrowed grey eyes that flicked past Nerys's shoulder before settling back on her face.

'Yes?' the woman said almost suspiciously, wiping her hands on a small towel that had seen better days.

'*Helo, Nerys yw fy enw i.*' Nerys introduced herself with a smile, explained that she lived in Traeth Coch, next door to Peter and Libby. She tried to keep her tone casual, apologetic, as if she were asking after a misplaced parcel. 'I was just wondering,' she said, watching the woman's face for a reaction. 'Were you living here when they were next door?'

The woman's mouth tightened. For a moment Nerys thought she might actually close the door in her face. Still clutching the towel, her hand stayed on the edge of the frame, knuckles white.

'Oh yes,' she said. 'But I try not to think about it these days.' Her eyes wobbled. 'About *him*.'

Nerys's heart quickened. 'Only, I found a letter mentioning him. A sort of . . . well, a warning. My nain had kept it. Even though it was anonymous, it was obviously sent by a concerned former neighbour.'

Glancing upwards, Nerys saw CCTV cameras, fixed beneath the eaves, watching the road, the front path, the gate.

'My brother put them in,' the woman said, following her gaze. 'It was him that sent the letter. He found out where they'd moved to. I think he was worried the man'd do something *really* bad eventually. He's dead now, poor Llew. Massive heart attack.'

'I'm so sorry.'

Seeing the anguished look on the woman's face, Nerys felt suddenly uncomfortable. As though she was being intrusive. She wondered how long ago her brother had died.

But then the woman sighed, a long, weary sound, and stepped back.

'You'd better come in,' she said.

Inside, the cottage smelled faintly of damp and wood smoke. Nerys followed her into a small sitting room, leading off the tiny, dark hallway. The ceiling was low and the space felt cramped, over-filled with oddments of furniture. The curtains were half drawn, despite the daylight.

'I'm Siwan, by the way. 'Scuse the state of the place. I don't get many visitors.' The woman sniffed, indicating a small monitor placed on a side table under the window. 'I don't really use the cameras any more. Probably no bad thing keeping them, though, bit of a deterrent if people think they work. But back then . . .' She shook her head. 'Back then we needed them.'

Siwan told her slowly at first, then in a breathless rush, as if once she'd begun it was impossible to stop. Years earlier, she'd moved back home to live with her brother, to escape an abusive relationship. Things had started small – odd, spiteful things. A neighbour's pond poisoned overnight, every fish floating white-bellied on the surface by morning. Scratches appearing along car doors, deep and deliberate. Tyres losing air. Fences damaged when the winds hadn't even been high. And always, somehow, Peter was nearby, sympathetic and willing, tools in hand.

'He seemed so . . . pleasant,' the woman said. 'Always smiling.

Everyone thought he was so kind. Most of the people round here at that time were quite elderly – a lot of them have passed away since he left.' She paused. 'It was difficult to pinpoint exactly when it started, or even anything that might've triggered it. But once Llew and I realised what he was getting up to, we were horrified.'

'So there was no obvious reason for him doing these things? I mean, nobody pushed his nose out of joint or anything?'

Siwan shook her head. 'It was bizarre. The old lady whose fish we suspected he poisoned was really upset. She said he'd painted a fence for her that same week and she'd been singing his praises. She just couldn't accept that it'd been him, and nor could a lot of the other neighbours. But once Llew cottoned onto him, we started watching him more closely. It was a real eye-opener. It was almost like, I don't know, like he felt *compelled* to do bad things. Like bored kids that vandalize stuff for no reason. As though he couldn't help himself. A sociopath, or whatever they call it.'

'And do you—have you got anything showing him doing things?'

She nodded vigorously. 'Oh, yes. Hours of it. For all the use it was. Llew saved it all on a DVD – he was good with stuff like that.'

Siwan rummaged through the scratched teak sideboard and held up the battered jewel case for a DVD. She switched on the old television in the corner of the room, slid the disc into the player beneath and began to fast forward with a grubby remote control. There were hours of nothing significant, until a figure appeared on the screen, the image by no means perfect, but distinct enough. The woman stopped forwarding and pressed *play*. Nerys recognised his form instantly: the squareness of the shoulders, the slightly bow-legged stance.

Peter.

On the screen he moved along the road in the early hours, stopping beside a car. His hand rose. There was a brief, violent motion, then he stepped back, almost leisurely.

Nerys felt a chill spread through her chest. 'Oh, my God.'

'We went to the police,' said Siwan. 'They agreed it was probably him. But "probably" wasn't enough for them to secure a conviction. It would've been a waste of their time and resources trying to get it to court, they reckoned. It's all about *money*, isn't it?' Anger flashed in her eyes.

'They said there was no clear view of his face in any of the footage, no proof beyond doubt. He was always very careful.' Her mouth set into a hard line. 'They did go and warn him, though. Told him the incident was on file. Said his card was marked and if anything else happened, they'd arrest him.'

Peter had painted Nain's fence, mowed the lawn from time to time; fixed the leaky tap in the kitchen. Jump-started Nerys's car when the battery was flat. Though she hadn't taken them up on it, she'd felt grateful when he and Libby had offered support after Nain died.

'*We're only next door. Don't hesitate to ask if you need anything.*'

Only next door. The words sent a chill through her now.

The woman let the footage run to the final clip. Nerys peered more closely at the screen. Her breath caught in her throat. This time it was a clear image of Peter, standing alone in the empty road, his face lit by the street lamp.

Nerys noticed that Siwan had begun to shake a little and felt suddenly guilty. It had clearly been traumatic for her at the time and reliving it all was stirring up unpleasant memories.

'This was captured the night before they moved away,' she told Nerys, lifting a hand to her mouth.

Peter was looking directly up at the camera, staring straight into the lens, his eyes piercing. He didn't smile. He stood very still, his lips moving slowly, deliberately, forming words without sound.

Nerys felt something roll in her stomach. 'What—what's he saying?' she asked, though a part of her didn't want to know.

Siwan hesitated. 'I couldn't tell, either. Not at first. But I have a friend who's hearing impaired – she can lip read.' She swallowed as her eyes searched the frozen image on the screen. 'He was saying, "*Fuck you. I'm gonna dance on your grave*".'

Nerys gasped. 'But the police – you showed them this, right? What did they say?'

Siwan chewed her lip. 'He wasn't saying it directly to our faces, so they said they couldn't do anything. It felt like he was laughing at us. Always staying just beneath the radar of the law.' She shook her head angrily.

'Whether it was aimed at me, or Llew, or both of us, I don't know. But I blame Peter Fowler for what happened to Llew. My brother wasn't a well man anyway. His mobility was poor. The strain of it all, the constant stress, having a *shinach* like that so close by, the sleepless nights wondering what he was going to do next. It really took its toll on him.' Tears filled her eyes. 'Even after they'd moved on, he was still so wound up about it all. That letter you found. It was just after sending that, he dropped dead. Right outside our front door.'

Nerys's heart went out to the woman. 'I'm so sorry. It must've been terrible for you.'

Siwan nodded wordlessly. Her gaze strayed to the window.

'I haven't clapped eyes on either of them since, thank God. His wife was a strange one. Barely said two words to anyone, unless he was with her. And even then, she'd be looking for his reaction all the time. It was like she was waiting for his permission or something. As though he'd told her to keep quiet unless he said otherwise.' Siwan took in a breath, her eyes widening suddenly. '*Aros*. I've got something of theirs. I just remembered. Wait there.'

She disappeared briefly, into what Nerys assumed was the kitchen. She could hear drawers opening and closing, before Siwan reappeared.

'The cottage next door has been sold now, but it's still empty at the moment. But when they were here, they'd been renting the place. There were another lot of people in for about six months after they left. Anyway, they found this in a cupboard and brought it round, asked if we had a forwarding address.' She held out a small shallow box, the lid embossed with the faded picture of a pink rose. The kind that once held notelets and envelopes.

Taking it from her outstretched hand, Nerys peered inside. She frowned, unsure initially what she was looking at. Odd bits and bobs, the kind of objects that might be kept to repair something at a later date. Fragments of splintered wood. The resin head of a dove, clearly broken off a garden ornament. Part of a slate name plate from a house, the wording ending where it had snapped clean in half. One hinge, which looked as if it had come from a gate. A hefty bolt. A jagged piece of plastic from a wing-mirror. A red collar for a cat, worn and frayed, with a tiny rusting bell. Four tyre valve dust caps. But Nerys's stomach dropped as her eyes landed on a sachet of something labelled '*WARNING*: *HARMFUL TO AQUATIC LIFE*', remembering what Siwan had said about the lady's fish. And beneath everything, a tatty, lined notebook. As she began to thumb through the pages, coldness prickled along her spine.

'I wasn't sure what it all was to begin with,' said Siwan. 'But when I read the notebook, it became as clear as day. It's like a log of some of the things he chose to break. But again, it's not proof. Not as if it's definitely his handwriting, even – and all those things, he could just explain them away as stuff he'd picked up that might come in useful. Stuff no one needed any more.'

Nerys shuddered, suddenly thinking of Nyten back at home. 'That collar? Was there a cat involved somehow?'

Siwan pursed her lips. 'There was an elderly chap. He passed away years ago, now,' she said slowly. 'He lived alone, a couple of hundred yards away. He only had an old cat for company, scrawny little thing, all skin and bone. She disappeared one day – he wondered if a fox might've carried her off. Really upset, he was. Never found out what actually happened to her.'

Staring at the words, etched angrily and deep into pages of the notebook, rambling and without context, Nerys realised that this was Peter's warped form of justification; his memory of 'why it had to be done'. Some perceived snub or minor misdemeanour that he had blown up in his mind, clearly believing it deserved retaliation. But no evidence that he had written it. Nothing concrete to connect him to it at all. She felt slightly sick.

Siwan nodded towards the box. 'Take it with you. If he starts his antics again, it's something to show the police. Maybe if things got bad enough, they'd analyse the handwriting.' She blew out her cheeks. 'Who am I kidding? I'm clutching at straws. I s'pose the coppers have got bigger fish to fry – they'd think it was all petty stuff. It would just be sweet to see him get some sort of comeuppance, that's all.'

Nerys nodded in agreement. Peter really was a vile, vindictive scumbag; that much was clear. How had she not seen through him before?

Thanking Siwan and clutching the box, Nerys left not long after that. She'd heard – and seen – more than enough. Outside, the air felt colder; the light was dimmer, the wind whistling through the leaves of the tall sycamores around the houses, the branches bending until they creaked. As she drove away, the image of Peter's upward-tilted face, the cold, unblinking eyes staring into the camera, the mouth twisted with hatred, pursued her down the lane.

By the time she'd descended the winding road to Traeth Coch, the sea ahead restless and a myriad shades of grey and green. Nerys's hands were tight and stiff on the wheel. The letter Nain had kept was no longer a relic to be consigned to the past. It was a warning that Nerys had found too late – or perhaps just in time.

Now that she knew what kind of man Peter really was, a cold, unsettling feeling crept through her. And with it came a single, dreadful thought: if he had been capable of all that before, what, as Llew had feared, might he do next?

Chapter 55

NOW – Saturday 27th May 2023

Elin

Elin put the letter down, a queasy feeling churning in her stomach. She lifted the lid from the stationery box and picked up a small notebook. Its once glossy blue cover was creased and dog-eared, the pages warped slightly as if it had been handled often, or squashed into a pocket. Even before she'd opened it, she'd guessed who it belonged to.

It was Peter's.

The writing was pressed hard into the paper. Names appeared on some pages. Addresses on others. Short, sharp sentences followed, heavy with bitterness, filled with unwarranted grievances. Someone who had ignored him. Someone who seemed to be smirking when looking his way. Someone who had failed to show appreciation when he'd helped them. Another who failed to maintain their front garden, dragging down the tone of the neighbourhood. Elin turned the pages slowly, appalled by the pettiness of what she was reading.

Beneath the notebook lay the rest.

A resin dove's head, ripped cleanly from a garden ornament, its blank eyes staring up at her. Valve caps from car tyres, greasy and dull. Splintered, creosote-coated wood, jagged where it had been snapped from a fence. A slate nameplate broken neatly in two, part of a house name still legible across it. A small sachet, its top rolled over, the picture of a skull and crossbones warning of its harmful contents. And at the bottom of the box, a red cat's collar, the rusty bell still attached. When she lifted it, it made a muted, rattling sound.

Elin's chest tightened.

These weren't random objects. They weren't rubbish. They were some kind of trophies.

Each item corresponded to something in the notebook, each grievance catalogued. People who had crossed him. People he clearly believed deserved something taken from them. His subsequent spiteful actions all justified in his twisted mind.

A chill slid through Elin. Peter's face rose unbidden in her mind: the amiable smile, the offers of help, the careful way he'd always seemed to be watching without looking. She had trusted him. Worse, she had liked him.

She closed the box with shaking hands.

Elin remembered suddenly the unease she'd felt when Valeria had called that day, the way it had stirred an old memory of Nain and Mam, years ago, pausing mid-conversation with arched eyebrows as raised voices spilled over the fence from next door. Arguments – heated, angry ones – nothing like the cheerful, easy-going front Libby and Peter presented to the world. Elin had been young, but the tension had lingered, tangible enough to make her sit up and take notice.

Peter had explained it all away, of course. He always did.

They'd met him on the track as they returned from the shop one day. Fliss was 'a bit headstrong,' he'd told Nain with an apologetic grimace and a laugh. Things hadn't been easy when she came to stay after they'd first moved to Traeth Coch and she'd returned to Spain sooner than planned. With his familiar grin, he'd said that 'normal service had been resumed'. Elin remembered wondering what that meant and it had stayed with her.

The phrase echoed in her mind now. What exactly *was* 'normal service' for Peter and Libby? The memory of what she'd seen that afternoon when she walked up their path, the way he'd reacted afterwards, had completely altered her impression of the man. And had Bethan been right about Libby all along, rummaging through Nerys's belongings? Had she been looking for something? That letter – or even Peter's box of trophies?

A horrible thought crept into her mind. *The dead gull chick.* She'd thought perhaps Tom Buckley could have been responsible. But from everything she'd learned, it seemed that it might have been exactly the kind of stunt that Peter would have pulled. But what had she ever done to him? And yet all of the evidence in that notebook pointed to the psyche of someone completely irrational. Delusional. It was quite possible she hadn't done anything at all.

*

That night, sleep came in fragments. Elin drifted in and out, her dreams muddled and disturbing. From nowhere, an image of Peter and Libby appeared, standing together outside Nain's garden gate, staring up at the house accusingly. And then, as though conjured from her subconscious, a scene as clear as a 3D film played behind her eyes.

Cai, standing in the narrow lane that led from the beach, the hedges closing in around him on either side. The place where he had died. The place she hadn't been able to face. He looked oddly solid, the way he had in life. She could even see the creases in his jacket. His face was almost lit from behind, his hair wind-ruffled and mud on his boots; that familiar tilt to his head when he was deep in thought.

He didn't speak. He just stared at her, his dark eyes solemn, then turned in slow motion, to glance up towards the overgrown fields beyond the lane at the land he'd been so excited about. The place where he was sure something important lay waiting to be discovered beneath brambles and turf.

Elin woke with her heart pounding against her ribcage, her throat tight. She was shivering, despite the warmth of the air. Convinced for a moment she could still feel him there, her eyes swept every corner of the room. Though she was all alone, it seemed as if someone had passed through; that she might have just missed them. The longing was almost unbearable.

The memory of the hologram surfaced again, unwanted but insistent. Cai's image, assembled from actual photos and audio footage, was intended to soothe her grief. To help her survive the dark days that had followed his death. But his words had strayed from the script. And what he *had* said had left her with more questions than answers. *It was no accident*.

At the time, it seemed so real. But as time passed, she'd tried to tell herself she'd read too much into it. Now, steeped in the sense that something was deeply awry, she wasn't so sure. The dream; Nerys's warning. Harry's knife. The recent unpalatable discovery about Peter. It all felt like fragments of a disjointed puzzle that she needed to fit together. But how?

The urge that followed was sudden and overwhelming. She knew now that she needed to go to the lane.

Elin spent the day trying to push down the feeling, telling

herself it was madness; that, however startlingly vivid, it had just been a dream. That grief did strange things to the mind. Elin cleaned the cottage from top to bottom. She made herself pasta salad for lunch, but it remained untouched on her plate. She picked up one of Nerys's Marian Keyes novels and tried to read, but couldn't focus. All the time, the lane was calling to her. She stood at the window and stared across the bay, to the gap between the grassy ridge where it began.

Cai had been an archaeologist. It was an integral part of him – his belief in the importance of the past, the way it linked inextricably with the present. The driver who killed him had never been found. Cai had been carrying a knife belonging to someone else. A stolen knife. Where had he got it? Had the police missed something? Was he trying to tell her to go and find whatever it was? Thoughts were bouncing around her head so quickly it had begun to throb.

By early evening, as the light softened, the sky beginning its gradual drift toward dusk, Elin could resist no longer. The low tide provided the perfect opportunity, and she needed to seize it. She pulled on her jacket, her hands trembling now with anticipation rather than fear, and stepped out purposefully across the sands.

Chapter 56

NOW – Wednesday 10th May 2023

Three weeks earlier

Libby

Rain pattered against the back door. Libby leaned against her kitchen counter, staring into a cup of untouched tea. She held the mug in one hand, rubbing absently with her index finger at a mark on the rim that had long disappeared.

The front door opened suddenly. She heard familiar, steady footsteps. Peter appeared in the kitchen doorway, ruddy-cheeked from the sea breeze. He shrugged off his coat and slipped it over the back of a chair. Meeting her gaze, he smiled broadly – but it was the kind of smile that was instantly summoned, not gradual. The kind that could vanish every bit as quickly.

'How's my girl? You look miles away. Everything all right?'

Libby stiffened, then painted on a smile, attempting to conceal her troubled thoughts. 'Just tired. It's been one of those days.'

Peter stepped up behind her, placing a cool, strong hand on her waist, a little too firmly. Libby didn't pull away, though her fingers tightened around the mug.

'Tell us what's up.'

She turned to face him, swallowing. 'I was speaking to Elin earlier. Over the fence. That Bethan's been stirring the pot. Saying I've been . . . interfering. Overstepping the mark. Like she thought I was trying to control Nerys.'

Peter's expression shifted, still smiling, but more thinly. Showing more teeth. 'Is that so?'

Libby nodded, a quaver in her voice. 'I did try to explain, told her how things had been with Nerys. But it felt like she'd already made her mind up, and I . . .' She shook her head. 'I hate feeling like I've done something wrong when – well, all we were doing was trying to help, wasn't it?'

Peter stroked her arm. To anyone looking on, the action might have appeared tender. But Libby remained rigid, her eyes flicking downwards warily.

'You did what you thought was best. We both did. Nerys'd be in an even worse state if you hadn't stepped in.' He paused. 'People often jump to the wrong conclusion when they don't know the bigger picture. And besides, Elin hasn't been around in ages. She's in no position to judge. She should be bloody grateful.'

Libby looked at him uncertainly. 'Elin wasn't being unkind,' she said hastily. 'Just a bit . . . cautious. But Bethan made me sound like some sort of busybody. Like I was poking around for the hell of it.'

Peter let out a bark of laughter, but his eyes remained cold. '*Pfft.* That Bethan's always been a gossip. As for Elin,' – he smoothed a lock of hair carefully from Libby's face – 'she must be really fragile at the moment, with everything that's happened. Grief affects people's judgement. Makes them imagine all sorts.'

His tone was soothing, measured: but Libby detected a simmering undertone. 'I don't want any trouble, Peter. I want things to be friendly, especially when Nerys comes home.'

Peter kissed her forehead – a gentle gesture, although it felt oddly possessive. 'And they will be, love. I'll make sure of it.'

He lifted the mug from her hands and walked past her towards the sink, rolling up his sleeves as if preparing to wash up. His back was to her, but the square set of his shoulders was unmistakeable: the tendons in his neck flexing, his jaw tight.

Peter's voice stayed calm, almost cheerful. 'People shouldn't go around accusing you of things they don't understand. I can see it's upset you. And I don't like you being upset.'

Libby watched him anxiously, her fingers twisting together. 'Peter, you're not going to say anything to them, are you?'

He glanced over his shoulder with another reassuring smile – the kind he always used to placate her, but which only left her uneasy now. 'Me? No, no. I won't say a word.' He paused for a moment. 'But that doesn't mean I can't sort things out. Quietly. Make sure they don't trouble you again.'

The colour drained from Libby's cheeks. 'Peter, please. I don't want any drama. Not . . .'

Peter turned the tap on, tipping the cold tea down the plughole. 'You won't even know I've done anything,' he said, raising his voice above the rush of water. 'You can trust me, love. I'll handle it. But in my own good time.'

As he scrubbed the mug with slow, deliberate movements, his eyes focused somewhere far away, calculating, cold; his mouth twitching.

Libby looked down at her quivering hands, steadying them against the worktop as she forced a small smile. But inside, a familiar knot tightened in her stomach. She knew that tone. She recognised that look.

And whatever Peter might be planning – neither Elin nor Bethan was going to like it.

Chapter 57

BEFORE – March 2023

Nerys

Looking up at the glow from Peter and Libby's window, Nerys felt suddenly apprehensive about going into her own cottage. It was evening now, the light dimming. She desperately needed to speak to someone about what she'd discovered from Siwan. Elin – well, it just felt like she was too far away to be much help right now. Bethan had so much on her plate with the shop and everything, but she was a good friend. And she was level-headed: she'd know what to do.

It was so awkward. She had no doubt that everything Siwan had told her about Peter was true – hell, that horrible video clip spoke for itself – but the police clearly couldn't do anything without concrete proof. Maybe she should have reported him herself for burning the rubbish, but it had all seemed rather petty when she'd thought about it afterwards, especially when he'd come round with the chocolates. Had that been his plan – to make her feel guilty so that she wouldn't say anything to anyone? An accepted gift would make her beholden to him in a way, wouldn't it?

The cottage had never felt so empty as Nerys closed the front door behind her. As she crossed the living room floor, her own footsteps echoed eerily from the walls. Every sound was amplified. The creak of the stairs as she climbed to the bedroom seemed too loud. Nyten was sleeping on the bed. She stirred, lifting her head, and gave a soft miaow as Nerys went over to stroke her. The little cat had almost fully recovered, but was nervous now, and not keen to go out for longer than a few minutes. It was probably for the best – Nerys didn't want to risk her being injured again, more so than ever now.

Nerys hurried through the house, checking the doors and windows, closing curtains. Once satisfied she had safely shut out the world beyond, she made herself a light supper of beans on toast and sat in the living room with it on a tray, picking at her food with no real appetite. She kept the TV on just loud enough that she could hear it, but not so much that the volume would drown out any suspicious noise. After everything she had learned, she felt the need to remain alert, tuned in to what was going on around her.

Nyten had come downstairs and stretched out next to Nerys on the settee, where she sat in a state of brooding anxiety all evening, staring at the TV screen but not absorbing the programme. She hadn't been able to stop thinking about Llew's letter, the box of bizarre trophies; about the tangible fear it had brought to Siwan's voice as she'd spoken of the sheer spite and cunning Peter had displayed; the way he'd always known how to stay just on the right side of criminality. Worst of all was that final clip the woman had shown her: Peter's cold-eyed stare, his face twisted with hatred as he mouthed words meant to instil dread.

'I'm gonna dance on your grave.'

Nerys tried to tell herself she was overreacting, to convince herself she was safe. She had locked both outside doors. She had checked them twice. And why would Peter suddenly do something to her, out of the blue? He'd lived next door for years, never done anything before. Maybe he'd held a grudge against Siwan and her brother, and the others in Mynydd Mechell, for some reason. Maybe more had happened to upset him than was recorded in the notebook.

No, she was being melodramatic. She poured herself a glass of white wine from the fridge to relax a little.

After washing up the supper things, she made her way wearily up to bed. It had been a very long day and the wine had been enough to tip her over the edge of tiredness. But she resolved to discuss everything with Bethan in the morning. Bethan was strong and resourceful: she'd be able to advise her.

*

The noise came from downstairs not long after midnight: a soft clink, like metal hitting the ground, followed by the unmistakeable scrape of wood across stone.

Nerys sat up. Her heart began to thud so hard it left her lightheaded. Nyten, who had been nestled beside her, stirred a little then curled into a tighter ball, as Nerys eased herself from the bed and to her feet. She strained her ears for further evidence of movement below. Every step quiet and deliberate, she crossed the room and took the stairs one at a time, wincing as the last couple creaked slowly beneath her weight. There was a distinct chill as she reached the bottom, as though a blast of cold air had recently gusted through. At the last step she paused, her hand gripping the banister, and listened again. Turning to her left, Nerys froze.

Someone was standing in her kitchen.

Her heart hammering, she stepped forward and flicked on the light.

Peter turned slowly from the counter, as though he had all the time in the world. He was still wearing his green fleece, zipped to the throat, his familiar, amiable smile settling into place before slipping, quite quickly, into something else. Something that made her blood run cold.

The breath left Nerys in a rush. 'How—how did you get in?' she asked, her eyes darting to the back door.

He lifted his hand, and there it was: a key, dangling between his fingers. 'Libby had one once,' he said benignly. 'From when she was feeding your old cat, remember?'

Nerys remembered. She remembered Libby pressing the key into Nain's palm with a smile, after they'd returned from a weekend in Llangollen. She remembered Nain hanging it back on the hook by the door. The box of fudge they'd given the woman as a 'thank you' present for looking after Llwyd.

Peter held the key aloft. The metal was the wrong colour, an unfamiliar piece of blue wool tied around the grip. Her stomach lurched.

'You got a copy cut,' she whispered.

He smiled again then, his lips thin and mean. 'I've always liked to plan ahead. You never know when things might come in handy.'

His eyes narrowed suddenly, pinning her to the spot. 'You've been prying, haven't you? Asking questions,' he said. 'About me.'

Nerys's mind flashed to the tree-lined lane in Mynydd Mechell, to the sense of eyes on her that she'd had briefly, and had too readily dismissed as she knocked on Siwan's door.

'I don't know what you're on about,' she said, though she could feel the tremor in her voice.

'Oh, I think you do.' He leaned back against the counter, utterly at ease. 'I spotted you, you see. I was driving back from Amlwch. I saw you coming the other way and turning left off the main road. I was curious, so I thought I'd follow. Not hard following someone – especially when they've got a bright red car like yours. People are too busy with their eyes on the road ahead. They don't expect to be watched.' His smile widened, though his eyes remained hard. 'You shouldn't believe everything you hear. That Llew and his bloody sister – nightmare neighbours. There're two sides to every story, you know.' He cocked his head. 'I've always been good to your family, haven't I? Helped your nain with all sorts over the years. Painted your fence.'

Nerys recalled the urgency in Nain's voice as she'd watched Peter through the window, thick with warning. Why the hell hadn't she listened? She thought now of poor little Nyten, attacked in the safety of her own garden. Was he the one responsible?

'What do you want?' she asked, a chill building from deep inside her.

'Did she give you something, by any chance? Something that belongs to me?'

Nerys swallowed. 'No. Why – did you leave something behind when you moved out?'

His eyes narrowed. 'I think you know I did. And I think that Siwan bitch gave it to you.'

Nerys shook her head, a little too vehemently. 'No. No, she didn't give me anything. We just talked.'

He tipped his head to one side again, regarding her with evident distaste. 'I think you're lying.'

His eyes flicked beyond her somewhere for a moment, then back to her face, holding her now in an unblinking stare with pupils that felt like drills. 'It might be best if you kept your little chat to yourself. And if she *did* give you anything – well, it wouldn't be a good idea for you to show anyone. I just thought I should mention it. Accidents can happen, you know,' he said, his voice quietly menacing. 'Things happen when people are least expecting them. I mean, it'd be a shame if you had to spend the rest of your life looking over your shoulder.'

Nerys felt her throat tighten. He went on, his manner conversational now, as if he were discussing the weather. 'And such a worry when it comes to others, too. The ones you care about. That woman you work for – Bethan, isn't it? Lovely little shop she's got there. The wiring in those old buildings can be such a fire risk, though.'

Nerys could hardly breathe. Remembering what Siwan had said about poor Llew, a queasy feeling turned in her stomach. She thought suddenly of capable, caring Nain; of how stupid she'd been to doubt her judgement.

'There's a knife underneath.' That's what she'd said. How right she'd been. She thought of her lovely Mam. Elin, so far away now. Of how quickly things could change. Life was fragile, transient: nothing could ever be relied upon completely. Time could swallow things whole, leaving no trace of what had gone before. Leaving her utterly alone and helpless.

'Get out,' she said, though her voice was barely more than a croak.

Peter straightened, the pleasant smile restored as though he'd called in to return a cup of sugar. 'Think about what I've said. I just wanted a friendly word, you understand,' he said, slipping the key into his pocket and patting it. 'Neighbours should look out for one another, shouldn't they?'

The door finally closed behind him, leaving an eerie, unsettled atmosphere in his wake. Nerys was rooted to the spot for a moment. It took every ounce of her strength to move. With shaking hands, she turned the old key in the lock. Pushing a chair under the door handle, she slid down the wall until she was on the floor, arms wrapped around her knees, rocking. The room seemed to pitch and roll. She felt sick.

Nerys knew she had no solid proof. If she spoke out, something worse might follow. No, something worse *would* follow. The knowledge closed in on her until it felt as if her head might explode.

After what felt like hours, she managed to prise herself up off the floor and stumbled her way back upstairs. Disorientated, she cast about until she spotted her phone. Her fingers were thick and clumsy as she dialled Bethan's number. Unsurprisingly, given the late hour, it went straight to voicemail. Nerys left a message. She didn't mention Peter's name. She didn't say anything about their encounter. She simply said, in a faltering voice, that she was struggling at the moment. That she didn't feel well and wouldn't be coming into work the following day. That she'd be in touch soon.

Outside, she could hear the wind buffeting the windows, the roar and hiss of waves breaking on the shore. Nerys sat on her bedroom floor, her quivering arms wrapped around herself, waiting fearfully. For something was sure to follow, and she didn't dare imagine what it might be.

Chapter 58

BEFORE – March 2023

Nerys

By the next day, Nerys hadn't slept at all. She felt a physical and emotional wreck. Her hands shook as she called Bethan again mid-morning and asked, stumbling over her words, if she could take Nyten for a while.

'Could you – would you be able to come and get her as soon as possible?' she asked, trying to keep her voice steady. 'Just for a week or so.' She kept her explanation vague, talked about the worry of Nyten not having another accident. About feeling unable to care for her properly at the moment because she felt so wrung out.

There was a beat of silence before Bethan responded. She sounded puzzled, but concerned. 'Is everything all right, cariad? I mean, apart from you feeling under the weather?'

'I'm just worried about her,' Nerys said. And she was.

Genuinely. 'You know, after what happened before. I really thought I was going to lose her.' She took a breath. 'I'd feel better if she wasn't here at the moment.'

Bethan agreed, telling Nerys that it was all fine; that she just needed to focus on herself and getting better. She promised she'd be round after work and to have Nyten's basket and litter tray ready. It would be nice, she said, to have the company. Nyten was such a sweet little cat.

When Bethan arrived later that afternoon, Nerys glanced around anxiously as she ushered her into the cottage, hurriedly closing the door behind her. Bethan studied her with a thoughtful frown. 'Have you eaten? Would you like me to make a sandwich or something?'

Nerys felt suddenly self-conscious. She was still in her pyjamas, her curly hair like a bird's nest. She was all too aware she could do with a shower.

She shook her head. 'I'm not hungry.'

'A *panad*, then?'

Nerys squeezed a smile. 'I'm okay. But I can make you one if—'

Bethan raised a hand. 'I won't, if it's all the same with you. I'll take the *pwtyn* and get back. I've got to pop round to Mam's to sort her supper, then I need to get on top of the bookkeeping for the shop.'

Nerys nodded, feeling suddenly guilty. Bethan had enough to contend with, without being left short-handed.

'I'm so sorry. To put all this on you . . .'

'Don't be silly. You've been through such a lot, these last months,' Bethan said gently, beaming as she scooped Nyten into her arms and scratching under the cat's chin. 'Your nain, everything else. Maybe it's all catching up.'

She told Nerys to take all the time she needed. That, if need be, she'd advertise for temporary help in the shop, although she was sure it wouldn't come to that. She even asked, carefully, if she could have Elin's number – whether she should call her. Suggested she might want to come and stay if she knew Nerys wasn't well.

'No,' said Nerys, a little too quickly. 'No, she wouldn't.' The image of Elin's face, open and unquestioning, rose in her mind, and with it the certainty that Peter would be watching the cottage constantly. At least she wouldn't have to worry about Nyten now, and if she kept her mouth shut, Bethan should be okay. The last thing she wanted was for Elin to be placed in any danger.

Bethan narrowed her eyes, cocking her head to one side. 'Have you two fallen out or something?'

Nerys shook her head, unable to explain without remembering Peter's thinly veiled threat. His twisted smile. Her stomach turned over.

Bethan stood at the door holding Nyten aloft in her basket, and threw a worried glance over her shoulder.

'If you need anything, call me. You take care now, cariad.'

Nerys gave Nyten one last tickle through the basket's grille before waving Bethan off, then bolted the front door. She checked again, making sure she'd pushed the chair underneath the one at the back properly, and blew out a long breath. She would stay put for now. Hopefully Peter would notice that she wasn't seeing anyone and be satisfied that she hadn't mentioned what had happened. Hopefully she'd be able to return to some sort of normality and just keep out of his way.

*

After that, she barely left the cottage at all. The days rolled into one another, passing in a fog of exhaustion and anxiety. If someone knocked, she hid, her heart hammering, breathing shallow. Sleep came in snatches and she woke night after night in a cold sweat, convinced someone was at the door. Sometimes there was – the rattle of the handle, the soft creak as it opened despite the chair she'd wedged beneath it. Once, she heard quiet laughter in the dark. He was playing games with her, keeping her reminded that he was the one with the upper hand. It was slowly driving her to breaking point.

Nerys rang the police more than once, never naming Peter, never quite able to force the words out. Each time they came, of course, they found nothing, and left her with reassurances, shooting knowing looks at each other. Each time, her sense of reality thinned a little more. She had become a prisoner in her own home.

*

But then, one morning she woke to voices downstairs. She could hear Peter talking, clear as day. Libby, responding eagerly. They were both in the cottage.

'I'm concerned about her mental state,' Peter was saying loudly. 'Living alone like this. Talking about people being after her.'

Libby murmured in agreement. 'It's not normal. Maybe we need to contact social services.'

Nerys lay rigidly, the walls closing in around her. Libby must know. She had to. Why else wouldn't she ask how he'd got in? They must be in it together.

When she was satisfied that they'd gone, Nerys called the police again, sobbing now, her words a tangle of everything that had been happening. The truth of it all. She realised she should have changed the locks, she said, but she'd been too scared, too broken to think straight or take any remedial action. She'd prayed that it would stop eventually, that he'd grow bored of tormenting her.

Although by now, of course, she had become recognised as a nuisance. The girl who cried wolf. And Peter was ostensibly a pillar of the community. This time, the police didn't come.

Instead, the knock came early the next day. A firm, official-sounding rap, filling Nerys with dread. When she came downstairs, two clipboard-wielding strangers wearing lanyards were already standing in her living room. A man and a woman. And behind them she could see Peter and Libby, sitting with pseudo-concern on their faces, as though it were their house and she was a lodger they wanted to evict.

'They're dangerous!' Nerys shrieked, backing away. 'They've been letting themselves into my house – he's got a key. They've been going through my things. He's—'

She felt hands reaching for her, restraining her shoulders. Panicked, Nerys struggled to free herself. 'Why aren't you listening to me? He's a *monster*.'

Calmly, the woman told her to sit down, to take deep breaths. Peter shook his head sadly.

'Poor girl. She's not well,' Nerys heard him say. 'We're only trying to help.'

Everything was a blur thereafter. The sudden, unexpected sting of a needle in her arm. The room swimming, voices fading in and out. The last thing Nerys saw before the darkness took her was Peter's face, composed and satisfied, as her home slipped away.

Chapter 59

NOW – Saturday 27th May 2023

Elin

The bay was quiet, with only a handful of people outside The Quay. No one seemed to notice Elin as she picked her way across the rocks, skirting the moored boats as she headed for the other side. The evening air was cool against her skin, the sky streaked pink and gold. Sand turned to dusty, gravelly soil as she crossed the coarse marram grass sprouting at the far edge, then left the beach to turn into the narrow lane. The light had that honeyed, mellow quality she always associated with the bay at this time of year, the promise of a long, lazy summer ahead. The thought might have smoothed over anything for her once, lulled her into a false sense of security. Elin gritted her teeth. She wasn't about to let it now.

This was the path Cai had taken that final, fatal night.

She moved slowly, retracing his steps from the memory of

where he'd once led her, her trainers crunching on shingle that sounded far too loud now in the quiet. The lane climbed away from the bay and closed in on itself, banks rising steeply on either side, thick with bramble and wildflowers. It was hidden from the main road and the view of anyone who didn't know the area. Elin felt the uncomfortable weight of that seclusion now, wrapping around her, making her feel hemmed in.

The police had declared it a hit-and-run. A tragic case of being in the wrong place, at the wrong time. Several weeks had passed since Cai's death, but now that she was emerging from her initial raw devastation, the unsatisfactory explanations for what had happened to him niggled at Elin, like a splinter buried in her finger. That dream had felt like a wake-up call; it had finally galvanised her into action. It was unlikely now that anyone would ever know the exact circumstances around Mam's disappearance. But before too much time had elapsed, she owed it to Cai to try to uncover the truth about what had happened to him. The more distance there was between her and the day she'd lost him, the deeper her questions about it all had become. *It wasn't an accident*. That was what the grief-bot had said. Was that what it had been referring to?

Elin's whole body became rigid as she reached the curve in the lane where the hedges grew taller, the sky narrowing overhead. She stopped, her heart beginning to thud, and tried to picture Cai here: his long stride, his distracted air, his mind already half-buried in the past. He'd spoken openly to several people about his plans to start the dig nearby. He'd been excited, animated; convinced the area was hiding more things worth finding.

An uncomfortable knot tightened in her chest.

What if there *had* been something else hidden here – something other than what Cai was so keen to discover? And what if not everyone had wanted that something unearthed?

Elin looked around, acutely aware of how quiet the lane was, how easily something could happen here without witnesses. The unease she'd been carrying was building now, becoming heavy and cloying.

Her eyes were drawn to the rise on the right, the area Cai had identified as a prime spot to excavate. Elin glanced about for a moment, then steeled herself to begin the ascent, her legs slightly unsteady. Remembering the knife in his pocket, without understanding its significance, she felt one thing with chilling certainty: whatever happened to Cai had been set in motion long before he ever set foot here.

Elin took in a breath. The undergrowth had been trampled, deliberately beaten-down even, gorse and brambles parting to create a clear path, implying that someone had definitely been here recently. Could this have been Cai – or was it someone else?

A rustling from somewhere to her left, followed by a muffled thud, stopped Elin in her tracks. Her eyes darted over her shoulder, gooseflesh prickling along her arms. The words that Cai's hologram had spoken rang in her ears now: '*Don't trust the—*' The what? It was a warning, wasn't it – and especially in view of all the things that had happened to her lately, Elin wasn't being careful.

Cai would never have sent her here, she realised that now. The last thing he would ever do was put her in any danger. This was all down to her own erratic, irrational impulses. She was an idiot, coming to such a deserted spot alone. What the hell had she been thinking?

Chapter 60

NOW – Saturday 27th May 2023

Elin

The lane had all but disappeared.

Brambles and gorse tugged at her from both sides, tangled together over the seam of earth that climbed away from the lane and towards the fields beyond. Though panicked now by the realisation that she might not be alone, Elin felt oddly compelled to push forwards. Her sleeves snagged on thorns, the smell of ferns and cow parsley filling her nostrils. Back there was where Cai had taken his last breath: down there, where the road kinked and rose. Though she hadn't been able to bring herself to visit the site until now, she had pictured the incident in her mind's eye with terrible clarity: his broken body on the rough tarmac, a smear of oil, the perpetrator's wheels screeching as they fled the scene. Had there been blood on the road? The thought was unbearable.

Elin paused to fill her lungs, her ears pricked, eyes darting. There was no one in sight. Maybe it had just been a bird, or a rabbit, even. She had finally reached it: the overgrown place Cai had been so excited about. '*There's something up there, El,*' he'd said, eyes bright, hands sketching shapes in the air. '*You can feel it.*' He'd talked, as he so often used to, about shovel test the pH levels of the soil; about the strata of history, layered like pages. Things that Elin had given no thought to before she met him. He had opened her eyes to so much. Now she scanned the ground for anything – the glint of metal, a piece of glass, the slightest evidence of disturbance; some clue that might tell her what had actually happened that fateful evening.

The earth looked wrong somehow. Not dramatically so, not freshly turned – just subtly uneven, as if it had been worried at and then smoothed over. Elin squatted, raking the soil with her fingers. Her chest tightened. She didn't know what she expected to find. She only knew she had to keep looking.

A twig snapped behind her.

'Elin.'

She started, her heart quickening, disorientated by the sound of her name breaking the silence. As her head whipped round, she was momentarily confused to see Peter, standing a few paces away. His broad frame blocked the view of the lane, his pleasant, familiar face pinched into something hard and unrecognisable. He held an old spade loosely in one hand, the metal edge dull and caked with dried mud.

'Oh!' Elin clapped a hand to her chest. She felt suddenly lightheaded with panic. 'Peter. You frightened the life out of me.'

'You shouldn't be up here on your own.' His tone was amiable, almost avuncular. 'It's not safe, you know.'

Though her pulse was still thudding, she tried to keep her tone level. 'I'm just looking around. Cai was planning—'

Peter cast about briefly. 'I know what Cai wanted to do.'

Both hands gripped the spade now, his knuckles white. 'That's exactly why I'm here. I heard you – telling Ianto Pritchard you were going to make sure the bloody dig went ahead as planned. You really should've let it go, you know.'

The air had grown heavy. His eyes bored into hers, cold and unblinking. Elin straightened slowly, every instinct screaming. Her gaze landed on the shovel. A terrible chill crept through her veins. 'Why—what are you doing up here with that?'

Peter's mouth spread into a rictus grin. 'Collecting fresh soil.' There was an odd, slightly manic edge to his voice. 'It's good for the garden.'

He took a step closer.

Elin thought of his ugly, furious expression as he'd seen her looking through the window that day. The fear he'd clearly instilled in his own wife. The warning in the letter that Nerys had found. Everything was closing in around her. She backed away, her heel catching on a root. 'Peter, please. Stop!'

His arms lifted now, his expression murderous.

She turned to run, but the uneven ground betrayed her. She went down hard, palms stinging, breath punched from her lungs. She scrambled, half-blind with panic, as the shadow fell over her.

Elin braced herself as the spade whistled through the air, her hands covering her head instinctively.

Peter gave a sudden grunt, the sound torn from him as his body jolted forward. The blow never reached its intended target.

Elin turned her face to see him pitch sideways, the spade slipping from his grip and landing with a dull metallic clunk. Behind him stood Libby, face ashen, both hands locked around a sizeable stone she must have picked up from the beach. Peter hit the ground with a heavy, final thud and didn't move.

For a moment, all that could be heard was the distant rushing of the sea and the sound of Elin's ragged breathing.

'Libby?' She ventured, her voice quavering. 'What—?'

Libby dropped the stone as if it was burning her. 'I followed him that night, the night Cai was killed,' she said breathlessly. 'I tried to warn you. I knew he was lying. I knew it.'

Elin's stomach turned over as she thought of the note slid through her door, the words she'd considered a threat. The words she'd too readily attributed to Tom Buckley.

YOU SHOULDN'T HAVE COME BACK

It made sense now. She pushed herself upright, her hands encrusted with dirt, a gash down one arm where her sleeve had torn. A shiver travelled along her spine. 'Lying about what?'

Libby cast around, at the patch of ground Elin had been studying, then back at Peter's motionless bulk. Her eyes welled, but she didn't look away. 'About why no one was allowed up here. He kept saying that the ground wasn't safe or some such rubbish. About why he got so *angry* when your Cai talked about his dig.'

A cold understanding began to creep over Elin, slow and dreadful. *It wasn't an accident.* 'He killed Cai,' she whispered.

Libby made a peculiar sound, somewhere between a laugh and a strangled sob. 'He killed them all.' She swallowed. 'My sister, Fliss, she didn't just disappear. And neither did Meinir.'

Everything seemed to swim around Elin, the name ringing in her ears. 'My *mam*?'

'I think they're here,' Libby said, her voice barely more than a croak. She pointed, her hand trembling. 'Under this soil. He must have buried them. Years apart, but in the same place. He thought no one would ever look.'

Elin stared at the ground. The grass and flora had suddenly taken on a different aspect, the rapidly dimming light creating sinister pools of shadow. Her knees buckled and she sank back onto the earth, clutching at it as if trying not to fall once more.

All this time. All her family's grief and anguish, the not knowing, and Mam had been here all along, so near to home. And what of poor Jac? Had he witnessed something he shouldn't have, and paid the ultimate price? The coroner's 'accidental death' verdict had never felt entirely satisfactory. Elin had always wondered if his death might have been connected in some way to Mam's disappearance. But not like this. It was all too much to take in.

Libby crouched beside her, close but not touching. 'I tried to tell myself it was my imagination. The way he'd behaved when Fliss left; how he was after that storm. Agitated, obsessive about really trivial stuff. On a short fuse. I tried so many times to contact Fliss – I felt in my gut something was very wrong. I was at the shops, the afternoon she left and Peter told me she'd just stormed out. They'd had another row, he said. But we'd always been so close – she wouldn't have just cut me off like that, no matter what. And then Valeria turning up, well it just confirmed what I already believed . . .' She shook her head.

'Felicity and Liberty – the irony of the bloody names we were both given.' The tears began to flow now. 'I've felt like a prisoner for so long in my marriage. I'd always known there was another side to Peter, something dark he couldn't control. It didn't do to get on the wrong side of him. Sometimes he really scared me. So I did things I'm not proud of, just to appease him. Turned a blind eye to stuff. Went along with him hassling Nerys, looking for things of his in the house he was adamant she'd taken. Just to have some sort of normality – which was impossible when he got into one of his moods.' She clapped a hand to her mouth. 'But I didn't want to believe he could've done anything *that* bad. So I carried on as usual, blocked it all out.'

She drew in a breath and bit down hard on her lip, a bead

of blood breaking through the skin. 'When Cai started talking about his idea for a dig, Peter panicked. I could tell. And when he saw you heading over here today . . .' Libby's voice broke. 'I was afraid of what he'd do.'

Elin closed her eyes, her mind reeling. Cai's voice echoed again through her head – '*You can feel it.*' Now she really could. The terrible, appalling weight of it all. It was as though the truth was crying out from below, demanding to be seen. The land had waited too long, holding its dead and ready to give up its secrets.

Eventually, Elin drew herself to her feet, barely able to look at Libby. At that moment she felt nothing but contempt for her, whether she'd been an abused wife or not. If the woman had come forward with her suspicions sooner, her mam might still be alive – Jac, too. And her lovely Cai would have been spared. Libby may have saved Elin, but it was never going to make up for her failure to protect the man that Elin loved more than life itself. She glanced, just once, back at the disturbed soil, then turned to head unsteadily back towards the lane, leaving Libby staring down at her husband. Elin wasn't sure if he was alive or dead; right now, she didn't much care. But whatever the case, the police would have to be informed.

And then she needed to go straight to see Nerys.

Chapter 61

Now – Wednesday 31st May 2023

North Wales Chronicle
Donna Price – Anglesey Correspondent

Grim Discovery on Anglesey:
Remains of Two Women Found After More Than a Decade

Police have released a statement following the discovery of human remains, confirmed to be those of Felicity Michaels and Meinir Owen, whose disappearances have cast a shadow over Anglesey for more than a decade. Ms Michaels had recently been reported missing from her home in Seville, Spain, by her partner. Although circumstances are not clear, it seems she failed to return after a visit to Anglesey some fifteen years ago. Ms Owen was believed to have drowned following a violent storm on the island almost ten years ago, in October 2013.

The remains were uncovered earlier this week in shallow

graves on overgrown land leading from a narrow lane above Red Wharf Bay (Traeth Coch). Officers searching the area described the site as densely choked with brambles and scrub, a place easily overlooked despite its proximity to a well-known beauty spot.

North Wales Police said initial forensic examination indicates that the victims had lain undiscovered for at least a decade. DNA samples taken from family members have confirmed that the skeletal remains belong respectively to Ms Michaels and Ms Owen, both of whom vanished from the locality.

Detectives are now hoping to question Peter Fowler, who is suspected in connection with the women's murders. A distinctive heart-shaped pendant, believed to have belonged to Ms Owen, was discovered among other items of potential significance, after a search of the Fowlers' home close by. Following more in-depth forensic analysis of samples taken from the scene, Fowler is also believed to be linked to a hit-and-run incident near Pentraeth that claimed the life of archaeologist Cai Rowlands in April of this year – a case that has remained unresolved and deeply painful for his partner, Ms Owen's younger daughter, Elin, her sister, Nerys, and the local community.

However, Fowler is currently unable to be interviewed. He remains in hospital in a coma after sustaining a serious head injury, reportedly inflicted by his wife, Liberty Fowler. Mrs Fowler is currently in police custody, and inquiries into that incident are ongoing. Medical staff have indicated it is not yet known whether Fowler's injuries will result in permanent brain damage.

In a further disturbing development, officers searching the land also discovered the skeleton of a large domestic cat interred in the same area. The animal is believed to have suffered a broken neck. While distressing, police said the find may assist in building a broader picture of the perpetrator's psyche.

Detective Superintendent Gareth Carew of Bangor Police said: 'This is a harrowing discovery and our thoughts are first and foremost with the families and friends of Felicity Michaels and Meinir Owen, who have waited many years for answers. The inquiry into the death in 2013 of twenty-five-year-old Jac Parry, originally ruled an accidental drowning, has also been reopened in connection with these recent discoveries. While this investigation is complex and ongoing, we are not currently looking for anyone else in relation to these findings.'

Local residents in and around Red Wharf Bay expressed shock that such a grim secret could have remained hidden for so long. One resident, who asked not to be named, said: 'You walk those lanes and never imagine something like that could be just beyond the hedges. It's really chilling.'

Police have confirmed that specialist officers continue to examine the site and surrounding land, though they believe all relevant remains have now been recovered. Further updates are expected as forensic work progresses and the condition of Peter Fowler becomes clearer.

For now, a quiet lane overlooking one of Anglesey's most popular bays has become the focus of a sombre investigation, bringing long-delayed answers – and fresh sorrow – to a community still coming to terms with this terrible tragedy.

Epilogue

TEN YEARS EARLIER – October 2013

The day before the storm

Peter

Peter stood at the edge of the wall, his hands sunk into the pockets of his waxed jacket, his eyes fixed on the horizon. Terns swooped and rose, while the omnipresent gulls circled, their mournful cries the only sound save for the lapping of the waves. He had imagined the island differently when they'd first arrived from the Midlands: cleaner, quieter; more welcoming. A fresh start. That was the phrase Libby had used; as if you could scrub a life clean by rinsing it in the salt sea air.

Behind him, Libby lingered in the car park opposite The Old Boathouse. She was pretending to read a noticeboard while watching him in the reflection of its plastic cover, he knew it. He could feel her attention like a wasp buzzing round his head. She seemed more cautious these days. Guarded.

At first, Peter told himself the locals were slow to warm to outsiders, that was all. Island mentality. A different rhythm. Yet he felt certain conversations dipped when he approached, that eyes slid away as though they wanted to avoid him. He was sure he'd overheard his name spoken in a tone that set his teeth on edge.

When old Sion's garden gate had finally succumbed to the elements, Peter had been the first to knock, toolbox in hand. When the Evans's fence had blown down one night, he had gone straight to the builders' merchants the following morning, returning with posts and concrete. He'd noticed it was on its last legs, anyway – given it the occasional wobble as he passed. He always worked hard, cheerfully, breaking sweat so they could see the effort, the selflessness of it. He made sure Libby brought tea, smiled at the right moments. Showed how devoted she was.

Some of them thanked him properly. Called him '*dyn gwych.*' A top bloke, his neighbour Mrs Owen had explained. That had made his heart swell with pride. He stored those words carefully, like little trophies. He didn't much care for Mrs Owen's daughter. Behaved like a proper slapper. But the old lady appreciated him. She would send over cakes from time to time, thank him effusively for any small job. And the people from the church welcomed the pair of them: praised his efforts to maintain the graveyard, mend the pews.

But some of the others. He could tell they watched him with ill-disguised hostility. Like the bastards where they used to live. Not gratitude. Calculation. As if they were weighing him up and finding something lacking. As if they were wondering whether the damage only existed in the first place because of him.

Libby said he was imagining things – that it was all in his head. That *of course* people liked him, that they were grateful for his help. That it wasn't like before. And yet it gnawed away at him.

He'd caught snatches of it one afternoon outside the pub; he thought he'd heard his name mentioned in a lowered voice. 'Convenient,' someone said. Another responded with a sarcastic laugh. Peter felt the sound land in his chest like a stone. *Convenient*. As if his help were a trick, his willingness to repair things proof of some ulterior motive.

They don't deserve me, he thought. *They'll have to pay*.

That night, lying beside Libby, he stared at the ceiling while the sea swished faintly through the open window. He replayed every sly sidewards glance, every smirk. The injustice of it ballooned until his mind was filled with nothing else. After everything: after his previous incarnation, after the humiliation of being observed with suspicion, reported, whispered over, he had earned this restart. After Leicester, Mynydd Mechell had just been a blip. He deserved a second chance. He'd chosen to be better. Hadn't he?

Libby was breathing deeply. She shifted a little, her back a careful distance from his. Though she had never given voice to her concerns, over time, he'd detected a change in her after the situation with Fliss. A certain look in her eyes: a wariness that hadn't been there before. *Fliss*. How he'd loathed that woman, interfering, putting ideas in his wife's head. Trying to make Libby think she was being manipulated, that he was some sort of control freak. A rampant bloody feminist, that's all her sister had been. He wasn't going to stand for that, not in his own home. It was a wife's duty to obey her husband and it was his right to assert himself – he wasn't about to be undermined by some bloody dyke. It was her own stupid fault. She should have kept her nose out of it. They were well rid of her.

His thoughts drifted once again back to the more present issue. He felt the old, familiar stir of righteous anger: the certainty that he was being constantly observed, that he had become a topic of conversation. He imagined the locals standing together outside The Quay, smug and damning in their judgement, hatching some sort of revenge, their precious boats bobbing gently behind them.

They think they know it all, he told himself. *They think they're better than me.*

He was up before the dawn. Taking care not to rouse Libby, he had slipped from the cottage and begun to walk. Walking was good: it helped to clear his mind. Helped him to weigh things up properly. The tide was out, the boats close now on the swathe of damp sand to which they were anchored. Each one represented a local household, a small, floating badge of exclusivity; a sign of being part of the community. Bitterly, he ran one hand along a hull, the other closing around the Swiss Army Knife he'd lifted from the pub in his pocket. Maybe he could use the corkscrew attachment – leave a few carefully placed scratches.

Peter glanced about, then looked out across the bay. The sea was calm, though flames of crimson and ochre daubed the sky as the sun rose. What was it they said – red sky in the morning, sailors' warning? He'd seen the forecast. A storm was due to hit later in the evening. The perfect opportunity.

A better plan had begun to form. If they insisted on seeing him as the man who fixed things only because he'd broken them, then he'd give them something to complain about. Let them wake to *real* damage – damage they couldn't ignore. Far more impact than a few minor gouges along the paintwork.

He straightened, his heart quickening with excitement. The anger had lifted, replaced by a driving sense of purpose, almost triumph: a way to get back at those who had dared to doubt him, without them even realising.

He would show them. He would show them all.

Glossary of Welsh Terms

Am y – For the
Aros – Wait
Aw bechod – What a shame
Bach – Small (also used as term of endearment)
Bacha byns – Butterfingers
Bara brith – fruit loaf
Bechod – What a shame
Bore da – Good morning
Bwthyn – Cottage
Cariad – Darling
Cawl – Soup/stew
Croeso – Welcome
Chwarae teg – Fair play
Dim problem (o gwbl) – No problem (at all)
Diolch –Thanks
Duw (anwyl) – (dear) God
Dyn gwych – Top bloke

Dw i wedi gweld e . . . – I've seen . . .
Fy enw i yw – My name is
Gorsaf Heddlu – Police station
Gwyliwch – Watch out
Helo – Hello
Hiraeth – Homesickness, longing
Iawn – Fine, good
Iesu (mawr) – Jesus (literally 'great/big')
Mam bach! – Oh my! (literally 'little mam' – think 'Mamma Mia!')
Meddwl, hogan! – Think, girl!
Naddo – No
Nefi blw! – Good grief! (literally 'navy blue')
Nos dawch – Goodnight
Panad – Cuppa
Pwtyn – Puss
Pwy sydd yna? – Who's there?
Shinach – Sly bastard
Sut mae? – How's it going?
Sut wyt ti? – How are you?
Sws mawr – Big kiss
Ti'n iawn? – Are you well?
Tyrd (ty'd) yma – Come here
Ysbyty – Hospital

Acknowledgements

Many and grateful thanks to my editor Anna Nightingale for helping to reshape the narrative with her insightful structural edit and to Siân Heap for a thorough and sharp-eyed copyedit. Their input and guidance have been invaluable. Thanks also to Laetitia Grant for an impeccable proofread. Not forgetting India Desai, and huge gratitude to Amy Mae Baxter and Billy Lindon for their kind patience and help with my last-minute dithering!

Diolch yn fawr iawn to Auntie Ann, who has been so helpful in answering queries about spellings and colloquialisms. Although Welsh was my dad's first language, I am not a fluent Welsh speaker and the majority of what I picked up as a child was learned phonetically, so I take full responsibility for any errors!

A massive thank you also to the wider Team Avon, who work so tirelessly in the background – they are all real troupers and their efforts very much appreciated! To Helen Huthwaite, publisher extraordinaire, sales team Sara Eusebi, Dom Brendon and Hannah Lismore, marketing superstars Emily Hall and Jessie Whitehead, audio editor Imogen Gordon Clark and Joey Yau in production. Not forgetting Megan Smith for the brilliant cover design!

Thanks as ever to the people central to my existence, my wonderful family: to my husband, Mark, my children, Gemma, Natalie and Christopher, and my grandchildren, Olivia, Josh, Isaac, Noah, Oliver and Gracie. You are what it's all about!

Heartfelt gratitude to all the bloggers and reviewers who are so generous with their time – we authors have so much to thank you for. To all the lovely writers and friends on X and Instagram, who are always so supportive and encouraging – writing can be a solitary pursuit and it's comforting to know we're all in a similar boat!

A nod to the magical Isle of Anglesey, my dad's home, and on this occasion especially Traeth Coch (with apologies for the geographical tweaks and irregularities – all for dramatic purposes, so I hope I'm excused!). The area is indeed rich in history – as a child, my dad actually discovered a Viking skull (now secreted away somewhere in Oriel Môn, the museum and art gallery in Llangefni) buried a short distance from Traeth Coch along the headland, which very much inspired the idea of Cai and his conviction that there must be more to find here – and I'm sure there is!

And last but most importantly, to you the reader – thank you so much for buying this book and I really hope you have enjoyed the story. Fingers crossed it has brought a little escapism from the turbulent times we are living in.

A dead husband. A creepy cottage.
A secret she needs to stay buried.

This gothic psychological thriller with a jaw-dropping twist is perfect for fans of Ruth Ware and Cass Green.

When a young widow's little girl vanishes, could a dark family secret hold the answer?

A terrifically dark and twisty tale that asks: *can you ever really trust those closest to you?* Perfect for fans of Ruth Ware, Cass Green and C.J. Tudor.

A mysterious figure.
A whispering community.
A deadly secret . . .

A haunting, twisty story about the power of secrets and rumours, perfect for fans of Ruth Ware's *The Turn of the Key* and Lucy Atkins's *Magpie Lane*.

Secrets won't stay in the dark forever . . .

An eerie, bone-chilling and twisty thriller about how far we go to protect our darkest secrets, for fans of C.J. Tudor, Riley Sager and Cass Green.